CAN
4/15
KT-479-509
WITHDRAWN
Books should be returned or renewed by the last date above. Renew by phone 03000 41 31 31 or online www.kent.gov.uk/libs
Libraries Registration & Archives
CUSTOMER SERVICE EXCELLENCE
CSE
Kent County Council
kent.gov.uk
WITHDRAWN
C333736233

SOPHIE AND THE SIBYL

BY THE SAME AUTHOR

Hallucinating Foucault

Monsieur Shoushana's Lemon Trees

James Miranda Barry

The Deadly Space Between

Seven Tales of Sex and Death

Miss Webster and Chérif

The Strange Case of the Composer and His Judge

Criticism

Sisters and Strangers

Writing on the Wall: Selected Essays

SOPHIE AND THE SIBYL

A Victorian Romance

PATRICIA DUNCKER

B L O O M S B U R Y
LONDON • NEW DELHI • NEW YORK • SYDNEY

First published in Great Britain 2015

Bloomsbury Publishing Plc
50 Bedford Square
London
WC1B 3DP

www.bloomsbury.com

Bloomsbury is a trademark of Bloomsbury Publishing Plc

Bloomsbury Publishing, London, New Delhi, New York and Sydney

A CIP catalogue record for this book is available from the British Library

Hardback ISBN 978 1 4088 6052 6
Trade paperback ISBN 978 1 4088 6053 3

10 9 8 7 6 5 4 3 2 1

Typeset by Hewer Text UK Ltd, Edinburgh
Printed and bound in Great Britain by CPI Group (UK) Ltd, Croydon CR0 4YY

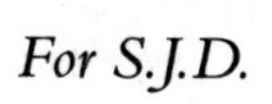
For S.J.D.

THREE EPIGRAPHS

She is an object of great interest and great curiosity to society here. She is not received in general society, and the women who visit her are either so émancipée as not to mind what the world says about them, or have no social position to maintain. Lewes dines out a good deal, and some of the men with whom he dines go without their wives to his house on Sundays. No one whom I have heard speak, speaks in other than terms of respect of Mrs. Lewes, but the common feeling is that it will not do for society to condone so flagrant a breach as hers of a convention and a sentiment (to use no stronger terms) on which morality greatly relies for support. I suspect that society is right in this . . . I do not believe that many people think that Mrs. Lewes violated her own moral sense, or is other than a good woman in her present life, but they think her example pernicious, and that she cut herself off by her own act from the society of the women who feel themselves responsible for the tone of social morals in England.

> *Charles Eliot Norton to G.W. Curtis, 29th January 1869. Cited in Gordon S. Haight,* George Eliot: A Biography *(Oxford: Oxford University Press, 1968), p. 409.*

It often astonished us what trash he would tolerate in the way of novels. The chief requisites were a pretty girl and a good ending.

> *George Darwin comments on his father's reading. Cited in Janet Browne,* Charles Darwin: The Power of Place, *Vol. 2 of a biography (London: Jonathan Cape, 2002), p. 68.*

What is the function of the epigraph? I always read them carefully. The writing which surrounds writing may well be written in code, but will also offer a key, a clue if you like, to the author's intentions. And in this case the two quotations above are particularly revealing. Our author is one of those sentimental people who need to admire their chosen heroes and heroines. She cannot bear it if her appointed gods turn out to be made of flesh and blood – with personal vanities and frailties as disappointingly tedious as our own. I think she has scores to settle with Mr. Darwin and Mrs. Lewes, but she adores them both. And that is her weakness. Her vindictive little game is undermined by love.

> *The narrator of* Sophie and the Sibyl *comments on her author's intentions.*

PART ONE

PART ONE

CHAPTER ONE

in which the Reader is introduced to two of the principal Characters in this History.

'Gnädige Frau Lewes, may I introduce my younger brother Max? He is writing a great work on the monuments of antiquity. I trust that his efforts will eventually see the light of day, but I think you're still stuck in the first volume, aren't you, Max?'

The publisher bowed to his distinguished visitor with a merry smile, revealing an unexpected bald spot that gleamed with all the neatness of a recent tonsure. His smile included the somewhat embarrassed Max, who resorted to effortless good manners. He raised her hand to his lips and murmured, '*Enchanté, Madame*,' in obsequious tones. Then he stood back to look at her. So this was the author of *Adam Bede* and *Romola,* the fame of whose *Middlemarch* was even then resounding through Europe like a triumphant drum. This was the woman considered too scandalous ever to be invited to dinner by respectable English families, all of whose members nevertheless read every word she wrote.

His first reaction was disappointment. She was old. Her liver-spotted hand and wrinkled skin smelt slightly of cinnamon mixed with an odd whiff of alcohol, that powerful preserving fluid sometimes used for scientific specimens. He raised his eyes to her face. A fragile veil was lifted away from her forehead, magnifying the long, thin countenance, the massive jaw and the vast, expressive eyes. The lady is old. The lady is ugly. The lady has wonderful eyes. Max met her unyielding gaze with a curious enquiry of his own. She represented a lucrative income for the family firm. Other writers chose their house and solicited their support because she was one of their authors. He glanced at his brother. Be polite, be charming. Impress this hideous, splendid dame. But he could think of nothing to say. The lady galloped unexpectedly to his rescue, giving him both the language in which the conversation was to be conducted (German), and the subject (his unfinished, indeed hardly begun, *Geschichte des Altertums*).

'Your brother tells me that you have been reading Lucian. I was a great admirer both of his philosophy and his poetry when I was a very young woman. My family, I am afraid, concluded that his influence was pernicious.'

She smiled slightly. The row of revealed teeth gleamed like tusks, yellowing, gigantic and uneven. Max inclined towards her, amazed by the scale of her remaining fangs. One or two gaps appeared, giving the untoppled columns the tragic aspect of a ruined temple.

'Yet I still regard his late lyrics and the famous *Fragment* as works that shaped my early thinking. The *Fragment* is really extraordinary. It has the power of a prophecy. We cannot read it now in any other light. How could he have known, in those early years of the first century, that this new religion, which he remained, nevertheless, pledged to exterminate, would rise and swell like a great wave, and that the destruction on its crest would sweep away all the gods he had so faithfully served? Lucian saw the terrible contours of the future; he grasped both the beauty of this new faith and the calamitous horrors trawling in its wake. Tell me, sir, what is your opinion of the *Fragment*?'

Max tortured his brains, still a little befuddled from a late night in Hettie's Keller, where he had enjoyed himself immensely, but run up some quite serious gambling debts. As he strolled into his brother's office, seeking immediate financial succour, his face carefully arranged in a smile of rueful penitence, he had not at first noticed the Sibyl, who was quietly seated by the fire, her ankle boots crossed, her umbrella neatly furled. Wolfgang's immediate introduction had taken him by surprise. The history of the early Christian Church in Asia Minor refused to break the surface of memory. He could not conjure up any recollection of the famous *Fragment*. Either this great lady, who was waiting, all patience and benevolent interest, for his considered opinion, had no trivial conversation at all, or she never deigned to discuss matters less consequential than the decline and fall of world religions. How on earth did she buy clothes? He examined the sober burgundy brocade and black lace, very little jewellery, and that awful veil, perched in raised folds upon the colossal forehead. She looked like a decorated statue.

'Ah yes, the *Fragment* . . .'

Had he ever read it? Max struck a thoughtful pose and stared at his brother's shelves of classics. They had been his father's books and he had known them all since boyhood, but now here they were, unhelpful, immobile, golden and embossed – Herodotus, Thucydides, Pliny, Livy, Tacitus – shouldn't Lucian, the Latin Lucian, not the Greek one – be in there somewhere? Or was he classed among the poets? Had Wolfgang separated out the Romans and the Greeks? But the lady, clearly amused by his hesitation, bought him a little more time.

'We cannot of course know what the *Fragment* would have been called, or how it would have developed. Perhaps it was originally conceived as a comparative study of religions in the ancient world? We know that Lucian was interested in the cults surrounding Mithras, and even in his own local water nymphs, for he compiled a list of sacred wells. But the usual title, *A Fragment Concerning the Origins of Early Christianity*, was bestowed upon the work by its first editor, Professor Heinrich Klausner, in 1782.'

Oh God save us all, that thing! Max gave an involuntary shudder of horror and relief. Lucian's rudimentary treatise, which he had immediately made every effort to forget, had given him a sleepless night. The Latin was elegant, indeed translucent, but the unfortunate encounter between history and what he had always enjoyed in church as a row of charming fairy tales had shaken him to the core. He looked straight at the great lady, ignored his hovering brother, and spoke from the heart.

'I must be frank, Madame, I cannot comment upon the *Fragment* as a scholar. I was disturbed, profoundly disturbed, when I first read it, both as a man and as a Christian. I realise that it is the great claim of our faith that God intervenes in history, that He made that final noble gesture, the sacrifice of his Son, an act that stands for all time, and yet – and yet – when I read those words, those cold observations made by Lucian, that the Christians were a set of artisans, tradesmen and merchants, that their faith originated in a Jewish sectarian heresy, that their young Prophet was executed under Pontius Pilate, and his reflections on the future of that fledgling faith, destined only for the eyes of the Emperor, I realised that I was more comfortable with myths than history. Myths are eternal, everlasting, and history is finite, indeed contingent upon particular, temporary forces. I wanted to cherish my beliefs in safety, without consequences. For if Lucian is right, and Christianity evolved out of a peculiar set of historical circumstances, then it will find its end in history, as he hoped it would.'

Max had never made so long a speech while still suffering from a hangover. The Sibyl's magnificent eyes widened in sympathy and surprise. His brother immediately intervened.

'Heavens, Max, I had no idea your studies involved such disturbing reading. The *Fragment* isn't on my shelves here, is it?' He gazed accusingly at his father's noble collection of classics. The great lady inclined towards her publisher, acknowledging his intervention, but never taking her eyes off Max.

'Your brother, sir, has just proved himself to be a man who reads with all his faculties attentive and alert. Such passion and engagement are rare in men of letters. For he is prepared to recognise, in his own flesh and blood, that Lucian is no abstract voice, lost in antiquity, but a man as full of faith and doubt as we are ourselves.'

She bowed her massive head. The veil was attached to a black cap, which covered her hair and, barren of trimmings, resembled an executioner's headwear. Wolfgang assumed a pious expression. Max shook himself, desperate to escape from his brother's airless rooms, the boxes of translations still in manuscript, the roll-top desk stuffed with invoices and account books, the classical library that loomed in menacing towers above him. The office suddenly smelled like a mausoleum. The lady stood up, her back very straight. Max then realised that the more arresting smell of freshly turned earth arose from her boots; the lady's footwear had left a little trail of muddy prints, from door to chair, and several clods, now drying in the firelight, had fallen from her heels. She had been traversing not streets, but fields. Max bent over her crisped hands, now encased in embroidered lace mittens.

'We are at home on Sunday afternoons, sir. And we will be delighted to welcome you then.' He did not mistake her tone. He was not being invited, but ordered to attend. 'Your brother knows the way to my door. He and Mr. Lewes are in constant touch.'

Her smile, faint, gracious, frightening in that the uneven teeth appeared once more, revealed in a theatrical lifting of the upper lip, stunned both brothers into silence. When the outer door thumped shut behind her Wolfgang gripped Max by the shoulders.

'Well done! Magnificent. She liked you. It's usually Lewes who hands out the invitations. If all goes well we shall have her new work at the price of the last. Sunday afternoon, my dear – mark – Sunday. You must be there. We shall go together!'

END OF CHAPTER ONE

CHAPTER TWO

takes place in the Sibyl's lodgings.
Max encounters the Extraordinary Herr Klesmer.

Be there by five. Max pummelled his way from his brother's apartments in the Jägerstraße, through the afternoon crowds, to the Sibyl's lodgings in the Dorotheenstraße, near the Neues Museum. Unter den Linden shimmered yellow and orange in the warm autumn sun. Babel towers of midges dithered in the milky air. The cobbles had blown dry, generating little puffs of dust beneath his boots. Did he look too funereal? Dark cravat, starched white shirt, coat brushed this morning before the early service, now becoming dusty. He paused at the corner to flick himself over with his new suede gloves. Elegance, sobriety and serious scholarship, this was the intended effect. He began to wonder if he did indeed look like an undertaker. Max harboured a satanic vision of the Sibyl's salon, a Last Judgement overflowing with fiery radicals and lady poets. He saw himself reflected in the café windows, pressed, trimmed, inappropriate, and fairly menaced with social disaster. Could he avoid the occasion altogether? But his brother, haring off to be seen again at church, where he was conducting one or two business deals, had descended upon him. Be there by five.

The double windows of the first-floor apartment, thrown wide open to greet the sunshine, swung gently back against the shutters. He could hear an animated roar of voices, expectant and ferocious, billowing to and fro within. The street door also stood open; a nervous young man, the appointed porter, bobbed his head, clutching the heavy right wing of the main doors, and pointed helplessly up the staircase. Max bowed slightly as he stepped over the threshold and removed his hat. A small hairy creature, with an eager, buoyant step, that had been heading up the stairs, turned back and bounded down to shake his hand.

'You must be Max! The Duncker brothers clearly duplicate each other right down to the moustache! You are most welcome, sir! Polly has been asking for you and your brother is already here.'

A huge bellow of shared laughter shook the building. This energetic ageing monkey must be the man himself, George Henry Lewes, the biographer of Goethe.

'I am honoured to make your acquaintance, sir,' said Max in English. Lewes burst out laughing, and with the brio of a much younger man, dragged him up the stairs.

Max feared the worst, murmured a little politeness and began planning his escape. Bow to the great lady, press her hand, drink one cup of tea or whatever is on offer, avoid all conversations with sculptors, musicians, actors and poets, and do a bunk as rapidly as decently possible. Don't, don't, don't get drawn into political discussions or religious debates. Avoid bluestockings. Pray that, apart from Wolfgang, you don't meet anyone you know.

The room bristled with joyous argument and knowing chuckles. Very few ladies, and two that he spotted, who announced that they were going on to a prestigious lecture followed by a concert, were of an age where their bare shoulders looked bulbous, wizened and unsuitable. The stove was lit; he could smell the coals beneath the mixed perfumes and heated bodies. Someone had pushed all the furniture back against the pale green-and-yellow-painted walls. A piano dominated the rug in the centre of the salon, and through the double doors, now folded back like an accordion, he saw yet another high-ceilinged space, and an untidy bookshelf, eight storeys high, packed with volumes, boxes and papers.

'Dr. Puhlmann offered us the apartment,' shouted Lewes, tugging Max's sleeve as if they had known one another for years, and making himself heard above the excited surrounding discussions. The little man sank immediately into the midst of a disputatious circle where he was called upon to adjudicate on a point of philology. Max felt someone helping him off with his coat, snatching his hat, and then found himself besieged by a booming pair of genial grey whiskers.

'Well, young man, here you are at last! Your brother's already here, you know, deep in talk with the great lady. She has not yet finished that marvellous book my girls have been reading in English. She intends to retire to the country to write the Finale. It's marvellous, quite marvellous. Haven't read it myself yet. I'm waiting for you Dunckers to bring out a decent translation.'

Max bowed, weakening at the knees, for here, full of jovial good humour, stood Graf August Wilhelm von Hahn, now something of a minor celebrity in Berlin and one of their authors. His military memoir, incorporating his own father's heroic participation in the Battle of Jena, caused something of a sensation when published by their house earlier in the year. The Count's critical stance towards the Prussian state apparatus transformed the gossip and general bravado into a distinctly chilly frisson when his publishers were visited by the intelligence services, who descended upon them, in plain clothes, unannounced, to inspect their autumn catalogue and boxes of stock. The Count, sanguine, optimistic and utterly fearless, pounded up the stairs to reassure them that he had visited everyone who matters, absolutely everyone, and there is no question of reprisals. We can contemplate a second edition with perfect equanimity. Wolfgang kept his nerve and *Erinnerungen und Erlebnisse: Lebensweg eines Liberalen*, 2 vols. (Berlin: Duncker und Duncker, 1872) went straight into a second, sell-out edition. According to Wolfgang, even the Sibyl – formidably well read in history, my dear, and remember the lady has met Mommsen himself, over dinner with the American Ambassador – well, she perused the work with astonishment.

The Count rattled on.

'You must pop round to see the girls, you know. Remember little Sophie, who chased you round the garden? We haven't seen you since the early summer and she was out at our old Jagdschloss then, bolstering herself up with fresh air and taking dreadful risks with those horses. Ready to jump anything! Goes straight at it! I think you'll find her quite grown-up. Herr Klesmer is going to play for us later on. I must finish my quiz. There's a good chap –'

The Count had invented a political quiz, which caused the most raucous laughter. There were no right answers. The wittiest or sharpest political response gained the most points. Max now realised that he had walked straight into a salon that actually flaunted its liberal inclusiveness. Here was the Count, encouraging subversion – 'Everything, yes, everything, my dear, can be discussed.' And Klesmer, a concert pianist and famous modern composer, acclaimed by Liszt and Wagner, made no secret whatever of his Jewishness. He actually declared himself a Jew! The very curtains of the salon shimmered with sedition. Max fingered his handkerchief.

Lewes danced up again, beckoning him to advance, and now he entered the inner sanctum. Behold the Sibyl, enthroned in elegance, a small table mountained with books at her side, her feet upon a cushioned stool. As he bowed, his smile becoming fixed, Max studied her velvet slippers. Were they too shedding mud? He caught the same whiff of spice and alcohol on her clothes. Was it linseed oil? The smell recalled his brother, aged twelve or thereabouts, lovingly polishing his violin. The Sibyl, flanked by young courtiers, who now withdrew to a safe distance, lifted her giant head, and gazed at him expectantly. Max blushed, feeling a faint, embarrassed tingle behind his ears.

'Thank you for coming to see us, Max. I hope I may call you Max. Wolfgang speaks of you so often. And with such affection. You must stay to hear Herr Klesmer play one of his own compositions. Let me introduce you to him.'

For there he was, like the catastrophe in an old comedy, conjured up by the ubiquitous Lewes who appeared to follow every conversation in the room, and anticipate every wish, like a successful circus impresario. Klesmer inclined slightly, a man smaller than Max with a mass of white hair, full lips, an unlined face and arresting grey eyes. He surveyed Max with sceptical contempt as they were introduced, then addressed himself entirely to the great lady, whose magnificent eyes held the two men in the same frame, an ominous image of Ugolino and his remaining son. Klesmer certainly took no prisoners. The discussion turned on the several merits of two different sculptures depicting the same subject: the abandoned Ariadne. One of the two had been misnamed Cleopatra and lurked in the Vatican Galleries in Rome, but the other, created by Johann Heinrich Dannecker, representing the unfortunate Ariadne stark naked, life-size, and seated on a panther, proved famous enough to have been viewed by both Duncker brothers, whilst in Frankfurt to attend the trade fair. They had visited both the Goethehaus in Großer Hirschgraben, draped with garlands on the poet's birthday, and the famous statue. Max simply acknowledged that he had set eyes upon the thing. He remembered prettier girls, just as naked, but with larger breasts and a good deal more friendly, in the closed rooms at Hettie's Keller, and had some difficulty comprehending this ecstatic appreciation of cold marble when warm flesh was to be had at the right price. The Sibyl and Klesmer, however, debated Nature and Art as if the two were in conflict, but closely related.

'Sculpture, like poetry,' the Sibyl declared, 'must generate the elements that engage its audience – tension and emotion. I maintain that Dannecker's Ariadne possesses both. Her head is lifted towards the horizon; she is gazing after her lost love. But she has been surprised while resting. The moment is clear. She has been unexpectedly awoken, one leg is so casually placed beneath the other, perhaps this is the very moment of her awakening consciousness? He is gone, and she finds herself alone. She knows that she is no longer loved. She has been abandoned.'

Max wondered how anybody managed to snooze on the back of a panther, but was too discreet to voice his literal-mindedness.

'Madame,' Herr Klesmer leaned towards the Sibyl and dared to contradict her. 'You spin a narrative from a gesture and a name. Now, the Ariadne to be found in the Vatican at Rome was originally known as the Cleopatra. Would your interpretation still be valid if the statue were simply to be renamed?'

'But it is not then the same statue. The name alone transforms the meanings of every fold in the marble!' The Sibyl demonstrated a pedantic streak. 'Cleopatra was the victim of her own folly. She was a queen who could love whom she chose. And she appears to have invested all her passion in the losing side. She is valued for her Oriental eroticism and her sexual power, not for the pathos of her fidelity to the man who betrayed her trust. Dannecker created his Ariadne in full knowledge of her identity and her fate. She represents the woman abandoned. He is interpreting her story.'

'Yet you loved the Roman Ariadne best, did you not?' Herr Klesmer raised one beautiful hand. His fingers were clean and tapered, the nails unbroken, as if he had never worked. He recited an English text unknown to Max. '"The hall where the reclining Ariadne, then called the Cleopatra, lies in the marble voluptuousness of her beauty, the drapery folding around her with a petal-like ease and tenderness."'

The Sibyl's eyes widened and glowed as if he had handed her a vast bouquet of roses. Max gazed at the illuminated lady, baffled. Klesmer suddenly poked him with one of his gorgeous fingers. Max lurched on his heels, a marionette whose strings vibrated into motion.

'And will you be publishing the English version in Berlin, sir? Or merely the translation?'

The unknown text clearly sprang from the Great Work, which the Count's wife and daughters were even then wolfing down in English. Max had no idea how far negotiations had progressed with the frisky husband. He hastily straightened his back and flattered the Sibyl, praying that the Ariadne – or was it the Cleopatra? – played a minor role in the Great Work.

'We are honoured and proud to publish any work by Mrs. Lewes, whether in English or in German,' declared Max. 'She is admired throughout Europe.'

Klesmer snorted. The lady smiled slightly, then put her unfortunate publisher on the spot.

'But, Max, you have not yet given us your opinion of the Ariadne. And we have been discussing her without reference to your views. Do tell us what you think about the two sculptures. Do you have a preference?'

This time, Max, no longer mesmerised by the peculiar company and the noise around him, let fly with his opinion. The girls at Hettie's Keller were the better sort of prostitute, not overeducated, but anxious to please and to enjoy themselves. When other men sneered at them, he often rose to their defence. And now, oddly enough, he felt moved to defend each and every Ariadne.

'The woman abandoned is traditionally regarded as the fallen woman, is she not? I have never understood what justice is to be found in that line of reasoning which serves only the desires and prejudices of men. She deserves our compassion. She is not to be blamed. Theseus is the villain of the piece.'

'Bravo, sir! Well said!' thundered the Graf von Hahn, appearing behind him. 'Klesmer old chap, aren't you going to play for us? I must get home to my girls and I don't want to miss a minute of you torturing that piano.'

The circle around the Sibyl parted. Max held out his arm to her and she accompanied him into the great salon where the piano loomed, menacing the roaring discussions, still orchestrated by the assiduous Lewes who buzzed from group to group. Max felt her small firm grasp and caught the rising scent of mixed spices from the appalling lace cap which covered her hair. This thick, heavy mane, now streaked with grey, emerged around the edges of her unsuitable headdress. He looked down upon her great forehead and the protruding nose and wondered if she could ever have been beautiful. But the hypnotic grey-blue eyes turned gratefully towards him as he arranged the cushions at her back in an upright chair. She became the centrepiece of the salon, with a clear view of Klesmer at the piano.

Was she beautiful or not beautiful? He never decided the question, for then he had his answer. The musician twirled the stool upwards, thus becoming master of the keys, and faced the Sibyl before settling himself to play. His gesture was clear. He intended to play for one person alone. The rest of the company merely counted as incidental spectators. And now she gave the composer her entire attention. It was not just the generous freedom in her manners, nor her lack of affectation and the clarity of her gestures that formed the basis of her charisma, it was the passion of her attention that made her beautiful still. No man is impervious to the flattering power of a woman's concentration upon him, however ugly she might be, and Max felt the drama of her listening, as if he could hear her soul breathe. He stood behind her like a soldier on duty, taking first watch.

Klesmer leaned over the keys. The rooms rustled, fluttered, then grew silent. Everybody waited.

Max rarely listened to a concert or an opera all the way through. Even famous singers in drawing rooms paused to water their vocal cords and adjust their robes. Max took advantage of the intervals. He slipped outside on to balconies, into gardens, or took a turn around the lily pads decorating fishponds, where he always found a quiet place to loiter, smoke and scratch his testicles. But now, pinned behind the Sibyl's luminous presence, he quailed within, displayed like a collected specimen, his wings skewered with pins to the green velvet of her open curtains. The expectant hush, prolonged by Klesmer's predatory pause over the black and white keys, pressed down upon Max's spirit. The only door to the salon, far away on the long side of the room, with two unknown young men leaning against it, remained firmly closed and out of reach. There was no escape.

Then Klesmer began to play.

Surely music should soothe, reassure, inspire, entrance, or at the very least uplift the weary spirit from its bed of pain? Music should not be experienced as a personal, visceral attack on the stomach and the genitals. No piano, in Max's hearing, had ever released such an unpleasant onslaught of violent sound. The power of Klesmer's passionate surge across the keys stunned and hypnotised the assembled company. An imperious magic in his fingers seemed to send a nerve-thrill through ivory key and wooden hammer, and compel the strings to make a quivering, lingering speech for him. Melodies strutted forth like maidens in stiff new dresses, only to be crushed and shunted away before the iron march of more subversive masculine themes. A scherzo of such tearful, ripening tenderness, surely, did not deserve to be followed by such outbursts of brash rage? Max could not hear the structure. Yet he still felt the power of Klesmer's playing. For long moments he was lifted into a desperate indifference about his own doings, or at least a determination to laugh at them, as if they belonged to somebody else. He gazed at the Sibyl's pendulous, protracted jaw, which loomed beneath him in profile. She sat with her head raised, her vast concentration fixed upon the shuddering form of Herr Klesmer. Her eyes had become brighter, her cheeks slightly flushed. Max sensed that he had been utterly forgotten.

Irritated and eclipsed, he retreated to a safe place in his own mind where scepticism and good manners provided him with an impenetrable cocoon. The explosion of applause as Klesmer flung back his white head and hurled his beautiful hands into the air, high above the piano, took Max entirely by surprise. Could anyone have derived any pleasure at all from this extraordinary performance? The Sibyl passed a handkerchief across her moist eyes. Max gazed intently at the door. Klesmer rose up, mobbed at once by enthusiasts clustering round him, and acknowledged the cheering acclamations, his forehead curtained with a sheen of sweat. The full lips trembled.

'Thank you, thank you. Gnädige Frau Lewes?' He pushed his way to the Sibyl's feet. 'Madame, I beg to be released. You alone will understand me. You alone.'

He bowed to the great lady, garlanded with deafening shouts of 'Bravo' and 'Encore'. The Sibyl returned his bow from her throne, her emotion undisguised, and away swept the extraordinary Herr Klesmer, cutting a path to the door, as if armed with a scythe. The uproar in the salon continued undiminished as he stormed down the stairs, through the hallway and out into the street. The Graf von Hahn pounded in pursuit, braying his praises, jubilant. As the musician's powerful strides carried him away down the Dorotheenstraße he collected an improvised following, young men from the salon, who could not bear to quit his presence, and a Bacchic train of street children, shouting in excitement. One of them pranced beside him, blowing a tin whistle. And so, magical as the Pied Piper of Hamelin, the pianist completed his fabulous departure.

Max leaned against the wallpaper, uncomfortable, obscurely upstaged and tingling with alarm. His brother appeared beside him.

'Remarkable, most remarkable,' breathed Wolfgang, as if they had just witnessed a convincing miracle. He paused, allowing a moment for intense reverence. Then his business persona returned in force.

'Max, listen to me carefully. I have had some conversation this evening with the Graf von Hahn, and we are contemplating an extended third edition. He has invited you to visit them this week. They are still at their summer house by the lake. I will organise a carriage for you. You are to complete the negotiations, but don't give too much away. Insist upon the political risks that we are taking, but remain positive and convinced. I am sending you because he has also mentioned his eldest daughter as a possible match. Now consider this seriously, Max. It would be a most advantageous connection. I must be father and mother to you now in these matters. No obligations on either side of course, not at this stage, but bear it in mind.'

A new vista opened up before the unfortunate Max, now obliged to take in too many ideas at once. He saw a long line of clipped yews, pointed at the top and filling out towards the base, neat as chessmen on either side of a weeded gravel path. He smelled the odour of hot green in the shadowless summer heat, and at the end of this avenue, a child dressed in white and blue, her fair curls shining in the spray, danced in the fountains.

END OF CHAPTER TWO

CHAPTER THREE

steps out for a stroll in the autumn sunshine.
Sophie von Hahn bewitches the Assembled Company.

The Jagdschloss stood on the edge of a forest, bordering a lake well stocked with carp. This handsome little hunting lodge, owned by the von Hahn family for over two hundred years, extended and modernised in the eighteenth century by ancestors in enormous wigs, now gave off the perfumes of a gentleman's residence. The alterations, transforming the building, had been completed in an era when the masculine décor of antlers, stuffed boars' heads and huge fireplaces had given way to paintings, vases and curtains. Flowers and soft sofas took the place of wooden settles, marble hallways replaced the dark passages cluttered with muddy boots and guns. Yet the family still referred to the house as the Jagdschloss, and this improbable title hung over the long two-storey building, whose yellow walls and white-slatted shutters suggested a Mediterranean villa, transported from a hilltop in sunshine to the dark edges of the North. After a rainy August harvest the September days shimmered with dry roads, sweetening grapes in the conservatory, and reddening apples tumbled into rough orchard grass. Max arrived in a fine cloud of dust, discomfited and irritable, harassed by the mid-morning sun. He had dressed up in the early cool, and now wore too many clothes.

The first thing he saw was the young lady herself, the eldest daughter of the household, the goods he had come to inspect, Sophie

Anna Elizabeth Constanza, Countess von Hahn. As the carriage swung round the half-circle of gravel in front of the Jagdschloss, he glimpsed a tall, fine girl, all green stripes and bare arms, her hair mounted in plaits, held in place with a black Japanese comb. The comb flashed through the front door, the last thing certain and in focus, for the apparition squinted at him through the carriage windows, then fled back into the house. In the moment of jingling, creaking silence as the horses stopped, stamped and snorted flecks of foam, he heard a thrilling scream shear through the Chinese boxes of one room after another, opening out into long corridors, where hessian runners muffled the thunder of her boots.

'*Maman! Maman! C'est lui! C'est lui!* He's here!'

Max smiled, flattered, touched, and began to dust himself off. The moment of personal welcome from the young Countess, who had clearly been spying on the approaching roads, now vanished in the rush of family overflowing into the hallway. The Count's hunting dogs, long-eared piebald hounds and two well-brushed English black spaniels, surrounded Max and snuffled at his heels. A gaggle of young girls pounced upon him and tugged at his sleeves. The Count had three daughters in fairy-tale succession and a household of accompanying cousins, all of whom caused the *Jagdschloss* to bulge at the corners. The entire house heaved with expectant energy, like an encampment before a battle. And here they all were, babbling, calling out, thronging the steps. The Count boomed greetings and gathered up the flood of little children.

'Let the poor chap inside, my dears! Sophie? Where have you got to? It's your old playmate Max. Come to chase you into the fountains. Do you remember Karin? My youngest. And this is Lotte. Here she is. Lottie! Say hello to Max.'

He pulled a long blonde plait to identify his third daughter and Max kissed a slightly grimy cheek.

'Will you play hide and seek with us in the gardens?' demanded Karin. Lotte chewed the plait, unable to speak.

'Nonsense, dearest! He needs a cold drink first. Come on. Let him in.'

Sophie von Hahn hovered just inside the doorway. She knows, thought Max, watching her cautious hesitation. She knows that her father has asked me to choose her, and she doesn't know whether to court me or treat me as if I was of no consequence whatever. The embarrassed hesitation infected both parties, for Max, usually self-confident with loose women, who fawned on his full purse and good looks, quailed before the feral glance of this young virgin. Who knows what forces of desire will govern a young girl? Obedience to her father? Submission to her own contradictory passions, or vanity wedded to ambition? Sophie von Hahn's dark green eyes, flecked with hazel, scanned Max with animal intensity. Max took the initiative. He mounted the last step and bowed, never taking his eyes from her still face.

'Countess?' Everyone else tumbled into the house, shrieking.

She hesitated again. 'Do you remember me?'

'Of course! You covered me with oily water from your father's fountain and I had to change my braces and my shirt!'

Sophie von Hahn, sixteen years old at the time, but still running, like a young hound, with the pack of smaller children. The Count's midsummer birthday party, here at the Jagdschloss, huge red Chinese lanterns in the gardens, the children unfettered with excitement, too much alcohol in the fruit cup, everyone screaming, so that you could hardly hear the musicians, and the stone seats by the lake still warm from the sun, long after dark. Sophie von Hahn, who had taken a shine to Max and his uniform, insisted on playing find me, chase me, catch me, in the formal gardens. Finding the hidden person was not enough, you then had to catch them. Darting in and out of the pointed ornamental yews, a gaggle of children in party clothes thundering after him, Max almost pinned Sophie up against the belly of a stone Amazon, who stood guard before the fountain. But she darted underneath his outstretched arms, blue ribbons flying, and leaped on to the basin's rim. Now she was above the children clutching at her shoes, and away she went, scampering sure-footed through the spray, faster and faster.

'Sophie! Come down!'

Max grabbed one ankle and arrested her flight. But she neither stopped, nor fell. Instead she squirmed away, revealing a white-stockinged leg, a bandaged knee and a shimmer of thigh, reached into the rippling pond with cupped hands and covered Max in water. The children shrieked, jubilant, as he let her go, shaking the drops from his forehead and moustache. The spectacle of Max, drenched, proved too temptingly wonderful to behold. Sophie did it again. And now his white shirt stuck to his chest.

'You can't catch me! You can't catch me!' Sophie danced in the fountain's spray, her arms flung wide.

Now the shared memory of that gaudy night united them in a delightful conspiracy.

'You remember that!' Sophie grinned in triumph, her adolescent victory flooded back.

'You wore white lace and blue ribbons.'

She frowned; clearly that dress, last year's fashion, had long been discarded. He gazed at her corn-gold plaits and the black Japanese comb, the high collar and the tiny sunburnt freckles spattered across her nose and cheeks. She stood quite still, alert, tense as a deer hearing a footstep in the forest. Max watched the extraordinary rising curve of her breasts. Surely the girl he had dragged from the fountain's rim, damp and screaming, had been no more than a scrawny, flat-chested child.

But here was the Count again, his little wife scuttling beside him.

'Max my dear, come in, come in. Sophie, what are you thinking of? Leaving your father's publisher standing on the doorstep.'

Sophie von Hahn acknowledged his importance with a perfect rush of good manners. She snatched his hat and cane, held out her hand for an instant, and then whirled round, flinging open the coat cupboard door, which was all but concealed in the panelling. The Count stroked his whiskers and collected Max's arm while Sophie bounced beside him. Her youth and energy streamed from every limb; she appeared to walk on springs. Max found her bounding stride adorable. She was barely half a head shorter than he; the black Japanese comb, he noticed, was covered in writing.

'Has Wolfgang told you?' boomed the Count. 'A third edition!'

And so they all headed for the drawing room where the younger children were banging out 'Frère Jacques' on the grand piano.

❧

Jellies for dessert! But would the trembling mix actually set in the heat? The von Hahn family had captured an English butler on one of their frequent shopping expeditions to London and he had the marvellous idea of transporting the tray of scarlet jellies to the ice house, an igloo of stone just inside the forest, filled with blocks of ice in sacking, where they set solid within half an hour. All the French windows stood open to the late-afternoon air and the long muslin drapes, which kept marauding insects from the lake at bay, stirred in the draught. Max and the Count, left alone at the table to talk business and finish their sweet wine – lovely flavour, don't you think? Imported from Portugal! – could still hear the children shouting from the lawn's edge, as they tried to launch the little rowing boat on the dark water. The Count talked about his extended third edition of *Erinnerungen und Erlebnisse: Lebensweg eines Liberalen*, now also described as his 'testimony', and at one point as his 'legacy'. Max realised that he was merely required to nod, agree, look grave and smirk depending on the Count's mood, but to become unflinchingly direct if money was discussed. He was quite unprepared when the Count suddenly changed the subject.

'Well, young man, what about Sophie? Do you think she might fit the bill? I'm prepared to do something very handsome so far as her settlement is concerned. And she has her grandfather's fortune, provided that she keeps her title and her own name. He's always hoped for a grandson, you see, so that the family name continued in the direct line of succession. I never minded my little flood of girls. But that's not something you'd bother about, is it? We'll have to get a special dispensation, but I'll do all the paperwork. I mean, the estate is surely the most important consideration, and were you to be blessed with a son then the names of Duncker and von Hahn could be combined. I was very fond of your father and I think he would have approved the match. He held Sophie in his arms when she was a baby, you know. And there you were, still in short trousers. Five or six at the time. And when he asked if you'd like to hold her, you said, "No thank you, Papa. I would rather not!"'

The Count let out a huge guffaw and sliced up one of his own apples with a blunt fruit knife. Max blushed, completely at a loss.

'I'm sure that I would answer quite differently now, sir.' He offered this as an apology, then realised that the lady in question was a rather different proposition from a babe in arms. But the Count did not appear to remark his indiscretion.

'Of course you would. Well, no hurry. Come and see us more often. Get to know her. She's a clever child. Full of English ideas. She'll be eighteen in November. Right sort of age. I married her mother when she was eighteen. Quite lovely, she was.' The Count handed Max part of the battered apple and they sauntered out on to the lawns.

The warm late-summer smell of sunshine on damp grass dominated the gardens near the house, but as the party approached the forest paths, a darker smell brushed the air, dead leaves, turned earth, cut meadows. The hay was all in, the distant stubble burned off, the cool of longer nights lingering among the trees. Shall we walk round the lake, following the edge of the forest? Yes, I'm going on ahead. And away the children bolted, their bright colours reflected in the dark lake and against the darker green.

'Not too fast! Mind the roots! Don't fall in! Konstantin, stay back from the edge!' The Countess tumbled after the younger children, her white cap slightly askew.

'No cigarettes, mind,' warned the Count, 'the woods are far too dry.'

Max found himself once more with Sophie on one side, plucking a pine cone, and the Count on the other. He felt under arrest.

'Father says he saw you at Mrs. Lewes's salon last Sunday afternoon.' Sophie's thrilled tone revealed her passionate adulation of the Sibyl, one of the unconditional disciples. 'She must be very frightening to meet. She is so wise and clever. Is she really as ugly as everyone says?'

Max did not mishear the premature rebuke in her tone. Beauty should not count in any palace where Genius had already taken up residence. Max rose to the occasion.

'Well, she is rather startling when you see her for the first time. She has a long face and a massive head. But very beautiful grey-blue eyes. And when she speaks she leans towards you so as not to miss a single word. That's very flattering. But a bit disconcerting. Especially if you have nothing very interesting or original to say.'

Max hesitated; it had just occurred to him that the Sibyl's habit of leaning forward and peering at her guests might indicate deafness and myopia. Sophie fixed him with a delighted mischievous grin.

'Then it's not fair that you should be one of the company and not me. I should have so much to say to her. About Dinah. And Maggie Tulliver. And why must she make Dorothea so stupid as to marry an old man who sucks his soup.' The Sibyl's characters walked beside them, utterly real and closely known. 'I think she is not on the women's side. Her blonde women are vapid, egotistical and silly. They are never as clever as the dark ones.'

Sophie shook her blonde plaits so vigorously the Japanese comb slipped sideways, almost completely dislodged. The Count gently pushed it back into place.

'But I weep over her books,' Sophie continued, almost talking to herself, 'and so does Maman. No one ever makes us cry as much as Mrs. Lewes does. Not even Mr. Dickens.'

'For which I am very grateful, my dear,' cried the Count. 'Imagine if you did. Masterly and eloquent as our author is, the floodgates are opened indeed whenever we reach an affecting climax. I can hear you in my study. You'd think we had suffered a bereavement, or that one of the horses had colic.'

'Oh, there are some passages that I have by heart,' sighed Sophie, 'they are so beautiful. And it is dreadful to wait for the next book. I cannot imagine how *Middlemarch* will end. Or how she will contrive the marriage between Lydgate and Dorothea. Perhaps the fair Rosamond will have an apopleptic seizure brought on by her own selfishness or by seeing her aristocratic cousin riding away, then turn purple and die upon the sofa. Or maybe she'll be carried off in childbirth and Dorothea will comfort him.'

Sophie clearly shared the Sibyl's taste for melodrama. She flung the plucked pine cone into the lake where it floated in the shallows before vanishing into the reeds. Max decided not to reveal his utter ignorance of the plot of *Middlemarch*. The Sibyl's creation that had moved him most was not one of her rural English dramas, but the austere historical tale of *Romola*, the scholar's daughter and her dangerous mentor, the megalomaniac monk Savonarola. He had passed five blissful days, mesmerised by the careless villainy of Tito Melema and the gorgeous fiery beauty of his betrayed beloved. Max had not in fact read anything else other than this great Italian fresco and *Adam Bede*, the first novel translated and published by Duncker und Duncker. If a novel was not written by Sir Walter Scott he had great difficulty picking it up again, once he had laid it aside. He had even argued with his brother on the need for '*une histoire vraie*'. He didn't care if characters that had never existed were declared bankrupt, sucked their soup or married women far too young for the match to be suitable. Neither pathos nor intrigue accompanied their fictive destinies. But Savonarola really had governed republican Florence in the 1490s, had indeed fallen from power and walked to his flaming death. This was history; these were the stories that mattered. Max never investigated the veracity of *Ivanhoe*. There must have been knights and jousting during the Middle Ages and festive events with flags and tents, just as Scott described them. And *Old Mortality*, he remained convinced of this, recorded the persecution of the righteous dissenters in the Highlands with documentary rigour and offered a true description, not only of a savage and glamorous landscape, but of a just war. History readily translated itself into myth; but this did not mean that these fabulous tales were therefore less accurate or revealing. Max often argued that if the archaeological explorers dug where Homer said they should, they would happen upon the ancient walls of Troy.

But at his side tramped Sophie, anxious that at least one fair heroine should triumph over misadventure and innate stupidity. He glanced at the petulant shudder in her shoulders and the graceful ease of her stride. A maiden huntress, a virgin deity! But could she ever learn to love him enough to make marriage a matter of genial companionship rather than a chilly set of formal daily meetings? And could he make her happy? Max seldom gave himself up to reflection on sexual matters, he had no reason to doubt his power to charm and to seduce. But something untamed shimmered in the figure of Sophie von Hahn, who now swung round to face him, her hand on his arm, her face all passionate importunity.

'Would you introduce me? You could. You're her publisher. Well, in a way you are. I would give anything to see her and to shake her hand. Just once.'

The old Countess appeared behind her daughter. Her dapper little figure skirting a muddy patch, where a tiny stream crossed the path.

'Now, my dear, we've been over all this. When you are married you can call on Mrs. Lewes every morning.' She looked significantly at Max. 'But until then you must be a little more cautious and listen to your parents.'

'Oh Maman!' Sophie stamped one boot down in the dry leaves,

turned on her heel, lifted her skirts and pounded off down the path after the children.

The Countess took Max's arm.

'I have the very highest opinion of Mrs. Lewes. Her work will live for ever. She is one of the immortals, but her entourage, well, August tells me that you never know who you might meet. And at this stage Sophie should be a little sheltered. Innocence is so fragile, don't you think?'

Max could see nothing fragile whatsoever about the beat of Sophie's boots upon the path. Her pale slenderness and the loosened plaits vanished into the pine trees.

END OF CHAPTER THREE

CHAPTER FOUR

in which the Story pauses a little.

What is the role of a Sibyl? She is ageless, immortal, suspended in a cage, over the smoking Delphic gulf. She is also the prophetess of catastrophe and change. And so this particular Sibyl proved to be. She unravelled our common past and foresaw the dark century to come. She also transformed the shape and nature of prose fiction in the nineteenth century and altered our understanding of the novel, its role, scope and possibilities, for generations of writers and readers still unborn. The Sibyl's extraordinary manifesto in defence of realism, which appears in the famous Chapter 17 of *Adam Bede*, that chapter 'in which the story pauses a little', seems to me to be exceedingly revealing. She equates realism not only with accuracy, but honesty. Her fiction mirrors a world without perfection. Her characters speak and act, as we do, not as heroes in ideal worlds. They make alarming mistakes, with evil, lasting consequences. She creates figures overflowing with human flaws, forgiven at the last by their author, given her complete understanding of all their circumstances, and her benign compassion. Her much quoted epigram, 'Falsehood is so easy, truth so difficult,' gives me pause. Why should the truth be difficult to write or to speak? The truth is often cruel and unforgiving, unless we cloak reality in a sentimental humanitarian patina, which the Sibyl certainly seemed inclined to do. The truth is only difficult when it results in exposure, humiliation and pain, and neither the author nor her characters have the guts to face it.

She uses the famous Chapter 17 to deliver a lecture on 'the secret of deep human sympathy', in which I, for one, have never believed. And were that all the Sibyl had to offer I might never have returned to her books. But she presents her readers with other lavish gifts, her garnered knowledge and her massive, cunning intelligence; she never abandoned her jolly taste for melodrama, and we love her for it. Yet the Sibyl insisted on maintaining genteel fictions in her life that she seldom countenanced in her novels. She was never really Mrs. Lewes; that respectable identity, as the old Countess well knew, was a sham. She answered to a multitude of names, Mary Ann Evans, Marian Evans Lewes, Polly, Mutter, Madonna, and she wrote under a masculine pseudonym, her most famous name of all. And the one that lasted. No one describes Charlotte Brontë as Currer Bell, unless they are constructing a literary argument in a learned journal. The Sibyl turned out to be a master of pretence. Her fiction championed the honesty she preached, but never practised.

Realism of course, as a literary mode, has largely degenerated into tired commercial cliché, produced by lazy writers out to make a fast buck and consumed by readers in airports. That high moral purpose, championed by the Sibyl in 1859, doesn't cut much ice now. And we are swamped by what she so memorably described as 'silly novels by lady novelists'. The tendency to discipline and punish errant or ignorant characters lasted all through her writing life, and therein she was no different from her contemporaries. But the sexual sins which resulted in grisly deaths for most of the fictitious ladies in male masterpieces – Anna Karenina, Emma Bovary, Lady Dedlock in *Bleak House,* Tess of the D'Urbervilles – I could go on and on – were by and large excused by the Sibyl, indeed often accommodated and forgiven. Tessa, the chubby little *contadina* in *Romola*, never knows that she wasn't really married to Tito Melema, and the Sibyl's portrait of Florence in the 1490s is riddled with coded references to sodomy, for which the city appears to have been famous. Take another careful look at Nello the Barber and his coterie, and there you will find the

Sibyl's queer community. Adultery, no, thou shalt not die for adultery, not in her novels. But you will be punished mercilessly for greed, misplaced ambition, hypocrisy, domestic cruelty, and moral betrayal. I am deeply impressed by the sins she refused to forgive. Grandcourt gets away with keeping a mistress and fathering four illegitimate children, but his creator refuses to condone his failure to marry Lydia Glasher when at last he could have done so. The discarded mistress turns all her thwarted rage on the new wife, Gwendolen. And the latter deserves all she gets, because she married him knowing that his wealth was infected with moral corruption. *You will have your punishment. I desire it with all my soul.* That is Lydia Glasher's curse, sent with the poisoned diamonds, and I have heard our own author muttering this splendid formula to herself in the bathroom, when she thinks no one is listening.

The Sibyl entered this world in 1819, a world moving at the slower pace of coaches, a world lit by oil lamps and candles upstairs. The railways had not yet reached her local town; the Channel was traversed under sail and no one had ever heard of the telegraph, the telephone or the bicycle. Lavatory paper had not been invented, and so it fell to her, when their kitchen maid succumbed to a bilious attack, to cut up the gazetteer, and the cattle auction posters into little squares, thread them into a plump and fluttering mass and suspend them from a nail on the inside wall of the jakes. No bathroom ever existed in that house. Everyone managed with enamel chamber pots, or a brisk dash through the walled vegetable garden to the little house above the septic tank. The faint scent of urine, faeces and dark menstrual blood drifted through the rooms in summer, but without central heating, human excrement seldom festers with flies, as it would now. The Sibyl felt the cold; she wrapped herself in shawls, mantles, woollen stockings, fur-lined boots. Thrift is an admirable moral quality, but she adored discomfort for its own sake, and only ordered a fire when the windows threatened to freeze on the inside.

Behold the onset of modernity! The Sibyl witnessed the inventions of Alexander Bell and saw the last years of gas light before the advent of electricity. And one thing supported her magnificent advance into the world of celebrity and the ranks of those writers who gained great wealth through their intelligence and genius. An increasing mass within the population could now read. No mysteries here. The Education Acts of the 1870s began with the creation of 'school boards' to construct and manage schools where they were needed, to build upon the work of philanthropic charities, religious foundations and working-men's associations. The 1876 Royal Commission on the Factory Acts recommended that education be made compulsory in order to stop child labour. And the 1880 Education Act did exactly that. Thou shalt attend school between the ages of five and ten. But of course the reforms took time to enforce. Most children worked outside school hours and their families could not live without that income. Revolution follows literacy with giant strides; if the people can read then they must be carefully influenced by the right opinions. They must also be brainwashed into making extensive purchases. The front and back pages of the newspapers were given over to advertisements for hoses, corsets, dental fixtures and tennis lessons. Look at the first printed versions of *Middlemarch*. The frontispiece and back flaps were surrounded with adverts for the very tonics, purges, vitamin tablets and chest expanders against which Lydgate inveighed with such fruitless zeal.

And here comes the age of cheap editions: pocket editions, abridged editions, one-guinea editions, with illustrations, and magnificent collected editions in embossed covers. Buy the lot for a knockdown price. Cheap wood-pulp paper and one-penny-a-week subscription libraries nourished a universal desire for self-improvement. Reading is good for the bowels and enlarges the soul. The self-help message proved unbeatable.

But what of the young Countess, Sophie von Hahn, whose vivid sexual energy enticed Max into a sequence of sentimental fantasies, which went no further than undoing her plaits and allowing his fingertips to brush her flushed and angry cheeks, as he rocked home in his brother's carriage? Sophie von Hahn was born in the Year of Our Lord 1854, the same year in which the self-styled Mr. and Mrs. G.H. Lewes first visited Frankfurt, Weimar and Berlin. Lewes achieved fame in Germany as the biographer of Goethe. He interviewed many friends and acquaintances of the Great Man. The Sibyl aided his researches. She had yet to write a word of fiction. The couple arrived in Berlin in November 1854, delighted with the city, when Sophie was barely a month old. Her father, driving home at speed, anxious to see his beloved wife and tiny daughter, actually passed before their very door, where they were reading *The Merchant of Venice* aloud to one another. Lewes took the part of Shylock, which, given his love of theatre, he performed with resonating gusto and exaggerated affectation.

Sophie and the Sibyl belonged to two very different generations of Victorian women. Thirty-five unbridgeable years lay between them. They were born in different countries, grew up in different social classes, and learned to think in different languages. The Sibyl earned her wealth; Sophie inherited cash and lands in plenty. The Sibyl taught herself languages and philosophy; Sophie studied at home, surrounded by tutors of every nation. One woman assumed her right to wealth and privilege, the other clawed her way back into Victorian respectability by denying her fictional women the satisfied ambitions and desires that she claimed for herself. Cautious, conservative, of uncertain health and confidence, the Sibyl peddled a sententious wisdom that proved utterly seductive. Her novels sold and sold and sold and sold.

And Countess Sophie von Hahn, bewitched by the writer's omniscient authority, lost in adulation and illusions, continued to be one of her most enthusiastic readers.

END OF CHAPTER FOUR

CHAPTER FIVE

in which Our Hero strives to redeem himself.

Wolfgang Duncker lurched to and fro between his desk and his father's towering bookshelves, fuming with wrath against his younger brother. The rage achieved parental dimensions. Too many piled books and boxes of manuscript cluttered the floor to allow the infuriated publisher an unencumbered free passage round his office. But his fury required movement. And so he blundered between the curved oak steps, which enabled him to reach the upper levels of the shelves, and the fireplace, which contained nothing but a few charred sticks. He kicked the coal scuttle, sending a little puff of black dust into the air. Max, cowering on the low chair in the corner, tucked his boots beneath him, and attempted to remain invisible.

'You live off this firm, Max. And I think you might try to contribute something useful rather than bringing us all to ruin.'

Wolfgang thumped the desk.

'Think of everything our father put into this house. All his time, all his savings. I don't think he ever set foot in Hettie's Keller. In fact I'm quite sure he didn't.'

Max agreed. His father didn't need to do so. He kept a mistress in some style, even purchased a new apartment in Leipzig for her. Rumour had it that she was still alive, furnished with an adequate pension, that she paid visits to and received them from respectable ladies of means, and worshipped her benefactor's portrait in the evenings. But Wolfgang had now reached his climax of righteousness.

'Where do you think I am going to dig up the ready cash to pay off these debts? The end of the rainbow? The terms you agreed with Graf von Hahn are far too generous. This is the third edition, Max. The third! Everybody who wanted to do so has already read it. It will sell, but slowly, and we have to cover our costs.'

Wolfgang began rubbing his tonsure and swallowing hard. The office closed in around him, small, hot, stifling. And the clerk, lying low in the first room off the entrance hall, which also served as a warehouse, was listening hard to every thundered denunciation of the spendthrift brother. Wolfgang thought about his original reasons for sending Max out to the Jagdschloss and the charming letter he had received from the old Countess, urging him to visit them all again very soon, and be sure to bring Max. Sophie will be delighted to see him. All going well in that quarter, at least. He glared at Max, and then lowered his head like a belligerent bull. Max saw the tonsure approaching at speed.

'And when you marry? Even if she does come with a handsome settlement? What are you going to do?' Wolfgang's hot breath billowed against his cheek. 'Get through it all at the card tables and let your wife live in the street?'

Max shrank deeper into his chair. Gambling, he assumed, flourished as a pleasure among bachelors and military men, one of the many delectable things he must forgo, when he entered that realm of enchantment, which surrounded the vivid, shimmering person of the young Countess, Sophie von Hahn. The loss of the card tables would be a small price to pay for the treasures gained. The brothers gazed at one another. That profligate sum for the continuing rights and expanded edition of *Erinnerungen und Erlebnisse: Lebensweg eines Liberalen* might well prove to be a prudent financial investment. And they both knew it. Wolfgang shrugged, bit his lip and prowled back and forth.

The promissory note for Max's gambling debts had fallen due and must be honoured. They had not yet settled terms with Mrs. Lewes and that canny, grasping not-quite-husband of hers. He managed her like a racehorse, well groomed and stabled and only brought out for races where the first prize was above one thousand guineas. *Middlemarch* had been sold for something like that sum to Osgood, Ticknor and Co. in America, who originally intended to bring out the novel in weekly instalments in a paper called *Every Saturday* – handsomely illustrated. But his spies informed him that the copyright must have been sold on, for the Great Work was even now appearing in *Harper's Weekly*. Lewes, impervious to irony, published the bimonthly English version surrounded by advertisements for cordials, tinctures and surgical corsets. He actually sold space to cures for every disease of the eye by Ede's patent American Eye Liquid! Hedging his bets, that crafty little ape of a man! The Sibyl loomed before Wolfgang, a great Atlantic ship, her funnels gusting steam, while Lewes leaped around the engine room, shovelling coal and pumping the bellows. What on earth could he offer for the Continental reprint? Before Tauchnitz sprang in ahead of him?

He inspected his brother through narrowed eyes. Max was folding and refolding his gloves. Max. Once more the Sibyl had asked for Max. He had a secret weapon tucked away in his office, which he wasn't yet using to his best advantage. The Sibyl manifested many little weaknesses, and one of them, which seemed bizarre to Wolfgang, who calculated her sales figures on a regular basis, was her craving for admiration and praise. She needed a young man, a handsome young man, attentive at her elbow, holding her shawl, and confirming her charismatic magnetism with every devoted glance. But could Max be trusted? Wolfgang glowered at the warm red rug and a hole bored by an escaped coal. Max must be sent on a mission and made to realise that this was his chance, his one chance, to redeem himself.

'All right,' snapped Wolfgang, 'I'll write you a cheque and you can pay your debts. But you'll have to earn the money. You're going to Homburg, either tonight or on the morning train. The Leweses are already there, drinking the waters and wallowing in the baths. They've rented the first floor at Obere Promenade 14. Here's the address. I heard from her today. They're besieged by the English, but you can deal with the adoring crowds. Her new work is all but finished, and we must have it, both the Continental reprint and the translation rights. I'll give you a margin and an upper limit. Never negotiate with Lewes if she's not there. He'll hound you into a corner. If he pushes you up, withdraw; say you need to speak to me. You can't shake hands on any deal without my consent. Is that clear? On the other hand we must secure the rights. She wants to come back to us. Loyalty means something to her; she has a sentimental streak. But he doesn't. And he's the business brain. He'll talk her up. Remember, they're rich now. And everybody wants to know them.'

Wolfgang fingered his first editions of her works, which were all still conspicuously displayed on green velvet, in anticipation of her last visit.

'And Max –'

His brother had risen to go, disguising the guilty sweat on his palms. He stiffened, expecting another onslaught.

'If I find out that you have so much as touched a card or rested an elbow on the black and red squares in the Kursaal I shall halve your allowance, confine you to the country house, whatever the weather, and write to the Countess von Hahn giving her the honest reasons for my decisions. Is that clear?'

Max went white. The twelve years between the brothers suddenly expanded into thirty, and he faced the balding patriarch his father had once been, stuttering explanations as to what he had done with the eggs. In the Duncker household there was a daily accounting. And it did not do to be weighed in the balance and found wanting.

When Max arrived in the not quite fashionable portion of the street where the Leweses had taken lodgings the couple were not at home. The housekeeper explained that they walked every afternoon in the parks and woods. She then added that the sure signs of their home-coming, clods of mud and leaves, littered her staircase every day. The town streets appeared quite dry, even the horse shit crumbled in the gutters, leaving the crossing sweepers with very little work to do. But the Leweses avoided the crowded promenade, headed off past the bandstand and plucked their way through brambles and woodland to the river. They even visited the outlying villages and returned bearing sprigs of late-flowering briar roses, all thorns and no scent, with which they decorated their rooms above. Max and the ruddy housekeeper inspected her freshly swept wooden staircase like a pair of private detectives, and concluded that Mr. and Mrs. Lewes were still at large. Max wrote his hotel address, the Grand Continental, exceedingly fashionable and littered with English tourists, on the back of his card and placed it carefully in the pottery bowl on a dresser in the hallway. He flicked through the other cards left by Lady Castletown, Mrs. Wingfield, and a folded message from a painter called Hans Meyrick. Could it be the same man he had met in the Neues Museum in Berlin, picked out by Wolfgang as a possible illustrator? He had discovered Meyrick carefully reproducing the statues of classical antiquity in a giant sketchbook; a jolly good fellow, according to his friends, often to be found in Hettie's Keller, and up for a laugh. Max unfolded the note and attempted to decipher the script, but gave up when the housekeeper peered suspiciously over his shoulder.

'Tell Mr. and Mrs. Lewes that I will call again tomorrow.' He strolled away down the steps and mingled with the passing crowds.

September turned out to be a popular month for the English in Homburg. The Casino overflowed in the warm nights; the throng in the Assembly Rooms crowded the dancers. Max paused in a quiet square before the Synagogue and watched the men and women separating at the entrance. He determined to resist the *Kursaal* and its gaming tables, for Wolfgang never delivered empty threats, but he now found himself at a loss, not hungry enough for supper and very bored. The hotel dining room gaped like an abyss, packed with vague acquaintances whose names he could not accurately remember, and aged military types, armed with manuscript memoirs, anxious to be as successfully published and as extensively discussed in the press as the now notorious Count von Hahn. Duncker und Duncker dealt in the very latest celebrities. Max decided that he had pandered long enough to the rich and famous.

He consulted his small guide to the spa, borrowed from his brother. The rudimentary map only showed the main sights: Thermal Baths, Konditorei, Gymnasium, Kursaal, Lawn Tennis, Theatre, Assembly Rooms, Royal Schloss with Gardens and Fountains, Churches (various), Synagogue, Concert Hall, Grand Continental Hotel, Pension (various), Parks, Open-air Bandstand, Freilichtbühne, Belvedere. He passed the street sellers hawking flowers, apples, plums in sugar, and the very first brazier, roasting nuts, that he had seen that autumn, all gathered round the market entrance. Even the smaller hotels bulged with visitors. He heard children playing on the swings, beyond the high brick wall of Frau Heide's Very Superior Pension. Should I go this way? Or this way? He halted at a crossroads and watched an empty cart lurching slowly over the cobbles and onward beneath the yellowing trees.

Dusk had settled on the little town as Max coasted carefully into the darker eddies, where carriages passed infrequently and gentlemen walking alone were honoured and anticipated. Even in the rural suburbs, remote from the main baths, the streets gleamed clean, the dust damped down and recently swept. Max began to doubt his informant's directions. He lit a match and consulted a handwritten address: Königgasse 8. Be assured of a royal welcome! Yes, here it is – the knocker on the door is a snarling lion, beautifully polished, and shining in the gloaming. Courage, comrades, joy awaits us! Max felt an erection rising against the buttons of his slightly-too-tight trousers.

The opening door revealed a huge expectant smile, and the warm smell of a female body, recently perfumed, gusted into his face. She barricaded the doorway, large, big-breasted, her teeth even and clean. Her arse blotted out the light. He brushed against her as he entered.

'Bonsoir, Mademoiselle.' Max set the tone and bowed low.

She giggled.

'Come in, sir, come in.'

The first rendezvous of the evening, but the fizzing Sekt was a little too warm and the rooms, in heavy patterned red silk, close and airless. The *Hausmutter* accepted his cluster of coins with a cordial nod and waddled away into her private chamber to count them. The overflowing bosom that had welcomed him into the bower of bliss oozed against his shoulder. She smelt of musk.

'My sister would like to dance for you. Shall I call her in?'

I'll have to pay off the dancer too, Max calculated, wondering what he would say if Wolfgang forced him to account for every last thaler.

'Perhaps we could get to know each other better first?' he suggested, chivalric even in a situation where the imminent transaction was utterly clear, the price already named and paid.

But the maiden presented little information beyond the fact that she had grown up in the country, loved her mother's farm and sent money home every week. Her mother believed that she was still in service at one of the big houses in Homburg; unfortunately she was obliged to quit her favourable situation, when her figure, seen to advantage while she was bending over a grate, attracted her master's unwelcome attentions. She explained the regrettable incident with great good cheer, from which Max deduced that she earned more as a prostitute than she had done as a housemaid, and had better working conditions.

The lady looked anxiously at the clock under its glass dome on the dresser and Max suspected that the second engagement might even now be approaching. The tariff rose alarmingly after the first hour. He gulped down his draught of warm bubbles and followed her into a dark closet. The bed was covered in russet shawls, the blinds drawn, the shutters closed. The air felt thrice breathed. He stumbled over a row of little boots. The girl's white thighs gleamed in the obscurity as she raised her skirts. Max gently lowered them again, patting her cheek. He decided not to take the risk of venturing into unknown canyons and gorges, only to find that many nations had already planted their flags. Instead, he settled himself on her mattress and deliberately undid the buttons of his trousers. She tucked her breasts between his thighs as she knelt before him. The bed shuddered a little as she began to suck and push, kneading his stomach like a hungry cat. But they lurched off together, rocking in rhythm, a brave little ship leaving harbour and catching the first wind.

Max felt the wonderful moment of approaching darkness as the lady's lips sucked his penis into a priapic arch. The delightful explosion ended in salvage, as the maiden expertly fielded every drop upon her handkerchief. Through his muttered groans Max heard her praising his Tremendous Engine, its magnitude and voracity; flattering practised phrases, which, nevertheless, were pleasing to hear. He kissed her forehead, and bending to undo the ribbons on her bodice, released both breasts into the fetid air. They swayed before him, gigantic and comfortable. Lying back upon the russet shawls he sucked both nipples into pyramids, resisting the temptation to forage further beneath her skirts and incur more substantial expense. He had spent all he could afford for one evening. But he felt neither guilt nor regret. During his unsteady progress in darkness, back along the unfamiliar streets, Max felt well disposed towards all mankind and a little in love with his farmer's daughter, whom he determined to visit again, as soon as his business with the Sibyl and her dancing whiskered husband should be concluded.

❧

But on the following morning, when he presented himself on their doorstep, he encountered Mr. and Mrs. Lewes dressed and ready to go out. Mrs. Lewes dipped her head and he found himself bowing to an enormous green bonnet trimmed with a deep red frill. The green shawl draped over her shoulders slipped a little and was immediately rescued and straightened by Lewes, who began gabbling cheerfully.

'Ah Max! We're on our way to your hotel to winkle you out. D'you know Meyrick? The painter? He's offered to conduct us round his studio. Wants to paint Polly of course, but we'll look at what he does first before we agree to anything.'

Max lifted his hat and stood aside, making polite noises of assent, and offering his arm to the Sibyl as she descended the steps like a recently awakened deity. He caught a glimpse of the slight wolfish smile as she peered cautiously up into his face. And so the little party set off through the still uncrowded streets, the dark-suited gentlemen on either side, the Sibyl cruising gently between them. The chilly air smelt of bonfires and dead leaves. Autumn now freshened the wet pavements and the street vendors seemed slower to animate their baskets and carts. The spa dozed in the early day.

Lewes chatted energetically, leaning across to Max, breaking off to greet the odd acquaintance, everyone bowed to the couple as if they were passing royalty, who had mysteriously mislaid their carriage. The Sibyl murmured the odd comment in German, but otherwise concentrated on picking her way over the cobbles as they descended into the old town and the narrow, secluded streets.

'You must excuse me, Max,' she whispered, when they arrived at the painter's door. 'I am suffering from an appalling attack of neuralgia, which came upon me in the night. But I am anxious to visit Mr. Meyrick. He has been so warmly recommended to us. Ah, we have found him at last.'

Am Mühlweg 17 towered above them, an immense wooden house. Pale, late roses mingled with Michaelmas daisies surrounded a veranda covered in dead leaves. A child eating an apple opened the door and pointed to an endless staircase lit from above by a dusty roof-light. Meyrick himself came bounding down two flights to greet them;

Max and Lewes adjusted the speed of their climb to allow for the Sibyl's toothache.

The painter leaped to and fro like an excited dog, his face encircled with very long ginger curls, but he was freshly shaven and clearly wearing his cleanest shirt. Max recognised him at once as the man working in charcoal before the blank-eyed figures of goddesses and gladiators in the winter halls of the Neues Museum.

'We met in Berlin,' he said, shaking hands. 'I am the brother of Mrs. Lewes's publisher.'

But Meyrick, clearly desperate to impress the visiting celebrities and secure his commission, merely nodded, bowed and welcomed him into the draughty atelier, then flung himself into captivating the silent Sibyl, whose prophecies and pronouncements remained suspended. The studio smelt of turpentine, mixed paints, linseed oil and burned vegetables. Meyrick clearly lived where he worked. An assortment of cooking pots littered the brick hearth surrounding a small black stove, apparently the only heating in the huge cavernous space. Coals glowed through a round gap in the lid and the hob chuffed gently like a stationary steam engine. Vast northern windows welcomed the autumn light. Unfinished canvases turned their faces to the wall, so that all they could see were the rough sketches and the brown mesh of the reverse sides. Meyrick led them straight to his easel where he had prepared a sofa, covered with a glaring white linen sheet, ready for Mrs. Lewes, who subsided thankfully, her skirts compressing like an expiring bellows.

'I prefer grand historical subjects,' declared the painter, 'but created in the spirit of that stern realism so admired by your English artistic brotherhood. Yet I also treasure that affecting tenderness that I fancy best illustrates my own style. Here is the last in a series of four: *Berenice Weeping in the Ruins of Jerusalem*.'

The painting revealed a beautiful young woman, her rich clothes ripped and torn, her feet bare, her gaze vacant and empty, the lovely breasts partially exposed. All around her lay a great city destroyed; the temple toppled and the roofs aflame. The eerie atmosphere surrounding the abandoned grieving woman gained in intensity from the fact that the city appeared to be entirely uninhabited. No other figure haunted the picture. Jerusalem, in Meyrick's vision, resembled ancient Rome, rather than an Eastern walled fortress, which, Max suspected, would have been nearer the mark. But the detail was extraordinary, crisp and sharpened like a photograph, each fallen brick and splintered column painted with a meticulous attention to shadow and weight. The city's calamitous destruction could have been caused by an earthquake, or any other act of God, as the victors were nowhere visible, nor were the bodies of the slain. Berenice herself appeared to be both agent and victim of the absolute ruin that surrounded her. Max thought he recognised the model, but could not be certain. The maiden in the painting was a dark-eyed beauty, representing the Jewish princess, whose tragic story now ended in catastrophe.

'Did she ever return to Jerusalem according to the legend?' asked Lewes, peering closely at the woman's delicately painted breasts.

'She was cast out from Rome,' murmured the Sibyl, drawing her shawl closer to her massive aching jaw, 'but no one knows where she died.'

'I like to believe that she returned to her people,' said Meyrick. Max now convinced himself that he had indeed recognised the magnificent breasts through the shimmering veil of convenient myth. *The Rape of the Sabine Women*, which Meyrick now displayed, contained naked breasts a-plenty and some extraordinarily convincing Roman thighs, partially covered in metal and leather. The artist's genius for creating surfaces and tiny, convincing details loomed out at Max: the thonged sandals of the screaming women and the bloody sides of white horses, wounded in battle. That much-praised stern realism now seemed menacing and uncanny. He found himself eyeball to eyeball with the inside of a woman's mouth as he shouldered the canvas on to the easel, with Meyrick supporting the other end. The entire painting writhed and howled. Even the blood appeared fresh and dripping.

'I completed this last year upon my return from Rome.' Meyrick began to explain the composition.

Max inspected the other, smaller canvases that Meyrick had prepared for them to see. Here was Echo fleeing from Narcissus and the Bacchae in thrall to Dionysus, tumbling after their erotic enchanter. The dancing god sported long ginger curls, his golden cup raised in ecstasy. Max half closed his eyes to absorb the energy of the gesture and the naked glory of the figure; he recognised the self-portrait of the artist by the intense stillness of the features. The first follower clung to his arm, and now Max smiled, quite certain that he was gazing at the very lips that had tasted his own body the night before. Here she was, the long blonde hair dishevelled and unfurled, the warm country cheeks, the vast magnificent nipples, and the abstracted glance of the professional prostitute. Meyrick's model is surely also his mistress. Ah, and here she is again, as Titania, or could it be Queen Mab? I see Queen Mab hath been with thee tonight! Well, sir, she has also been with me. Max ogled the naked Fairy Queen, imagined his lips on her breasts, and then bent to study the picture, obscurely embarrassed by the opulence of the woman he shared with the painter.

'My Shakespearian studies are taken mostly from the tragedies.' Meyrick was anxious to present himself as a serious painter. '*Othello*, *Macbeth* and *Lear*. Here is Lear with Cordelia murdered, cradled in his arms. But ah, sir, I see that you have uncovered my Titania.'

Max raised the painting from the dusty floor to the easel.

'Goodness,' cried Lewes, snatching up the offered magnifying glass. 'Polly! Come and look. Never in my life have I seen so many fairies.'

'There's a good-natured competition among the painters here,' explained Meyrick, 'to see how many fairies we can squeeze on to one canvas. Would you believe that there are one hundred and sixty-five fairies in these Athenian woods? All busy about their queen! I won the Fairy Prize for this painting,' he added with a smug flourish, handing the glass to the Sibyl, who rose unsteadily and approached the picture.

The visitors sniffed the flamboyant varnished surface, peering at one tiny, grotesque figure after another. The little people belonged to several different species. Some marched in ranks, wearing uniforms with tiny golden buttons, others, bizarrely clothed in savage grass skirts and adorned with garlands of minuscule flowers, whirled in circles, holding hands. Two little elves with pointed ears approached bearing a parade of exotic fruits on silver platters: pineapples, apricots, oranges, dates and pears, the flesh of each delicacy painted with exquisite care. A couple galloped past on miniature donkeys and a wizen-faced crone in a cap of bells danced all alone in a corner. The surface of the painting quivered with activity and movement. Three tiny ladies peered at their faces in even tinier mirrors, others melted disturbingly into half-human, half-animal forms. A little row of blue-skinned goblins played on cithers, lutes and a large tuba. A gaggle of junior fairies, one picking his minute nose, clutched their slates, attentive to their elfin master, whose ferocious bobble eyes bulged out of all proportion to his face and reddening ears. One creature with hooves and hairy legs dived into the ground beside the giant fingers of his sleeping queen.

'My word, Meyrick,' cried Max, genuinely impressed, 'only an overdose of laudanum could have produced these delicate and scaly beasts! How did you dream them all up?'

'Oh, there are fashions in fairy painting,' said Meyrick, unabashed.

'I have seen your Titania before, however,' said the Sibyl. 'She is there in your Roman canvas, grappling with the soldiers, and here beside Dionysus, clinging to her chosen god. If I am not mistaken she is also Echo and Pandora.'

'You are very perceptive, Mrs. Lewes.' Meyrick bowed his assent. Max stared at the discerning Sibyl, suddenly feeling exposed and accused, as if the all-seeing Sibyl had watched him, oiled with lust, sucking Titania's breasts.

She smiled slightly, raising her deeply lined face and glowing eyes towards the painter.

'I suffer from toothache, sir, and my hearing is not what it was, but my powers of observation are undimmed. And here is a lady who has not always been an artist's model. Your stern realism, Mr. Meyrick, betrays her earlier professions. She was either in service, or has worked on the land. Look at her hands. Those are the hands of a woman who works. They are beautiful, but they are also calloused and hard to the touch.'

The Sibyl sank back once more on to the white shroud, while all three men examined Titania's roughened hands.

'The Fairy Queen did not, I think, scour her own doorstep,' continued the Sibyl from her throne, 'but I love the busyness of this painting. It exudes the energy and bustle of a street scene in Fairyland, the more so because their ruler, even in her gigantic sleep, appears to dream their presence. This work is a miracle of varying scales, like Piranesi's vaulted staircases, ascending into darkness.'

Lewes spun round and gazed at her with affectionate concern. 'Shall I take you home at once, Polly? That toothache has not eased at all. You already look exhausted.'

The Sibyl raised her gloved hand to his. 'I fear we are obliged to discuss the question of the portrait on another occasion, Mr. Meyrick.'

Max offered his arm to support her, while Lewes rearranged her shawl. She looked up at him gratefully, but remained silent.

❧

'Anyone who hates faults, hates mankind.' This assertion was delivered in sweet, firm tones. Nobody dared to dissent.

The Sibyl sat in the light by their window, reading aloud to Lewes when Max entered their sitting room. She completed her sentence and looked up, every gesture slow, patient, careful. Max found it impossible to imagine her hurried or alarmed. He bowed and lowered his eyes to avoid the terrifying smile. Lewes sat by the fire with his feet perched on a low stool, balancing a currant bun on a toasting fork. The tea tray stood ready on the table by the lamp. He bounded over to shake Max's hand, wielding the steaming bun like a Devil's prod.

'Come in, Max, come in. I hope we can dispense with all the formalities. You find us revisiting Lucian. Rather upon your account, I gather. Polly is gathering her forces to complete the Finale of her Great Work and then we shall celebrate.

'For now the matchless deed's achieved,
Determined, dared and done!

'Well, almost done.'

Max clasped the Sibyl's mittened paw, with, he hoped, suitably submissive reverence. And then settled down to listen to more of the odious Lucian, whose sinister *Fragment* now clearly rested in her lap. The Gothic script facing the Latin original announced the existence of a German translation. Max feared the worst. The Sibyl's voice, low and persuasive, resumed the narrative, left floating through history by the provincial governor of Mysia and Lydia, marooned far from Rome, battling with corrupt officials, insurgent slaves and disturbing news from the frontiers. He spent his days in court and the evenings coaxing his resentful wife to sample the local spices. But he found himself confronting a new religion, which threatened to undermine the state. For the altars were deserted; no one purchased sacrificial doves or votive silver offerings for the Temple of Jupiter. The gods ceased to speak, the augurs fell silent, the entrails lay bloody upon the altar slab of prophecy, uninterpreted, meaningless and blank. Something new had arisen from the gutter, something irrational and inhuman, a heresy slithering out from beneath the wreckage of Jerusalem and the slaughter of the Jews. The thing proved as tenacious as an Asiatic infection, spreading slowly, like lichen on damp stones.

'I was asked to investigate the Christians by the Emperor Trajan, who suggested that we should interrogate the servants of the main households under suspicion. At first we had imagined that the new religion remained confined to the artisan class and located near the docks, but various accusations brought before me suggested that some of the major households in the town had become tainted by the sect. My informants revealed that Christianity originated with the Jews, who await a saviour, or a messiah. The Christians believe that He is come. This is unlikely, as their young Prophet was executed by Pontius Pilate, during the reign of Herod in Judaea. So far as I was able to ascertain, no major insurrection against Rome was ever planned by these disciples. The Christians meet on the first day of the week to say prayers, chant devotional verses, and share a simple meal of bread and wine. But preachers of the hotter sort made themselves known at Ephesus. And a riot is recorded. The struggle appears to have taken place between the Christians gathered in the theatre and the silversmiths, whose business, located in the streets below the temple of many-breasted Diana, consisted of making silver images of the god and offerings to her for healing and protection during childbirth. The Christians proclaim One God, all-powerful, invisible and transcendent, who needs no idols or incessant blood sacrifice. Nor presumably any expensive, delicate, silver shrines. The silversmiths are reported to have got the better of the encounter, racing through the streets shouting, "Great is Diana of the Ephesians!" and pillaging shops supposedly owned or run by Christians.

'It was upon the Emperor's wise insistence that this growing flame should be quenched. This, therefore, became my mission, and I began by handling the interrogations personally. I demanded of the accused whether or not they subscribed to the new religion. If they denied the charge and offered prayers to our gods, and gifts of wine and incense to the statue of the Emperor, they were pardoned and set free, whatever the nature of the accusations made against them. If however, after persistent warnings, they refused to deny their faith, I ordered them to be led away to execution. The Emperor himself advised me that an infallible test was to demand that they spit upon the name of Christ, as no genuine Christian would ever do this. I was loath to inflict that test upon the citizens before me, many of whom were mere children, women and slaves. In fact the sheer variousness of the people brought before the courts roused my instincts of alarm. The new faith respected neither sex, nor caste, nor indeed class, for the usual hierarchies in households where the infection had taken root became unstable or were even dissolved. A maid and her mistress went to their deaths together, supporting one another, singing praises to their invisible god. This scene took place in the public arena, and caused much widespread and unfortunate scandal, engendering seditious discussions in the marketplace, for the woman had been a notorious benefactor in the town, contributing substantial sums to a variety of causes. Adepts of the Christ claim to be sinners, guilty of various spiritual crimes that I could not understand, and yet to have been made perfect through the grace of their god. I have not resolved this contradiction.'

The Sibyl laid down the *Fragment* and looked up.

'I rather think we have not either, not in our own age. It is the misfortune of Christianity to insist, not on the fallibility of human nature, a quality even Lucian acknowledges in his gentle acceptance of our weaknesses, but on its criminal wickedness. As for the doctrine of original sin, I see no conclusive evidence in its favour. Either in the types of humankind, or in individuals.'

Lewes popped a tea cake on his toasting fork and handed the steaming bun to Max. 'Lucian ruled Mysia with an iron fist, did he not?' remarked Lewes calmly. 'He never gave original sin a chance to take root. If he discovered anyone afflicted with that inherited disease they were in breach of Roman law.'

'Lucian was an atheist. Religious convictions have never been a prerequisite for moral excellence,' smiled the Sibyl, coming to the tea table. 'But I agree. He prided himself on the fact that he was a ruthless governor. Lucian took no chances.'

'Could a just ruler conduct a moral reign over his citizens or his subjects without any religious principles at all?' Lewes clearly enjoyed a good dispute.

Max rarely troubled himself with intellectual speculations concerning ethics, let alone metaphysics, but something he had discovered in his researches for his all too easily abandoned *Geschichte des Altertums* now clanged like a rising bell.

'Was the main city of Mysia called Sardis or Pergamum?' demanded Max, to the general astonishment of the Leweses, whose teacups froze in mid-air. Max had sat silent, attentive and decoratively pleasant to the eye for so long that his voice boomed into the warmth of their food, carpets and furniture.

'Both Sardis and Pergamum were situated inland, I believe,' said the Sibyl, manifestly capable of conjuring all biblical history out of her massive brain in an instant. 'Lucian mentions both cities. But at that time Ephesus was a considerable port. The earthquake, which buried the town, filled the land between the arena and the sea with rubble from the mountain. Many of the great cities on the Anatolian coast ceased to exist because they became separated from the Mediterranean by increasing undredged silt. Lucian speaks of the docks in his comments on the Christians, and he certainly embarked at Ephesus when he returned to Rome by sea. The Seven Churches established by the time of Trajan's campaigns between AD 98 and 117 were often located in ports, and St Paul travelled frequently by ship. He was shipwrecked on the rocks of Malta and immediately set about converting the island to this new faith.'

The Sibyl sipped her tea and took a moment to reflect.

'Lucian compares the new religion to a plague, spread through the waterways. All seven churches of the Apocalypse were established in the provinces over which he was governor: Ephesus, Smyrna,

Pergamos, Thyatira, Sardis, Philadelphia and the unfortunate lukewarm Laodiceans.'

She stretched forth her cup towards her husband and uttered a rich, warm laugh.

'My tea is in imminent danger of becoming a Laodicean!' Her huge pendulous face lit up like a young girl's, mischievous, merry and comical. '"I know thy works, that thou art neither cold nor hot: I would thou wert cold or hot. So then because thou art lukewarm, and neither cold nor hot, I will spue thee out of my mouth!"'

Max dreaded the fate of all those found to be lukewarm.

'Poor Lucian,' continued the Sibyl. 'The infection clung to his rocks and terraces, taking root and growing fast. The games were eventually banned; the temples ruined and abandoned.'

'But was the old religion worth saving?' asked Max, thinking aloud. He gave up trying to follow the Sibyl's sympathies and set about wolfing cake.

'Now there's a good question, Polly! And posed with the candid open-mindedness of a free-thinker, if I may say so, Max!'

The unfortunate Max munched his cinnamon and raisin cake in horror. For here was conclusive proof that he sat among advocates of that dark doctrine, which teaches that man is dust, and nothing but dust.

'Yes, it is a good question,' said the Sibyl, unperturbed, 'and much depends upon how we understand the rise of Christianity, for if we view all new religions as a voyage towards the idea of God, then the Jews hold a special place, not only because of their unusual monotheism but because of their emphasis on human responsibility. The great strength of the Olympian gods lies not only in their all too human fallibility, which reflects the imaginations of their creators, but also in the pagan emphasis on the holy nature of the earth in their representation of divinity. We have sacred groves, sun gods and water nymphs. The ancients worshipped the world before us. Poseidon and Apollo rule the waters and the skies.'

She turned confidingly to Max.

'Since Mr. Lewes purchased a microscope we have not ceased to wonder at the miraculous organisation of those tiny worlds hidden from our ordinary sight. Not unlike Mr. Meyrick's paintings, although we have never yet come across the little people. I believe that in a remoter time the gods represented and celebrated our link to those unrevealed worlds within worlds.'

She paused to accept another cup of tea, smiling tenderly at Mr. Lewes's fingertips.

'And the earth is filled with treasures that we would be wise to treat with reverence. But in our own time we see them clearly with the eyes of science: our geologists, naturalists, and, of course our extraordinary Mr. Darwin, the beauty of whose *Origin of Species* never ceases to enthral us. No, it is the human endeavour of shaping our own history which determines the rise and fall of our religions. We create the gods we need.'

Max wondered if he would actually survive the conversation. He changed the subject.

'I am to join an archaeological expedition to Anatolia led by Professor Kurt Marek in the spring. Pergamum is one of the places where we obtained permission to begin our researches. We shall hunt down biblical truth by digging it up.'

Both Lewes and the Sibyl turned upon him with expressions of transfixed and startled interest.

'Well now, Polly, here's a turn-up for the books! Our Max is not content with challenging received opinions of antiquity, he intends to retrieve his own version with a shovel!'

And the whiskered little man leaped out of his seat to extinguish a flaming tea cake, pounding his guest on the shoulder as he did so. The Sibyl's calm gaze rested upon Max, intrigued and intent, as if he had translated himself into a phenomenon that surpassed all her expectations.

END OF CHAPTER FIVE

CHAPTER SIX

records the Narrator's speculations on the Mysteries of Marriage and reveals one or two Interesting Possibilities intrinsic to the Plot.

Max had in fact agreed to join the archaeological expedition under some pressure from his brother, who put up the necessary funds. Wolfgang engaged both an artist and a photographer to accompany the troop of historical scholars, and intended to publish the first photographs of the great temples unearthed, should they be as glorious as was generally supposed. The publisher had cleverly spotted a method of making his recalcitrant brother useful, and, with one stroke, removing him from Berlin's more immediate temptations. Off you go, Max. I'll buy you a splendid set of trowels, picks and boots, and suitable clothes for a different climate. The Turks did not countenance gaming tables outside Constantinople, where they supposedly existed for the sole amusement of tourists and visitors. Max's travelling allowance would be strictly rationed, thaler by thaler, or, if the much-heralded new currency should ever come to pass, a fixed amount of Reichsmarks, donated every month to the Embassy account, and not one pfennig more.

But for Max, as he sauntered away from the Lewes household in the early evening, both consideration of the terms Lewes himself had written out for the Continental reprint and the translation rights of *Middlemarch*, now so nearly completed, and, indeed, the archaeological spring expedition, had all but faded completely from his mind. Two things disturbed his youthful complacency: the sudden, casual emergence of that modern philosophy of atheism, whose contaminated air he had inadvertently sucked in, and the nature of the bond between the Sibyl and her married lover. No god sanctified this union. They stood alone before an ungoverned universe, braided with meaningless accidents and mysterious unseen laws, visible only to science. The Sibyl had staked her all on one man's faithful trust. And she seemed very far from being a lost and fallen woman. Indeed, she gave every indication that she enjoyed contented happiness with her loquacious, energetic husband, her social celebrity and obvious wealth. Was she one of the wicked, who shall flourish like the green bay tree? This was completely improbable. The Sibyl gleamed from afar, a moral lighthouse, benevolent and wise. She dispersed her radiance to a higher moral circle, far above the general populace, whose ignoble desires rose no further than a moment of sweaty fumbling on the dance floor or an elbow resting on the gaming tables. But if no God watches, judges and foresees our every deed, then why should not evil flourish? For who shall stop us? And the faintly guilty flush Max felt about the throat as he tapped away over the cobbles of the Königgasse was infantile and irrelevant. Take your pleasures, sir, enjoy. Morality is simply the limit of what you can get away with. The God of his childhood either did not give a damn, or did not exist. True, the Sibyl could not be received in decent, English bourgeois company, but actually, who cares? She kept company with ambassadors, intellectuals, aristocrats and princesses on the Continent. Writers travelled from America to sit at her feet. The casino still stood, for a few more months at least, littered with all sorts and conditions of men, peacefully rubbing shoulders at the roulette table, eyes narrowed and fixed, not upon each other, but upon the red and the black.

Max, you will remember, has received a proposition, if not a firm proposal of matrimony, to which he is not averse. But neither is he inclined to follow it up with any degree of haste. He is a conventional man, but lacks those spots of commonness, with which the Sibyl adorned one of her fictional heroes, who chose his wife to match the furniture. Respectable virgins, at least in Max's eyes, prowled the Assembly Rooms like panthers, dangerous, supple, on the watch. He always took care to dance with every pretty girl in the ballroom. Two dances each. His habits never changed, he loitered, bowed and vanished, wary of the circling mothers, who closed in at once if he led a girl out on to the balcony, or into the dining room to look for ices on the buffet. Max never underrated women's passions or their cunning. How these unstable waters could be negotiated in matrimony remained a mystery to him.

And indeed, they are a mystery to me. What qualities in a man and a woman allow a marriage, legitimate or otherwise, to prosper and endure? Never underestimate the power of habit. Most men cease to see or listen to their wives in all but the most general terms fairly early on in the engagement. If the deal has been arranged, as it often was in the nineteenth century, he is more likely to be wondering if he can live with her perpendicular nose and podgy hands than listening to her statements of desire with any great attention. If he has married for love his central preoccupation will be with his own powerful feelings, and the sad necessity of keeping his prick in his pants before the appointed day. If indeed he does. The Welsh have a wonderful tradition called 'bundling' – that is, courting in bed. And presumably the knot is hastily tied if the woman falls pregnant. With the lady's fertility established and the inheritance secure, the marriage may then proceed with celebrations and blessings.

John Fowles, in the first of many books to assault the nineteenth century with the sensibility of the twentieth, which then indeed opened the Neo-Victorian gates to the pornographic gusto of the twenty-first century, mentions the fact that among Dorset peasants in the 1880s, 'conception before marriage was perfectly normal. Thus premarital sexual intercourse *was the rule, not the exception.*' (Italics in the original.) Fowles goes on to assert that, in the Victorian period, when a man and a woman of the middle classes were introduced, shook hands and conversed, the possibility that they would go to bed together remains simply inconceivable and not on the table, as he supposes – or hopes – that it is in the modern world. Fowles, writing in the midst of the so-called sexual liberation of the 1960s, 1967, an iconic year, set his novel, *The French Lieutenant's Woman*, precisely one hundred years earlier. Now, the usual point of writing an historical novel is to measure the distance travelled between those previous generations, and ourselves; sometimes we contemplate the roads not taken, and expose the reasons why. But sometimes we venture down precisely those unknown, un-chosen roads, rewriting history as fiction. This is what might have happened, should have happened. Even if it didn't.

But Mr. Fowles doesn't do that, he gives us a good story and a just account of mid-Victorian attitudes, sexual, political and religious. But, in tones that are often patronising and contemptuous, his narrator uses a 1960s set of sexual prejudices, all, to my mind, male, misogynistic, lecherously and vigorously heterosexual, and pre-AIDS, to bash the Victorians as a just punishment for their rampant hypocrisy and sexual confusion. It's easy to crow, isn't it, if you imagine yourself in possession of superior sexual hindsight? But I want to challenge Fowles on his own territory. Did middle-class men and women in the 1870s approach one another without a sexual thought in their heads? Surely Max speculated freely on the bizarre idea of the magnificent Sibyl, who radiated *noli me tangere*, except to kiss my gloved hand, and the hairy little scientist, making the beast with two backs? Lewes had three sons, but the Sibyl appeared to be childless. Did the couple use some form of contraception? And if so, what? Had babies been concealed, smothered at birth, or smuggled off? Every gesture on both sides indicated that they were a couple devoted to one another, courteous, fond, and conciliatory to a fault, fussing over each other's health, comfort and headaches. Max observed it all, at close quarters.

Happy middle-class marriages in every age usually work best with a degree of geographical distance: separate domains, consisting of drawing rooms and gentlemen's clubs. The Leweses achieved an almost supernatural harmony, whilst maintaining a degree of domestic intimacy, which, in every other couple, leads to a tournament, fought out between Spite and Contempt. Spite is usually the woman's weapon; many of us have been burned, hanged or battered into pulp for being unrepentant bitches. Contempt is the prerogative of power.

The Sibyl often referred to her 'sacred bond' with Mr. Lewes, a holy act of union, an echo of that unfortunate Act which still, at the time of writing, binds Scotland to England. In her letter announcing her changed status to her brother Isaac, she employed a little necessary subterfuge. But she used that fatal and mendacious word – husband.

Rosa Cottage
Gorey
Jersey
26th May 1857

My dear brother

You will be surprised, I dare say, but I hope not sorry, to learn that I have changed my name. And have someone to take care of me in the world. The event is not at all a sudden one, though it may appear sudden in its announcement to you. My husband has been known to me for several years, and I am well acquainted with his mind and character. He is occupied entirely with scientific and learned pursuits, is several years older than myself, and has three boys, two of whom are at school in Switzerland, and one in England.

We shall remain at the coast here, or in Brittany for some months, on account of my health, which has for some time been very frail, and which is benefited by the sea air. The winter we shall probably spend in Germany. But any inconvenience about money payments to me may, I suppose, be avoided if you will be kind enough to pay my income to the account of Mr. G.H. Lewes, into the Union Bank of London, Charing Cross Branch, 4 Pall Mall East, Mr. Lewes having an account there.

I wrote to you many weeks ago from Scilly, enclosing a letter to Chrissey, which if you received it, you would of course put by for her, as it was written in ignorance of her extreme illness. But as I have not received any intimation that my letter reached you, I think it safest to repeat its chief purport, which was to request that you would pay £15 of my present half-year's income to Chrissey.

I shall also be much obliged if you will inform me how Chrissey is, and whether she is strong enough to make it desirable for me to write to her.

Give my love to Sarah and tell her that I am very grateful to her for letting me have news of Chrissey.

[...]

We are not at all rich people, but we are both workers, and shall have enough for our wants.

I hope you are well and that Sarah is recovered from her fatigues and anxieties. With love to her and all my tall nephews and nieces,

I remain, dear Isaac
Your affectionate sister
Marian Lewes

Notice that she claims her rightful income, and insists on the importance of her family relationships. All that loving care for her ailing sister Chrissey, who had married a hopeless failure and had her health ruined by constant childbirth. But none of this solicitous obfuscation worked. Isaac Evans smelt a rat. She said that she had changed her name, but not that she had married. If Lewes had three sons and was indeed the respectable scientist and intellectual she said he was, then he must have had some form of a wife. Would it not have been prudent, honest and sensible to mention the fact that he had been, for many years, a widower? But, as in a more famous contemporary narrative, the gentleman possessed 'a wife now living'. Isaac Evans handed the letter over to his solicitor, and demanded concrete evidence of marriage in a church, a shrewd tactic, which forced Marian Evans to waffle on about sacred bonds and legal contracts in her dignified, unflinching, candid reply. But she still signed herself, defiantly, Marian Lewes. Isaac Evans broke off all communication with his abandoned sister, and forced the rest of his family to do so.

And herein lies the problem. Marian Evans Lewes, or whichever of her many names you wish to use, insisted upon the value of an integrity she did not actually possess. She wrote thousands of pages defending the so-called sacred bonds, all of which proved in need of sharper definitions. No one could argue that Miss Evans was seduced and betrayed in true nineteenth-century fictional fashion. The writer may have hidden behind a complex web of sexual moralities, a labyrinth that we are still decrypting, but the woman herself stubbornly brazened it out. She insisted on calling herself Mrs. Lewes, never mind the other Mrs. Lewes, whose sons she supported and whose bills she paid.

Mr. Fowles never bothers with the daring and courageous women of the mid-nineteenth century who fought for social and sexual reform: Caroline Norton, accused of 'criminal conversation' with the Prime Minister, who campaigned for the transformation of the divorce laws, Barbara Bodichon, who founded the *English Women's Review*, and visited Marian Lewes and to hell with decorum and appearances, Elizabeth Gaskell, who wrote *Ruth* (1853), championing the virtue and innocence of the young woman seduced. Actually, Gaskell insists so fanatically upon Ruth's utter innocence that I, for one, have never been able to identify the moment when the wicked Mr. Bellingham makes himself Master of her Person. But possess her he certainly did, because she gives birth to a son, who lives to be proud of his heroic mother. The latter dies in a burst of sanctimonious religiosity. Saved at last!

The Sibyl saved herself by writing fiction.

END OF CHAPTER SIX

CHAPTER SEVEN

spins the Wheel of Fortune in unexpected ways.
The Reader is invited to place her Bets.

Prostitutes, gorgeous as princesses, rubbed shoulders with the recently rich around the roulette tables, but too many of their Berlin acquaintances, there to enjoy the gambling, had already greeted him. Max decided to play safe. Forbidden to enjoy himself in the Kursaal, and disinclined to float gently in the baths, Max decided to pay for one whole night of bliss in the arms of his farmer's daughter. She fulfilled all his expectations, and if not as weightless as the Fairy Queen Titania, nevertheless performed an exotic variety of magical tricks, some of which startled her worldly young gentleman into yelps of joy. Sated, washed, brushed and perfumed, he strolled back towards the populated promenades in the early morning, inordinately pleased with the intensity of his night's bought pleasure. He paused to light his cigarette, not ten paces from the Israelite's pawn shop, when a familiar young figure swung out into the street before him. Her plaits were tucked into her hat, so that her pale neck shone smooth as a statue above the embroidered collar and the bold green stripes of her walking dress. Max was so close that he saw the light gleaming through the fine blonde hairs at the nape. Her laced boots, black with white trim, hammered away over the cobbles. She kept her eyes down. She wasn't looking for trouble. But there was no doubt about it; out of the Jew's den flounced the Countess Sophie von Hahn.

Max froze, his face boiling with embarrassment and shock. Her receding virginity reproached him for that one night of love, and he stood, denounced, as guilty as any young husband caught *in flagrante delicto* with the housemaid. What on earth was she doing in Homburg? And did she know he was already here? Max dived into the Aladdin's cave presided over by a tiny bearded Jew. The shop was darker than he had expected; the pocket watches, bracelets, necklaces and precious stones luminous on black velvet squares beneath locked glass.

'May I be of service to you, sir?' whispered the Jew. He laid down an elegant necklace of opals and rubies surrounded by diamonds, that he had been examining through an eyeglass, which he now carefully extracted, and set down beside the languorous jewels.

'The young lady who just came in – what did she want?' Max blurted out his alarm.

The Jew seemed to shrink a little. All transactions on his premises remained confidential. He murmured apologies. Max loomed over him. Without speaking, the pawnbroker simply lowered his eyes to the necklace and Max grasped the transaction at once. Sophie had borrowed money against the necklace, almost certainly without her father's knowledge. But where was the Count? Would no one step forward to reprimand this wastrel daughter? What troubles had engulfed her? Blackmail and Vice hovered in the wings, awaiting their chance to drag down his adorable Sophie. Max mounted a metaphorical charger and lowered his lance at the Jew.

'I understand you perfectly, sir,' he snapped, although nothing had been explained. 'How much?'

'One thousand thaler.' The Jew's voice sank to a barely audible vibration. He glanced nervously into the rooms behind him, hoping for reinforcements if the gentleman before him, clearly a near relation of the lovely young lady, turned nasty. Max shivered slightly. The jewels glowed on the velvet between them. This necklace must belong to the old Countess; surely these jewels formed part of Sophie von Hahn's dowry and inheritance. One thousand thaler barely touched their value and the Jew knew it. Redeeming the thing then and there drifted into Max's brain, but without Wolfgang's authorisation the project was impossible.

Max turned on his heel, threw open the door, with not one further word to the Jew, and bounded away down the street. He flung himself into the awakening watery sunshine of the little town and pounded after the woman he intended to honour with his own hand and his brother's money. So far as Max was concerned Sophie von Hahn already counted as his wife, and never mind the fact that he hadn't actually asked her. But she had vanished into air, as decisively as the fairies, dissolving at daybreak. He rang the bell of Frau Heide's Very Superior Pension, but the sleepy maid informed him that they didn't have rich people like the Count von Hahn staying there, and why didn't he try the Grand Continental Hotel? Out of breath and temper, edgy and flustered, Max stormed the reception desk, only to be informed that the Graf von Hahn and his daughter had indeed arrived the day before, had left several messages for him, including a pressing invitation to dine with them on the previous evening, but had not yet emerged from their suite to greet the day. You little minx, Max fretted and bristled. Not dressed yet? Not gone out? He was quite prepared to hunt her down himself and give her a wigging. Had she got herself into debt? Surely the Count gave her a generous allowance? Was she supporting some indigent relative? The indigent and the undeserving remained indistinguishable in Max's imagination. Or maybe she had become too deeply involved in good works of a religious nature?

Standing there, undecided, in the great foyer of the Continental, beside the palms in giant Oriental vats, Max poured out his apologies to the Count von Hahn on the back of his visiting card, which he left with the porter to be sent up with their breakfast. Then he marched out into the gardens to read his letters just arrived from Berlin: one from Wolfgang and the other from Professor Marek, inviting him to attend a series of lectures in preparation for the Anatolian expedition in the spring. Wolfgang outlined a counter-proposal for Max to negotiate with Lewes, which gave their house both Continental reprint rights and the translation copyright on the Sibyl's next masterpiece, whenever she might choose to create said work, certain to be even more excellent and extraordinary than the present magnificent and amazing magnum opus. Max abandoned his brother's hyperbole. Yet more negotiations with the inflexible hairy husband! Max almost mowed down an elderly English lady, her companion and their little dog, parading round the fountain. His self-satisfied mood of sexual accomplishment dissipated before a row of irritating obstacles.

And so it was that Max, disgruntled and anxious, presented himself at Obere Promenade 14, equipped for battle with the publisher's counter-proposals. But the scene which greeted him in the comfortable first-floor apartments suggested a peculiar and alarming scientific experiment. Lewes, he assumed that it was Lewes, sat at the table, still wearing his *robe de chambre*, an ample towel draped over his head, so that his voice, hoarse and stifled, emerged faintly through the folds. A sinister balsamic mixture filled the room with odours of menthol and verbena. A brown bottle containing the tincture stood beside the jug of boiling water, which the Sibyl poured carefully into the basin before her husband, causing the vapours to surge upwards, like mist evaporating from the valley bottoms. She nodded earnestly at Max.

'Pull the towel right over the basin, dearest, and breathe deeply, so that you get the full benefit.'

Lewes bent forwards, as if intending to be sick.

'I am sorry, my dear fellow,' groaned the voice, hoarse and indistinct. He echoed like a reluctant spirit guide, discovered beneath linen drapes at the climax of a seance. 'You have caught me at a low ebb.'

Max attempted to excuse himself and backed towards the door, but both the Sibyl and the muffled Lewes insisted that he should settle and be seated.

'It's only a chesty sore throat,' gasped the voice, 'and Polly's wonderful inhalation may put a stop to it. I don't want her to succumb to this as well.'

The closed rooms, stuffy and airless, with the fire banked up and blazing, produced a dreadful claustrophobic fug, smelling equally of illness and cloves. The Sibyl gazed at Max, the marvellous grey-blue eyes filled with beseeching tenderness and anxiety.

'George wondered if you would be so kind as to escort me round the park. He is sure to be better tomorrow and is convinced that my headache will reappear if we sit here with the windows closed.'

'Give Polly a run in the sunshine, won't you, Max, there's a splendid chap,' croaked the scientist, suspended over the fumes. 'And fight off the English. We've already turned away Lady Castletown this morning, and her daughter Mrs. Wingfield, who pours forth confidences to Polly. The English are kind and convivial, but also very wearing. Polly needs a brisk canter *à pied* and a dose of fresh air, or she'll buckle under the strain.' Lewes vanished again beneath the towel and the steam mounted around him as if he were sniffing hell-fire, well in advance of his appointed time. Max assented politely to every suggestion.

Here she was, the Sibyl, in bonnet and cape, neatly packaged with gloves and shawl, ready to step out through the wilder reaches of the park, beyond the prying eyes of the English guests at the Hessischer Hof, with Max as her guardian knight. The lady set a cracking pace. Max realised, in some alarm, that his charming promenades as a *flâneur*, through Berlin's welter of amusements, did not equip him to pound down damp paths beside the Sibyl, who leaped bare roots like a champion racehorse, engaged on winning a steeplechase. They strode purposefully away towards the pine forests, carried on a light wind, beneath the reddening leaves. At first their speed permitted no more than sparse conversation and the occasional observation, but once they reached a safe distance well beyond the morning crowds circling the bandstand and the pavilion, the Sibyl slackened to a steady little trot and accepted his arm with a grateful inclination of her huge white forehead. The disordered bonnet slipped back a little, revealing a thick mane of chestnut streaked with grey. Max immediately felt embarrassed and intimidated by this unlooked-for tête-à-tête. The great trees around them blew leaves of many colours, as varied as Joseph's coat, across their path. He kept an eye out for brambles snatching at her shawl, and lurking murky puddles, for the path, less frequented here in the outer reaches of the park, roughened and dipped. But the Sibyl knew where she was going. Her gentle pressure on his arm guided him on to woodland trails, unvisited. They startled a hare on the edge of a meadow, which leaped away into the undergrowth, ears flattened. The path now rose upwards and they began to climb. The trees thickened and darkened, the way before them flecked with sunlight.

'I feel so peaceful here,' remarked the Sibyl, scraping mud from her boot on a dead branch. The earth peeled off in one piece like the shavings from an orange. 'We never meet anyone.'

Max bowed, terrified of small talk. He felt sure she had already notched him off as insincere and stupid.

'I came out here to meditate the Finale to *Middlemarch*.'

Now he had to say something.

'Your readers will be both grateful and distraught, Madame. For every ending is both a resolution and a parting. Especially for those who have followed you through this long and enthralling year. Your characters have become living people to so many of your readers, who fear for their final destinies.'

He thought of Sophie's putative endings, and remembered that she found none satisfactory. Suddenly the end of the story mattered more than anything else. He longed to hand his bride both the pawned necklace and a happy ending. But the Sibyl stepped ahead of him.

'Conclusions are the weak point of most authors, but some of the fault lies in the very nature of a conclusion, which is at best a negation.'

Max did not understand her. He adopted an exceedingly grave expression, and navigated a wrinkle in the mud with exaggerated care for his pale grey trousers. She drew him after her into the forest. The Sibyl looked up at the whispering trees; sycamore, ash, birch, oak, giving way to an eternal, darkening green. They stood side by side, listening to the soughing pines. Their onward steps made no sound, cushioned by pine needles, and they drew closer together as the path narrowed. Immediately, they both lowered their voices, as if entering a church.

'Every limit is a beginning as well as an ending,' murmured the Sibyl, her head tilted, as if listening to the rhythm of her own words. 'Who can quit young lives after being long in company with them, and not desire to know what befell them in after years? For the fragment of a life, however typical, is not the sample of an even web: promises may not be kept –'

She stopped and looked directly at him, her great face sombre and worn. Max felt judged.

He had flourished and bloomed, grown tall and strong, his father's favourite son, the Benjamin of the family, that wonderful miracle – a healthy child, after several tragic infant deaths. His sister fled away into the shades, carried off by scarlet fever, and his mother had despaired of ever giving Wolfgang a sibling. But here stood beautiful, joyous Max, with his dark eyes and powerful bounding limbs! He saw himself, galloping fearless on his first pony, speaking both English and French fluently at seven years, rattling along beside his stringy, austere tutor, reciting the names of all the plants, as if the earth belonged to him. He remembered eating too much cake at his tenth birthday party and being violently sick all over his rocking horse; carrying a giant cone of sweets to his master on the first day of school, sitting for his portrait in his cadet's uniform at fifteen, that painting still hanging in the hall. Had he lived up to the golden promises of those first days? He had not only wasted his brother's money, he had disappointed Wolfgang by refusing to finish anything.

If any project proved difficult or irritating, Max instantly manufactured an excuse to abandon the field of endeavour. He stood surrounded by attempts and beginnings, rather than achievements, all his beauty and charm fraudulent and spoiled. Even Hans Meyrick, with his effeminate curls and effusive desire to impress, had won the prize: he had painted more fairies into one canvas than any other artist.

The Sibyl sensed his discomfort. Her antennae flickered like a praying mantis registering a disturbance in the air. The luminous grey gaze swept across his face, conciliatory, generous and forgiving. He could hide nothing from her.

'I sometimes feel –' Max commenced his confession, then ran out of words, as well as feelings. The forest breathed quietly about them; sunlight spattered across the Sibyl's bonnet and shawl.

'You see, Mrs. Lewes,' he gathered speed and began to gibber, 'I am like your Tito Melema. Or at least I am in danger of becoming like him. *Romola* is your book, that is, the one book that meant most to me, or at least so far –' Max was not prepared to admit that he had not read one single word of *Middlemarch*.

'You see, Tito Melema wasn't an evil man. He simply didn't like rows, unpleasantness or decisions. I recognise that. He liked everything to be as pleasant and as beautiful as he was himself. And he procrastinated. He did intend to save his father from slavery and to purchase his freedom. Just as soon as he had set himself up properly in Florence, and got a bit of influence. He didn't mean to forget the man to whom he owed everything. And he really did love Tessa, the little *contadina*, not because she was undemanding and naïve, but because she believed in him, unquestioning. He just didn't possess a strong enough character to comprehend Romola's finer moral sense, or indeed to be worthy of her love –' Max petered out, sensing that his situation had degenerated into the ridiculous. Here he was in the middle of a forest, describing a fictional character he had recognised as an awful personal warning, to the very woman who once created him. Tito, the laughing

Greek, loomed merry and menacing, amidst the sharp shadows of the pines, and Max stood, hesitant, between this phantom of himself and the traitor's only begetter.

'I know Tito,' he blurted out. 'I know all his weaknesses. I found it appalling that I knew him at once, and so well.'

The Sibyl smiled slightly, without uncovering her fearful teeth, and offered her arm to Max. They stepped onwards down the forest trail, whose edges now appeared fluid and nebulous among the dead needles.

'I am very moved and honoured that my work should speak to you so clearly, and that you read Tito with so unerring an eye. You are right. He is not a criminal; he simply wishes to follow a path through life that is always littered with adoration and roses. But the moral life, that best part of our own souls, is neither so rosy, nor so simple.' She paused, looking up at the earth's breath, which stirred the pine tops. 'That book is indeed dear to me. I was a young woman when I began, but an old woman by the time it was finished.'

'You were unflinching in your justice.' Max contemplated Tito's end, and the grim fate that awaited all those incapable of rising to the awful demands of the moral life. 'The traitor died by his own adopted father's hand.'

The writer nodded, her face sombre.

'But revenge, however just or apparently noble, is persuasive only in fiction, Max.' She used his Christian name with warmth and intimacy, her hand on his arm pressed him gently onwards. 'In our human world, revenge leaves nothing but the taste of ashes in its wake. My first source for that part of the intrigue in *Romola* came from General Pfuhl, nearly eighteen years ago. We met at Fräulein Solmar's salon in Berlin. He told me of a wealthy nobleman, who was cheated out of all his property by a villainous adopted son. The man killed the thief he had taken to his bosom – killed him on the spot. He was imprisoned, tried and condemned for the murder. It is said that on the eve of his execution he refused to accept a confessor, and cried, "I wish to go to Hell, for *he* is there, and I want to follow out my revenge."'

'Was killing the traitor not enough?'

And here Max was graced with the Sibyl's disconcerting yellow smile with the red gaps, gleaming at uneven intervals.

'It seems not. Revenge, you see, binds the avenger irrevocably to the person who has wronged him. They are doomed to seek one another for ever through the shades of Hades. Baldassare never freed himself from Tito. His hatred grew, commensurate with his former love.'

Max suspected that the Sibyl, who spoke of Hell and Hades with such eloquence, did not actually believe in the existence of either place. A fresh puzzle presented itself to him for the first time. Why, if she walked the earth without faith in Providence or the Beyond, did she praise religious fervour with such discriminating conviction? Was it possible to live openly with a married man and still preach morality and righteousness from the pulpit of her fiction? Wolfgang assured him that all her first readers, when her identity was so well concealed that not even her publisher knew who the mysterious friend of Lewes was, remained convinced that the author of *Adam Bede* must be a clergyman, in charge of a rural parish in the Midlands. The Sibyl raised her extraordinary eyes to Max, paused, and then pronounced her absolution.

'Reflect for a moment, Max, upon your interpretation of Tito. You have recognised his nature as a dangerous one. You have seen where that kind of moral laziness may lead. You are not Tito and you need never duplicate his ways. You have a choice.'

And now, in her priest-like presence, Max felt himself illuminated, reassured. He was being given a second chance, but he did not know how, or even why. The arched cathedral of the forest and the Sibyl's grave authority, that uncanny sensation of having been not only heard, but chosen, conspired to meddle with the fragile roots of his complacency. Something intangible in her company lifted him from the swamps of his own selfishness. He vowed never to visit a prostitute or gamble at the tables again.

But Max was led into temptation before that day was out.

❧

They returned home to a pile of visiting cards and Mr. Lewes, peacefully prostrate upon the sofa. Lady Castletown had besieged him with Irish bronchial remedies, and sent meat broth and soft, steamed vegetables from her own kitchens. Furthermore, she insisted that my dear Mrs. Lewes and her charming German publisher, that handsome young man who has such a sweet German accent, should join them for dinner, with a view to visiting the Kursaal later on to watch the gambling. The mercurial little showman was laid low and the great lady novelist must not only be amused, she must nurse him in as remote a fashion as possible, for that cough is certainly contagious, and she was sending her very own private physician, with his efficacious assistant, to ensure the dear man's speedy recovery. At first the Sibyl refused. She would not leave her husband's side. But Lewes added his persuasive croak to the general clamour.

'We'll dine here together, Polly. But you must go out a bit or you'll succumb to morbid thoughts. I'm feeling better already, and a long peaceful night will set me straight.'

He closed his eyes. Max pressed the Sibyl's hand gently and nodded his farewell, then crept out of the room. On the stairway he remembered Wolfgang's revised publication deals. Renewed negotiations were out of the question at present, he had bought himself a little time. But suddenly another memory intervened: a torrent of opals, rubies and diamonds poured across the Jew's counter. Both of these peremptory thoughts framed themselves into commands to act, and disconcerted his new-found composure. He burst into the autumn sunshine, clutching his hat.

Back at the Grand Continental Hotel a row of messages fluttered towards him from the reception clerk. Count August von Hahn and his daughter longed to see him, after a session in the baths for arthritis (the Count), and a gallop in the meadows (the Countess), come and visit us in our suite, my dear Max, when you have sufficiently buttered up the famous lady and closed the deal. My little Sophie is quite rabid with desire to meet her, and thinks that she'll get round her doting father while her mother's still at home. I'm counting on you not to bend a whisker, Max, or to engineer an introduction. It would all come out at the dinner table, and I'd be in for a hell-fire lecture.

The Count and his daughter occupied five adjoining rooms on the second floor, with views overlooking the royal castle and the park. The maid flashed past him, bearing two jugs of hot water for the Countess to refresh her toilette, after her fiery ride out to the hunting lodge, surrounded by an escort of admirers. But here she was, the young lady herself, still in her riding habit, with her veil thrown back, her bright cheeks flushed and her eyes dancing.

'Why didn't you come before?' she demanded. 'I wanted to see you and tell you lots of things.'

'You were galloping around the countryside, and I am engaged upon my brother's business,' smiled Max, beguiled. She grabbed his arm and dragged him into a gorgeous expanse of gilt mirrors and chandeliers, with four French windows and a long balcony, from which he glimpsed the fountains and the gardens.

'Come in quick! Father! He's here!'

What things does she have to tell me, thought Max. Certainly nothing about Jews and jewels. He decided not to probe the mystery. Or at least, not yet. Sophie flung off her jacket and swung on the bell rope so that all the tassels shivered, her enthusiasm unbounded and unfeigned.

'I've ordered chocolate. My fingers are freezing. You must take a glass with us.'

Could she have negotiated a price on that necklace for someone else? The soft smell of wealth perfumed the rooms. How could the

Countess be in debt? At eighteen? Sophie offered him a cigarette and hauled the double windows open.

'Blow it out on to the balcony. That's what Father does. Mother makes him smoke outside at home, or in the winter garden. And we call that the Fumarium.'

The autumn air, rushing into the warm salon, smelled of bonfires. But here is the Count himself, dressed in a blue silk waistcoat, festooned with medals and ribbons, explaining that he is due to address a small political society, nothing subversive, you understand, just a group of like-minded chaps. And here is the waiter, wearing white gloves, armed with a pot of chocolate, extra cream, orange biscuits, tall delicate glasses in the Russian style, embedded in silver frames, standing perched on the threshold. No one heard him knocking. Max subsides into luxury, gazing at the smooth, translucent countenance, tiny earlobes and glossy pearl earrings of Sophie von Hahn. She is all movement and vivacity. She cannot sit still. She flickers past him, corn blonde and blue, like a ripe field. She flings herself into a chair so that the flower-filled vase on the rosewood table shivers and wobbles. Then she raises one boot towards her father for him to unbuckle and unlace, then the other. Max observes this cheerful domestic intimacy, and steals a glance at her white-stockinged toes. He is quite unprepared for the smooth curve of her instep, the gentle rise of her ankle, the intricate twitch of her calf muscles as she stretches and flexes her foot. All her youth and beauty, suggestive, glimmering, floods into the long stretch of her body, as she leans back in her chair and yawns. Max ostentatiously presses against the cold stone of the balcony and blows smoke into the crisped chestnut leaves of the nearest tree. He manages to mask his erection.

❧

In the hushed deep stillness of the Kursaal, sixty or seventy people gathered around the roulette tables, many standing in outer rows, peering forwards to watch the gambling. Some of the aficionados had been there, slouched on gilded chairs, since mid-afternoon. The reverent concentration of those seated at the tables remained fervent and undisturbed, the hush broken only by a light rattle, a faint chink, and the occasional monotonous murmur in French: *Faîtes vos jeux, Rien ne va plus*, as if an ingenious automaton had been constructed to officiate at the ritual. For gambling does indeed resemble the Holy Office, the repetition of a sacrament charged with the particular mood of the congregation, optimism and desperation, laced with curiosity or boredom. Some are there merely as observers, while others are engaged, with all their souls, in the deadly pleasures of the game. Max had played both parts in his time, at these very tables, and now he stood well back as if to avoid contamination, holding the Sibyl's shawl, while she conversed in whispers with Lady Castletown. Here before them, lounged or poised, lay the great world of men, and women too, old and young, wealthy and skint, some leaned over the tables, ignoring one another, utterly lost in the deep, hypnotic trance of risk. These were the big players, staking all on the red or the black, barely aware of the impoverished dilettantes placing small bets with an absurd flourish. Rank, age and sex vanished in the long chequered space before the wheel. Were these lovely painted women, with their little jewelled reticules, ladies of pleasure or daughters of the rich? No one cared. *Faîtes vos jeux, Rien ne va plus.*

Max watched the gamblers. He felt the adrenalin precision of that tingle in the thighs, chest and neck, as you begin to win, and the quiet sighs from the watchers, never from the table, as you begin to lose. The whole point of gambling is to lose. You always lose in the end. You go on till you lose.

But someone at the far table was on a winning streak, and causing a small stir in the phalanx of onlookers. He could see only the back and shoulders of her blue jacket, and her hair pinned up into a jaunty matching cap with a darker velvet band around the rim. She wore walking clothes indoors, as if she had sauntered in from the Schlosspark, to pass the time between dinner and the dancing among the clique at the tables, her dark blue gloves luring the napoleons out from other fingers. Here they come, swooping towards her across the red and the black as if magnetised. She won, again and again.

Was she beautiful, or not beautiful? Max could not see her face. He craned forwards. He glimpsed the blue cap, emerging and vanishing as the crowds closed round again to watch '*la belle qui gagne*'. The blue gloves, tapering to points, pushed the chips away across the board as if they were too filthy to touch. Back came her stake carrying the contents of the board in its wake. Max rose on tiptoe, his view of her magical fingers suddenly frustrated by two fat silken backs. The Sibyl, sensitive as a butterfly to every gust and shift in the air, immediately sensed his defection.

'Who is it?' She raised her giant head to look, but the far table, now surrounded like a fort under siege, hid all its secrets.

'A young lady, playing recklessly, I believe. And winning.'

The Sibyl followed his curious glance and they proceeded to the far side of the Kursaal to watch. Lady Castletown, waylaid by one of her many English acquaintances, paused in the gangway. They took up their positions by a sofa on the angle of the stairway, commanding an excellent view of both tables. Max settled the Sibyl first, bending to make her comfortable, then swung round to scrutinise the face beneath the blue hat. He recognised her at once, swallowed hard in disbelief, and glared across the little distance between them. For there, bent forward to deposit her stake, the blue glove firm on her little tower of chance, sat the Countess Sophie von Hahn.

His first idea was to abandon the Sibyl, who was now also gazing, fascinated, at the gambling belle, and drag the feckless wench out of the Kursaal and back to her hotel by the hair. What did she think she was doing, flinging down her money like a drunken professional? And where was Fräulein Garstein, the chaperone, who was supposed to accompany Sophie on a march round the park and a session with the dancing master, while the Count talked politics? But even as they watched, Sophie won again, her pointed avaricious fingers raking the pile of chips across the green baize towards her. *Faîtes vos jeux*. She divided the *jetons*, canny as a Frankfurt banker, hesitated, then shovelled the lion's share on to the black. A soft gasp ruffled the hush. She had doubled her stake. Her eyes devoured the spinning glint of the wheel.

Roulette is a game of pure chance, if the house has not bugged the machinery. Win or lose appears as random as the accidents of birth: one child has shining eyes and long lashes, the other a hare lip. Ah, Sophie, you see nothing else, with your hot glance, bent head and that defiant set of your shoulders, braced for whatever comes. The girl's whole body rocked, clamped to the board and the wheel. The other hands that placed their stakes did not exist for her. She saw nothing, only the wheel's turret and the spinning rim. She won again. A small whispered tinkle of pleasure and astonishment accompanied the rustle of shifting ivory stakes nuzzling the actual cash on the green baize. Max tensed; the crowd solidified around her. He eyed his prey, a cheetah preparing for the leap.

The Sibyl laid her hand gently upon his sleeve. He saw the ivory lace mitten clamped on to his dark coat and recoiled, the moment lost.

'I take it that this young lady is an acquaintance?'

Max remembered where he was, bowed politely, and bent his head to hers. No one would have overheard their exchange.

'I am afraid she is indeed. That, Madame, is the eldest daughter of the Count August von Hahn. But I am at a loss to explain her presence here in the Kursaal, without her father or her usual chaperone.'

The Sibyl's ironic smile of recognition bought him a moment to stifle his fury, now directed primarily against Fräulein Garstein, who had mysteriously allowed Sophie to slip the leash.

'This is quite unaccountable. What can –'

'Do sit down for a moment,' suggested the Sibyl.

Max obeyed.

'Do you know why she is gambling with such passionate abandon? She lives mostly in the country, I believe, and can hardly have done this before? Although Fortune, at present, clearly loves her dearly. Do you have any idea why she is here?'

'I do.'

Suddenly Max gave in to that universal impulse to confide all, seduced by the benignity of that great prophetic forehead, and the vast tenderness in the writer's eyes. Max's narrative, carefully absorbed by the Sibyl, revealed itself to be a masterpiece of omissions. Yes, he had played with the Countess when they were children. And of course, Wolfgang had always been a close friend to the Count. Max adopted a careful strategy, which would give the tale a sentimental spin, and would also explain his evident and possibly excessive feelings of indignation and concern. The Count himself was like a father to us when my own father died. And so I have always known the little Countess. (That makes me sound like the brother she never had.) I had no idea, until yesterday, that they were visiting Homburg. He decided not to mention the recent visit to the Jagdschloss, or the proposed engagement cooked up between Wolfgang and the Count. This morning, when I was walking in the early day (I had just spent the night with a prostitute), I saw her in an odd part of town. And here he disclosed everything he had witnessed concerning the necklace and the cautious Jew. Opals, rubies and diamonds flowed on to the Sibyl's lap. Yes, Sophie von Hahn had laid down part of her inheritance upon the Jew's velvet counter.

'Ah, she must have visited Herr Wiener,' nodded the Sibyl. 'His shop is in the Judengasse. He is a friend of ours. I know him through other connections.'

Max immediately regretted his incivility to the clearly alarmed pawnbroker, and gazed at the Sibyl, astonished. Surely she was omniscient, all-knowing and forgiving, given that her acquaintance stretched from chateaux to ghettos. What if the Jew revealed he had been rude? Max now overflowed with speculative drama concerning Sophie's motives, to conceal his own embarrassment. Why did the Countess need to raise money in the first place? Was she in terrible trouble? The Sibyl presented only rational explanations.

'Either she needs one thousand thaler to nourish her gaming streak, my dear Max, or she owes more than that sum and is busy winning it back before you at this very moment. But soon, she will begin to lose, and we must stop her before she does. We must also remove the need – or the debt – she is concealing from her father. The Graf von Hahn has championed my cause in his time. And that kindness I will now repay. Her relationship to you makes her all the more interesting to me. But one of us must save her from this evil vale of temptation. I will send to Herr Wiener for the necklace. He will accept a credit note from me.'

Max stared, open-mouthed, at her decisiveness.

'Go on. Be quick. Stop her. Her luck won't last.'

The Sibyl rose to greet Lady Castletown and retreated in the direction of the supper tables. Max thrust himself into the fray. Sophie, leaning forward, elbows on the table, had by now accumulated an Ali Baba's cave of winnings, piled up before her. Max grasped her shoulder, none too gently, and hissed:

'Countess von Hahn, I believe you should now rejoin your father.'

Her eyes widened in shock as she recognised Max.

'You! It's not possible! Wolfgang told us he had banned you from the tables.'

'I'm not playing, Sophie. You are. Just collect that pile of money and get up. Now.'

Murmurs of disappointment surrounded them as he dragged the gambling belle away by the elbow. Belligerent with righteousness, Max stood fuming while Sophie translated her *jetons* into cash, then swept the girl out of the Kursaal and into the swift chill of early evening, regardless of numerous fascinated glances, and a trail of gossip, burgeoning behind them.

'A striking girl – that Sophie von Hahn – unlike others.'

'I hear that the Count is negotiating her price with the publishers. That was Max Duncker I saw, dragging her away from her pleasures. Is the marriage arranged between her and the younger or the elder brother?'

'Oh, she must always be doing something extraordinary. She is that kind of girl, I fancy. Do you think her pretty?'

'Very. A man might risk hanging for her – I mean, a fool might.'

'You like a *nez retroussé* then, serpent-green eyes and that wonderful boyish stride? She really does not present herself like a lady.'

'I saw her this afternoon in the water meadows, at full gallop, riding a bay horse. Quite fearless, she was, all her veils flying!'

'Very becoming that – a girl who can master a horse.'

'The younger Duncker son used to be here every night at the tables. Haven't seen him this year. He must have been mastered by the little Countess.'

'Well, I gather she's taken his place, and had a luckier swing at Fortune's Wheel.'

Max dragged Sophie through the lighted streets towards the Marktplatz, nodding to the odd acquaintance. He glowed with rage, and never noticed the social sensation caused by their rapid progress. What irritated him most? The fact that the Sibyl could write out a credit note for a thousand thaler without a flicker, and he couldn't? His prospective bride rubbing shoulders at the gaming tables with men who were hardly gentlemen, and ladies who were certainly not ladies at all? Sophie von Hahn exposing herself to gossip, comment and impudent glances? The delinquent behaviour of Fräulein Garstein? The irresponsible Count? Or was he incensed by the bitter truth that she was winning, and winning large sums, whereas he always lost every stake, without fail?

'You don't need to hang on to me as if I was a criminal, Max. Let me go.'

'You're coming straight back to the hotel. How could you be so indiscreet?'

'In what way? By winning?'

Sophie pulled herself free, and shaking with pink-cheeked resentment, took her stand on the steps of the Grand Continental, and declared, for all the world to hear:

'How dare you spoil my game? I was well ahead. I know when to stop. Unlike you, by all accounts. You haven't even asked for my hand and yet you think that you can treat me as if I were an abject wife, to be bullied and pushed about. You have no right to tell me what to do. And you never will have.'

Max hurled her and her ill-gotten gains through the hotel doors. And behold Fräulein Garstein, rushing towards them, a respectable middle-aged bundle of grey silks.

'Ah *ma chère*, there you are! I was most anxious. The reception clerk told me that your headache had quite gone and that you had stepped out. I looked for you in the gardens. But I am so relieved to see that you were not alone! Indeed, you have discovered a most acceptable escort!'

She smirked at Max, the fiancé-in-waiting. Sophie laid down her heavy bundle of notes and cash on the marble table in the foyer, turned her back upon him, and began, with slow and ostentatious care, to unpin her hat. Max bowed low to both women, speechless with fury, and stalked out of the building. He pounded back down the Obere Promenade to the Kursaal, cutting several people dead en route and causing lasting offence.

The Sibyl stood in the hallway, buttoned, cloaked and muffled, gently acknowledging curious little troupes of admirers, her washed eyes anxious for home and her beloved scientist. She drew him aside, pulled forth a cambric handkerchief from her *nécessaire* and opened her palm to reveal a glittering shaft of colours. The pure stones flickered and swam in the gas light.

'There are the very jewels, I believe?' Max gasped. How had she conjured them up in so short a time?

'They must be returned at once. And, I rather think, delivered up to the hotel safe.' The Sibyl reflected for a moment. 'For her to accept them from either one of us, my dear, would be utterly compromising, and extremely humiliating. She has taken control of her own destiny and here we are, robbing her of all her freshly awakened powers.'

The Sibyl flashed him a glance of pure mischief.

'I took the liberty of writing this note. She will not know my hand.'

She handed him a scrap of torn-off notepaper, on which was written with a pencil in clear, but rapid handwriting:

> A stranger who has found the Countess von Hahn's necklace returns it to her with the hope that she will not again risk the loss of it.

Max reddened and gazed at the Sibyl, trumped, upstaged, and quite unable to speak. She handed him the necklace and the message, then took his arm in hers, as if they belonged to one another.

'And now, my dear Max, I have enjoyed a sufficient number of adventures in the Spielsaal for one evening, and would be delighted if you would see me home.'

END OF CHAPTER SEVEN

CHAPTER EIGHT

in which Our Author sorts out Several Muddles.

Max slouched in his chair, eyeing the new arrivals in the breakfast room, and nibbling thin slices of buttered brioche, while the Count deciphered the English newspapers. The papers were all out of date, but still vigorously fought over by the early guests in the Grand Continental. Had Max calmed down overnight? As we all usually do? Not a bit of it. His emotional temperature had risen ten degrees. A reprise of the previous night's rage engulfed him while he composed a brief note to the Sibyl, enquiring after her husband's health. Should he mention the apparition of Sophie in the Spielsaal? No, be oblique. Nothing specific or incriminating. And I thank you for your kind comprehension concerning last night's incident. That will do.

But it didn't do at all. He sat facing the Count, compromised by his own silence concerning Sophie's gambling escapade, convinced that the Count would hear of it anyway. Most of the visitors in Homburg had watched her gambling. But that now appeared to him as by no means the worst moment of the night's events. He sat there, appalled that the young Countess had refused him, point blank, in public, before he had even got around to proposing, on the hotel's front steps and in ringing tones. Surely the Count would get to hear about that too? Why hadn't he said anything? Here he was, combing the columns of *The Times*, a paper he described as detestable, and gently chuntering to himself.

'Home of democracy indeed! A second Athens! They forget themselves. Athenian democracy was an oligarchy, based on a slave state. And no question whatever of votes for women.' None of the random, irritated expletives were directed at Max.

'Ah! Here you are, my dear!'

The boyish stride, criticised as unladylike, crossed the sunny breakfast room in two bounds, and a large kiss descended upon the Count's whiskers. She wore her riding habit, the blonde plaits wound round her head, like a true rural maiden, bent on pigs and harvests. Max immediately stood up and bowed, peering at her dimples from beneath his lowered lids.

'Countess,' he murmured. Sophie von Hahn flushed brick red, and merely bowed in return. She sat down with a thump.

'I'll just order your chocolate. Max and I have been drinking coffee.' The Count noticed their mutual embarrassment and grinned, ah, *Bonjour, l'amour*, how perfectly suitable for young lovers to blush and tremble in each other's presence, and we were all young once. He began waving at waiters.

The supposed lovers looked at one another, mortified. Nothing could be said in front of the Count. Sophie recovered first and mouthed her apology in dumb show. I'M SORRY. The shape of her lips and the downcast glance shimmered with genuine repentance. Max sat bolt upright and mouthed back, I'M SORRY TOO, disarmed. The silver pot of chocolate and a rack of fresh toast scurried towards them, but so did the hotel manager, with a packet for the little Countess, handed in late last night, delivered by a young boy he didn't know. Max, standing just outside, smoking on the steps, had paid said young boy to deliver the package to the reception clerk, then sauntered in himself, giving no sign of recognition, and insisted, as a responsible family friend, that it should be locked in the safe until morning. He dare not let the jewels, so recently redeemed, slither out of sight.

Sophie, unknowing, innocent, dropped the packet beside her plate and chomped the toast, avoiding Max's eye. He sat quite still, transfixed by the packet, and pretended to listen to the Count's political commentary. Finally Sophie reached over and slit the packet neatly open like a fish fillet, with her slightly buttered knife. The jewels flooded out from their shroud, bound and muffled by the Sibyl's handkerchief. And here lay the fatal note, a torn slip, containing the gentlest of reprimands. The Count leaned over, astonished.

'What on earth are you doing with your mother's necklace at breakfast, Sophie? I told you to lock it up in the hotel safe when you weren't wearing it. It's much too valuable to carry about.'

Her eyes flickered across the note. She reddened again, then turned white. Her fingers trembled on the butter knife. Was she consumed with vexation, or wounded pride? She must have realised at once that the clear straight lines of writing before her were not from Max. He would never write to her in English. But did he know who this stranger was? She raised her savage green eyes and searched his impassive face. He began fiddling with his cigarette case. Then who? Who knew? Or had the Jew himself returned the jewels?

'Sophie? Are you listening?'

'Oh yes, Father. I'll put them back in the hotel safe at once.' She gave no sign that they had ever been anywhere else.

'You might wear them tonight for the dinner and the ball. Your mother would be pleased.'

So the necklace wasn't even hers to pawn. Max transformed an indignant snort into a cough. Sophie tucked the crushed note up her sleeve, and swept the guilty necklace on to her lap, out of sight. He watched her fasten the button on her cuff one notch tighter to secure the note. She'll pore over that in her bedroom, later. And she will scan the English here in the hotel, wondering, which one, which one. Nothing, however, interfered with her appetite. She wolfed down two more chunks of toast, a large bowl of pears in honey, and then swigged her steaming chocolate, two cups, at speed.

'Please excuse me.'

She rose, clutching the jewels in both hands, and made off towards the hotel office. She'll interrogate the manager, thought Max, and then have it all out with Wiener. Would she go that far, he wondered? Of one thing he was completely certain. Sophie von Hahn believed that the unknown stranger, who had returned her jewels, and whose identity remained a mystery, was a man. A man who was probably watching her.

Did the young Countess feel compromised, humiliated, exposed? As she should have done? Max had no idea. The Count turned to Max, but his thoughts were so saturated with Sophie that the Count's sudden change in demeanour and proximity, a shift in tone and rhythm, generated a gentle shock in his brain.

'Will you take care of Sophie? There's a good chap? Just for a couple of hours while I amuse myself in the Kursaal?'

Gambling? The Count? The elderly gentleman lurched forward like a predatory owl spotting a mouse, and thrust his whiskers into Max's face. 'And not a word at home, eh? You can tell Wolfgang I stopped you coming with me.'

Everyone traipsing round the shops and streets in Homburg vor der Höhe, or taking the waters, with their extraordinary curative powers, an amazing tonic which eliminates arthritis, lesions and psoriasis, was actually there for the Spielsaal and the roulette tables. Those canny French entrepreneurs, the brothers Blanc, François and Louis, negotiated the thirty-year concession with Landgraf Ludwig von Hessen-Homburg to build the Spielbank, and ensure an annual turnover of at least one hundred thousand gulden. The Casino opened on 23rd May 1841. And thus an insignificant country town, capital of a tiny principality, with an elegant chateau on a hill, surrounded by farms and woods, became an international spa with a fashionable Spielsaal and high stakes. Dostoevsky named the place 'Roulettenburg', for the Kurhaus did indeed resemble a miniature castle, all columns and decorative turrets, with the fatal wheels turning in the left wing. The town flourished and filled up with the wicked and the dissolute; they too prospered, like the biblical green bay tree. Streetlights glowed in the thoroughfares, and a direct train link to Frankfurt united Homburg with the great world. By 1866 the three most opulent Prussian casinos, much visited by the British, were Wiesbaden, Ems, and Homburg. But puritanical Prussian morals kicked in, and with the founding of the Deutsche Reich came the order to close. The brothers Blanc decided to play on until the last possible minute – the twenty-third hour of the last day – 31st December 1872, before returning to their other profitable little enterprise, the Spielbank Monte Carlo.

The urgency of imminent closure packed the Spielsaal in the Kurhaus with passionate addicts and curious tourists. If pressed to explain himself, the Count August von Hahn would have offered two motives for disappearing in the direction of the card tables and Fortune's Wheel. He genuinely did wish to partake of those Silenic pleasures, before the unkindly Prussian harpies whisked them away, but he also wanted to arrange a little tête-à-tête between his innocent, vivacious daughter and her intended. Let the young people get to know each other better. He never doubted Max's honour or his intentions. Of course Max wanted to marry Sophie. Every young man with means and ambition would want to do so. The Count was prepared to place all his stakes on that square. Well, young man, here's your chance.

'Yes, of course, sir, of course.'

Max rose and bowed, as the Count slipped away, in search of his wallet and coat. Sophie reappeared a moment later.

'Where's Father?'

'Heading off to the Kursaal,' said Max, and met her eye for the second time that morning.

'No, really?'

A moment of mock horror engulfed them both, and then erupted into shaking giggles. They clutched each other's hands and rocked with laughter. The breakfast room stared; the unmentionable could now be discussed.

'He'll find out, Sophie. Someone will tell him.'

'I know. I'll have to come up with some dreadful excuses. But you'll back me up, won't you? You saw me win.'

'I can't say that I encouraged you. I pulled you out of that place.'

'Well, at least you weren't playing. Wolfgang would have a fit.' She smothered a fresh wave of laughter.

'Come on,' commanded Sophie, 'I'm engaged to go riding before dinner and I've got something to show you.' She snatched up an apple from the fruit bowl.

'I hope you're going to give me some explanations for your behaviour yesterday. Even if you aren't in the least repentant.'

She paused. They were already striding down the Dorotheenstraße, and a gust of cold air flooded his unbuttoned coat. It was warm in the sun, but nowhere else. She grinned up at him.

'I'm going to reveal all my secrets!'

Then she took his arm and laughed, laughed as she had once done when she guided him through the bushes in the woods near the Jagdschloss, to their secret cabin, a little wooden shack with real curtains, built with her own hands, where the children carefully arranged their broken crockery for dinner. Max noted with some alarm that they had marched out of town in the same direction as the Königgasse, and feared the worst, but she turned off into a mucky cobbled alleyway, where the stables looked out over the meadows. The Schlosspark with the new Tannenwaldallee now lay behind them, and the fresh damp mass of fields stretched out, the cows wandering into the distance. Sophie turned abruptly into a narrow lane and they both leaned back against the hedges as two ladies on horseback, veiled against the dust, trotted past. Max felt the prickle of twigs on his back. He had forgotten Sophie's refusal to marry him, and already begun to imagine their life together. She attended the Berlin charity subscription concerts with her mother, but he had never seen her at the theatre or the opera. He hoped she wouldn't insist on spending all their days in the country. Would she be content dealing with farmyards, gardens and stables?

'You don't ride much, do you, Max?' He detected a note of puzzled reproach, and experienced a ripple of panic; she clearly imagined him strolling down an eternal boulevard.

'Wolfgang keeps a carriage, but no saddle horses,' admitted Max, alarmed that the Duncker brothers appeared to be living well within their means. But here they reached the stables. Sophie leaped a puddle at the corner, hauling up the skirt of her riding habit and revealing her boots. Max noticed her tiny silver spurs and heels flecked with mud. He observed her frank and cheerful manners with the head groom, who immediately strode out to meet her. She shook his hand warmly, as if she were concluding a deal. Then he realised that she was in fact doing exactly that, concluding the deal.

'Tell Herr Halmers that I have arranged for the money to be paid directly to his agent. The balance is already waiting for him at the hotel. And I shall expect the signed papers, including the documentation and the bill of sale, to be delivered to me by the end of the day, so that I can arrange transportation by train.'

She swung round to Max. 'Come! Look.'

And she pranced into the long dim tunnel of the stables with loose boxes ranged on either side. His eyes gradually adjusted to the dark; the sweet warm smells of crushed hay and horses mingled and thickened in the gloom. Sophie gently opened a box door and spoke quietly to a huge bay mare that raised her head and snorted slightly. Behind the mare stood another young horse, a smaller bay with two white socks, perhaps a yearling. Max caught the flicker of the creatures' startled, retreating eyes. Sophie fastened a halter on the mare; the animal bent her neck and shivered. The Countess talked softly to both horses all the time.

'There you are. They're mine now. Both of them.'

Max stood well back, open-mouthed, batting the flies away with his hat.

'Are you telling me that you were gambling in the Kursaal just to win money and buy horses?'

'Yes. And I won a lot more than I needed as it turned out.'

Was she thinking of the redeemed necklace? Max couldn't ask without giving himself away.

'Mind. Stand back. I'm going to lead her out.'

And into the warm autumn sun stepped the dark bay, her neck arched, her powerful flanks trembling slightly as she raised her tail and deposited a pile of steaming golden turds dangerously close to Max's recently polished boots. Sophie laughed out loud at his elegant withdrawal to safer ground, and stood back herself to let the young filly trot out past her mother, nickering with excitement in the fresh air. The still-stabled horses began to stamp and neigh, calling to their two companions, now smelling freedom and open fields. The head groom slapped the yearling's rump and she circled the yard rapidly, her unshod hooves slithering on the cobbles. Both animals shimmered with unspent energy and strength.

'I'll let them loose in the meadows this morning and ride her tomorrow. I have to get a wider side saddle that fits. Herr Halmers keeps his horses shut up in boxes. But they are like us. They need to gallop and roll in the sunshine.'

Max concluded that Sophie would hate to be shut up in crinolines and drawing rooms. What could he offer this Daughter of Artemis? A wave of doubt almost drowned his restored confidence. He acknowledged himself a man of hesitations, while Sophie glowed with decisiveness. Here she stood, gloating over the magnificent bay and her foal, stroking their black manes and surging shoulders as they danced about her, the mare nuzzling Sophie's fingers, eagerly pulling on the rope, their breaths generating huge gusts of steam. The groom threw open the gates and Sophie slipped the rope from the mare's halter, turning her loose. The two horses, freed at last, raised their heads high, and clattered forth into the meadows, their excitement palpable with every stride. They felt the soft earth beneath them and shuddered. And then they were galloping, tails raised like streaming flags, calling to each other, away down the slopes to the river, a straight trail charted their course through the damp grass, their dark forms sharp against the silver of the willows.

Sophie swung on the gates, crying out with excitement.

'Look, Max! Look at my horses. Even I – and I chose them – hadn't thought they were so beautiful.'

Her green eyes filled with tears and she snatched at his shoulder for balance with her gloved hand. This utter abandonment to the moment enchanted Max. The girl galloped with her horses, unaware of his presence, lost in the glamour of their excitement, power and joy. He stood beside her, steadying the gate.

'Wouldn't your father have bought them for you?' The Count granted his daughter's every wish, like an elderly djinn in a lamp.

'Oh yes, but then they wouldn't have been mine. Really mine. And I wanted them so much. And I thought I had to get the money from somewhere. Then I saw women playing in the Spielsaal. And the idea came to me. I could win what I needed at the tables.'

'But what if you had lost all your savings?' Max prompted carefully; the origins of her original stake remained her secret, and his.

'I won. And I'll win again,' retorted Sophie, jumping off the gate. Her spurs rattled on the cobbles.

Max strolled back into town, wondering if his smart coat smelt of horse and needed to be brushed. He promised himself an emergency dose of cologne when he reached the hotel. His last glimpse of Sophie, disappearing at a brisk, dusty trot down the lanes, filled him with determination. He would court her, win her, earn her confidence, and deserve her love. He wished to see her always, coming towards him, her green eyes filled with the same passion that had possessed her when she beheld her horses. Max saw something tangible and precious in her face, and he wanted that ardour for himself. No man could ever desire a more potent reward – that love poured out unmeasured, profligate. But first he must persuade her, and himself, that he was a serious man, capable of genuine scholarship and distinguished achievements. He settled in the hotel library to peruse the most recent issues of the *Edinburgh Review*.

He was dozing comfortably over an article on natural history in a quiet armchair by the window, when he received a note from the Sibyl, delivered in hushed tones.

My Dear Max

Thank you for your kind enquiry. My husband is much recovered this morning, but we have consulted Dr. Schöngraben who has advised a mild water treatment in addition to the mineral tonics we are both already taking. We have every confidence in him, as he was a pupil of the famous Dr. Gully at Malvern, who worked such wonders for Mr. Darwin some years ago, and whose treatments were not ineffective when we tried them in the past. Would you be so kind as to call upon us this evening? My husband is anxious to finalise the proposals for subsequent reprints and publications with your brother's house.

Affectionately
M. E. Lewes

PS. I trust there have been no difficult repercussions with our gambling belle, and that she has received our little packet. I confess I am eager to hear more of her adventures. She is a young lady who interests me greatly.

Max decided to draw a veil over Sophie's horse-trading. Her motives still appeared obscure, unintelligible. He could not understand her need to act independently of her father. The Count's famous generosity overflowed; his household, family and friends lived brimful with comfort and riches in the wake of his excess. The hotel staff flung themselves into action whenever he appeared and fought over his gratuities. Had she so wished, Sophie von Hahn could have demanded an entire stable of racehorses. This complex doubleness in his fiancée-to-be troubled him greatly. Was she in fact a reckless, headstrong girl, capable of impatience, temper and deceit? Was her affectionate and docile obedience to her father merely a calculated performance? And were all those kisses and caresses a way of blinding the old gentleman to her real aims and purposes? And what on earth did she actually want? Most men think they want a wife with spirit. But the challenge, usually unacknowledged, is to break that spirit, and bend her will to his own, for the real issue, as Humpty Dumpty so eloquently put the case, is this: who is to be master?

Max replied at once to the Sibyl's message, adding that the package was received at breakfast with baffled embarrassment, but that Herr Wiener could rest assured that the matter would go no further. Privately, he doubted that the bumptious Mr. Lewes would be up to any robust discussion of figures and reprints after the fearsome ordeal of the water treatment. Hydrotherapy and its sister cure, thalasso-therapy, commonly known as sea bathing, had both gained a terrific reputation, in the 1840s and '50s, for miraculous improvements, no matter what the ailment; the Homburg cure followed the English model. Each patient was placed on a strict regime of copious vege-tables, little meat and no alcohol, which purged the body of all noxious toxins. Then, a pattern of soaking and washing different parts of the body, to awaken sluggish organs within, would be prescribed, depending on the seriousness of the complaint. Lewes was diagnosed as 'liverish', and therefore wrapped in wet sheets for hours, then 'sweated' with a lamp under a blanket. But his nervous system was considered by the resourceful Schöngraben as too sensitive to be plunged under a douche. The douche consisted of a huge tank of icy water, suddenly released upon the patient from a great height. The resulting shock worked wonders apparently, both for the circulation and for anyone with a delicate digestion, and had been known to ease the suffering caused by dreadful, persistent vomiting.

Max, like all young men blessed with good health, mistrusted all drugs and doctors, and put his faith in two things: eating less and going for walks. He was proved right about the water treatment. The unfortunate Mr. Lewes, flattened by the sweating and the wet sheets, proved quite incapable of receiving visitors that evening.

Nothing for it then, but to scrub himself down and dress himself up, trim his fashionable moustache into points, wax his opulent curls, cram himself into a fresh white shirt, stiff-starched white collar and cuffs, a deep white waistcoat decorated with tiny gold studs, and determine, well beforehand, to ask the Countess Sophie von Hahn for the first dance. Max checked the visitors' list at the hotel. There were no very dangerous virgins of his acquaintance, accompanied by their mothers, married sisters, cousins or aunts, lurking in Homburg, attempting to get the season off to a flirtatious start. Had the Countess von Hahn returned from her ride? Yes, the young lady, ensconced in her suite, had already sent down to the kitchen for copious refreshments. As the lamps came on in all the houses, the hotel braced itself for the evening's festivities. Much rearrangement of furniture and decorating of tables went on during the day, and now came the time for lighting the gaseliers in all the hallways and down the main corridors. The ballroom, famed as a *Prunkkammer*, shimmering with gilt and mirrors, remained golden in candlelight, untouched by modernity, and, as yet, empty of music, satin slippers and leather soles. The parquet smelt strongly of beeswax.

Years later, people in Homburg still recalled that evening of celebration, which became known as the Architect's Ball. Schloss Homburg vor der Höhe, once the residence of the ruling Landgraf von Hessen-Homburg, now belonged to Kaiser Wilhelm I, whose grandson Kaiser Wilhelm II became cheerfully known to the British at a later date as Kaiser Bill. He decided to make Schloss Homburg his regular summer residence, and after perusing various estimates and proposals, transformed the *Königsflügel* into luxurious modern living apartments, with English water closets discreetly hidden in cupboards. The town, already galvanised out of its medieval torpor by its position as a fashionable Kurort, now prepared itself for royal visits. Great expectations were entertained on all sides: fresh stables, horses, hunts, hotels, building projects, a new brewery, landscaped gardens, parks laid out in the English style, lakes dug, new housing, roads relaid, an extension of the gas streetlighting, clinics, quacks and haberdashery, dressmakers, jewellers, tailors from Berlin and full employment. Upholsterers from Frankfurt arrived in full cry; surely there would be an orgy of refurbishment, a great measuring for new curtains and a rising middle class, bellowing for fine porcelain?

The extension of gas lighting in the town proved uncontroversial. The Kurverwaltung had already built a gas factory on the Frankfurt Landstraße near Gonzenheim; all the streets and squares glowed brightly at dusk and the Kurhaus sported gas lights in every room. Sophie von Hahn repeated her mother's views on gas lighting. She wouldn't have it in the house, because all the dirt she had been scraping from side to side over the years with the aid of the housemaids would suddenly become visible. The Count, all in favour of every modern development, no matter how outlandish, grunted, and folded his arms. All the English households took gas light for granted. Even in the kitchens.

The Architect and the Baumeister from Darmstadt visited the Schloss, to draw up preparatory studies for the Kaiser's state apartments. The Court comes to Homburg, and these fine, anticipated visitors will leave a trail of wealth in their wake, rich pickings for all, an earthly abundance of prosperity and happiness. The invitations arrived, printed on ivory cards. *You are cordially invited by the Town Council to a formal dinner and a ball at the Grand Continental Hotel (Louisenstraße 12).* But an undercurrent of anxious desperation simmered beneath these bright declarations of confidence. Spare the Spielsaal, wailed the Council, smelling disaster; but there was no reprieve for the gambling. The Großer Spielsaal would be closed by the end of the year. The town lived in terrible fear of the consequences. The number of visitors would probably halve in one season.

The Architect's Ball was a last-ditch attempt to salvage the town's economy from the jaws of the oncoming Prussians.

A select number of guests, Sophie and the Count included, attended the dinner, but invitations to the ball were less exclusive, and all manner of men and women sauntered through the doors of the Grand Continental. Several decorated doxies, unaccompanied, excessively rouged, skimmed past and made straight for the ladies' dressing room. Max, lurking in the lobby, and hoping to apprehend Sophie, ran into an acquaintance; the artist arrived in acceptable, if slightly shabby clothes, curls tied well back, no hat.

'Meyrick! How are the fairies?'

'Capital!'

They shook hands.

Hans Meyrick looked startlingly young and scrubbed. Max noticed, disconcerted, that he appeared to know everyone who came through the doors. The painter stood in a little swirl of dead leaves, surrounded by happy smiles of greeting.

'I've been very fortunate,' confessed the artist, leaning against the very marble table upon which Sophie had banged down her gambling gains. 'Mrs. Lewes has agreed to sit for me, but only for a series of portraits in chalks and silverpoint. Her husband does not consider her strong enough to endure the lengthy studio sittings necessary for a portrait in oils. Nevertheless, it's an important commission and I shall do my best. However, the Count von Hahn is not at all satisfied with the photographs recently taken of his daughter. All of which, he says, fail to capture the dynamic energy of her glance. And so I am to paint her portrait, in her blue riding habit, with whip, boots and spurs visible, in a style that radiates her vivacity –'

But at that moment the lady herself interrupted him. She pounded towards them, holding her skirts high above her dancing shoes. Sophie had discarded Fräulein Garstein in the dressing room and now stood her ground on the flagstones, fabulous in pale green, the controversial necklace at her throat, her hair dressed in a massive cascade of curls, a starched green waistband with large ribbons magnificent in her wake. She thrust her face up to Max, indignant with bottled rage and disappointment.

'She is here, here in Homburg! The author of *Middlemarch*! You knew and you didn't tell me. My spoken English and French are quite good enough for me to be introduced. I've read every word she's ever written, and you haven't. You must have been visiting her and you could have taken me with you. Mama's silly prohibitions count for nothing when we're not at home.'

'Good evening, Countess,' said Meyrick diplomatically, snatching up her hand and kissing her white-gloved fingers. The young lady nodded, but concentrated on her quarrel with Max.

'Your mother may not be here, Sophie,' he replied, with no intention of humouring this fresh outburst of folly, 'but your father is. And he would not approve of you calling upon Mrs. Lewes if your mother did not wish it.'

'Oh, you take their part against me!' Sophie chewed her thumb through her glove. 'Why should I care what is proper or not? And in any case, if any one of my actions was improper of course I should know, for I should feel no pleasure in doing it. Hans is going to take her likeness, you are able to call upon her every day and I am not even allowed to shake her hand, or to tell her what joy she brings to our house. Nothing could be more morally uplifting and improving than her books. They are proof of her nobility, and the greatness of her soul.'

Max decided instantly that they proved nothing of the sort, but did not choose to take the argument in that direction. He did not think that the Sibyl needed defending on moral grounds, but he saw, quite clearly, that despite her avid consumption of the novels, Sophie and her beloved author occupied different worlds. He could not even imagine them sitting opposite one another. And he did not like to hear Mrs. Lewes discussed in a public place, as if she were common property. The moment of absolution in the forest haunted his unconscious mind. This writer moved in a sphere beyond the petty judgements of ordinary men and women. No words could contain the Sibyl. He had fallen under her spell.

The great world surged past them, and some, who had witnessed the gambling belle in action at the tables, paused to enjoy the argument. The hotel manager, in charge of the ball, and clearly overtaken by the magnitude of events, had already settled the musicians, ready for the first set, and they were tuning up as the guests poured in. Max, Meyrick, and the explosive little Countess, still standing in the foyer, were objects of amusement and remark.

An evil pause settled over all three. Meyrick gazed longingly in the direction of the ballroom. Sophie fingered her necklace, scanning the crowd. She's watching out for him, thought Max, the man who redeemed her jewels. She is wearing the necklace as a signal. He squinted at her dance card, which dangled from her wrist, and saw to his alarm that several names were already entered in a cheerful scrawl. The orchestra, now perfectly audible above the turbulence in the hallway, contained both a trombone and a tuba. A bandstand thump could be heard from the far end of the ballroom.

'I hope you're not already engaged for every dance.' Max tried to sound conciliatory.

'Not quite.' She glared at him for a moment, then suddenly relented and smiled broadly. She held out her hand. The full-length gloves covered her elbow, but above that her upper arms, soft, unmarked, vanished into the green lace of her sleeves, only to emerge again, her white shoulders rising to her naked throat, the jewels warm against her skin. Max had never seen so much of her uncovered. He caught his breath.

'I'm sorry I shouted at you. It's very rude. I'm just so frustrated. Mrs. Lewes seems so near to me and yet withheld – like a god, whose presence is everywhere, but never seen.'

She looked at the dance card. 'Good heavens, Hans. I'm engaged to dance with you!'

Meyrick held out his arm to her and grinned apologetically at Max. 'The Countess is doing me the honour of the first quadrille.'

Sophie called over her shoulder, 'Come and ask me in the refreshment interval. You used to be brilliant at the waltz. My dancing master, who was also yours, said you had real grace.'

And away they went, the obsequious Meyrick bowing to right and left.

Max realised that he could not enter the ballroom and avoid dancing. Too many young ladies wanted partners, and so, rather than risk incivility, he stepped outside into the dusk and the flare of the gas. All the hotels in the Louisenstraße gleamed in the dark, yet all the carriages and walkers headed fiercely through the windy damp towards the Grand Continental. The Architect's Ball sucked everything towards it, a tornado with the dancing at the core. He stepped down one of the side streets into the dark, under the eaves of a large house with carved doors, and vanished.

Max's temperament, actually so far distant from that of the Countess von Hahn and her impetuous rapidity as to suggest an incompatible gulf, demanded time, not only to think, but also to feel. Max stood smoking in the dark, safely out of range of the hotel steps and the faint drizzle. He had imagined married life as a coronet of smiles, sexual convenience, and excellent domestic organisation. Children would appear from time to time, washed and diffident, respectfully addressing him as 'Papa'. They would then be swept away to the nursery, awaiting a suitable moment to be reintroduced. Calm reigned throughout an orderly house, a port of still waters, and at the core, gardening, supervising, decorating and managing the kitchens, but above all smiling, stood the little Countess, her wonderful golden hair secured beneath a modest cap. This conventional fantasy, no sooner conjured up, was just as rapidly dismissed. A quite different Sophie von Hahn stood before him in his mind, her brows drawn together and her head thrown back. This apparition showed no signs of settled calm. Nor did obedience to her father and mother appear to figure very strongly in her moral landscape. In a mere two days Sophie von Hahn had undergone a startling metamorphosis. Max had never envisaged marrying a woman already so firmly wedded to her own opinions, still less one that proved more fortunate than he was at roulette.

Wolfgang ordered him to consider his childhood companion as a suitable future wife, and he never questioned his brother's judgement. But Sophie was, and was not, still a child. She sharpened all his senses, she possessed everything he desired: beauty, intelligence and wealth. But now, equally clearly, she presented an appalling vista of extraordinary domestic disruptions, and unpleasant rows. She danced across his imagination, luxurious in green, swirling, turning, clasped in the arms of men he didn't know and had never met. How long had he stood, skulking in the drizzling dark, well away from the glare of gas jets and carriage lamps? How many cigarettes had he smoked? Max began to feel defeated and stupid. He had abandoned the field to a far lesser man in Hans Meyrick, who, even now, might be turning her head with tales of the Fairy Queen. He stamped on his cigarette, shook himself alert, and marched briskly back to the Grand Continental, to gain possession, if he could, of the Countess Sophie von Hahn, and set about taming the beast.

The ballroom, stiflingly hot, overflowed with dancers, observers, flunkeys, gossips and English voices. He craned his neck and insinuated himself into a corner. His mirrored image immediately appeared at his right shoulder; arrestingly handsome, he decided, and pretended to straighten his white tie for the pleasure of a longer look. But even as he indulged this moment of harmless vanity he caught sight of her flying curls and Meyrick's open hand, spread firmly across the green gauze of her waistband. The artist's long hair, partially escaped from the controlling velvet ribbon, strayed across her face. Oh, you should see me dance the polka! The painter swung the Countess into the air with bravado and panache.

'Sir,' brayed the hotel manager, who had hunted Max down, even into his temporary, mirrored cave, 'may I introduce you to a young English lady who would be an ideal partner for the next set?'

'I should be delighted.'

Max confronted a plump, simpering Englishwoman, at least five years older than he was, draped in swathes of orange taffeta. His alarm deepened when the lady, a confirmed admirer of the ubiquitous Mrs. Lewes, also proved to be a fan of Mr. Darwin. Had Herr Duncker read *The Descent of Man*? A remarkable volume. And was it already translated into German? I gather that Mr. Darwin is very particular about his translators, but that he is in constant correspondence with numerous members of the *Versammlung Deutscher Naturforscher und Aerzte* and many have been quite converted to *Darwinismus*. Wolfgang, with an eye to the main chance, had in fact published numerous works on popular science, both for and against *Darwinismus*, ever since he had grasped the tiller of the firm. The ongoing controversy sold well, and most people purchased both sides of the argument. But Max hadn't ever bothered to read any of the tracts and pamphlets, and thus remained blissfully ignorant of the details concerning evolution and natural selection which swept the educated world. The relationship between apes and men appeared to him self-evident, but just as one does not always acknowledge distant relatives, Max did not feel called upon to investigate further. Classical antiquity, sufficiently remote to bear exhumation, without discovering flesh on the corpses, seemed unsettling enough. The bluestockinged mound of taffeta danced him briskly round the crowded mass of seething couples, with never a word concerning the weather, the Kaiser's arrival at the summer Schloss or the heat of the room. He handed the lady her fan, as he secured her a seat after a strenuous half-hour of heaving bosoms and increasing perspiration.

The Countess von Hahn, devouring an ice in a goblet, materialised at his elbow in the refreshment room.

'Did you survive Miss Gibbons? I saw you getting the scientific treatment. She has tested the Homburg waters with her travelling chemistry laboratory, and our doctor says she is spot on in her mineral analysis.'

Max took Sophie's hand and shuddered. He desperately needed a sofa. The damsel leaped to the rescue.

'Let's run upstairs and eat ice cream in Father's suite.'

Decamping from the ballroom proved neither polite, nor simple. They ran into endless rows of curious acquaintances, including the Count, who had cornered the Kaiser's Architect and pinned him down on the question of improvements to the Orangerie. Sophie and Max bounded up the stairs hand in hand, affectionate and open as any young couple happily engaged, secure in the family's approval. Sophie held up her green gauze in her left hand, careful not to tread on her lace flounce. Her little white dancing shoes rattled on the tiles, then muffled into damp thumps as she scurried down the corridor.

Ice cream in different flavours triumphed in the refreshments room and remained all the rage, whatever the season.

'A jug of iced water, two tall glasses, *et deux petites corbeilles de glaces, s'il vous plaît*. Please send them up immediately. Thank you.'

The waiter raised his eyebrows slightly at the young Countess, alone with her father's publisher in the Count's private suite, but withdrew at once to tell everyone downstairs. The staff took the pulse of the hotel. They knew whose doors opened softly in the night, which boards creaked and when the last lamps had been blown out. The Countess von Hahn turned out to be a favourite, not just with the kitchens, but also with the chambermaids. Her manners, frank, democratic and decisive, went down well everywhere. Knows what she wants, that girl, never wastes your time with whims and caprices. Eats up too, never seen such a good appetite. And she drank a spoonful of wine at supper. Yet she's got such a neat little waist. It's all that riding, and she sits her horse well. Do you know what I heard? She's already spent all that money she won in the Spielsaal. And on what? You'll never guess. She's up there now with the younger son.

Unchaperoned, I've seen Fräulein Garstein wandering around like a lost cow. Aren't they engaged to be married? Well, if they aren't, they ought to be. She danced more than once with the artist, Hans Meyrick. He's just as handsome as the publisher, but not so rich. Is he really so rich? I thought it was his brother's money. Well, he'll never want for anything again if he marries the Countess. And whatever they need, she can win at the tables.

Sophie von Hahn shook off her dancing shoes, propped her feet up on a footstool, shoved her father's papers aside and gobbled her ice cream. Max marvelled at her wolfish voracity. He nibbled a biscuit, careful not to drip crumbs and ice on to his shirtfront. He could not keep pace.

'You'll dance with me when we go downstairs again, won't you, Max? Like we used to? Especially the last galop. I kept that free with you in mind. I don't much care for the quadrille. Somebody always muffs it up.'

Max gazed at her smile, utterly disarmed.

'I'll help you escape from Miss Gibbons. An awful lot of the English ladies read volumes I can't pick up, they're so heavy. But Miss Gibbons is the only scientist. Did you know that she's visited Mrs. Lewes? At her house in London, which is called the Priory. I suppose she's the abbot. Have you ever been there?'

Her tone became obscurely accusing. Max confessed that he had never set foot in the Priory.

'Miss Gibbons says that they have a beautiful secluded mansion and that the garden is filled with roses. All sorts of famous and not so famous people go to see her, and not just gentlemen. I think I might go with Father –'

Max shrugged impatiently.

'We've already discussed this, Sophie.'

The necklace, gleaming at her throat, seemed to wink at him, the dark-eyed stones malevolent as watching toads. Sophie changed the subject.

'Did you admire my horses? And did I do right to buy them? They came when I called them this evening. I think they know my voice already, but I was carrying a bucket of oats and molasses and they could smell that.'

Max examined his fear of this unpredictable and dangerous beauty. All the women, whose skirts he lifted and whose bodies were landscapes marked by many men's hands, were paid to serve him. This girl expected to rule. He discovered in alarm that his reverence for her innocence actually concealed his terror at her virginity. Like the Sibyl, she would be told no lies. Now she was looking straight at him, green-eyed, merry and radiant, waiting for an answer. Max spoke from the heart.

'I thought your horses were beautiful. And I thought you were too when you watched them galloping away. Your eyes were full of tears.'

Sophie leaped to her feet, knocking over her empty ice-cream bowl, which rolled under the armchair, seized both his hands and kissed him on the lips, a huge resounding smack of pure, boisterous affection.

'You darling! You do understand me. You think I did right.'

At that moment the salon door flew open and there stood the Count, resplendent in his campaign medals, his lace cravat rakishly askew.

'Sophie!' His daughter leaned over his publisher, her curls falling into his face, as if she had been riding astride his knees. She bounced upright, uncompromised, pink-cheeked and smiling. Max shrivelled to the length of an earthworm. He sat transfixed among the cushions, electrocuted by Sophie's kiss.

'What's this that I've been hearing downstairs? The hotel is full of it. Is it true that you were in the Spielsaal, gambling, all yesterday afternoon, in public, unchaperoned, winning indecent amounts of money, all of which you've used to buy horses? Speak, child. Now. Explain yourself.'

'It's all true, Father. But I didn't spend it all. I won enough to pay for their transport home myself.'

Thus spoke Sophie, unrepentant.

'You monstrous little baggage! How do you think that makes me look? Like a man who can't afford to give his daughter all the horses she wants.'

'But I wanted them to be mine, Father. Paid for with my own money.'

The Count marched round the rug in a circle, mopping his forehead. Max tried to make himself invisible, slithered out of the armchair, and took up a position in the shadow of the French windows. He was still holding his goblet containing the remains of melted ice, but could find nowhere convenient to abandon the thing.

'I'm sorry if I embarrassed you, Father. I didn't mean to do that, and indeed, I never thought of it. Please forgive me.'

She looked up at the Count, expecting absolution. The Count had started worrying about greater matters.

'I can't settle your inheritance until you're married. You can use your own money then.' He suddenly remembered Max, slapped him on the shoulder and collapsed on one of the sofas.

'Well, Max, I've been looking into the question of Sophie's inheritance and it's damnably complicated if she marries a commoner. Her grandfather never thought she would, but he was a very old-fashioned gentleman. Not at all modern in his views. And it seems that the only way to fulfil her grandfather's wishes and ensure that she keeps her title, name and privilege is to appeal to the Kaiser himself. Or the König, whichever title he prefers. He uses both, you know. But I've got wonderful news. His first secretary will be down at the Schloss tomorrow to meet with the Architect, and I've been granted an interview. I've set the whole thing in motion! I'll have to swallow my politics of course, but that's a minor sacrifice, if it will make you young people rich and happy.'

Max felt himself vanishing into a long dim space, with horses, their heads suspended over doors, neighing on either side.

'Max, my boy, you'd better marry this girl at once and take her off my hands. As you can see I've lost all but the most nominal control.'

Sophie cut in:

'But, Father, he hasn't asked me yet.'

And she grinned broadly at Max.

END OF CHAPTER EIGHT

CHAPTER NINE

visits the Museum.

But Max didn't propose that night, or the next day either. He told himself that he needed camellias or a conservatory with glowing oranges, and the lady, modest, flattered, glancing downwards, and then raising her eyes to his in grateful adoration. He simply could not imagine proposing marriage to the bracing girl who bounded through the mêlée on the dance floor, lost a lace flounce in the final galop, while swinging round in his arms, and didn't care, then stood clapping her hands at the last blast of the tuba, hot with sheer youth and dancing joy. But who could grasp the spirit of Sophie von Hahn? She soared and slithered away, laughing, teasing, shimmering with haste. Would she ever stand still long enough to listen to a marriage proposal? How could he declare his love if the lady seemed likely to laugh at him? And did he really love her?

The jury, still locked in conclave, had reached no decision.

Therefore, Wolfgang's latest letter, recalling him to Berlin, arrived like a reprieve. His brother wrote informing him that Mr. and Mrs. Lewes, wearied by the persistent English claiming their acquaintance, rather than the exhausting water treatment, had decided to decamp in the direction of Stuttgart and Karlsruhe, where flatterers, milords, and autograph seekers seemed unlikely to pursue them. The contracts, now settled and drawn up, awaited signature. Mr. Lewes has been invited to attend a joint meeting of the *Goethe-Gesellschaft* and the

Society for the Promotion of Scientific Knowledge, where he is to take part in a lecture and discussion on the subject of Goethe as a man of science. You know how antiquated these societies are, Max. Ladies cannot become members and are therefore not admitted. But don't worry; there have been plenty of protests. I would therefore be most grateful if you would conduct Mrs. Lewes on a tour of the new collections. Your affectionate brother etc., etc.

In the years immediately following the founding of the Kaiserreich, Berlin boiled and churned with the fever of building works. The Franco-Prussian War brought the National Gallery project to a standstill. But now the work had recommenced; huge holes in the earth regurgitated workers, and armies of stonemasons swarmed over great white blocks, left lingering in piles on the roadways. Max picked his way through the boom of hammers and chisels, skirting the grimy mounds of discarded rubble. The creation of the Museumsinsel, well under way, produced tornadoes of dust, which, in dry weather, coated the queue of passengers waiting for the omnibus. Those perched on the upstairs seats remained at risk from gusts of fine grit. The Bavarian workhorses, who pulled the omnibus, stood patiently, like man and wife, their coats speckled with stone dust and wood shavings. Armed with his umbrella Max fought his way to the Museum steps, where he picked out the Sibyl, resplendent in a new astrakhan jacket, with a muff to match. Lewes, pale and jittery, danced about, looking in all directions. Max hurried to meet them.

Midweek, but the Museum still sucked in dozens of hurrying visitors. Max heard English voices and shuddered. He led the Sibyl into the sculpture gallery, determined to save her from her own celebrity, and guided her down the long cool march of colonnades. The alcove spaces stretched away before them, peopled by white statues, many larger than life-size, an occupying army, all colour drained from their veins. Some figures bowed, bending their heads and hands down towards the visitors; some, arrogant and detached, ignored the upturned, wondering faces. Marble satyrs grimaced and snarled, clutching their enormous phalluses; fleeing women flung their faces to the heavens, gazing upwards at falcons and descending gods. Olympians hurled javelins, or crouched over the discus. A belligerent Hercules brandished his club; Diana, a Roman copy of a Greek original, mastered her hounds. The Sibyl said little at first, her gloved hand rested lightly on his arm. She seemed preoccupied and distressed by Lewes's rapid departure.

'We are now at that age, Max, when every parting, even for a few hours, seems to foreshadow the moment that must come,' here she braced herself slightly, 'that moment when we must part at last. If you knew how I dread that fearful day; were I to be left –'

She sighed and turned her face towards the windows; the skin, shrivelled and carved into lines of pain, moved him to pity. He pressed her hand gently, and as if only then becoming aware of his presence, she raised her great head towards him and her countenance transformed before his eyes into an oval of benevolent gentleness. Max hastened to reassure her.

'But he seemed, I mean, when we parted from Mr. Lewes just now, and he was bolting away across the square, he seemed more than well. He was animated, no, really excited at the prospect of vindicating Goethe's *Metamorphosis of Plants* in such exalted and distinguished company. He has completely recovered from that brief bout of bronchitis in Homburg.'

'Indeed, he has. And we have been walking out by the Spree with such pleasure. We have settled into our old apartment and are really quite comfortable. I should push aside my anxieties – or use them to nourish that fine tenderness which unites me to Mr. Lewes. I think of him with such gratitude, Max, for whatever success I have had is due entirely to him. Without him I would have been quite unable to work. He has defended me against all comers.'

Max carefully rearranged his expression. He did not like to think of Lewes as indispensable.

The Sibyl gazed at the goddess Athena, whose nose, smashed flat, gave her the fierce appearance of a warrior who has just lost a battle. Her helmet, however, remained intact. The Sibyl's yearning for her absent husband appeared to ebb as she turned from the Athena towards Kresilas's famous statue of the wounded Amazon. The bare-breasted maiden leaned against a marble column, her white feet disturbingly naked in the daylight of the gallery. Two artists, perched on stools beneath the windows, their backs against the hall walls, concentrated hard on the muscled bodies of the athletes. Is this where I first saw Meyrick? Max faced a disconcerting row of tiny penises and tense buttocks. Surely women seldom gazed at naked men, or at least not quite so intently as did the Sibyl, who, unembarrassed, approached the gorgeous Antinous and smiled. The statue of the Emperor Hadrian's boy lover stood tall, heraldic, potent, fixed in a magnificent gesture, which usually represented Apollo.

'Ah, the beloved boy,' said the Sibyl, walking round the statue, her eyes at the level of the genitals. 'It is extraordinary, is it not, how Hadrian's cult of his lost love spread throughout the Empire? Antinous had cities named for him, temples built, an entire religious sensibility thrived upon Hadrian's grief. Antinous surpassed his destiny as just one more lost boy, and became a Hermes of the Underworld. He never grew old.'

Max stared at the statue's proud nakedness, the reared arm cresting the world. The blank eyes interrogated posterity. Max decided that the beloved boy looked arrogant and sulky, and had he lived would surely have developed an enormous double chin. The signs were there. This glossy Antinous will run to fat. Max decided to pay attention to his diet and the amount of port wine he consumed at dinner. But the Sibyl had begun to moralise. He stood to attention. Duty called. His function, on that October morning, was to incline his head devotedly, and keep his views to himself.

'Hadrian lost that classical poise, so typical of wise rulers in the ancient world. He fell victim to quacks and charlatans, and sank into credulous absorption, giving ear to any cult which proclaimed eternal life. He could not accept that his beloved boy had chosen to leave him and that they would never embrace one another again. For Antinous was found drowned in strange, indeed inexplicable circumstances. Some say he gave his life for Hadrian, a bizarre, primitive sacrifice on the banks of the Nile. At that time Egypt bristled with mystery and resurrection cults, including that of Isis and Osiris.'

The Sibyl, clearly used to addressing a rapt audience, usually consisting of one spellbound individual, and clearly possessed of a pedagogical streak, treated Max as if he were in urgent need of instruction. Max dared to question the Sibyl's patronising dismissal of all Egyptian spiritual quests.

'But seekers after truth might well have been adherents of those cults.'

'Of course, and I do not despise them. Nor do I disparage Hadrian's noble grief. He made his Antinous a god.'

Max gazed dubiously at the naked marble foot, inches from his nose. He could not imagine loving a man with the unmeasured passion Hadrian had poured out over Antinous. The Sibyl continued.

'But our relationship to those belief systems has been transformed by the serious scholarly challenges, led by German writers and thinkers, to our own common faith. Nothing has seemed more remarkable to me than the spread of scepticism, or rationalism if you will, during the latter part of my life. Any person who has no assured and ever-present belief in the existence of a personal god, or of a future existence with retribution and reward, can have for his rule of life only those impulses and instincts which are strongest or which seem to be the best. We have the power of reflection and our highest intelligence commands us to act for the good of others. This is undoubtedly the deepest pleasure on this earth: to deserve the love of those close to us, and to see that diffusive goodness spreading ever outwards.'

Max did not share this Olympian perspective of universal benevolence, which bore little relation to the deep-rooted iniquity he observed all about him, and often perceived, to his alarm, within himself, but he decided not to argue, and, while giving every impression of complete attention, he guided her towards the Hall of Classical Roman Portraiture.

The marble faces, which had, until then, appeared unchanging and remote in their abstract loveliness, suddenly aged, creased, and frowned. The blind gaze of their still features shifted, intensified, and became disturbingly real, concentrated and intent. Eternity, which had left Antinous untouched, notched lines around these eyes and mouths. Death and Time held hands with the Romans. Here stood the Emperor Augustus in marble relief, and here a bust of Caracalla, his naked chest crossed with his sword belt, and his cloak wrenched aside for battle. They paused before the tomb relief of Publius Aiedius and his wife Aiedia: two aged faces peered forth from their monument, as if it were a window carved in the wall of their final home. The figures turned a little towards each other, their shoulders touching, their hands clasped. The Sibyl gazed at the shrunken mouth and chicken neck of the old man, and murmured, almost to herself:

'That long, late afternoon of love. To be desired above all else.'

Max decided not to hear, obscurely jealous of each solicitous reflection directed towards her husband. The Sibyl's strange gift of being wholly present in her listening never was withdrawn. But her absorption in Lewes covered every thought with a patina of wifely devotion. They lived each other's lives, and from that claustrophobic intimacy all else remained excluded. No one could be admitted to the Presence, except as a converted worshipper, and Lewes, as gatekeeper, checked out all the applicants. How odd, thought Max, to find himself within the walls, without the aid of a Trojan horse. They paced the gallery slowly, arm in arm. Max kept an eye on the other visitors, but no one approached them, or attempted to accost the Sibyl.

'Here it is at last,' she exclaimed, 'the face I have come to see.'

And before them, next to an animated struggle, which represented

Theseus dealing with the Minotaur, a bust on a plinth gazed away out of the window. The temporary handwritten label peeled slowly off the polished oak stand: *Der Dichter Lucian, Erworben 1871*. The Poet Lucian. The face, reflective, absent, was that of a bored sitter forced to remain still, while the clay mould of his features took shape beneath the sculptor's hands. Was this a noble, scrupulous face? Max had expected Lucian to resemble the Sibyl, and found to his surprise that he did not. Shrewd rather than handsome, austere rather than generous, and that kind gentleness which so often animated the Sibyl's glance formed no part of this man's character, concluded Max. But like the Sibyl, he was no beauty. The hawked nose loomed from his lined face. Beneath his folded hands, apparently written on a tablet, emerged the words: 'SUAVE MARI MAGNO'. Max didn't recognise the lines, but the Sibyl gently indicated the text and completed the verse, first in Latin, then in English. *Pleasant it is, when on the wide sea the winds stir up the waters, to gaze from dry land at the great troubles of another.*

'Those are the first three words of the second book of Lucretius's *De rerum natura*. Lucian and Lucretius were not contemporaries, for Lucretius died in 55 BC, and while we are not certain of Lucian's dates, we think that he was born in Southern Gaul a hundred years later, perhaps around AD 50. But Lucian is known to have admired the poem, although he considered its contents subversive, and possibly damaging to the state. Many of his comments seem hostile to the philosophy of Epicurus, whom Lucretius revered. The Epicureans seem so modern to me now. But Lucian knew all his predecessor's poetry well, and that verse, which if the sculpture is genuinely a portrait, and we believe that it is so, must be one that he chose, for it describes what Lucian did. He retired from public service to his country estates by the sea, and concentrated on farming and writing. So far as I know, apart from that early period when he studied in Athens, he never travelled for pleasure. He lived in quiet retirement and gazed upon the sea and other people's troubles.'

'But if the *Fragment* is authentic,' said Max, intrigued by the face of the ancient atheist, 'then he had enough close contact with the changing mores of the Empire, even when he ceased to be Governor of Bithynia and Phrygia, to write what he did with authority.'

'Indeed.' The Sibyl never ceased to gaze upon the pensive countenance before them, lost in the wastes of nearly two thousand years, and now polished and gleaming amidst Caesars and famous gladiators. Like the Sibyl, Lucian had transformed himself into a celebrity. 'He lived close to a busy Mediterranean port. Christianity spread rapidly across the waters.'

She gazed critically at the portrait; then walked round it twice.

'This bust was created for a public building, to honour the man. I think he must have been past fifty when the likeness was taken. The provenance of the sculpture must be secure. The archaeologists seem entirely confident that this is the poet philosopher Lucian. That unique voice, contemplating his own times and the future of all peoples, rings as clear and truthful as if he were speaking to us now. His extraordinary organic theory of societies and religions influenced Herder, I believe. He thought that, like plants, a society may be born, grow, flourish, blossom and mature, but that it will then inevitably fade, decay and die away, so that new worlds and new ways of thinking may be discovered and reborn. Do you know the story of Lucian and the slave girl? She was a Palestinian woman, possessed of extraordinary healing powers, whom he purchased at the very moment when, unbeknown to him, as master of the house, the new religion had already crossed his threshold.'

She turned to face Max, who shook his head. And there, standing in the gallery, the Sibyl told the story of the first meeting between Lucian and Myriam.

The old philosopher had arranged for his agent to purchase several household slaves in the market at the local port, but before allowing them to enter his service he insisted that they should be inspected for vermin and disease. Then the new slaves were brought before the master who questioned them himself, concerning their origins and talents. The young woman from Palestine could read and write Latin as well as Greek; this was extremely unusual in a woman sold into bondage. The head cook vouched for her; he claimed she understood the medicinal qualities of plants, and that her power to heal wounds, agues and skin diseases was little short of miraculous. Intrigued, Lucian demanded to know where she had learned these things. The cook glared at her, but the woman stood mute, her head thrown back, defiant. Was she too frightened to speak in the presence of the master? Lucian called for a slate and chalk. Could she write? Would she be useful?

'Let her write down the source of her power.'

The woman snatched the slate, scrawled a single shape across the surface and handed the image back to Lucian. He found himself gazing, for the first time, at the secret Christian sign of the fish. The slaves grouped around him recoiled, frightened for their lives. For the new religion, widespread within the philosopher's household, could never be safely acknowledged. Lucian simply nodded, and dismissed the group, stipulating that the woman should be treated well and brought to him again when she had regained her tongue. And so began that curious connection between the old Stoic philosopher and the Palestinian slave, the argument between classical antiquity and the new religion.

'Lucian realised at once that Christianity could not be stopped. And he foresaw its power. The old religions managed their gods with a system of bribery and wheedling, and bloody offerings of sacrificed animals. The Christians claimed to love their god, and, despite the evident insanity of the proposition, argued that their god loved them in return. Lucian felt the full force of this argument. And I can never forget the poignancy of his words when he wrote: *I returned to my sacred groves, only to discover that the nymphs had fled*. The old religion could not evolve to confront this threat, and would therefore wither and die.'

'But he thought that Christianity would vanish too,' Max objected, shaken by the Sibyl's fearlessness, and sensing that he was being challenged. 'And paganism didn't just fade away gracefully. The old religion was put down by force.'

'Not many people were prepared to die rather than relinquish their faith in Aphrodite, Max. That made no sense. The old religion was distinguished by ritual. What you did mattered more than what you believed. The Christians were prepared to die for their hidden faith, for something unproven, unseen. Persecute and torment a people for their beliefs and some will certainly recant, but others, the most intensely fanatical, will prefer to die, however horribly, thus bearing witness. And I do not think that Christianity as a religious system will pass peacefully away in our lifetimes.'

She smiled calmly at Max, concealing the fearful teeth.

'The old religion continues to glimmer through the centuries, my dear. In the sixteenth century most people in England were hedging their bets by visiting sacred wells and attaching locks of their children's hair to holy trees. We visited a little chapel in Brittany, which was once dedicated to St Venus. There she stood, emerging from the waters, surrounded by fishes, her lovely breasts uncovered. But in the Middle Ages the chapel was rededicated to St Agatha, who sacrificed her breasts for god. And so the beautiful naked breasts of the goddess simply changed sides, and the old religion metamorphosed into the new faith.'

Max had never discussed the erotic and religious potential of breasts with anyone, even his fellow officers, and no woman of his acquaintance ever talked with such open frankness. He bowed slightly to Lucian and the Sibyl, a ploy devised to mask a faint but rising blush. The Sibyl took his arm, mightily amused.

'Come. I have something else to show you that I noticed when we were last in Berlin.' They approached a red sandstone tomb of a Crusader and his wife, laid side by side, their gloved hands clamped in prayer.

'Look carefully, my dear. Do you notice anything odd about this dead, devoted couple?'

Max didn't. They were both fixed in carved stone, their blank eyes raised to heaven. At the knight's feet lay a snarling lion, the long mailed shoes curved over the creature's body, ending in neatly fettered points. Beneath her feet lay a greyhound, foetal and quiet, nestled in the final folds of her stone drapery. Nothing was amiss. The tombstone seemed remarkably well preserved and intact. Husband and wife had been dead for nearly five hundred years.

'Look,' insisted the Sibyl.

And then he saw it. Protruding from the folds of her gown, shrouded a little by the embroidered cord at her waist, lay a sword. The lady had carried her sword to the grave, and no ordinary sword; this was a broadsword, with jewels carved into the handle, a sword carried only by knights in battle. The lady lay for ever armed, like her husband; she too was a knight.

'Good heavens,' said Max. 'How peculiar!'

'I wonder,' replied the Sibyl, satisfied by his surprise, 'what story lies behind this curiosity, which is nowhere mentioned in the guidebooks.

'Indeed,' said Max, proffering his arm. He did not like to think that a wife, capable of decapitating her husband in life, would continue to take the precaution of retaining her weapon after death.

The Sibyl possessed an odd knack of noticing disconcerting facts or objects; she was on the watch for the peculiar, and the graceful irony of her manner as she enjoyed sharing her visions of the freakish and the weird enchanted him utterly. He was granted an audience, standing before her inner world, a museum of observations, selections and judgements. Her public would have expected to view a noble array of sentiments, ranked like statues of the antique gods in the upper gallery. Instead he was privileged to view a cabinet of curiosities, where the bizarre triumphed over the moralistic and the beautiful. He had been granted permission to meet the Sibyl on her own ground.

'No one but you would have seen the sword.' He gazed at the Sibyl's extraordinary profile. They paused before a gigantic Renaissance Madonna, startled by the arrival of a floating angel with rainbow wings.

'I think that the sword has often been noticed, and then ignored. We tend to ignore the unaccountable. Look at this Madonna's expression. What do you see? I see surprise, incredulity and disgust. The mother of Jesus of Nazareth would almost certainly have been illiterate. Yet now that we women have been allowed to learn how to read we are perpetually disturbed in that precious, silent meditation, rarely by angels, but sometimes by men.'

She gleamed wickedly at Max, who reddened, remembering his intrusion at Homburg when the Sibyl sat reading Lucian.

'Forgive me, I would never intentionally intrude –'

'Don't apologise! I only said that for the pleasure of seeing you blush again. You radiate such an endearing modest glow.'

Max inclined his head to hers, flattered and trapped.

'Shall we look in on the Byzantine sculptures? A second-century sarcophagus has been added to the collection. I didn't see it in the spring, but Mrs. Harleth tells me that the frieze is in perfect condition.'

As they left the Museum at the appointed hour the Sibyl thanked him graciously.

'We shall spend the rest of our time in Germany visiting Karlsruhe and Stuttgart, but I hope that we might see you there before we return to England. We have an affinity with what the world calls dull places and always prosper best in them.'

She declared herself too tired to walk to the Dorotheenstraße, and so he hailed a cab. As he took her gloved hand to help her up the step she reached into her pocket and handed him a small note, with an air of conspiracy.

'I have received a letter from the Countess Sophie von Hahn. As you are mentioned therein I think it perfectly correct to put the matter in your hands. You will give her an answer for me, Max. I would have been quite unable to avoid making mention of a certain necklace or moralising on the evils of the Spielsaal.'

Max took the note. Ripples of alarm shivered down his arms and back. What had Sophie dared to say to Mrs. Lewes? The Sibyl, sharp as an owl on the hunt, noticed his discomfiture at once. The mischievous smile, which she delivered at the last, finally revealed her monstrous teeth, and abruptly transformed her from the Grandmother into the Wolf. Max, abandoned on the busy pavement, watched her cab rattle away down the wide streets. Then he swallowed hard and opened the letter Sophie von Hahn had written to Mrs. Lewes.

END OF CHAPTER NINE

CHAPTER TEN

builds to an Unfortunate Climax,
leaving Our Hero in a Desperate State of Mind.

Sophie wrote in German on headed notepaper filched from the Grand Continental. The letter, clearly dashed off in haste, for the handwriting flowed over the edges of the line and dipped downwards, had been composed on the very night of the Architect's Ball, five days earlier.

Sehr geehrte Frau Lewes,

I hardly dare to write these words as my heart is overflowing. Indeed, you must receive so many letters of admiration and gratitude from your readers that I must content myself with adding to the pile. But I cannot bear to know that you are so close to me here in Homburg and that I am forbidden to see you. What pleasure and delight you have already given me. When I read your words I imagine myself in your company, and throughout all the hours I pass, turning your pages, I feel that you are speaking to me, and only to me, as if we were alone, together in one room. And I have listened, all attention, to your wisdom and forgiving tenderness. You see into all hearts and read our human souls. Forgive me if I speak only of myself. I cannot know who you really are, and yet I feel that I do. I long to have the strength always to do what is right, and yet I cannot always discern what this would be in my particular circumstances. I have always found the loving judgement that I seek in your words. And that is why I appeal to you now.

I am promised in marriage to Max Duncker, the younger son of your publisher here in Germany. Yet I cannot tell whether this would be right, for me or for him. Could I ever love him as a husband? And does he have the power to make me happy? For I do not even know if I want to be married at all. I have never travelled or lived my life, just for me, made my own choices, tested myself against the world. Would I be content with the duties of a wife? Or with a life tied to a household and children? I cannot imagine myself as a mother, because I want more, more than ordinary women of my rank and station appear to do. I want to visit other countries, study their histories and peoples, just as Max has done. Perhaps I could be an explorer or a scientist, for this would be the fulfilment of a dream, especially if I could visit Egypt, India, Africa – or ride beside herds of bison on the plains of the American West. You see, I have longings and dreams. Surely women have a right to want more than they are offered or permitted to desire? The right to lead extraordinary lives that have some purpose and meaning? Just as Dorothea yearned for some great cause to which she could dedicate her days? To be part of that greater kingdom of human endeavour? To live as you have done?

I pray that you will not think this letter impertinent and I beg you to grant me an interview, however brief. If I have overstepped the mark, then the only atonement I can make is to resolve that whatever words of advice or warning you may give me shall not be lost. I will treasure them for ever. For I believe in you, my dearest Frau Lewes, I love your novels with all my heart and I love you too.

I remain, sehr geehrte Frau Lewes, your affectionate and obedient servant

Sophie, Countess von Hahn

Standing there in the street with all the crowds in flux around him, the first idea that erupted in Max's brain was to tear the letter into tiny pieces, scatter them in the gutter, ride like the Devil to the Count's country Jagdschloss, where the family remained, still settled in their summer residence, and spank the feckless Countess till she screamed. Or was she with her father, still in Homburg, arranging transportation for the miraculous and dearly purchased steeds? Max stared at her handwriting, furious that he was not the recipient of this unguarded torrent of confidence, admiration and love. She should be writing passionate letters to him, and to no one but him. What unmitigated madness could have entered the girl's head and induced her to write to the Sibyl in this fashion? And what insolence possessed her to describe herself as 'promised in marriage'? Surely nothing so certain had ever been agreed? And then to suggest that she might not be satisfied with him as a husband! Max bit his lip in fury. He feared that he might awake one morning and discover himself married to the boisterous Countess, without any action on his part. Would he be pleased at this prospect? Or outraged? He simply did not know. One thing loomed in his mind, with utter clarity. Any attempt on Sophie's part to approach the Sibyl must be stopped. Their paths must never cross. Max, not at that moment sufficiently self-aware to understand his own motives, did not realise what he feared. The Sibyl, with her great washed eyes and noble ageing countenance, knew too much about him. He feared that freemasonry of the sex, which resulted in confessions of a most intimate nature. He shuddered lest the Sibyl should describe him in terms of hesitation and weakness. She possessed the means to tarnish that self-portrait he had so carefully polished, and therefore to betray him. Was Sophie's outburst of self-revelatory ardour handed over as a warning? And if so, who presented the threat? Sophie or the Sibyl?

Why did Max set such store by the world's eyes? He was twenty-three years old and had, as yet, done nothing of any magnitude, apart from running up enormous debts. His knowledge and his reading, random rather than profound, would not pass muster among the members of various learned societies he sought to join. His studies in antiquity were best described as rudimentary. He cast no shadow; like Peter Schlemihl, he was a man without substance. But not a man without ambition. He desired a name in the world and he wanted to be remembered. He imagined himself honoured with memorials for doing great things, so great that they were not yet even conceived, let alone executed. His mind resembled a bell jar, with all the oxygen sucked out.

❧

The Duncker establishment in the Jägerstraße stood four storeys tall. The servants amounted to one butler, who managed everyone, including the two brothers, one cook, one kitchen maid, one scullery boy, two housemaids and a groom. Most of the household observed Max, storming into the house, abandoning his coat on the chest in the hall, and locking himself in his father's library, where a fire was always laid, even in summer, to prevent damp invading the books. With whom had he quarrelled: the Countess or his brother? His present studies, with photographs of the proposed site in Anatolia, reproached him with their neglect. A dead fly lay on the distinguished essays by Professor Marek. He flicked it into the flames, then flung himself into his father's chair and reread Sophie's letter.

Distance, familiar surroundings, time to consider alternatives, all these things encourage calm judgement, informed by reflection. But not in this case. Max became steadily ever more furious. The Countess von Hahn had deliberately, knowingly, cunningly disobeyed him. The fact that the young lady's behaviour should not yet concern him to this degree simply never occurred to Max. Her business was his business, of course it was. He rummaged among Wolfgang's papers scattered across his father's desk and fell upon the corrected proofs of the first translation of *Middlemarch*. The unfortunate Chapter 29 began thus: 'One morning, some weeks after her arrival at Lowick, Dorothea – but why always Dorothea? Was her point of view the only possible one with regard to this marriage?' Max read no further. Had he done so he would have been confronted by the awful consequences of neglected scholarship, and the eternally unfinished key to all mythologies. Instead, he felt justified in his rage, his personal point of view for ever vindicated. And confirmed by the Sibyl herself. Yes, there was another way of reading Sophie's letter and recent events in Homburg. The Countess von Hahn had insulted his integrity and challenged his sense of self-worth. Moreover she had revealed her personal ambitions to a complete, if influential, stranger, and those ambitions were in direct conflict with her duties as his wife. He snatched up a sheet of Wolfgang's writing paper and scrawled a savagely brief and formal note to the Count von Hahn, in which he requested the Count's permission to seek a private interview with his eldest daughter at her earliest convenience.

This note, instantly dispatched to their Berlin residence at Wilhelmplatz, where the family was every day expected, then travelled another sixteen miles to the Jagdschloss on the lake, and passed at once from the hands of the Count into those of his wife, who was digging in bulbs with the gardener. She pulled off her gloves and beamed at her husband. A private interview! Well, my dear, it's not like our Max to be so formal. And so soon after the visit to Homburg, where they were every day in one another's company. Practically tied to each other with ribbons! She danced the last set with him, and I caught them wolfing ice cream together upstairs. His brother will arrange a handsome settlement of course. The Dunckers own a good deal of property, from the mother's side. I haven't settled the business of Sophie's title and inheritance, but I've had a good deal of encouragement from the Kaiser's personal secretary, and I've been called to court as usual, never mind the Memoirs. Well, what do you think? Shall I write and ask him to come out here? Or will the end of the week in Berlin seem soon enough? The old couple linked arms and gazed at their gardens, remembering that wonderful moment, decades ago, when the Countess's own father, God rest his soul, the dear man, had totted up the figures, studied the young Count with suspicion, and then given his consent.

Sophie, Countess von Hahn,
will be delighted to grant a private interview to
Maximilian Reinhardt August Duncker.
She will be at home on Friday morning at ten o'clock,
Wilhelmplatz 2, Berlin.

In the course of three days Max developed a tremor in his left cheek. Sophie, radically undecided on the wisest course of action, and helplessly watching the post, lest the Sibyl should choose to break her sinister silence, ordered a new dress in pale blue silk. A precaution, just in case the result of the interview required new clothes. She spent hours talking to her horses. The creatures replied in kind; they lifted their heads and snorted at the sound of her voice, or the clatter of her boots crossing the yard. Her younger sisters teased her mercilessly and made up silly rhymes, which they chanted in chorus.

Sophie and Max
Went off to Saxe
In heavy weather.
They looked the same
When back they came
Huddled together.

The songs ended in stifled shrieks and raucous giggles. The household buzzed with expectation. Her mother wondered if eight months might seem too indecently short an engagement and if her husband could find out exactly when Professor Marek intended to spirit the archaeological ingénue away to parts of the world where the food makes you sick.

Max said nothing whatever to his brother.

On Friday morning Max appeared in the hallway dressed for battle: dark as an undertaker, starched white cuffs and collar, black waistcoat, long coat, top hat. He stood before the mirror, obscurely convinced that he would emerge by midday, master of the field.

'Where on earth are you going?' Wolfgang looked up from the scientific journal that he was reading with a magnifying glass, and stared.

'Out,' snapped Max, and left the premises.

❧

But when he got to Wilhelmplatz, and saw the square, drenched in cold sun and changing colour beneath a steady descent of browning leaves, he lost his nerve completely, and began circling the gardens, overlooked on all four sides by the great town houses. Other people roamed the gardens; a child followed her nurse, pulling a little toy wagon. Someone chased a small white dog. Two muffled old ladies, whispering in French to one another, tottered past. Carriages banged along the roadway. He heard the bells of the Wilhelmskirche declaiming ten times in the distance. Max increased his speed, fingering the fatal letter in his pocket. Should he just forget all about it and go home again?

At that moment he was spotted by the Count and his wife, who were peering anxiously out of the French windows from the first-floor drawing room, which overlooked the square at the front of the mansion and the private gardens at the back. Why had Max come on foot rather than in the carriage, given the formality of the occasion and the October chill?

'What in heaven's name can he be thinking of? He must know we're here!' The Count watched Max executing a shifty dash across the damp grass only to disappear into the autumnal bushes.

'Where's Sophie?'

The little Countess, panic-stricken with stage fright, had abandoned the downstairs salon, her chosen theatre of confrontations, and, without gloves, hat or coat, tramped at speed round the French gardens, crunching the gravel and kicking at the box hedges as she pounded down the little *allées*. Why is he late? It's gone ten. He's never late. I'm the one who's always late. The great house, bristling with the anticipated encounter, now stood like a fortress between the two main protagonists. Max screwed his courage to the sticking post and charged. The bell shook the house. The porter, standing just inside the door, had watched his rapid advance across the inner court and flung back the heavy draught-excluder. The fire in the hallway belched and stuttered.

'The young lady was waiting for you in the salon, sir. But now, I believe, she's taking a turn in the gardens.'

Max walked straight through the house, down the steps and out into the gardens, still wearing his gloves and clutching his hat. Indignation suddenly warmed him up. There she was, wearing her short red jacket and blue riding skirt, her boots thudding on the pathways, striding away from him towards the still fountains.

'Sophie!' he bellowed into the quiet air.

She skidded on her heels like a polo pony, and galloped towards him, her face glowing pink with pleasure and excitement. They stopped short and stared at one another. A truly frightful pause ensued, and Max, torn between shy love and insulted *amour propre,* almost lost sight of his rehearsed script. But alas, he did not rethink his strategy; he gathered up his courage and fired the first shots.

'Mrs. Lewes thanks you for your letter, which, given that its contents concerned me in important ways, she invited me to read before returning it to you. Here it is. She regrets that she is unable to offer any specific advice.'

Sophie's blank incomprehension drained all her colour away. Max held out the unfolded letter in one black glove, the other remained clamped to his hat. She looked down at her own handwriting. He stood like the messenger of death, ready to deliver the terrible news, and then depart at once. Sophie snatched the letter and began to read it again, with a baffled intensity, as if she had never seen the words before. When she looked up, she was brick red and shaking.

She took one fatal step closer to Max. He thought she intended to hit him.

'This letter is addressed to Mrs. Lewes and is intended for her eyes only. And it does not concern you. How dare you assume that it does! You have no right to read my private correspondence.'

'Be careful what you say, Sophie.'

'Careful! You dare tell me to be careful?' Her voice rose and her breath came in smoky blasts, as if her inner organs had begun to roast on a flaming spit. 'I had not expected you to be so underhand. Or so dishonest. You are spying on me. That's what it feels like. My feelings for Mrs. Lewes are mine. And mine alone.'

What about her feelings for him? Max turned away and put down his hat on the rim of the fountain, realising, too late in the day, that he had expected contrition and embarrassment from his beloved Sophie, not unchained rage. He stood prepared for tears and a little screaming. Perhaps even many minutes of judicious silence. Then the lady would raise those beautiful green eyes towards him and beg forgiveness. At first, he might be haughty and offended. But one or two beseeching looks and the increasing certainty that her whole happiness depended on his every glance would surely win the day. He had not imagined the final moments of this scene; the narrative ended with his apotheosis as the magnanimous arbiter of her destiny. This careful script, of which he had composed both speaking parts, floated away into the milky sky. For the Countess had been unexpectedly transformed into a malevolent harpy. He fiddled with the fingertips of his black gloves. Sophie grabbed his sleeve, utterly beside herself. The flood of love and trust poured out in the offending letter was clearly undergoing a rapid and dramatic revolution. Now she was screaming, both at Max and the absent Sibyl.

'She has betrayed me and in such a way that has made you despise me. Just as I now despise you. But it's not only that. She has ensured that I hate you and can never trust you again. No gentleman would ever have read my letter. And no woman who honoured her own sex would have given that letter to you. I shall never read her books again. I don't care how her novel ends. She has raised a wall between us. *And she meant to do it.*'

Did Mrs. Lewes intend to sow division between two childhood sweethearts? That certainly was the predictable result from the way in which she had chosen to return the letter, given the characters of the two young people involved. And Mrs. Lewes, however observant and astute she might have been, did not know Sophie. Mildly flattered, her mind elsewhere, she had mistaken youthful passion for immaturity, and, used to adoration, had missed the questioning critical intelligence beneath Sophie's spontaneous overflow of powerful feelings. The French gardens, evergreen, symmetrical, laid out with the precision of playing cards, presented an ironic ordered calm against which the alienated lovers confronted one another by the cold fountains. A girdle of little towers, neatly clipped in box, surrounded them. Max stared at the pointed cones of reason with chaos in his heart. He struck back.

'Before you judge, condemn and dismiss Mrs. Lewes, whom you once so much admired, Sophie, there is something you should know. She was with me that day when we saw you gambling. And she was the stranger who returned the necklace. She paid your debts and protected you from disgrace. You owe her everything.'

Sophie's face stilled in shock. Max seized the advantage.

'I saw you leaving the Jew's pawnshop. I knew what you had done. That necklace belongs to your mother. You had no right to borrow money with those jewels as your security. You charge me with dishonesty. Consider your own behaviour.'

Sophie stood trembling, open-mouthed, speechless, her humiliation now complete.

'Excuse me, Countess.'

Max bowed, snatched up his hat and stalked away down the raked gravel paths. He avoided the house and strode up to the gate in the wall, the secret gate through which he had often escaped, hand in hand with Sophie, to avoid the smaller children, and play hide and seek, just the two of them, in the square gardens. The gate was locked. He swung upon the bell until the porter appeared, and stood, white-faced, unflinching, while the bewildered old man fetched the key.

'And are we to congratulate you, sir?'

Max stared down the unfortunate porter, as if he had gone mad, then vanished away down the Wilhelmstraße, dispensing neither gratuities nor farewells. He had covered several hundred yards before he realised that not only had he taken the wrong direction, but also that his face was soaked in tears.

The Count and Countess sat upstairs, waiting, mystified, expecting the happy couple to appear at any moment, assured of joy and blessings. Their daughter, however, stormed into the house and locked herself in her room, where she was later heard howling, then sobbing, and finally, quite unaccountably, ripping pages out of her treasured books. Her little sisters, round-eyed, wedded to the keyhole, reported violent grief on a scale as yet unwitnessed in the household. When Sophie sent back her supper, a thing unknown throughout her entire history of childhood tantrums and punishments, the Count decided to write at once to Wolfgang.

Wolfgang old chap,

We came back to town yesterday hoping to see Max, who had, as you no doubt know, requested a private interview with Sophie. Well, after all that dancing in Homburg we imagined that the two of them had come to an understanding, just as we'd hoped. He didn't need to see me beforehand, as I'd already spoken to you. And of course we were delighted when she told us he was coming. I didn't want to rush things, but it would be good to have everything settled and arranged. After all, they grew up together! But some sort of altercation occurred in the gardens. Max stormed off without speaking to either of us, and that's most unlike him. And now Sophie is locked in her room and won't eat. Do you have any idea what's going on? If you do, let me know at once so that we can put it right.

Your Affectionate Friend
August, Count von Hahn

But Wolfgang had no idea whatsoever. And this was the first he had heard of the famous private interview. Why had he not been consulted? Wolfgang considered his younger brother to be a frustrating, if charming, wastrel, with a good heart and a cunning streak. But Max began to behave in a very strange and singular fashion. His metamorphosis into a nocturnal creature meant that he spent the days shut up with his studies in the library and, politely but firmly, dined out. A curious correspondence grew up between the Count and his publisher. Sophie's behaviour was equally peculiar. She had thrown all Mrs. Lewes's books out of her room. Quite extraordinary. She worshipped the celebrity author, but she had ripped her favourite pages out of *The Mill on the Floss* and vandalised *Adam Bede*, over which she once adored having a delightful, uninhibited weep. What did it all mean? The great mansion in Wilhelmplatz rumbled with disorder and discontent. The young lady made infrequent appearances at mealtimes, picked at her food and grew thin. The Count brought her horses into town, but although she spent hours in the stables, murmuring all her troubles to them, she refused to ride. Her bright cheeks faded. The old Countess wanted to call in a doctor, possibly a specialist.

Had Max been seen in Hettie's Keller? Wolfgang made discreet enquiries. No sign of him. Not since he came back from his mission in Homburg. Was the young gentleman ill? Madame Hettie, who now passed herself off as French, cooed at Wolfgang. Had Max finally abandoned vice? A broken heart – that is the only possible explanation! Sophie has refused him. And now the little Countess regrets her decision, but is too proud to undo her refusal. And given that the Countess is so far above him, Max dare not renew his suit. Wolfgang and the Count, convinced by this erroneous interpretation of events, set about inventing a remedy. Good novels always end happily. All you need is a pretty girl and a good ending. Hence the repudiation of the Sibyl, for this is the writer who separated Adam from his one true love and drowned the fabulous Maggie Tulliver, a victim of thwarted passion who had committed no moral wrong. How should Sophie's story end? Surely not in rejection and dismissal? A new chapter, charged with dramatic reconciliations and perpetual joy, must be invented and composed.

I will send Max down to Stuttgart to visit Mr. and Mrs. Lewes with the latest version of the translation, before they return to England. And Sophie's godmother, who is something of a sporting soul, will have her to stay out in the country, before the bad weather sets in. Then we will cook up a musical or a theatrical evening to welcome them both home. How's that? Lots of people, some sort of event, a performance by Herr Klesmer will hook in a crowd. I'll fix a date with him. And we'll hold it here in Wilhelmplatz. Some time before Christmas, when the season is properly under way. Well, Wolfgang, what do you say?

And so the true but disappointed lovers were dispatched in different directions by their immediate male relatives, determined that young hearts must be given occupations and not allowed to brood. Sophie took her horses with her on the visit to her godmother's estate, and by the end of the following week could be seen galloping across open country without a hat, and returning in the early dusk, very hungry indeed. Please do not imagine her as a fickle girl with shallow feelings. Young shoots rise inexorably towards sunlight. It was not in her nature to nurse a grudge against someone she had always loved, nor to remain angry and ashamed. When she thought about Max it was with the old childhood affection. In her heart she forgave him. And she waited, confident of his return. She never doubted her love for him or that he loved her as of old.

But that evil scene in the French gardens worked a dangerous course, subtle as an underground river, through Max himself. He no longer regarded Sophie von Hahn as his future wife. She did not understand him and the Sibyl did. He caught the train for Stuttgart.

END OF CHAPTER TEN

CHAPTER ELEVEN

takes the Train to Stuttgart, which allows the Narrator a Closer Look at Max.

Sophie forgave Max. But she was not inclined to forgive the Sibyl. Nor did she enquire too closely into the Sibyl's motives. She has betrayed me, and I will neither forget nor forgive. Thus determined, Sophie felt unchristian, but clean. She needed someone to blame for this emotional disaster, and to hate whoever that was, from the stomach upwards. When she blossomed again among the yellow leaves and muddy fields of Mark Brandenburg, flying along the rutted paths, leaving the groom well behind her, the poison tree of resentment and bitterness nevertheless grew strong in her heart. She never did read the end of *Middlemarch*, when the final episode, specially ordered by her mother, arrived at the great house in Wilhelmplatz. And so she never appreciated Dorothea's revelation concerning the oneness of humanity, and universal human suffering, after her night of similarly disappointed tears, nor did she learn of that latter-day St Theresa's championship of Lydgate when all the town turned against him. Sophie decided that the Sibyl's advocacy of self-sacrifice and discriminating morals boiled down to a lot of tedious sententious waffle, and she was having none of it. Down with the Sibyl and her hypocritical morality! Who believes in a prophetess who doesn't practise what she preaches, especially when it all comes seasoned with an atheistical gospel of scientific rationalism.

Sophie, however, being far more interested in horses than in Darwinism, or visions of the perfect Right that included all humanity, soon relegated her disillusion with the Sibyl to a far corner of her heart. She looked forward to seeing Max again, after a suitable lapse of time in which everyone recovered their tempers and their dignity. Sophie never doubted that Max would renew his proposals and fling himself at her feet. For this man, who had once hurtled after her vanishing plaits in the damp forest, risked his Sunday best in the fountains for her sake, strolled through her life, not as a guest or as a suitor, but as a permanent resident, part of her domestic landscape. Her interesting doubts, contained in the letter to the Sibyl, reflected the influence of her once beloved author's work rather than her deepest feelings. Sophie could not imagine marrying a man who did not put her first or regard her desires as his commands. She loved Max unconditionally and without reflection, as if he were already an inmate of her stables, needing grooming, fodder and the whip.

But what of Max? I have noticed one thing he has clearly overlooked. The Sibyl may never have intended him to read that letter. And certainly never to reveal that she was the stranger who had delivered the necklace. For had she replied to Sophie's eighteen-year-old torrent of adoration, her handwriting would have given her away. Did she, like Sophie, think that gentlemen do not read a young lady's private letters? Was her conscious intention, when she handed over the unsealed missive, to throw these young people together? Or maybe she wasn't even thinking clearly? Even genius suffers from its cloudy moments. Max was to answer the letter on her behalf. But how was he to do that if he hadn't read the letter in the first place? Sophie declared that she was promised in marriage to Max; therefore they were an engaged couple, were they not? A few crisp words might have been exchanged, but serious matters, which involved money and familial consent, had surely already been settled? Did the Sibyl think that Sophie's unguarded outburst and declaration of her deepest hopes would touch Max to the core, and move him not only to propose marriage but a life of camaraderie and adventure, discovering the world?

Who knows? But one thing is certain. Max had become, in the Sibyl's vast expanding consciousness, an object of special interest. I have no conclusive evidence that the Sibyl cared for men more deeply than she did for women. She inspired a lifelong passion in the heart of Edith Simcox, and young persons of both sexes flung themselves at her feet, confessing all. But an ungenerous comment from Mrs. Jebb does rather stick in the mind.

'She has always cared much more for men than for women, and has cultivated every art to make herself attractive, feeling bitterly all the time what a struggle it was, without beauty, whose influence she exaggerates as do all ugly people.'

Well, that Sophie, Countess von Hahn, possesses youth and beauty in abundance brooks no dispute. Is the Sibyl simply jealous, after all? I think not. For the Sibyl's fame and wealth stood crowned by something magnificent and intangible – the sense of her own entitlement to judge others and yet still to be adored. Is she guilty of that fatal vanity which often overtakes celebrities, whatever their talent, who are sought after, lionised and flattered? Had she begun to believe, not what she thought of herself, but what others said of her?

Poor Blackwood, her devoted publisher, upon receiving *The Legend of Jubal, and Other Poems,* wrote in pitiful tones: 'If you have any lighter pieces, written before the sense of what a great author should do for mankind came so strongly upon you, I should like much to look at them.' Poetry isn't her strongest suit, I'd agree. But her reputation was by then so colossal that the poems still sold, hand over fist.

The train bound for Stuttgart has not yet departed from Berlin. The conductor sees me coming and holds the door. The ladies' compartment is full. No matter. I am looking for Max. Of course I have been watching him intently throughout these pages. I even dream of him. But we have never shared the same weather, breathed the same stale air, and certainly never sat opposite one another on a Continental train. If I can get a closer look at him I shall have a clearer idea of how to proceed.

He rises as soon as I enter his compartment and makes space for my small suitcase, hatbox and umbrella. He bows, and waits until I am conveniently seated. He closes the window to avoid the invasion of smuts. I am not used to being held up straight by what feels like a surgical corset, nor am I accustomed to wearing so many layers of clothes. I am hidden behind a thick muslin veil. He cannot see my eyes, but I continue to observe him, unobserved. He has two laughter lines at the corners of his eyes. And he looks older than he is. His moustache is beautifully trimmed, pencil-thin, like a gentleman pirate, and he has white hands, with clean, short fingernails. Is he handsome? Yes, ah yes, he is far more beautiful than Antinous. I am well known for my iron heart and cold head. I have worked with many authors who can provide excellent testimonials, praising my wintry self-control. I am never bewitched by men, but this man, troubled, romantic, arresting, has captured my attention. His rich, cropped dark curls tempt my fingers, damp in my crocheted white gloves. No wonder he annoys Wolfgang, who cannot hide that bald patch. I am forbidden to touch Max, for I am someone in some future time. But I long to do so. And now he senses the intensity of my gaze and shifts, uneasy, disconcerted, in his seat. No respectable woman scrutinises a man like that. He consults his watch. I inspect the buttons on his waistcoat. At the same moment we raise our faces to the window; the train blasts a long hoot and shudders forward with a ferocious lurch, before heaving itself away down the line. I search for his reflection in the glass, but see nothing, nothing but a wash of steam.

END OF CHAPTER ELEVEN

CHAPTER TWELVE

in which Max seizes his Opportunity and does Something Very Silly.

'Sir, do I have the pleasure of addressing one of the Duncker brothers? Why yes, I believe I do. Your brother Wolfgang, sir, I have the honour to number among my close acquaintances. What brings you to Stuttgart?'

Max wheeled round, alarmed at being so easily recognised, and found himself confronted with a giant hairy paw and a large black beard. The voice, guttural and rumbling, completed the image of a Canadian bear in a tall top hat and black frock coat, with mud-splashes on his trousers.

'I'm afraid I don't recall . . .?' Max wavered.

'Carus, sir. Julius Victor Carus. We met once in Berlin at your firm's offices in the Jägerstraße, when I was negotiating terms for a translation of Mr. Darwin's famous work. Come now, you must remember.' Carus set off again, with Max under his arm, as if he had effected an arrest and was herding the culprit towards his destined incarceration.

'Yes, I have the honour of being Mr. Darwin's German translator. His second translator, mind. Old Heinrich Bronn did the first edition, published here by Schweizerbart, and I was engaged to repair some of the old boy's more fanciful additions. Couldn't do it though until the good chap popped his clogs. Five or six years ago, it was, and I discussed every delicate point with the Great Man himself by correspondence. Sometimes two or three letters a day. Your brother shied off publication though. You see, he had enough controversy on his hands with all those pamphlets, *Darwinismus: For and Against.*'

The bear boomed onwards, leaving Max no opportunity to reply.

'You were quite a young man then, just out of short trousers. Saw you since though – out in the park by the bandstand last summer with the von Hahns, on the arm of an uncommonly pretty young girl. That will be their eldest, eh?'

Carus marched Max across the cobbles and swivelled round, presenting his teeth in a slightly lecherous smile. Max winced, noting that he was observed on the arm of said pretty girl, rather than the other way round, and that, in this instance, the damsel was clearly leading the amorous dance.

'Ah yes, that would have been Sophie, Countess von Hahn.' Max tried to sound indifferent.

'Blooming, blooming. Mind you, her mother outshone all the other girls in her first season. A handsome family, all of them. You're engaged to her, I take it.'

Max suffered an internal seizure and turned white, then red. But Carus neither noticed nor paused.

'I assume that we're going to the same place. No other reason for you to be here in the Rote Gasse. And the lady is one of your big foreign authors, isn't she? Alongside Walter Scott. Mind the muck.' He steered Max round an oozing pile of horse shit.

The Leweses had chosen a rural corner of the town, close to one of the smaller hotels, where they took their meals. The streets were sufficiently bucolic to harbour a troop of geese and a multitude of farmyard odours. Carus thought this very suitable and declared himself a fan of the early rural novels. He fancied that Mrs. Lewes longed to return to the deep countryside lanes of her childhood.

'You feel that on every page. *Adam Bede*, that's the ticket. Written with love. You know, the one with that adorable kittenish little woman making butter in the dairy.' Max could remember nothing whatever of Hetty Sorrel and Captain Donnithorne in Mrs. Poyser's dairy. But he did remember a woman preacher delivering sermons in the open air.

'I have the translation of her latest here,' said Max, indicating a substantial package that bulged beneath his arm. 'She wishes to read all the text that we have already completed. I am to take the Finale back to Berlin.'

'Delicate business, translation,' growled Carus. 'Just as serious in the Sciences as in the Arts. Old Bronn had his own axe to grind when he set about translating poor Darwin. You see, the big question for Bronn was this: must every living being come into existence through the agency of another living being or could life emerge from disconnected organic materials? He was following the French. No shame in that. Many people did. And Bronn spotted at once that Darwin's theory did away with any notion of a Creator God. Out go the six days and let there be light! Can living creatures be made out of inorganic matter? That's the issue. The first origins of life! Where do we come from: God or Nature? Darwin's very cautious, you know. Very circumspect. He doesn't make any great statements. Wait a minute, we've gone straight past their door. Here it is. Do you know Lewes? First-rate botanist in his own right. That's why he has such a convincing handle on Goethe.'

The front door swung open to reveal a dark stone passageway that traversed the house. Carus had clearly tramped through on other occasions.

'Out the back!' he roared, his huge bass echoing off the elderly woodwork. A young boy chasing a black-and-white dog charged past them yelling his excuses, and as the door at the far end blew open Max glimpsed the golden colours of an autumn garden, stirring in the sunny wind. The door banged shut and the garden vanished. Carus thundered through, holding his arm out to Max.

'Mind the steps. Three down.'

The formal garden had once been laid out in geometric patterns, but now the tiny hedges, little lines of sportive wood run wild, poured out at peculiar angles. The ornamental hermitage, a rustic summer house coated in wisteria, yellowed at the edges, lay buried under seasonal colours, and the roses, sun-drenched in the washed light of these last warm days, fluttered in frail banks of red, orange, pink. Their petals showered down in the draught from the passage. The charm of this overgrown garden immediately convinced Max that it was the Sibyl who had chosen this last residence in Germany. No one, unless specifically invited, would ever find them out. Indeed, had he not met Carus, he would probably have patrolled the Rote Gasse for some time, searching for the secret passageway, the bundle of translated sheets growing ever heavier.

'That's their place. Little cottage at the back.' Carus crunched across the weeds and gravel, then shook the bell until it shuddered on the chain. A trio of bobbing maids appeared; all three stared at Max, entranced.

'*Sind Herr und Frau Lewes zu Hause*? Get along there then and announce us!' He snatched Max's card, slapped it down on the first maiden's hand, and sent her scuttling off into the interior, her clogs scuffing the tiles. The other two lingered for a moment, wide-eyed, transfixed by Max's curls as he removed his hat.

'Real find, this place. They rented the cottage through the hotel. You know, Zum wilden Mann on the Marktplatz. Marian tells me that it reminds her of Goethe's Gartenhaus in Weimar. That's built in a little park, all vines and hedgerows. There's a back door here, leading out into the fields and woods. And believe me, they go out walking, whatever the weather.'

But at that moment George Lewes interrupted the grand monologue, bounding towards them, arms flung wide, his universal bonhomie filling the hall. He ripped off their coats and gathered them in to Polly and the blazing fireside.

Max raised his eyes to greet the Sibyl. And now he saw her, as if for the first time. She rose, entwining her thin hands, slender and hesitant, nervous as a girl unused to company. The lace at the throat of her black, high-bodiced velvet dress matched the little lace cap perched on her opulent, grey-streaked hair. She gazed at Max, beseeching, her deeply lined face and massive features transfigured into beauty by the pleasure with which she clasped his hand. Max indicated the package.

'Your great work, gnädige Frau, translated.'

She lowered her head in gratitude, and bowed. Max felt obscurely comforted, and understood. He laid the treasure on her table.

But there in those warm, low-ceilinged rooms, with the sound of church bells and children crying in the distance, Max once more found himself rocked, not by intellectual pretentiousness, comfortable waters he negotiated fearlessly, but by unfettered speculation on the nature of things, which left all known ports astern. Lewes and Carus had heard the Gospel according to Charles Darwin, seen the miracle of evolutionary theory in all its majesty, recognised this great and mighty wonder, and become not just passionate believers, but evangelists. Carus's new translation of the *Origin of Species* formed the centre of the discussion. Surprisingly, Lewes defended the elderly Bronn, and forgave his shameless additions to the volume.

'Bronn drew out the implications of Darwin's theory. He saw what a ferocious blow the book had delivered to conventional religions and bigoted orthodoxies. What arrogance motivates the bishops to argue that we are descended from demigods and set just a little lower than the angels? We are animals. We behave like animals and we think like animals. All wars begin as fights over mates, territory and resources.'

'Agreed,' thundered Carus, 'but he had no right to insert his own views into the book and attribute them to Darwin.'

Lewes appeared to view translation as something of a two-sided debate between the author and the translator. The Sibyl deliberately shifted the direction of the argument.

'Darwin's Doctrine of Development,' she asserted, 'created an epoch. There is no doubt of that, but to me, the Development Theory, and indeed all the other processes by which things come into being, still produces a feeble impression compared with the mystery that lies beneath those processes.'

Max dipped a toe into the torrent.

'But surely if we can reflect upon our origins, maybe even account for them, we are not subject to the inexorable laws of development and progression. We can choose not to be.'

'And that,' declared Carus, 'is what distinguishes the civilised races from savages.'

'Indeed,' cried Lewes, digging in the pile of books scattered across the table. 'And I have actually marked the passage in *The Descent of Man*, for he uses your words, Polly, your very words. Listen.

> 'With savages the weak in body and mind are soon eliminated; and those that survive commonly exhibit a vigorous state of health. We civilised men on the other hand, do our utmost to check the process of elimination; we build asylums for the imbecile, the maimed and the sick; we institute poor-laws; and our medical men exert their utmost skill to save the life of everyone until the last moment ... Thus the weak members of civilised society propagate their kind ... the aid we feel impelled to give to the helpless is ... the instinct of sympathy, which was originally acquired as part of the social instincts, but was subsequently rendered more tender and more widely diffused.'

Lewes closed the book and gazed at the Sibyl with unguarded affection.

'I thought of you, Polly. *Be the sweet presence of a good diffused.*'

Carus, however, was not inclined to bow down before the Doctrine of Sympathy.

'But sympathy may then signal the undoing of our race since it ensures the continuation of weakness. Perhaps the white races will sink while others rise.'

Here the arrival of teacups and cake intervened. The company sank into afternoon reflections. The maid bearing hot water stopped dead before Max as if her feet had taken root. Lewes gently relieved her of the kettle. The Sibyl watched this little drama, mightily amused, and then renewed the discussion.

'Darwin feels, as I do, that sympathy represents the noblest part of our nature. Even as the unclouded light of truth streams in upon us, we are called not to neglect that higher moral life which impels us to strive towards the Perfect Right. We seek the True, the Just, the Good. That is our highest and most sacred calling, and we find our way towards this, our true destiny, through serving others.'

The old woman glowed with her own inner radiance. Her declaration affected the three men in different ways. Max sat incredulous and dumbfounded. Carus toned himself down and stroked his beard. Lewes pressed her hand gently. No one spoke for a moment. Max suspected that the Sibyl had a limited acquaintance with real vice, or else she would not disown the menace of damnation quite so cheerfully. Her hopeful assessment of human nature and the greatness of which we are capable, forever loving, tender and saturated in forgiveness, failed to take account of a more savage reality, which he sensed and feared. Max heard the brutal drumbeat beneath his otherwise civilised skin.

Then the Sibyl began to prophesy, her voice low, solemn and compelling.

'That we should claim kinship with the beasts is not in question. And we know that the substance and object of all religion is altogether human. Divine wisdom is human wisdom. But to reject the despotism of religious systems is not to deny the holy power of all our most intimate and sacred bonds. That source of true living emotion, the heart of man itself, is sucked away from its rightful object, and given to the God who wants for nothing. But in our earnest search to discover what is Right, we need no incitement or support from above. He, to whom the Perfect Right is not holy for its own sake, will never be made to feel it sacred by religion.'

'But, Madame, you argue on behalf of a natural morality that informs all social relations –' rumbled Carus.

Max intervened.

'No, you talk as if all men were brothers and had only to realise the necessity of loving one another to do it! That just doesn't happen.'

He addressed Lewes and Carus directly, astounded at his own daring in contradicting the Sibyl.

'And while it is quite clear that you all regard original sin as outmoded nonsense, simply declaring that it doesn't exist never prevented slaughter on the streets. Surely, when you abandon the Christian faith you pull the right to insist on Christian morality out from under your own feet?'

'I do not underestimate the difficulty of the human lot,' replied the Sibyl, her Olympian calm floating above Max's passionate objections, 'but in whatever I have written I have tried to widen the English vision a little, and to rouse the imaginations of men to an understanding of those human claims that are the just demands of their fellow men. No matter how different or repulsive they may seem.'

And into the midst of this portentous statement scurried the smallest of the three bobbing maids, clutching a message. She curtsied to each member of the company in turn, and then handed the folded slip of paper to Lewes. He leaped up, delighted.

'Polly, my love, we are all invited to the opera tomorrow night. And that includes you, Max. Herr Klesmer is in town, baying with desire to see his favourite author. Isn't that marvellous!'

❧

Max therefore had twenty-four hours in which to fester with confused indignation. He was mildly aware of the Darwin debate. He had even sat smoking beside Wolfgang, while the publisher corrected the proofs of various tracts, for and against, listening to his brother's fulminations, without ever absorbing the arguments. For it is perfectly possible to saunter through life, especially if you are wealthy, young and in good health, taking the view that the intellectual controversies of the age are there for you to enjoy, dip into from time to time and ignore at your pleasure. He had peacefully nodded at Miss Gibbons's breathless enthusiasm for the Development Theory as they careered round the ballroom in Homburg, accepting her torrent of evolutionary certainties as something peculiar, which occasionally poured forth from English spinsters. Above all, this rigorous discussion happened elsewhere, and did not affect him personally. Now it had. And without his consent.

Max simmered with unspoken disagreements. The Fall of the Roman Empire, in so far as he understood the causes of its slow demise, led him to believe that steam engines, gas lighting, new markets, numerous wars, and a general improvement in education and living standards, were no guarantee of national survival. Progress, far from being inevitable, remained a precarious business. The littleness of humankind, the meanness of our understanding, and the viciousness of our habits, both in modern Berlin and in Southern Gaul, during Lucian's peaceful withdrawal into retirement, impressed him with their similarities. Lucian and the Sibyl, noble giants on fire with their misguided faith, walked the world, confident that Reason and Truth would triumph for all eternity. Max saw no grounds whatsoever for this benevolent optimism. The evidence supporting that ancient, unfashionable doctrine of innate evil, against which our better natures struggle if they can, galloped towards him, transformed into a host of grinning demons, waving banners. He passed an uncomfortable rainy morning in his hotel rooms, drinking coffee, smoking and staring at tiny patterns in the wallpaper.

Herr Klesmer and the sun arrived in the early afternoon. The musician stormed in, barely announced, his white mane shaking, and his head thrown back, like an orator reaching a climax. The peculiar manner of his entrance arrested Max in mid-stride. He had begun to pace from the fireplace to the furthest windows, from which he could see nothing but gabled roofs and yellowing trees. Max had last seen Klesmer plunging through the streets of Berlin, followed by a Bacchic train of admirers. Now the musician appeared once more, as if he had walked the world since then, gathering garlands of praise and prodigious roars of eulogy.

Klesmer froze in a dramatic attitude, his ferocious glare fixed upon Max, as if he was taking part in a game of charades, and had achieved the perfect pose for the tableau.

'Good day to you, sir!' He suddenly bowed, as an afterthought, then, holding his hat at a theatrical angle, he delivered his request.

'I wish you to be on your guard tonight, sir. I am counting on your support, for there may well be trouble. I do not court controversy. But when a stand must be taken, I am fearless. I tell you, sir, fearless!'

Max bowed, hoping that the musician's courage was thus sufficiently acknowledged.

'Tonight you will witness Wagner's sublime tale of passion and damnation, *The Flying Dutchman*! I am creating the performance tonight as the composer intended. There will be no interval. You will hear the music of the future – *das Kunstwerk der Zukunft* – uncensored, unfettered – the true musical drama of which Liszt and I have dreamed. An opera should not be a mere mosaic of melodies stuck together with no other method than that which is supplied by accidental contrast, no trite succession of ill-prepared crises, but an organic whole, which grows up and spreads, like a palm.'

At this point, casting his hat aside, Herr Klesmer flung his arms apart, indicating the huge spreading fractals of the Phoenix.

'And the germ must be there from the first seething notes in the strings through to the triumphant catastrophe.'

He paused, hesitated, then declared:

'But I have heard rumours that there will be opposition present. Of Carus I am quite certain. He will be bold in my defence if necessary. But Madame Lewes is fragile, sensitive. She is easily overwhelmed. I look to you, sir, to take care of this great lady, and to anticipate her anxieties, to remove her from the theatre should the public become unrestrained, chaotic, abandoned.'

Max, intensely surprised by this fervent intrusion, stood leaning against his desk.

'But Herr Lewes will be present, if, as you fear –'

'Ha! Lewes! He understands nothing. He comes only to jeer. Wagner demands submission, dedication; the whole soul of his audience must be laid at his feet. To hear truly is to believe. And you are the younger man. You must stand strong, sir, and take his place at her right hand. I shall hold you to account. And now I bid you farewell.'

He whirled out of the rooms with a flourish, leaving Max in a dense cloud of his own cigarette smoke. Had he hallucinated the entire interview? And how had Wagner escaped the clutches of Weimar? Wagnerismus seemed even more controversial in Bismarck's Germany than the arguments smouldering around Mr. Charles Darwin, the gist of which had long been accepted by German scientists and intellectuals. Indeed, Wagner's operas, consigned in many places to the Index Expurgatorius of theatre managers, had so dramatically failed to please the general public that Max had never heard one. Now the composer's supporters, organised, militant, began to move outwards from Weimar into other towns and theatres, seeking converts and champions. Klesmer and Liszt, linked like hounds fixed upon a scent, roved the salons and concert halls hunting down their audience and bullying them, until they surrendered.

'No interval?' Max ruminated upon the implications of Klesmer's speech. 'Well, the sorbet sellers won't be pleased.'

A wonderfully warm, still evening, dry underfoot, brought out the crowds. Here were the last days of promise in an Indian summer, a breath of unruffled serenity that could only end in driving sleet and blown leaves. The women came with their cloaks untied and their hoods thrown back. While he stood waiting on the steps of the freshly painted theatre Max heard one or two English voices. The playbill announced Julius Klesmer as the Director of the Orchestra and Herr Süßmann as the baritone, singing the lead, his lovely wife supporting him as the noble maiden Senta, prepared to die for her great love. Süßmann's name gleamed magnificent in huge black letters, far larger than Wagner's, which the theatre manager in Stuttgart still considered a discouragement to large audiences. They love Süßmann. He'll draw 'em in. But the legend of the opera itself proved to be the greatest attraction. *The Flying Dutchman*! Who does not know Heine's passionate ballad of the sailor doomed to sail the seven seas for all eternity, until he finds a woman prepared to sacrifice her life for love, and remain for ever faithful unto death? *Treue bis zum Tod*! Max noted that the playbill promised spectacular scenery and special crowd-pleasing effects: a haunted ship, its ghostly crew of damned sailors, and a brand-new diorama, created for this very production. The theatre, recently refurbished, advertised itself as 'luxuriously equipped with all the appointments that safety, comfort and elegance dictate', the front stalls freshly padded.

But here comes Lewes, bounding up the steps.

'Ah Max! Polly hoped you'd dine with us. Didn't you get our message? No matter! A little supper afterwards perhaps, if we all survive the ravages of damnation and immortality granted by eternal love.'

Behold the Sibyl, shimmering in eerie gas light, her fine veil thrown back, her wonderful eyes raised towards him, intense with sympathy and concentration.

'I fear that you were distressed by yesterday's discussion.' She spoke so that only Max could hear her as she took his arm. 'I would not see you unhappy. No, not for the world. And to think that I had any part in your unhappiness would give me great pain. For we have become such friends.'

Max pressed her gloved hand; his irritation vanished and he felt infinitely reassured. He had been heard, and noticed, by someone who mattered. The Sibyl understood and anticipated every current in his thoughts. Wherever he looked, he saw her, patiently waiting for him, her countenance overflowing with counsel and forgiveness, her presence all-embracing, like the Everlasting Arms.

'Liszt regards *Der Fliegende Holländer* as a transitional work,' she continued, 'in which Wagner seeks only to escape from the idols to which he once sacrificed. He has not yet reached the point of making war against them. So you may rest tranquil for this evening. There will be a mighty wash of dramatic situations and affecting melodies. You will not have to suffer as we did with *Lohengrin*.'

Here they were, facing an ornately gilded picture-frame stage, and heavy swags with tassels, new cane chairs for the orchestra, red plush for the front stalls and fresh flock wallpaper covered with paintings of famous moments in Shakespeare. Lear staggered forwards, his eyes rolling, with Cordelia dead in his arms, Beatrice and Benedict flounced away in different directions, misunderstanding one another in a garden, Juliet leaned over her balcony, Rosalind strode the forest in breeches, and Banquo's ghost summoned Macbeth away from the feast. The company settled into the second row beneath the slips, a little discomfited by a noisy crowd on the hard benches above them. Carus glared up at the malicious faces, sensing trouble.

'Don't worry,' cried Lewes, 'Klesmer will drown them all out.'

The theatre filled up to the gunnels like a great ship transporting expectant emigrants seeking New Worlds, and many sat munching pastries as the rumoured lack of an interval did the rounds and caused some digestive alarm. How can we get through three hours without ice cream or sweetmeats? The audience, noisy, hot and cheerful, anticipated an astounding spectacle and a riot of emotions. Two ushers fled round the auditorium, lowering the gas light, a trick upon which the Maestro had insisted, as essential to his emotive effects. The orchestra trooped in, greeted by unsteady applause. An army of brass and timpani assembled in too small a space. Klesmer clearly intended to lift the roof off the theatre. Well known in the town for his concert performances, he proved something of a favourite with the audience, and two squat candles balanced either side of his score threw his face, lit from beneath, into a dramatic mass of shadows. He resembled a demon, risen from the depths.

'Klesmer! Klesmer! Klesmer!' bellowed a rowdy section far above the stalls.

This enthusiasm was rapidly dowsed by a collective intake of breath as the curtain soared upwards, revealing two gigantic ships rocking, dangerous in moonlight, before an implausibly vertiginous precipice, with distant cliffs reaching to infinity. Simultaneously a terrifying gust of wind blustered through the strings. The catastrophe of imminent shipwreck seemed inevitable. Sailors, apparently swinging from the rigging, appeared in little bursts of limelight, then faded away into shivering gloom. Throughout the overture the stage shuddered, gleamed, darkened, and the audience gasped, thrilled to their stomachs. The rollers on the diorama were inaudible above the blazing orchestra, and as they shifted and slithered, the black ghost ship with wonderfully red-painted ripped rigging loomed above Daland's smaller trader, like a vampire apparition encircling its victim. Then, in the far depths of the stage, a pale face, leery as Mephisto, hovered high on the mast of the black ship with ripped sails. The pale man stared out beyond the limits of the diorama into eternity. The audience recognised Süßmann, and screamed in unison. Klesmer urged the orchestra onwards, the grand outline of his face and floating hair flung into sinister relief by the stage lamps, as if he was in pursuit of his own shadow. Then, for one second only, the audience glimpsed the soprano, perched on the rim of the cliff, her arms outstretched, as the Overture thundered to its close. The emotional narrative of the opera, condensed into a few precious minutes, now unfolded at greater length. One or two people set off towards the foyer in search of drinks and pastries.

The Dutchman's long opening monologue wooed even the doubters standing at the back. Tragic, white-faced, Herr Süßmann transformed himself into the Solitary Wanderer, terrifying, corrosive, predatory, heart-rending in his longing for peace.

'Bravo! Bravo!' screeched someone close to them, longing for an encore. But Klesmer continued, inexorable.

'I was delighted with this opera when we were with Liszt in Weimar,' murmured the Sibyl. Her shawl fell across Max's arm.

The mighty conflict imaged in the two ships proved to be a metaphor for the entire production. Daland's dapper modern waistcoat and fob watch, his scrubbed sailors and natty trading vessel smacked of profit, successful capitalist ventures and domestic prosperity. The sea, raving against his native rocks, remained simply an inconvenient antagonist. But for the Dutchman, that cursed image of white-faced damnation, the sea, the storms, the flood tides and the infinite horizons formed his only element, as one of the eternal undead. And between him and the voyage that has no end stood one young girl and her peculiar passion for a legendary man she had never seen.

But how does a revolutionary composer wean a conventional audience off their customary diet of operatic song? The public longs for arias, duets, *romanza*, *cavatina* – for three whole acts, yea, sometimes four acts, with a ballet in the middle. And how do you stop them walking about, taking the air in the foyer, looking up their acquaintances and chatting, stepping out for a cigarette or a mislaid shawl, and then nipping back inside just to hear their favourite solo? Abolish the intervals and tighten the plot; if they so much as shift a leg they will miss something crucial!

Those two threads, the Dutchman's curse and Senta's promise of redemption, shrill tremolos on the high violins, diminished seventh chords, a mixture of diatonic chromatic figures in the basses and ah! that familiar, endlessly rising motif in fourths and fifths, they saturate the score, bending the pale man towards his own salvation. No one can step into the shadow where grace cannot reach them, nor can they ever escape the compassionate grasp of the Everlasting Arms. It is the stage manager's business to transform the scenery, rapidly and in secret, as the music rages onwards, firing the singers, pulverising the audience into their seats.

And on that night it worked. There they all were, sweating, breathless, gripped. Will she be true to her pale-faced wanderer? Can her handsome huntsman lure her back to a safe life, where nothing more will happen to her, but days of marriage, children, peace and happiness? Will she choose one supreme moment of glorious sacrifice or the patter of long summer days? She has been sold to the Dutchman! Daland's cupidity made him sell his daughter to the captain of a ghostly black ship with ripped red sails. She is promised to another, but here at last, risen from the ocean's depths, stands the man she loves.

Klesmer knew that subversives lurked in the audience. The author of the *Wagnerfrage* and his friends had pinpointed the Stuttgart production as a crack in the dam of orchestrated prejudice, which had so far successfully kept Wagner's operas out of the provincial theatres. But Liszt and Klesmer had triumphed in Dresden. Their friendship and their adulation of Wagner stood revealed for all to see! The Jews have joined forces with the Wagnerians! This creeping evil must be stopped!

How far through the score had they actually got?

Steuermann, lass die Wacht! Steuermann, her zu uns! Helmsman, leave the watch! Come to us, come to us.

A ripple stirred the slips. Three young men had risen to their feet. No, they were being dragged down and drowned out by a detonating chorus of Norwegian sailors apparently based in the row just behind them. Max noticed the disturbance and its rapid suppression. Nothing could stop Klesmer now. Here from the belly of the phantom ship came the eerie hollow cries of the Dutchman's crew, spectral lights flickered in the rigging like will-o'-the-wisps. Max worried about the incendiary nature of the extraordinary stage effects. The Sibyl tucked her arm through his. Yes, the climax approached! Every part of the scenery, including the flats, appeared to shiver and undulate. The singers, unwavering, plunged onwards, keeping pace with Klesmer. The heat in the house soared to levels equal to that of a tropical rainforest. Max loosened his collar, and noticed that Carus and Lewes had already done so. The Sibyl's massive upper lip shone gently with perspiration. Then, suddenly, a smoking object, the size of a gin jar, flung from above, sailed past them and landed amongst the cellos. The sizzling odour of sulphur, accompanied by dense clouds of smoke, engulfed the musicians.

The huntsman, closely observed by the Dutchman, had almost completed his *cavatina – Willst jenes Tags du dich nicht mehr entsinnen*? – and the Finale loomed in sight. Klesmer, his lips compressed and his head flung back, stood proud of the belching smoke emerging from the bomb in the pit. He had no intention of losing a single note. Not one member of the orchestra flinched or dared to move.

Du kennst mich nicht, du ahnst nicht, wer ich bin! You do not know me, you do not suspect who I am!

The Dutchman bared his soul, at last and in a thundering declaration, boomed the truth of his identity to a horrified cast and the sweating public, most of whom believed that the sulphurous stench and dense, rising clouds of yellowish smoke constituted yet one more bold stage effect, intended to enhance the performance. A fight broke out in the slips as the two factions closed upon one another. A shoe flew through the air and struck Lewes on the forehead. He leaped to his feet, staggered, and then collapsed upon Carus.

Klesmer increased the pace.

I am the Flying Dutchman! bellowed Herr Süßmann to the enraptured mass. The Sibyl suddenly noticed that her husband lay bent double bleeding on Carus's lap. She let out a little smothered cry, which vanished in the wash of the soprano's ecstatic vow.

Here I stand, true even unto death!

A shrill gasp rose from the audience as she appeared to fly from the cliff's edge into the arms of the Dutchman, who then soared away from the mast up, up, up into the murky dimness of the painted sets. They vanished as the mighty ship of ghosts collapsed in a series of gigantic crashes, echoed in the orchestra, all of which drowned out the fight now raging throughout the slips and bursting out on to the staircases.

'Klesmer! Klesmer! Klesmer!'

The conductor's supporters took up the chant as the entire auditorium filled with nauseous smoke. The crowds in the stalls, now thoroughly alarmed, burst the doors asunder and poured out into the foyer and the autumn night. Some abandoned coats and hats in the *vestiaire*, seeking safety in the streets. But some never actually noticed what was happening at all in the lowered gas light, and remained on their feet, flinging flowers at Herr Süßmann and the soprano, who had descended from the heavens unobserved, and re-emerged from behind the tabs, bowing to left and right. Klesmer and his orchestra now barely visible in smoke, sank out of sight into the pit. Lewes drew himself upright, and wobbled a little, clutching a handkerchief to the wound, which was now bleeding copiously. But, ebullient as ever, he snatched up the offending shoe and waved it around his head, anxious to swing a punch at whoever had made him their target.

'Dearest, we must go home immediately,' cried the Sibyl.

'Bravo! Bravo!' yelled the ascendant Wagnerians.

Max batted the smoke, using the Sibyl's shawl like a bullfighter's cape, and peered into the surrounding fog, desperately seeking the exit.

They rattled back to the cottage in a cab, squashed against one another, handing clean handkerchiefs to Lewes whose wound still dripped. The Sibyl, now a little blood-spattered and ruffled with maternal concern, pressed each one to his head, then passed the bloodied improvised bandages to Max. Lewes never stopped talking. He praised Klesmer's courage, but thought the staging full of self-indulgent pantomime trickery, designed to amuse infantile minds. Carus raced away in search of the doctor, who arrived in full evening dress, also replete with opinions about the night's operatic events. By the following morning the incident was being reported as a full-blown riot, with opposing factions fighting it out, first in the theatre, and then in the streets. Lewes ceased to bleed and the doctor galloped away into the night to conduct an emergency surgery for the embattled contestants.

Max disliked the stifling anxiety flooding forth from the Sibyl. After all, Lewes wasn't badly hurt. Give him a cordial and a chance to sleep it off and all he'll have to deal with is a headache in the morning. Max strolled in the night garden; the air, perfectly still and warm, even at that late hour, stirred as he passed and then settled around him. He lit a cigarette and wandered down the little gravelled paths, crushing the weeds and brushing against the overgrown lines of box. Small squares of light illuminated the house behind him.

At first he did not hear her coming. The Sibyl, wrapped in her Indian shawl over her astrakhan short jacket, floated towards him on a cushion of warm air. He felt her gloved hand on his sleeve.

'Thank you, Max,' she murmured softly, 'for all your kindness. George is lying down quietly now. Carus is with him. I came to say goodnight.'

She took his arm and Max placed his hand upon her own. They set off round the long walk, talking quietly, like old and confidential friends. The emotions of the night brimmed over into their conversation: Wagner's endless passion for the love that braves death itself, Klesmer's miraculous triumph, and the jubilant Wagnerians, ransacking the town, Lewes's unfortunate accident, a supporter caught in the line of fire.

'He is so full of energy, my dear Max, that you would not think him frail in health, but I often fear, when I am not laid low by toothache or by bilious attacks, that his constitution is yet more fragile than my own. I must seem excessive in my concern for him. Indeed, I know I do. And I am sorry for it. But, Max' – and here she paused by the dead fountain – 'your friendship is too precious for me to be less than honest with you. I have been blessed with nearly twenty years of unchanging happiness, and I dread, dread with all my being, that final parting, when we are separated for ever. Wagner dreams of an eternal union, but we know that cannot be.'

Max shivered slightly. He saw Senta and the Dutchman, transfigured, ascending to the heavens.

'And yet, we need to grasp the meaning of that last farewell, for it gives the utmost sanctity of tenderness to our relations with each other. For even our own deaths are as intimate and natural as the approach of autumn or winter.'

Death, and an eternity of being dead, had never before figured in Max's calculations. And the Sibyl, enraptured by the depth and conviction of her own teachings, had quite forgotten the thirty years that lay between them. Max had yet to live his life. She stood, gazing at the end of her own journey, leaning against his youth and strength, and yet her gentle and inspiring tones, speaking of the four last things, her soft voice filled with certainties, offered a vast consolation, tender, passionate, infinite in its mild calm. They paused in the summer house, still warm, dark and dry. The Sibyl spoke of sympathy, friendship and the unbreakable power of human bonds. She convinced Max that nothing mattered more to her than that moment in the dying gardens. He was her knight errant. And his lady's grace and beauty, luminous in that strange twilight gloom, had never seemed more eloquent and necessary. But into this momentary calm the Sibyl flung down one sentence like a spear that poisoned all the earth.

'As soon as George has recovered we will return to England.' Panic engulfed him as she spoke. His compass and guide threatened to absent herself, possibly for ever. They stood inside the little summer house, surrounded by faint odours of damp and rotting vegetation. The Sibyl ceased to speak and gazed beseechingly at Max, who began to gibber.

'I can remain silent no longer, Madame. I must speak. If I seem impertinent it is because you have overthrown all barriers between us. I no longer see my way forward with any certainty or conviction. I believed myself a man of faith and now I doubt. I have always pleased myself, rather than seeking out a mission or a purpose in my life. There seemed to be no urgency in my decisions. Now my very identity is in question – and I cannot continue as I am – washed ashore with every tide. I tell you that I must speak.'

Max circled on the spot, his voice low, violent and agitated, stubbing the toes of his boots. He plucked at the fading leaves trailing from the wisteria, which mounted above them. The trunk spiralled upwards, coiling the trellis like a serpent, more massive than his forearm. Max braced himself against the uncomfortable helix and stared down at her shadowed face. The Sibyl settled her skirts and raised her massive chin, complacent, attentive, and utterly tranquil. She awaited the outcome of his impassioned incoherence. She had no premonition whatever of the declarations that were hurtling towards her. She made herself comfortable during the terrible pause in which Max found himself quite unable to voice the emotions bubbling in his chest. He suddenly settled for Shakespeare.

'"You have bereft me of all words."'

'That's unfortunate,' smiled the Sibyl. He saw her white face, leprous in darkness, the voice amused and detached. 'Our intimacy is based entirely upon words, for the most part judiciously chosen.'

Max suffered a curious implosion. He had reached the brink of rational discourse and a vast dark staircase stretched away before him, following the Sibyl's vanishing cape as she ascended into the realms of eternal light. He could not – would not – let her go. He flung himself upon the tomb-cold stone before her and gabbled like a madman.

'Madame Lewes – Marian – you cannot be unaware of how deeply our friendship has touched me – how unqualified my admiration – in short how much I love you. I beg you – do not cast me adrift.' He seized her gloved hand. With astonishing strength she took hold of his wrist and hauled him back on to the wooden seat beside her.

'Max. Take a deep breath. Sit still. And stop talking.'

But alas, Max, now quite beside himself, could not stop. Fixed in his brain was the idea that he had to propose to someone. And the woman in front of him had shaken him to the core. He raced to the edge of his own operatic precipice.

'Madame! I adore you. I tell you I must speak. Make me the happiest man that ever lived. Marry me. I beg you to marry me.'

The fatal words quivered in the air between them like a descending flight of arrows. Sincerity rather than sanity clamped Max firmly in her jaws. He meant every word of it. The Sibyl drew herself up like a tower under siege; her white lace shimmered with the unintended insult, and she rose, shaking.

'Sir, you appear to forget that I am already a married woman.'

But the fact that she was just as free to marry whom she chose as the ardent young man before her incinerated her flesh, draining all remaining colour from her face. The abyss yawned between them.

'Forgive me.'

Max plunged into the waters of abjection. The Sibyl clutched the twisted wisteria for support, ignoring his outstretched arm.

'Can you ever forgive me?' The wheel of fire to which he was now bound churned onwards, desperate and unhinged. 'My feeling for you cannot and will not ever change.' And in the unspeakable pause that followed both the old woman and the young man poised above her knew that this would remain true for ever. The Sibyl lowered her veil. Her recovered self-possession tolled his doom.

'I bid you goodnight.'

She rustled away down the paths between the renegade box hedges, the dark triangle of her moving form becoming one with the deeper darkness of the autumn garden. Max stood, truly speechless at last, gasping in the sudden night cold, his white breath booming in the damp air. The pain of her departure hung round him like a shroud. He stared at the muted shapes of greening statues, withered roses and clever blocks of yew, subdued into twilight animals with raised heads. The fountain, now mute, lay damp and fetid, blackened with dead leaves. The distant door banged shut as she entered the house, and he beheld his heaven, empty of a god.

END OF CHAPTER TWELVE

END OF PART ONE

PART TWO

CHAPTER THIRTEEN

in which the Reader bears witness to various irrevocable steps taken by Characters we already know. Herr Klesmer and Miss Arrowpoint accompany the Singer.

Meanwhile, Wolfgang and the Count von Hahn remained blissfully oblivious of the Stuttgart catastrophe, or even of the company's presence at the victorious performance of *The Flying Dutchman*. But news of that event reached Berlin, where the evening, now described as 'a riot' from start to finish, made the headlines. Wagner and his music were blamed for everything. His dissolute tonalities spurred on his equally unbalanced followers to initiate skirmishes in the theatre, which spilled into the streets and led to drunken running battles far into the night. George Henry Lewes, the famous English scientist and distinguished biographer of Goethe, we are amazed to learn, took the side of Herr Klesmer, who directed the orchestra. Mr. Lewes was seen bleeding from the temple and wielding his shoe as a weapon in the battle for Wagner. But who could resist Herr Süßmann's affecting performance as the doomed sailor, etc. etc. Wolfgang fired off an anxious letter to the Leweses, enquiring after their injuries, and hoping that Max had acquitted himself well in the fray that ensued. Should he send a telegram? The Count advised against this. After all, nobody was actually killed in the riot. And if any of our people were seriously hurt we would have heard from Max by now.

And so those undaunted romantic conspirators, the Count and his

Publisher, bent on engineering a satisfactory reconciliation between the estranged young lovers, and convinced that a discreet and gentle push would overcome all opposition, plunged into a campaign of unfortunate arrangements. The Count took the lead. Everything is decided! We'll hold a smashing mid-season ball on New Year's Eve. Sophie will come thundering back from the country, well before Christmas, and desperate to dance. Lots of handsome young fellows and some of the old guard to give us a bit of ballast. All our set from the Journal and any elderly female relatives we can winkle out from behind the ovens. Then the intelligence services can't accuse us of organising a radical gathering. It's a family celebration! What do you think, Wolfgang? Clever, eh?

But the whole thing had to be scaled down to the size of the large drawing room in Wilhelmplatz. An early bout of cold, snowy weather and blizzard winds destroyed a tree and part of the roof on the garden side of the ballroom. The repairs, costly and slow, forced the Count to draw in his horns. A New Year's party, intimate sort of thing, just fifty guests, lots of singing and music – Klesmer on the piano, of course – have you heard that he's engaged to an English heiress, money not blood, I gather, and that the family won't have it because he's a Jew? Well, he may be very famous, but he's still a Jew, and you can't change that. Actually, I think he's already married her. She was one of his pupils and a very gifted pianist. My dear, can you find out what her name was? We must invite the entire family. Then after supper and the midnight fireworks, that's all in hand, I've got an expert Chinaman who knows how to put on a bit of a show, without setting fire to the summer house, we can roll back the carpets and pound these fine old boards. Now what do you say to that, Wolfgang old chap? The Count insisted on paying for everything, including Klesmer's fee. After all, she's our little girl, and we want the misunderstanding between her and Max cleared up as soon as we can. No point being young, in love, and miserable.

Wolfgang, who had apparently never suffered from any of these things, agreed.

Max slunk back to Berlin and rendered himself invisible in archaeological museums, archives and consultations with Professor Marek in the nether bowels of the university. He took no strong drink, deserted Hettie's Keller and his old army comrades, rarely joined Wolfgang for dinner, and slept little. His steps could be heard, circling his father's library like a caged vampire. This kind of behaviour tallied perfectly with that of a man who has been disappointed in love.

But what has Sophie been doing all this time? She has taken up hunting and archery. She is even learning how to shoot and cuts a very fine figure before her elderly uncle, the retired colonel, and her father, the Count. Here she is, clad in Lincoln green, with a ruffled white shirt, the sleeves folded back, poised, turned sideways towards her target, her loaded pistol raised. Aim, relax, don't tug at the trigger, squeeze, balance, Sophie, balance, even out your weight, don't lean, steady now, – FIRE! Good heavens, the girl's sliced his head off. The target was a paper pheasant taking off, coloured in by her younger sisters, stuck to a broomstick, lodged on top of a plinth. Admittedly the thing wasn't actually moving, but Sophie's accuracy unsettled both gentlemen. The shredded pheasant's head could not be found.

The New Year's party plans blossomed and flowered despite the winter weather, and in mid-December the Count published an invitation programme: order of music on the front, supper menus on the back, with a list of the wines to accompany each course, and a special mention of the midnight fireworks.

The household disagreed on the domestic arrangements.

'We'll perch the orchestra here, my love, on a small stage between the great folding doors.'

'So everyone will have to troop out into the hall first, dearest, to seek out their supper. If you put the musicians at the other end the guests will just walk directly through the small salon.'

'But what should we then do about the fireplace? I've ordered large logs and holly surrounding the portraits.'

Julius Klesmer came round with his new wife, Miss Arrowpoint as was, to introduce her to the old Countess, who had sent a charming note of congratulations, wishing them every conceivable happiness. The Countess received the couple very graciously, tuning her excessive welcome to a higher pitch. She had never knowingly thought of Herr Klesmer as a Jew and did not intend to do so now. The Maestro inspected their rooms and fussed about the acoustics. Sophie gazed at Miss Arrowpoint, who bowed and smiled. Here was a plain, solid, amiable woman who had opposed her family in dramatically romantic terms and married for love. In fact, faced with an obstinacy equal to their own and a music tutor whose name was hardly ever out of the newspapers, the family had caved in and produced marriage contracts, dowry, trousseaus, carriages, a rural residence in Gloucestershire with stabling for eight and a town house in London, both free of mortgages. None of this figured in Sophie's imagination. Miss Arrowpoint stood statuesque and proud, a heroine who had leaped o'er the traces of convention, and galloped free.

'Will you help me prepare my ballad for the New Year's concert?' ventured Sophie, clutching her little sheaf of music. 'Mother says you have a great talent.'

'If I am worth anything at all on the piano,' smiled the heiress, in flawless German, 'it is thanks to Julius. He was, and is, my most exacting Professor of Music!'

'Oh,' gulped Sophie. Miss Arrowpoint instantly became even more glamorous and interesting. There she sat, plump and luminous on a silk sofa, her whole body diffused with satisfied love.

I want to be as happy as she is, thought Sophie, and hatched a plan.

The two women ordered their hot chocolate and fresh candles in the music room. Miss Arrowpoint worried about the proximity of the piano to the fire and pattered up and down the keys listening for heat-induced imperfections. Sophie cast off her shawls and stood, ferociously erect, before the music stand.

'I want to sing this.'

Miss Arrowpoint unfolded 'The Ballad of Tam Lin'.

'Ah.'

She nodded at the music that accompanied the traditional Scottish Border ballad, collections of which were all the rage across the drawing rooms of Europe, and immediately wondered if it was quite suitable for an unmarried girl of eighteen to sing in mixed company. No doubt about it – Berlin society, unbuttoned, easy-going and more open to difference and debate than her usual provincial circles in England – would probably sit listening to a tale of maidenheads and seduction in the open air without batting an eyelid. Miss Arrowpoint gazed at the vivid young girl before her, who stood loosening her tight knitted jacket and taking a sequence of deep breaths.

'I tried the Schubert arrangement. And I didn't like it. The traditional one is really the best. I can vary the characters and make it more dramatic.' Sophie had placed her bets and was going for bust.

A ballad always tells a story. And the themes are usually tragic: unrequited love, betrayal, sudden death, murder, jealousy, revenge. Fairies and ghosts dispute the terrain with mortal souls. Evil often goes unpunished. Cunning and trickery win the day. This amoral world, lavish and enticing, lurks at our fingertips. 'The Ballad of Tam Lin' bears a dangerously accurate message, destined for the hearts of all maidens: women, beware women. At first this is not clear. Maidens are confronted with the usual threat of predatory, but in this case fatally enchanted, knights.

Janet, our feisty and intrepid heroine, goes to Carterhaugh, where two rivers meet, although this secret, sacred place is expressly forbidden.

> 'O I forbid you, maidens a'
> That wear gowd on your hair,
> To come or gae by Carterhaugh
> For young Tam Lin is there.'

The price of passage demanded by the enchanted knight, should it still be yours to give up, is your maidenhead. Oh well, thought Miss Arrowpoint, feeling her way into the rippling introduction, if she sings it in Scottish dialect it may well be unintelligible to large parts of the company.

Janet goes out alone to Carterhaugh, suggestively dressed, in other words, asking for it, and plucks a double rose. Tam Lin immediately appears and threatens her. She stands her ground. Her tone is defiant throughout.

> 'Carterhaugh, it is my ain,
> My daddie gave it me;
> I'll come and gang by Carterhaugh,
> And ask nae leave at thee.'

Upon which he rapes her. Miss Arrowpoint remained fairly clear concerning the sequence of events, but wondered if Sophie had grasped the significance of raising her skirts a little 'aboon her knee'. Janet returns to her father's castle 'as green as onie glass'. The ghostly knight has planted his seed in her womb. But, marvellous to relate, she faces down the court and declares her love for Tam Lin.

> 'If that I gae wi child, Father,
> Mysel maun bear the blame;
> There's neer a laird about your ha
> Shall get the bairn's name.
>
> If my love were an earthly knight,
> As he's an elfin grey,
> I wad na gie my ain true-love
> For nae lord that ye hae.'

And off she goes to Carterhaugh to find out who her lover actually is. All is revealed. He is the grandson of Lord Roxborough, so far, so respectable, who came a cropper while out hunting and fell into the claws of the Queen of the Fairies. But his time in the lascivious glades of Fairyland is almost up. Sophie sang the knight's voice with genuine tragic conviction. He is the Queen's lover, but she is perfectly willing to hand him over to the Devil as her usual seven year's due tithe to Hell, on the grounds that what makes him delicious to the Fairy Queen – I am so fair and full of flesh – will also appeal to the satanic underlord.

'But the night is Halloween, lady,
The morn is Hallowday;
Then win me, win me, an ye will,
For weel I wat ye may.

Just at the mirk and midnight hour
The fairy folk will ride,
And they that wad their true-love win,
At Miles Cross they maun bide.'

Sophie fluffed the words while attempting to convey a scary atmosphere with a dramatic gesture. She had begun to perform to the empty music room. Miss Arrowpoint as was paused on a trill and suggested a return to the mirk and midnight hour.

'I'll have it by heart for the next rehearsal,' cried Sophie. 'I won't have the music in front of me on the night. It's too distracting. I want the audience to see me becoming one character after another.'

Miss Arrowpoint found herself already very fond of this young woman and her unhesitating, strident innocence. Tam Lin rode past on the milk-white steed and Janet pulled him down. The magic is unleashed as Tam Lin writhes in the grip of the Fairy Queen's power. He is translated into a lion, a bear, a serpent and a red-hot band of iron, a burning gleed! But Janet, alone at midnight on the crossroads, clings fast to the man she loves.

> 'Again they'll turn me in your arms
> To a red het gaud of airn;
> But hold me fast, and fear me not,
> I'll do to you nae harm.
>
> And last they'll turn me in your arms
> Into the burning gleed;
> Then throw me into well water,
> O throw me in wi speed.
>
> And then I'll be your ain true-love,
> I'll turn a naked knight;
> Then cover me wi your green mantle,
> And cover me out o' sight.'

Victory! The tables are turned on the Fairy Queen, for she has lost the most handsome knight in all her train of mortals held in thrall. For the story doesn't end with the lovers, rejoicing in one another's arms. Sophie turned upon Miss Arrowpoint, her eyes ablaze. She is transformed into her arch enemy, the older magic woman, the wise Queen of Shadows, who consumes men, any man, but preferably beautiful young men, at her pleasure.

> 'Out then spak the Queen o' Fairies,
> Out of a bush o' broom:
> Them that has gotten young Tam Lin
> Has gotten a stately groom.'

The accompaniment really does remind me of the 'Erl-King', thought Miss Arrowpoint, as she exploded, arresting, sinister, into the major key.

'Out then spak the Queen o' Fairies,
And an angry woman was she:'

Chin up, Sophie! Chest out! Breathe! This is the best bit. Fling it in their faces, no holds barred. Become the Queen. That's it! That's it!

'Shame betide her ill-far'd face,
And an ill death may she die,
For she's taen awa the boniest knight
In a' my companie.'

Sophie drew her breath from her very bowels for the last verse.

'Had I known, had I known, Tam Lin,
That I would lose thee,
I would have taken out your heart,
And put in a heart of stone!'

For the heart is the rapacious betrayer. Tam Lin spent seven years in the Queen's train, wreaking her evil vengeance on mortal women. Tam Lin, the rapist and the seducer, bound to this task until he saw the maiden in the green mantle, who risked her life to save her lover, the father of her son. His human heart secured his salvation. Had I known, had I known, Tam Lin – all the ferocious menace of the older woman, tricked and abandoned, surged forth from Sophie. She played both parts with equal conviction: the courageous maiden in the green mantle and the ancient witch with her white face of damnation. Miss Arrowpoint slammed out the triumphant conclusion.

'Bravo, Sophie,' she exclaimed, and burst into solo applause. Sophie, pink with effort and relief, surged round the piano in a flurry of lace and kissed the English lady with passionate gratitude. The applause continued in the doorway.

'My dear,' exclaimed Julius Klesmer, 'what follies are you tempting the Countess to commit? And who has chosen this seditious little ballad? Charming, and very dramatic. But it will not do. Not yet. We will go over the whole thing again. From the beginning.' Klesmer gently moved his wife further down the settle and commandeered the piano.

❧

When the invitation to the New Year's ball, addressed to both Duncker brothers, arrived in the Jägerstraße, Wolfgang found himself able to pretend that while of course he was aware that a ball, party, or entertainment, something of that sort, was in the offing at the von Hahns', he had taken no part in any kind of romantic-reparation conspiracy. Holding the card at arm's length he nerved himself up to play the responsible older brother. The scene took place at breakfast. Max, his face pinched and his hair in need of scissors, nibbled his toast, expressionless.

'I'll reply for us both, shall I?'

Max grunted.

'They'll be very offended if you don't go, Max.'

Max shrugged.

'The Count is not only our father's oldest friend; he's our best-selling author. Right up there alongside Mrs. Lewes.'

Max swallowed his coffee and looked straight through Wolfgang, as if he hadn't spoken. Wolfgang felt his blood pressure beginning to rise.

'Look, Max, I have no idea what has happened between you and the von Hahn girl, but I can see that something has discomposed you entirely. Ever since you came back from Stuttgart you've been a bear in the house. I'm not prying into your personal affairs. I can see you're upset and I've left you to it. But you can't live like St Jerome for ever. People are asking for you. And damn it, I miss your company. Come on, old chap. Chin up. You can put things right.'

Max studied the empty coffee cup and said nothing. Wolfgang decided to take the risk and confront his brother directly.

'Did you ask her to marry you? And she refused you?'

Max stared at his brother in horror, his lips white. Wolfgang pressed home his advantage, while his brother sat shuddering before him, as if suddenly hypnotised. At least I have his entire attention, thought Wolfgang. He allowed himself a jubilant moment of misguided triumph. Well, well, I do seem to have hit the mark.

'Forgive me, my dear. I had no right to enquire. Affairs of the heart, things like that, I know, it's all very personal.' So he and the Count had guessed correctly, a proposal that failed to please. We jumped to exactly the right conclusion. Poor Max, clearly a blow to his self-esteem. 'But listen, it's not the end of the world. Come on. Other people will be there. It isn't as if we are invited to dinner. And the first encounter is always the worst. Once that's over, things will settle down. And then, who knows?'

Women always expect to be asked twice, thought Wolfgang. We'll have them engaged by Candlemas.

'Excuse me.' Max rose, his toast abandoned. 'I find it very difficult – that is – it's not quite as you think –'

He gave up on explanations, and rushed out of the room. Wolfgang helped himself to more coffee and began planning a little letter of mutual congratulation to the Count.

Max, locked upstairs, alone in his rooms, sailed through an emotional hurricane. Before the ill-fated expedition to Stuttgart he had weathered many a squall, and odd days of turbulence, but the scene with the Sibyl had undone him utterly. He felt stupid, humiliated, diminished, and completely out of his depth. He understood neither Sophie nor the Sibyl, both of whom now took on a monstrous aspect. He was trapped between Scylla and Charybdis, the sea monster or the whirlpool, from whose swirling centrifugal force protruded great lumps of wreckage. Too late, too late, he saw the justice of Sophie's rage. No gentleman would ever have read that letter. And had he handed her the note, in its original envelope, unread, he would never have hesitated in his passion for Sophie, nor ever known that she had questioned her own love for him. He, and not Sophie, had been weighed in the balances and found wanting. He faced yet another evil reckoning. And yet, and yet, he still could not accept Sophie's conclusion, that the Sibyl had intended him to read that unguarded confession. What motive could she possibly have? Sheer spite? A perverse desire to make trouble? No, surely the Sibyl could not be responsible. He alone was to blame. He had treated his childhood sweetheart abominably, out of mere affronted vanity. Nothing could now be unsaid, undone, forgotten. He faced himself and loathed what he saw.

But what had he done that was so very bad? He had taken offence where none was intended, misread an ardent girl's outpourings to the writer she idolised, and got everything out of proportion. Then, falling under his icon's spell, and steered well off course by a catastrophic combination of Darwin and Wagner, he had sought security and salvation in the motherly folds of the great lady's gown. Who could save him? She could.

And oddly enough – here Max banged down a clothes brush on his dressing table – he still believed this. The Sibyl's uncanny power to illuminate and forgive glowed as strong as ever. But she was not free. And he had been a brute to suggest that she was. Marriage, of course, given those thirty years between them, was out of the question. But he could adopt the role of '*cavalier servente*', her courtly adorer, carrying gloves and shawls around opera houses, becoming the butt of Lewes's jokes and innuendoes. No shortage of applicants for that role, however. Max had watched the fawning hordes creeping towards her at Homburg. No wonder the celebrated couple fled to dull places and rented obscure country houses, where the chimneys smoked and the wallpaper gave you nightmares.

Max confronted his abiding sensation of shame. He abandoned the moral high ground and sank into the dust. Yes, he must accept the von Hahns' invitation, and set forth, magnificent but sombre, to attend the New Year's Eve festivities, and to face the music.

Snow fell on New Year's Eve. By midday the city, coated in quiet white, echoed with soft thuds, as accumulated snow abandoned the rooftops in little avalanches. Bare trees in formal gardens, all picked out in white on the windward side, resumed their former shapes, handsome in winter colours. The box hedges at the house in Wilhelmplatz, white above and evergreen beneath, circled the dug beds like untouched elevated roadways, free from slush and underlying mud. The great pond froze over, but not hard enough to skate.

'Oh no,' cried Sophie, gazing at the descending white curtain, 'no one will come.'

'Nonsense, my dear.' The Count glowed with confident hospitality. 'Rain keeps the guests indoors, not snow. Besides, your mother's menu will have them all here by four, salivating. And God knows, we have sufficient rooms. If anyone's nervous about the late-night ice they can spend the night with us. I'll have the fires lit upstairs.'

He stamped outside in his greatcoat, teetering behind his estates manager. Was the ballroom roof holding up? The repairs, still incomplete, were covered with sacks, canvas sheeting and a weighty layer of tiles. Inside the house swags of yew, adorned with red ribbons, pine cones and glittering crystal bells, carried the winter scents of outdoors through the halls and salons. The great drawing room, polished in festive readiness, flickered with candles and firelight. The huge ceramic oven in the corner, stoked up since dawn, smouldered and glowed. The Countess lit the logs in the fire at the other end of the room herself. Fruit cup and *Glühwein*, a great silver vat, smelling of cloves and cinnamon, stood steaming on a tripod; sugared pastries laid out in patterns tempted the first arrivals. Two rooms were set aside for coats, boots, capes, hats and galoshes, with selected chairs and sofas designated for each party. The young seamstress who made Sophie's dresses lurked in the ladies' dressing room to execute repairs as necessary. She peeked out at the great hall and the furore bubbling in the kitchen. The Countess inspected every servant's hands and nails before issuing fresh white gloves. 'If the gloves are clean then the flesh should be so too.' She made it sound like a divine imperative. The younger staff, wildly excited at the prospect of a party, didn't mind having their nails trimmed and the dirt dug out. The Countess, a lady of the old school, knew all her people by name and provenance. Her reputation for generosity flourished in the kitchens. Her mania for hygiene was generally considered insane.

Wolfgang and Max arrived early and stood in the hall shaking the snow from their shoulders, mobbed by the younger children. The Count gave no sign whatever that anything had ever been amiss between Max and his family or that he had not set eyes on the younger Duncker brother for over two months.

'Ah! There you are, young man! Capital! Sophie's dying to see you and tell you all about those blasted horses that we acquired in Homburg.'

At a stroke, all offence, error and misapprehension stood erased. Max found himself embraced by the old Countess, whose warm sugary smells welcomed him back into the heart of the family stronghold. He opened his eyes, and found himself at home. And there in the rumbustious bustle of the great hall, with the porters struggling to close the huge draught curtains across the double doors, he made out the hesitating figure of his wronged maiden, and bowed, never taking his eyes from her shadowed face. This gesture of acknowledgement and humility produced an electric response. Sophie stepped boldly through the mob, reached up and grabbed his shoulders, none too gently, pulling him down face to face, and then she kissed both cheeks in turn with gentle violence. Her bright freckled nose brushed against his own as she bounced on his boots. For one moment he held a scented armful of satin and ribbons.

'I'm very glad to see you,' declared Sophie, deliberately rising into detonating decibels, so that everyone could hear. 'We've all missed you dreadfully. But I have more than anybody else. Come and see how we've decorated the drawing room. And don't touch the crystal bells. Father's already broken one and they all come from Venice, and cost more than my annual allowance!'

Sophie von Hahn refused to be cowed, embarrassed, resentful, dishonest or passed over. Max gazed at her in grateful adoration. Had he really chastised and abused this guileless, ardent girl? He deserved a long session inside the Iron Virgin, until his bared chest, sprinkled with pricks of blood, hurt enough for him to merit her affection. He strode after her, prepared to inspect the decorations, lured by that torrent of loosened gold, her ribboned mane of hair, which shook out behind her, boisterous, uncontained. For Sophie stood upon her threshold of possibilities. She intended to bewitch her straying childhood lover all over again, and free him from whatever noxious enchantment had induced him to be censorious and horrid. No fear, no guilt, no shame. She set out to win.

The Klesmers, given unfettered encouragement by the hospitable Count, brought along a jolly host of English residents, settled in Berlin, in addition to their Christmas family visitors. And so, alas, there was a moral majority, perfectly able to grasp both the plot and all the implications of Sophie's ballad. This occurred to Miss Arrowpoint as was, who wondered if she should recommend a little judicious editing, but the English presence never struck Sophie as anything untoward. And indeed, the heat of the room, the roaring good cheer of the company, the opening salvos of festive drink and food put the guests in a mood to enjoy more or less anything.

Herr Klesmer stretched their good will to the limits, however, by playing a piano reduction of Siegfried's 'Rhine Journey', followed by one of his own compositions, which left everyone shaken, apprehensive and faintly menaced. Max whispered to Sophie:

'Oh dear, I hope the spirit of 1873 isn't going to resemble Herr Klesmer's creations.'

'Father's not pleased. He says that the Wagner is a lot of triumphal Prussian bombast. And not in good taste. He's gone to spice up the fruit punch with more brandy. Oh good, look.' Sophie stood on tiptoe. 'Frau Klesmer is going to play something more cheerful.'

A virtuoso performance of Scarlatti delighted them all and ended in laughter and applause. The beaming little apple of a woman stood up and announced, with unfeigned enthusiasm, that the eldest daughter of the household, Sophie, Countess von Hahn, would sing them a Scots ballad to the traditional tune and in the original tongue. All the English cheered. Sophie turned a little pale, squeezed Max's hand and then marched to the piano, ribbons flying, head high. Max edged himself close to the windows so that he had a clear view of her profile. The white night cloaking the terrace remained just visible through a crack in the drapes.

'Shhhhh,' Klesmer snarled at one of the English ladies for asking who she was.

Miss Arrowpoint stroked the keys. A little sigh arose from all the guests who recognised the tune. Then Sophie began to sing, gathering confidence and strength with every verse. Klesmer had transformed her performance from a girlish star-turn into a declaration of sexual freedom, confident, lurid, and as disconcerting as Vashti's burning performance in *Lady Macbeth*. Her green eyes raged as she clutched her enchanted beloved and defied the Fairy Queen to do her worst. The extraordinary denouement – *Had I known, had I known, Tam Lin* – bewitched the guests. A thrilled hush enveloped the company as Sophie, the last transformation past, sank back, breathless against the piano, her crisped fingers clutching the braid on her patterned silk. She raised her head, and a red stain crept across her neck and collarbone, but her eyes, blue green and snow-cold, faced the audience, unrepentant, defiant. Her eldest aunt, very deaf, and therefore seated in the front row, now incapable of understanding words in any language, began to clap with touching recklessness. The drawing room roused itself from the shocked stupor induced by Sophie's ballad, and joined in.

Wolfgang set about saving the day. 'Well, what a dramatic tale! One woman's courage in rescuing her love from the clutch of the evil fairies. And wonderfully performed, Countess. Bravo! Janet is quite the heroine.'

Klesmer's visiting mother-in-law swiftly objected.

'But she went out to Carterhaugh looking for trouble. I'm sorry for the Fairy Queen. She's the older woman here and she's been wronged. One of her knights – and the prettiest one too – has been stolen away.'

Immediately conversation and argument ignited the room.

'My dear, you have a quite beautiful voice, but I don't think you should sing about maidenheads in mixed company.'

'Oh, stuff and nonsense. Those verses are perfectly genteel.'

'Carterhaugh is a real place in the Scottish Borders, where two rivers meet, the Ettrick and the Yarrow. We were out with a shooting party near there last year, and came home very cold, clad in mud.'

'Gloomy ballads make for disagreeable entertainment in the festive season. You should sing something more joyful, child. Drink some mulled wine, you look quite flushed and done up.'

Sophie accepted a large red glass, which smelt like a cordial for curing coughs. She sensed an odd breathlessness in her chest, as if she had removed her dress in company and stood there, all exposed, in her shift and stockings. Max stared at the receding blush on her cheeks, which matched his own.

He had understood her perfectly. But it was his beloved who took the lead.

'There's a fire in the library. Come with me.'

The heroine of Carterhaugh refused to negotiate. The encounter, this time, would take place on her territory and her terms. The sound of male laughter from the dining room followed them into the chillier spaces of the Count's leather-bound collections. Max bumped into the globe, which lurked beside the armchairs. Sophie dragged him into the firelight, pulled the heavy wrought-iron guard aside and wedged two more logs in the grate. Wood shavings clung to her gloves.

'Did you like my ballad?'

She stood at his elbow, unnervingly close.

'I thought you were magnificent. And never more beautiful.'

'But what did you think of the ballad?'

Max felt trapped and challenged.

'It's traditional, isn't it? Or was it written by Sir Walter Scott?'

'I sang it for you.'

No way out or back. Sophie swung round to confront him, her face blurred. He smelt the heat of her body through the white powdered dust on her breasts and upper arms. Her shawl trailed from her bare shoulders. La belle dame sans merci hath thee in thrall.

'Can you ever forgive me?' Max heard his own voice, low, pleading, coming towards him from a great distance. The corners of her mouth began to tighten.

'I can never deserve you, Sophie. I'm not good enough for you.'

'You could try.' A huge grin and a bubbling merry chuckle erupted from the Countess. She smothered her amusement with a muffled gulp. If I propose to her now, thought Max, she'll laugh at me.

'I-I, that is –' he stammered.

'Look,' cried Sophie, 'I've as good as told you, in front of all my father's guests, that I love you and I want to bear your children. You know I'd do anything for you. And I'd defend you with my life. So the very least you can do is ask me to marry you.'

'I love you with all my heart, Sophie.' Max blurted it out. 'And I always have done. But can I ever make you happy?'

'I'll take the risk.'

They stared at each other.

'So, go on. Ask.' Sophie grinned.

Max took her hand, kissed it gently, creaked down on to one knee, so that he was looking up at her, and delivered the goods.

'Sophie, Countess von Hahn, make me the happiest man in the world and say that you will be my wife.'

'Yes,' she cried, jubilant, unsentimental. 'I say, can you get up? Your knee made an awful groan as you went down. Have you been doing nothing but sitting in libraries?' She hauled him to his feet and flung her arms about him. All the worst things that had plagued Max night and day and prevented him from sleeping at all, let alone well, dissolved into the snow.

'Shall we tell Father and Mother at once? Or keep it secret? And are you hungry? I am. Does being engaged mean that you can come round every day? Like you used to do? And will you come riding with me as soon as the snow melts?'

Max saw an endless, tree-lined avenue of happiness unfolding before him.

END OF CHAPTER THIRTEEN

CHAPTER FOURTEEN

sets out on a Perilous Sequence of Adventures, archaeological and otherwise.

The Sibyl wrote to Wolfgang in January 1873 with a detailed list of corrections, suggestions, and alterations to the German translation of *Middlemarch*. She took advantage of the Continental reprint to correct some small errors in the new English language edition. And she enquired warmly after Max. Wolfgang, euphoric, announced the glad tidings: Max is engaged to Sophie, Countess von Hahn. The arrangements were concluded on New Year's Eve and the young people, who don't want to wait, are to be married in June. Well, gnädige Frau Lewes, they have known each other all their lives, so there is no need for a long engagement. Wolfgang then oozed forth a little flattery on the magnificent and very well-deserved reception of *Middlemarch*, to ginger up the great lady, his eye firmly fixed upon the next extraordinary work, with which you, madam, will delight the world.

The Sibyl replied:

> The Germans are excellent readers of our books. I was astonished to find so many in Berlin who really knew one's books. And did not merely pay compliments after the fashion of the admirers who made Rousseau savage – running after him to pay visits, and not knowing a word of his writing. You and other

good readers have spoiled me and made me rather shudder at being read only once; and you may imagine how little satisfaction I get from people who mean to please me by saying that they shall wait till *Middlemarch* is finished, and then sit up to read it 'at one go-off'.

Please do tell me exactly when Max is to be married. I should like to write to him myself.

And so, in his next letter to her, Wolfgang named the day in June.

Domestic arrangements, and extensive purchases of plate, linen, rugs and curtains plunged Max into a flurry of decisions and large bills. No expense spared. Duncker und Duncker of Berlin flourished and grew through several very lucky hits: a run of pamphlets for and against Wagner, a very expensive book of ethnographical photographs – savages from New Guinea, covered in braids of teeth, Moroccan tribesmen, veiled, on camels, naked women from the South Seas, unselfconsciously gap-toothed, glaring at the camera – and a daring sequence of memoirs in imitation of the Count von Hahn's seditious declarations. The memoirs, rather than the Tahitian pornography, kept Wolfgang awake at night. He expected another visit, at any moment, from the secret police. But nothing happened.

Wolfgang made Max a full partner in the firm and gave him the historical list to develop, with fresh commissions. The archaeological expedition languished for lack of funds. In a blaze of scholarly generosity the Count volunteered a large gift with the small condition attached, that another photographic book, *Images of Ancient Monuments*, should form part of the project.

The formal betrothal and the marriage contract, signed and settled in February, transformed Max into a rich man. He could now dedicate himself to antiquity without even bothering his future wife for a handful of Reichsmarks. The lease on the old Duncker family home, three doors down from the house in the Jägerstraße, fell due for renewal on the 1st of April. Wolfgang undertook the redecoration expenses, vastly amused by the fact that the only parts of the house Sophie desperately wanted to see before they took possession were the stables.

The winter hardened into long gleaming points of ice, suspended like executioners' swords, from the eaves of all the buildings. The young couple went skating in the blue days of cold sun, rode out in the Count's sledge, accepted congratulations from people they hardly knew in their box at the theatre, spent hours talking about nothing in particular. Everyone loves a young couple and a fairy-tale romance: he's handsome, she's rich as well as beautiful, and here they come, brimming with affection and wealth, hell-bent on lifelong happiness. Only the witch, uninvited to the feast, harbours her generous malevolence and saves it for the moment where both parties have reached the point of no return.

Did the Sibyl intend to unsettle Max in his headlong flight towards matrimonial bliss? Who knows? But her timing was perfect. The early days of June 1873, marred by odd blasts of sleet pulverising the tulips, and hailstones, which actually shattered two panes of glass in the conservatory at Wilhelmplatz, filled everyone with fear for the weather on the wedding day. Would it be too cold for the open carriage? Should Sophie set forth on her father's arm, swathed in shawls? How could they negotiate that pond of mud below the church steps with a wedding train?

A state of nervous hysteria seized the entourage of the old Countess. But nothing bothered the bride.

'If it rains we'll just leave off the train,' she declared, careless, magnificent, 'and then everyone will be able to see that I am wearing Mama's wedding dress, layers of French lace with the bodice stitched in real pearls! No one's worn a wedding dress like that for over twenty years.'

'Thirty years,' sighed the old Countess.

'Don't take on so, my dear,' urged the Count.

The Countess initiated a confidential tête-à-tête about the wedding night, but Sophie breezily waved her aside.

'That's all fine, Mama. I've read a very modern book in English that has diagrams. I know what little boys are made of. And I dare say that Max has lots of experience. He was, after all, in the army.'

Her mother scuttled away, dumbfounded, and full of apprehension concerning the nature of the diagrams. She ventured a brisk hunt through Sophie's rooms for the very modern English book, while her daughter was out riding, but found it not. Some things simply did not turn out according to plan.

On the evening before his wedding day Max received a brief letter from the Sibyl. He opened it without even noticing that it had been sent from England.

The Priory
1st June 1873

My Dear Max,

Mr. Lewes and I would like to wish you every happiness on your forthcoming marriage to Sophie, Countess von Hahn. Please do give her our congratulations and best wishes. You are so often in my thoughts, and I think of you with great affection.

I remain, as ever, your true friend
Marian Evans Lewes

And thus the long silence, unbroken since that warm but dangerous night in Stuttgart, finally lifted, and the Sibyl stood before him, her intense presence permeating every corner of his rooms where all his possessions, now being rapidly decanted into crates and boxes, stood sadly naked and displaced, bearing witness. He could hear her voice, low, resonant with insinuation. *You are so often in my thoughts.*

Max panicked. He grabbed his hat and coat, fled downstairs and clattered out of the building. Wolfgang, brushing his frock coat in preparation for the morning, and inspecting the lining for moths, heard him go and strode to the window. Yes, there was Max, hurtling down the Jägerstraße, into a grey sheet of drizzle, with the Devil at his heels.

Wolfgang summoned his butler.

'I see that my brother has gone out. Do you know where he's going?'

'No, sir.'

'He didn't say?'

'No, sir.'

Wolfgang could dismiss neither his unease, nor his butler.

'Was there anything missing from his luggage or his toilette for tomorrow?'

'Not that I know of, sir.'

'Very odd,' sighed Wolfgang.

The butler risked delivering a little further information.

'He had just received a message, sir, which appeared to be the cause of his abrupt departure.'

'Ah. Was it from the young Countess?'

'No, sir. A letter from England.'

Wolfgang still stood, baffled, gazing at the miserable rain, while Max arrived, damp and shaking, at the great house in Wilhelmplatz. His bride and her seamstress were engaged in a last fitting of the pearl-bodiced wedding gown. Were the sleeves a little too tight? Here, beneath the arms? I will be carrying my bouquet of white roses and my arms will be raised. So.

Tumult at the door! The bridegroom must not see his lady in her gown before the day itself. For if he does, who knows what misery may result. Sophie! Sophie! She heard him calling in her chamber. Sophie swiftly shed the gown, which she piled on top of her dress-maker, pulled on her *robe de chambre*, an embroidered housecoat covered in swirling green leaves, and swept into her sitting room, hair loose, buttons undone, feet bare. Max had never seen her in this state of undress before, but hardly noticed her naked throat and the erotic streams of white silk.

'What is it, Max? You sound really alarmed.'

Suddenly Max felt ridiculous, racing through the rain and wet streets, pursued by a demon he had already beaten back into its cave.

'I wanted to see you,' he gulped, 'just to make sure you were still here and hadn't changed your mind.'

'Changed my mind?' She laughed, and dragged him close to the fire. 'Warm yourself up, my love. You're ice-cold. Of course I haven't changed my mind.' Her face, suddenly serious, darkened.

'I'm not the kind of person who loves one minute and not the next. Never doubt me, Max. Never.'

He drew out the note.

'I received this. From England.'

Sophie scanned the note. Then moved the lamp so that she could read it carefully.

'She sent this message so that it would reach us before our wedding day,' murmured Max, calculating distance, dates, post. He left the Sibyl's motives open to Sophie's interpretation.

'Ah. Did she indeed?' murmured Sophie. She raised her eyes to Max's face, then, carefully and deliberately, she ripped the letter into tiny pieces and flung it into the fire. As each morsel fed the flames the light flared across her cheeks and forehead.

'There. She is nothing but ash. Ash and dust.' She whirled round to face Max, with a wonderful white smile. 'Now we can be happy.'

Ignoring her dressmaker's shocked expression she snuggled into Max's damp arms.

❧

Their wedding day, tearful at first, rainy at dawn, suddenly bloomed into hesitant but hopeful sun. The tulips in the formal gardens righted themselves, the open carriage was ordered, the full train decided upon, the shawls discarded. The Count and his wife, luminous in their finery, medals, satin, trimming and brocade, went out early to gather white roses for the bridal crown. In the lee of the walled garden grew the climbing rose they had planted when their first child was born in 1854. Look at that rose now, nineteen years later! Robust, tenacious, busily strangling the ironwork trellis. That rose, pruned, tended, loved, might well live for hundreds of years. No scent, but thousands of suckers, reaching up, holding fast, loyal to the gardeners, spangled with thorns. Sophie's rose braced itself for matrimony. Our little girl, married at last, and to her childhood sweetheart. The old couple came indoors, slightly chilled, their eyes moist, their arms overflowing with roses.

Sophie, anxious in her wedding dress – we let it out last night – why does it still feel too tight – here? – forgot every tiny niggle in her delight at the crown and sprays of white petals, barely opened, tipped with the soft breath of pink. Oh Mama, she embraced her mother, leaving the old Countess breathless from a slightly too ferocious hug.

And here she comes down the aisle on her father's arm, stepping out ahead of the music, her own spring beauty challenging that gorgeous shower of roses. As the minister opened his book and smirked down upon their fresh faces, the bride's expression changed slightly, her joyous glow sank just a little into discomfort. Do you, Maximilian Reinhardt August, take Sophie Anna Elizabeth Constanza to be your lawful wedded wife? Sophie handed the bouquet to her little sister Lotte, who crouched at her side, shifting from foot to foot, still clutching the train, and then rubbed her bare neck beneath the veil with sinister energy. There was no doubt about it; the bride had begun to scratch beneath her own ears.

'Sophie, what's the matter?' muttered Max, as the minister urged God to bless the rings.

'I'm covered in greenfly,' hissed the bride, 'the church has warmed them up, and they're pouring off the roses.'

❧

Rome, city of visible history, where the past of a whole hemisphere seems moving in funeral procession with strange ancestral images and trophies gathered from afar! Sophie rubbed her eyes, bent down, tightened the laces on her boots, and braced herself for an afternoon in the Vatican Galleries. For she was beholding Rome, where the arrow of their wedding journey finally attained its target. They occupied an enormous suite at the Hôtel d'Angleterre. Sophie reduced their entourage to two. Karl to deal with the luggage, tips, hotels, carriages, customs officials, alterations in the tickets and the train timetables, and the seamstress, Margareta, to deal with Sophie's travelling costumes, hatboxes, jewellery case, numerous sets of shoes, scarves, silk and lace petticoats, evening gowns, morning gowns, riding jackets, stockings, slippers, and ladies' unmentionables.

But how had they travelled and what terrible obstacles had they overcome? Sophie's boisterous and practical good sense served them well on their wedding voyage to Italy. Max expected everything to be perfect. Sophie dealt with matters arising when it wasn't. They travelled by train from Berlin to Paris, leaving the old house in Jägerstraße invaded by decorators, and managed by Wolfgang. Then after a suitable passage of time spent goggling at famous art works in the Louvre, they settled in to study the antiquities. Sophie's skill with languages suddenly became a traveller's asset in her marriage trousseau. She spoke and read three tongues perfectly. Her French poured forth as fluent as her native German, and apart from a faint accent, which her family described as charming, her English, bolstered up by a parade of governesses, did more than pass muster. She chirruped away at Miss Arrowpoint over the wedding breakfast, idiomatic, faultless. Now she got them all better rooms with gorgeous views and their stamped documents returned – immediately, Countess, yes, of course – with bows and compliments.

And what of those first days of marriage? Were they blissful treasured hours, or an embarrassing, unfortunate couple of weeks, best forgotten in later years? Well, neither description suits the case. Remember that Sophie and Max have known each other all their lives. He teased her when she was first learning to walk, delighted whenever she fell over. She bit him on the shoulder when he held her too tightly. She ate his share of cream gateau, that slice he had saved, specially saved, to celebrate his first birthday meal at the adults' table. He found himself facing a slicked empty plate, barren even of crumbs. And then he had chased her into the fountains. No, Max Duncker and Sophie, Countess von Hahn, her name, title and inheritance intact, according to her grandfather's wishes, by special dispensation from the Kaiser himself, no, this young couple squabbled their way into a happy marriage. They conducted a decorous sequence of disputes about almost everything. And both of them enjoyed every minute. That wedding night, which should have been assisted by modern English diagrams, collapsed in affectionate, exhausted slumber. And the first serious bedroom wrangle took place when Sophie announced:

'Max. Listen to me. This is important. I don't want any children for at least two years. And I have all these devices and techniques to stop it happening. Look!'

Max didn't object to devices and techniques, some not unfamiliar, if they presented no impediment to his desires, but he did object to Sophie knowing about them. She decided this was unreasonable.

'You don't risk your life in childbirth. I do.'

He felt overtaken and rejected. She thought this was an excessive burst of egotism.

But the possessive love of good companions, who passed every waking hour either looking at or thinking about each other, always carried the day. Their servants got used to the Master and the Countess racing up and downstairs in search of one another, and shouting out from windows.

Well then, Sophie's cleverness at languages is earning her a good deal of respect. But she has never studied Latin or Greek. Max has studied both. And suddenly, in the fading shadows of the Museum in Florence, where they paused on their way south to Rome, surrounded by sarcophagi, Sophie resented the limits placed on her education.

She determined to mount an assault against the dead languages covering the tombs.

'What does this say?' She flashed a gloved hand at the dedication beneath a seated woman on a small box, built for ashes.

'I don't know,' said Max, 'it's written in Etruscan.'

He's lying, thought Sophie in a rage of ignorant frustration, and stalked off down the dusty aisles, leaving Max amidst the alien tombs of the Etruscans.

For now here she was in Rome, puzzled and impressed by the unfolding ruins, toppled columns, marble pavements and colossal shattered grandeur, which poked through the tissue of the modern city like dead white ribs. They stood on the steps of the Palazzo Senatorio, gazing at the massive calm of the colossi, strangely streaked and disfigured by the blackening weather. Confronted with something strange, vast and extinct, Sophie realised that the safest path to understanding led through patience, study and the capacity to sit still and listen. But very few young girls, aged not yet nineteen, and recently married, actually possess these skills, that are the gifts of maturity. Those who have looked at Rome with the quickening power of a knowledge, which breathes a growing soul into all historic shapes, will not easily grasp Sophie's dilemma. She gazed upon the wreckage of antiquity, baffled. How had a complete world with a language, a religion, wealth and land without boundaries, and an enviable, arrogant identity, simply ceased to exist? Why were these particular fossils declared significant? And what, exactly, had destroyed this empire and then strolled onward through history without so much as a backward glance? Max rejoined his young wife later that night and found her buried in an enticing mixture of Bulwer-Lytton and Gibbon.

But if the nights were dedicated to *The Last Days of Pompeii* and *The History of the Decline and Fall of the Roman Empire*, and thus to the earnest acquisition of scientific information concerning the cycles of history, then the days must be given up to viewing the wonders that remain. They wandered beneath the hollow arches of the Colosseum, with giant fennel luxuriant among the crumbling brickwork, and the Baths of Caracalla, amidst whose abandoned halls and tunnels dwelt a sinister mixture of starving cats and importunate beggars.

❧

She was invited to a special evening viewing of the treasures in the Vatican, but the afternoon turned sultry and airless. Sophie therefore lay down upon her bed after luncheon and immediately fell asleep, volume 2 of Gibbon open upon her breast. Six o' clock gone before the little maid tapped upon her door. The light glowed, grey and ugly behind the still curtains. Sophie rubbed her eyes, bent down, tightened the laces on her boots and braced herself for the Vatican Galleries.

Enter Professor Kurt Marek. Sophie had never set eyes upon the famous Professor of Archaeology, History, Ancient Languages, Greek Law and Religious Philosophy from its earliest beginnings, Philology, Linguistics and All Kinds of Knowledge. But here he stood before her. As she stepped into the salon he appeared to grow up out of the carpet, dapper, tiny and vivid with quick movements. He bowed, skimmed across the room, kissed her fingers, drew himself up, so that she could appreciate his burgundy waistcoat and emerald tie pin, nodded in acknowledgement of the fact that he was at least a head shorter than she was, stroked his goatee and proclaimed:

'Countess! I am honoured, honoured. I am here to escort you to your husband, who has, I imagine, spent a difficult afternoon in the Galleries. The air outside is intolerably close. I fear we may be in for a thunderstorm. The fiacre awaits us. May I carry your cloak?'

He whirled her down the stairs.

'Too oppressive, my dear, to wear anything but the lightest of jackets, yet I fear that we shall need our weatherproofs before the night is out. You are wearing boots? Good, good. But that little hat will not protect you. Ah, your cloak has a hood? Well then, we are secured against all eventualities. Drive on.'

He tapped the roof of the cab with a vigorous bang and they lurched away towards the distant dome of Christendom, embraced by Bernini's colonnades. The river's lead stream matched the sky. Sophie noticed with distaste how poor many of the people lurking in the streets near the banks seemed to be. Filthy children hung with rags, who wore no shoes, picked their way through piles of discarded waste and rotting vegetables. The smell of fresh human faeces and urine drenched their path. Professor Marek snapped the windows shut and they jolted onwards in the airless black box, stifled.

How welcome then were the gardens and fountains of the Vatican! Many of the daily visitors surged past them, warily glancing at the descending sky, their faces shiny with sweat. Professor Marek patted his brow with a handkerchief soaked in lavender as they paused inside the fine spray from the fountains. At the high doorway he produced a letter for the guards covered in purple stamps and declaimed a short paragraph in rapid Italian. The result was instantaneous: peremptory bows and formal greetings, then they were whisked through the arching halls at an extraordinary speed.

Max, seated on a camp stool before a fabulously decorated sarcophagus, from which he was copying the inscription, rose at once to meet them. Sweaty and dishevelled, he shook hands with the Professor, kissed Sophie, and then began to button up his collar. As the two men stood talking Sophie wandered away between the tombs and statues. The giant, cavernous galleries echoed above her, cooler than the outside world, but filled with torpid, stagnant air. Beyond the rows of eternal stone tombs, the inhabitants of which had long since dropped to dust, and through a high wooden doorway, loomed the white shapes of blank-eyed statues, crowding one another, like a mob frozen in flight. Gods and men jostled each other aside. A row of busts lurked at eye level, backed against the wall. But the great statues, larger than life, all faced towards her, uncanny, unbending, rigid. An athlete cradled a discus; another stretched every marble muscle, flinging an absent javelin into empty air. Here stood one of the Gorgons, her head a mass of broken snakes, her giant hand curled around a pot. A dying man, one stone arm raised across his face, reached out to her with his other arm. She noticed that two fingers, whiter than marble, even in the murky dusk, had clearly been restored. Her soft glove stroked his expiring foot. She peered at the contorted body above her, as he sank down in pain, his shrinking genitals disguised by a plaster fig leaf. These torsos, buttocks, straining throats, knees buckled, arrested in stillness, nevertheless disturbed her, like an oncoming army, arms lifted, heads thrown back.

'Sophie!' Max called through the galleries. She must see the best pieces: the Apollo, the Sauroktonos, or The Boy with the Lizard, the sitting statue, called Menander, the Faun of Praxiteles and the old Faun with the Infant Bacchus. A selection of marvels awaits us! As they strolled, perspiring, through the vast halls, cluttered with the reliques of antiquity, Max and Professor Marek talked incessantly in lowered voices. When they reached each artistic phenomenon the torrent of learning crystallised into dates, details and the informed observer's pedantic commentary.

'These portraits are Roman copies of Greek originals. The dates are of course approximate. Apart from this one, which is indeed a very famous statue. Also a copy –'

Sophie looked up and stared into a particular face, austere, severe, the face of a judge; but there was a detectable tremor in the mouth. She leaned against a neighbouring plinth and concentrated. The blank eyes gazed into hers; a courageous face, immediate, modern, uncorroded by time.

'Who is that man?' she demanded.

Professor Marek also gazed at the face, reverent, and for the first time the little man ceased to fidget and stood quite still.

'This, my dear, is the poet and philosopher Lucian, Governor of Bithynia and Phrygia, later of Caria and Lycia. A native of Gaul. He survived Nero's reign and spent his last years at his villa in the south. He left some wonderful descriptions of his beloved estate in his personal letters, his fish ponds, olive groves and vineyards. But my colleagues working there in France cannot locate the site with any certainty.'

'He was a Stoic,' Max added quietly, 'educated at Athens in the Greek schools. He never embraced the new religion, but it is known that he protected the Christians in his household.'

Sophie swung round to face Max.

'You know him? You've seen him before?'

'Yes. This is a copy of the original statue. We now have a duplicate in the Museum at Berlin. The original was larger than life-size and the sculptor was Greek. But so far as we know the portrait was taken from life. The first statue stood in the middle of the temple complex at Miletus guarding the way to the marketplace. It is said that he used to teach there, in the open air. He wrote in Latin and Greek, but knew many other languages. I've read all his work, all the writing that has come down to us, at any rate. And he is one of the first commentators on the early origins of Christianity. Some say that his future vision of our religion was prophetic.'

'When did you go to see the statue in Berlin?' Sophie persisted. Max blushed.

'Last year.'

'And was Mrs. Lewes with you? Did she explain who he was?'

'Yes. How did you know?'

'It shows. In the nature of the information,' snapped Sophie. Professor Marek missed the significance of this exchange, but not the writer's name.

'Ah, Mrs. Lewes! The famous writer. A very great lady, my dear. Max, you are her publisher, are you not? Her knowledge of the Greeks is second to none. And she cares for scholarship, as a man would do. The deepest questions matter to her. She has earned my most profound respect.'

Sophie glimmered before the white statue, humiliated by her own ignorance. She had never read the Romans or the Greeks. And until that moment she had never heard of Lucian. But now, standing there in the Vatican Galleries, she made a unique and strange decision. Facing Lucian, and stepping back so that his stare encountered hers, and no one else, she made a silent vow. I will learn your languages and read your work. Then we'll see what you have to say to me, and only to me. First hand, and not through the minds of others.

Max gently touched her elbow. She shook him off, but just as she did so the great windows blackened, as if a curtain had fallen, and a blaze of white light lit up the crowded halls of white figures. The thunder crashed over them, the building appeared to heave and sway, and the statues shook, frozen before their empty sepulchres. One of the Vatican guards, a blazing torch held aloft, flickered towards them down the long corridors. They hastened through the great halls, abandoning the lifeless marble bodies. The torchlight illuminated moments in marble, a swirling robe, a naked breast, a tense, extended nostril. By the time they reached the portico the rain, blowing grey sheets of water, flooded the gardens and pavements. The majestic piazza, abandoned, empty, became a rushing gutter of storm rain.

Professor Marek continued to astonish. He reached into his little briefcase and drew forth a gadget that looked like a telescope. Two rapid clicks and the thing unfolded into a vast black umbrella with a shooting-stick handle and a metal cap at the crown.

'Voilà!' he cried, a contented magician whose best trick has worked. 'We shall attend the evening service at St Peter's, for the candles are already lit.'

And far above them, mingled with thunder, they heard the pealing bells.

Sophie kept her vow. She sat down in the library at her own house in the Jägerstraße and attacked classical philosophy, poetry and theology. She burrowed into the commentaries and variorum editions. She attended an intricate series of public lectures on ancient bas-reliefs and black figure vases at the Humboldt-Universität. She learned Ancient Greek. She found Latin easier, because many grammatical structures resembled Italian – she had even been hailed in Rome by leering hucksters crying '*Salve, Madonna*'. And the alphabet danced before her, strange, but not alien. By Christmas she could read both Propertius and Homer in the original, with very little hesitation. Max found himself delighted and menaced by this burst of classical scholarship, and assured her that she would be welcome to assist him in his studies.

'Well,' she smiled, 'let's see if I can spare any time from my own. And from my horses.'

Why was she doing this? Max had no idea.

'And are you going to produce a pamphlet on problems in Homeric grammar?' he teased her, rearranging one of her coiled braids. Sophie smiled again, but her expression, enigmatic, reserved, gave nothing away.

Max's young wife, glamorous, fashionable, busy, and in demand, ran his household like a stringent quartermaster. He returned neither to Hettie's Keller, nor to the card tables. Too many events, of an interesting and unexpected nature, occurred at home. Sophie welcomed anyone to her table who had something important and original to say. Pretentious fools or women with affected manners were not suffered at all, and some high-society people, who took enormous offence at the fact, were never invited again. And they whispered their criticisms: *Mon cher*, she fills her salon with Jews and painters, and you can have no idea who you might meet. This was true. Many of the dramatis personae that had flocked about the Sibyl now sought out the young Countess. Klesmer and his wife became frequent musical visitors, but so did the rapid Professor, whose growing friendship with the Countess was as powerful as it was unforeseen.

Professor Marek never ducked controversy. When Heinrich Schliemann's first ecstatic newspaper reports reached Berlin in 1873, claiming that he had discovered Troy, using only Homer as his guide, the philologists and scholars roared with condemnation and derision. Two voices in the German Academy supported him, Professor Wilhelm Dörpfeld and Professor Kurt Marek. The latter faced a challenge concerning his views, proclaimed from university podia and in copious newspaper columns, across Sophie's supper table, and declared for all to hear:

'The professional mistrust of the successful outsider is mediocrity's mistrust of the genius. And the mediocrities,' here he fixed his antagonist with a savage glare, 'are in the majority, and usually, comfortably settled on the seats of power.'

'Hear, hear, sir,' cried Klesmer in English, who happened to be sitting next to him. The two men shook hands, like conspirators. Frau Klesmer, Miss Arrowpoint as was, hastily called attention to the vast, engraved silver samovar, which had begun to bubble gently, and enquired after its exotic origins. The company marvelled at the samovar, a wedding gift from Russian admirers of the Graf von Hahn, who were (shockingly) rumoured to be anarchists.

Professor Marek, although already in his early fifties, remained unmarried, and having no immediate family to impede him, turned up at odd hours, bringing Sophie gifts of books, pottery and antique jewellery. A serpent bangle from Crete which polished up well gleamed golden on her arm, a treasure she removed only at night.

'The Professor claims it was once worn by Aphrodite herself,' laughed the Countess as she stood in her dressing room, admiring her reflection, then she flung Max a seductive glance. Max could not sit quietly in his wife's presence without touching her, her hair, her shoulder, her elbow, her fingertips. What a peculiar relief he had discovered in retreating to the uncomfortable austerity of his almost empty rooms in Wolfgang's house. He laid out his books and set to work. But always, as soon as he reached home, he bounded into the hall, bellowing Sophie, Sophie! Has the Countess returned from her ride? Has she gone out to Wilhelmplatz? Is she in her sitting room? Or in the library? Or is she ordering everybody into action in the kitchens? And once he had found her he stood back, bashful as a boy, glancing sideways, as she hurried towards him.

❦

The archaeological expedition to Miletus and Priene, now handsomely funded by the Graf von Hahn, set forth by sea from Marseille, early in March 1874, with a mountain of crates stacked in the hold. Professor Marek had at last gained permission to investigate the temple complex of the lost city, and the shrine to Athene on the hill, supposedly part of a little town, never excavated or even built upon since its destruction, probably by earthquake, for all the columns of the temple had fallen at the same instant. The layers of paper required in order to gain access to this place, accompanied by bribes, politely described as fees, eventually reached depths that resembled the earth and rubble that littered the site itself. Professor Marek placed more faith in Pausanias's descriptions than in the rhapsodic beauty of Homer, who declared that the gods themselves had built the walls of Troy. Pausanias, pounding through Greece in the second century, described many of the ancient cities as already ruined. Sheep, tinkling with bells, roamed the courts and palaces where great kings had once ruled. The estuaries silted up and the sea level dropped; so the Greek cities on the Aegean coast shifted their ground. They either moved closer to the sea, or curled inwards, and lay abandoned, their fine, chiselled stone becoming houses, mosques and barns. Pine trees sprouted through the marble pavements, goats grazed in the baths and theatres. The stadium returned to fields, covered with flowers in the early spring. The ruins, peacefully overwhelmed by the natural world, presented an image of irresistible decay, mutability incarnate, a fulfilment of that unbroken promise that all things must pass.

A small guest house in the fishing port, commandeered to host the visiting Europeans, put out several flags, one Greek, captured after a set-to with a Greek vessel that had trespassed into Turkish waters, and one American of unknown provenance, which was all they had.

Professor Marek thanked the landlord in perfect Turkish. Max fervently hoped that the beds would be clean, and watched the maids, abject before the young Countess, as she stalked the terrace, entranced by the glittering aquamarine of the Aegean.

'Miletus flourished for more than a thousand years. It is one of the twelve Ionian cities on the western seaboard of Anatolia.'

Professor Marek, a specialist on the work of Thales of Miletus, had written a controversial tract outlining the philosopher's belief that all things belonged in and to one another, that life and matter were inseparable, and that even the wild orchids, that now grew in the ruined sanctuaries of the philosopher's city, possessed living souls.

'I've looked him up in the library,' cried Sophie, 'and none of his writings survive. So how do you know what he thought?'

Professor Marek urged his favourite pupil to try the Turkish coffee.

'You drink it very sweet. Like a liqueur.' Sophie wrinkled her nose.

'No, my dear, that's correct. We have nothing signed exclusively by him; five theorems are attributed to his hand. But philosophers are like planets. You see the influence one has upon another, even if the original celestial phenomenon remains invisible. Where would Socrates be without Plato?'

Sophie had not yet tackled the philosophers. Instead she wolfed down bread and olives, while the smell of fresh fish on hot coals drifted across the veranda. Max listened to his wife jousting with her Professor and smoked a cigarette in the rocky gardens just below them. A flight of steps cut into the stone foundations of the guest house ended in the soft rush of waves against a small jetty. He watched a little purple rowing boat with a trim white prow, recently painted, rising and falling in the blue water.

The Professor's voice floated through the slats.

'Well, Miletus must have been abandoned once the harbour ceased to be navigable. The estuary is gorged with alluvial deposits. But the shadows of decline and desertion can be very gradual and inconstant. We have no record of the earthquake that destroyed Priene. And the two towns are very close. The port was still being used in the fourteenth century when the Ottomans traded with Venice. But the main ruins now lie some two hours' ride from the sea. And the protective digs on the river have been neglected. The site is partially flooded in winter.'

'Really? So how are we going to get there?' demanded Sophie, desperate for her dinner.

'Mules and carts. That's all arranged. Some of the workers who dug last year with my French colleague, Olivier Rayet, have been engaged to work with us. I am counting on the foreman's experience.'

'Max,' shrieked Sophie into the golden light of evening, 'where are you? Here comes dinner!'

❧

The long jolting ride down rough tracks in bursts of light rain and sun hardly seemed worth the trouble, for Sophie's first glimpse of Miletus, the ruined city of philosophy, revealed a vast, marshy flood plain. Columns and walls rose from the storm waters. The dead streets lay outstretched, sleeping, the geometric grid clearly visible through the brackish flood. The remains lingered beneath the murky levels in that very section of the city where they had permission to excavate, but Professor Marek had no intention of wasting time. He set up the campsite on high ground, marshalled his workers, and began digging behind the ionic columns on the sacred way where the damp ground sloped. The first trench, at least fifteen metres by five, at once revealed fresh walls and filled several crates with broken pots, but the pits immediately overflowed with rising water, and had to be baled out, like a sinking boat.

The foreman's son, a fifteen-year-old boy called Mustapha, was assigned to Sophie as her companion and guide. He fell helplessly in love with the beautiful white lady in the green hooded overcoat who sat astride her mule like a man and appeared indifferent to mud, rain and hot weather. She began teaching him French. Soon they gabbled cheerfully at each other in a mixture of languages as they trotted round the site.

Mustapha led his captive Europeans up the flank of the wild hill to see the ruins of Priene for the first time. That day exploded into spring brilliance and heat. Here the only tracks through the pine woods and spiky flowering bush were made by goats. They left the mules in a clearing and battled up the steep ridge. Max followed Sophie and Mustapha through the fragrant mass, stumbling over broken white rocks.

'*Le pin d'Alep!*' cried Sophie, pointing out the Mediterranean pines and transforming the landscape into a French lesson. '*Le bois est très résineux, mais fragile, car hautement combustible.*'

'*Combustible? Was ist combustible*?' The boy's dark eyes went blank.

'*Feu!*' roared Sophie, miming terror and asphyxiation in the middle of the bush.

'*Feu!*' yelled Mustapha, delighted by the charade. 'Run!' And he hauled her up over the rocks.

'*Romarin*! Rosemary, and in flower.' Sophie broke off a sprig, pausing for breath, and handed it to Mustapha who accepted it with reverence. 'And that is *primevère élevée*. Look, Max. Primulas, here in the wild.'

Purple floods of dwarf iris ringed the ancient stones.

'*Églantier*, a wild rose. And *épine noire*. That's also a rose.' She stood like a god in her garden, dispensing names. 'Broom. The yellow flowers are broom. Repeat after me, Mustapha!'

But the boy wanted to show them the small secret theatre, overrun with sheep, who scattered to the left and right, hopping up the aisles like an audience, dissatisfied with the performance. Here was an entire city, buried in foliage. The dissolving white walls, fluted columns, broken neatly into segments, as if sliced by giant armed hands, a strange ornate stone seat, still fixed in the pavement, the clear remains of narrow roads, guttering, doorways, small rooms, now filled with rubble, crickets, birds, and the spreading wilderness of scentless rose. Sophie and Max walked the lost streets, arm in arm, anxious not to lose their footing in the unstable mass of white stones. The antique world, instead of coming closer, leaping to greet them across the centuries, suddenly became unreachable, a vanished place, which left no whispers and no echo. Sophie felt the strange mystery of receding time most strongly in the theatres, the markets and the baths. The voices and songs of the people who lived there had sunk into eternal dark, united with all things for ever lost.

She shivered in the warm sun.

'Max, this place is empty. Even of the ghosts. Let's go back. Mustapha! *Viens, viens vite!*'

They set off back down the hill.

❦

About a month later, Professor Marek, yelling with unchecked euphoria, pounded across the sunny wastes of the Greek city, now free of winter floods, followed by a stream of workmen, all dusty and delighted. A bas-relief of extraordinary beauty had emerged from the trench inside the *temenos*, the sacred spaces of the sanctuary. A draped thigh and a colossal sandalled foot came surging out of the damp earth. As the afternoon wore on a woman's arm, clamped to a shield, reeled backwards into the gouged cavity. An Amazon? Athena herself? The workmen scraped gently at the murky stone. The Professor himself, small trowel and grimy brush in hand, deliberately uncovered the clenched marble fingers. The resurrection continued, day after day. They had discovered the frieze encircling the altar. And it must be extracted, piece by precious piece. Max set off, armed with financial incentives, to negotiate the immediate removal of their treasure. Sophie and Mustapha sat on the crates, drawing each article for the excavation record, as it rose up from the grave.

'But what does it represent? What is the story in the frieze?' Even as she sketched each partial figure, every weapon and each severed limb, Sophie could make no sense of the violent action accomplished before her.

'Hermeneutics, my dear Sophie,' said the Professor, busily wiping a filthy hand on a rag, 'is merely the art of not being fooled. It is our method of determining the genuineness and the history of an artefact from a diversity of signs. I have my own ideas concerning this battle. For that this frieze describes a battle I have no doubt. But we are in no hurry and we do not need to speculate. We will wait and see what secrets the earth has yet to give up.'

A plague of mosquitoes settled on the marshy site in the early evenings. Max insisted that Sophie should retreat from this danger and return to the guest house by the sea, despite her protests, buttoned gloves and veils. Professor Marek agreed with Max, the site was now no place for a lady; the decision became suddenly inexorable. And so she spent her days dawdling in the pretty rowing boat with the white prow, too hot to read, while Mustapha fished in the shallows.

And it was during one of these expeditions that the boy offered to show her the basilica. A small Greek Orthodox community still worshipped there, although part of the church, now ruined, staggered towards the cliff, destroyed by an earthquake of uncertain date, which everyone could describe but no one could authenticate. They set out by boat down the coast. Sophie shielded herself from the sun, with hat, veil, gloves and parasol, perched in the stern, her covered fingers drifting in the wake.

Their first sighting of the basilica, easily visible from the sea, revealed a collapsed wall and a row of seven perfect Corinthian columns, shining pure marble, the pediment still in place above the central entrance. All around the church wild yellow flowers bloomed in abundance, butterflies circulated above the lavender, grass poked through the cracked walls. The foundations of a larger building protruded through the green, like cracked teeth. They tied up the boat to an unsteady wooden step and climbed the stony path, covered with sheep's droppings. The sanctuary materialised above them, growing more tragically magnificent as they approached. Standing on the levelled forecourt before the basilica Sophie paused, amazed by its extent.

Surely this building once stood massive on the headland, a white landmark for shipping. Now, all around her, buried in long grass, lay a mass of finely chiselled stone, an inscribed slab, a shattered column, the beautiful curve of a basin half-filled with yellow rainwater. Where was the church? They advanced towards the row of seven columns, and sure enough, in the shadows, behind a decomposing wall, stood a small white dome, peeling, but intact, with a wooden door.

'*Fermez, fermez*!' insisted Mustapha, for she left the door ajar, as her eyes darkened in the bare, airless space. '*Oiseaux, oiseaux*.'

'Oh, I see. The birds get in.' But once the door thudded shut behind her Sophie found herself inside a small cave, quite dark, for there were only two slits carved in the dome's flanks, which let in two blazing splinters of light. Mustapha lit a taper from one of the candles, trickling a faint smoky glow into the dark. The stale odour of incense clung to the walls. Her steps echoed on the stone paving, the dome seized the sound, damped it slightly, then flung back the leather slap of Mustapha's sandals. And there in the taper's sudden flare, she began to see them, the icons of the saints, face after face, encased in silver and gold, their vast eyes staring steadily into the dark, their hands raised in formal blessings.

Pax vobiscum. I am Alpha and Omega, the beginning and the end. He that believeth in me, though he were dead, yet shall he live. For thine is the kingdom, and the power and the glory, for ever. World without end. Each icon, radiant with certainty, gazed, unyielding, at Sophie, who steadied herself with her parasol, and returned the holy stare, curious and unafraid.

'They are saints,' murmured Mustapha, indicating row after row of still, identical, shining faces.

'But you're not a Christian,' said Sophie, 'so how do you know?'

'It is a holy place for all peoples,' said Mustapha. '*Sacré*. It is tradition.'

Sophie shook herself slightly and touched the smooth walls, which were covered with some sort of white lime. There were no chairs or benches, only a small row of steps and stone shelves on which the icons rested. As she stepped back her shoulder nudged a plinth, the top of which unsettled her hat. Turning round she found herself gazing at a marble row of bare toes, larger than life-size. A gigantic statue, squashed into the corner to the right of the door, took up all the space, and reached right to the roof.

'Mustapha, bring the light. Who is this?'

'He too is saint,' declared Mustapha, scampering across, waving the taper. 'He is famous saint. Worshipped here. Everyone else is massacred. But he defends and protects the Christians.'

And so at last Sophie looked up and found herself staring into the blank, marble eyes of the philosopher Lucian.

END OF CHAPTER FOURTEEN

CHAPTER FIFTEEN

results in a Disturbing Revelation. A Statue is transported to London and Two Characters in this History, destined never to meet, against all the odds, actually do.

In February 1876 two events electrified London's intellectual circles: the final authentication of the statue of Lucian, discovered in a ruined basilica near Miletus – the very statue that had once stood before the market gates for centuries, guarding the way to the sanctuary – and the first episode of a new novel by the author of *Middlemarch*. The statue, destined to rest in an honoured alcove somewhere inside the British Museum, raised a frenzy of excitement among the learned societies of archaeologists and historians. Was it genuine? Or not genuine? After all, identical copies of Lucian's image abounded throughout antiquity. Lucian became as ubiquitous as Antinous. Just as the beautiful beloved of Emperor Hadrian transformed himself into an archetypal image of lost youth, so too had the grave authority of the philosopher come to represent wisdom, endurance and the ancient values of the republic.

The circumstances of the statue's discovery, so piquant and so glamorous, cast a spell over the newspapers. Photographs of the beautiful young Countess and her handsome husband, standing beside the mighty form to give it scale, did the rounds of all the journals. Professor Marek, the acknowledged expert on ancient Miletus, bounded off on lecture tours. The Great Professor, now mighty and famous on the basis of three huge trenches, eighty boxes of coins, pots, miscellaneous jewellery, curved masonry and inscriptions on stones, included passionate demands for money in his discourses. We must save the fragmented giant frieze depicting the Battle of the Amazons, which once surrounded the great altar in the *temenos*! Funding flooded into their expedition account, sponsors popped up like tulips; the ancient world became fascinating, mysterious, and above all, fashionable.

The novel also roused a good deal of turmoil and ferment, for unlike her earlier work, which dealt in ordinary lives, rural truths and the drama of everyday emotions, the Sybil's masterwork, *Daniel Deronda,* addressed the social struggles of the rich, the not-so-rich and the would-be-rich. The opening, set in a Continental gambling resort, identified as Leubronn, but everybody knew it was Homburg, uncovered a society in flux, the class hierarchies shaken, the pursuit of wealth a naked necessity. And that first encounter between Gwendolen and Deronda across the gaming tables generated a babble of intrigued speculation. Mrs. Lewes wrote to her British publisher, John Blackwood, on 17th March 1876:

> We have just come in from Weybridge, but are going to take refuge there again on Monday, for a few more days of fresh air and long, breezy afternoon walks. Many thanks for your thoughtfulness in sending me the cheering account of sales. [...]
>
> Mr. Lewes has not heard of any complaints of not understanding Gwendolen, but a strong partizanship for and against her. My correspondence about the misquotation of Tennyson has quieted itself since the fifth letter. But Mr. Reeve, the Editor of the *Edinburgh*, has written me a very pretty note, taxing me with having wanted insight into the technicalities of Newmarket, when I made Lush say, 'I will *take* odds.' Mr. Reeve judges that I should have written, 'I will *lay* odds.' On the other hand, another expert contends that the case is one in which Lush would be more likely to say, 'I will take odds.' What do you think? I told

> Mr. Reeve that I had a dread of being righteously pelted with mistakes that would make a cairn above me – a monument and a warning to people who write novels without being omniscient and infallible.

Quietly satisfied by the universal adulation that descended upon her, although anxious at how the Jewish theme of the novel, nowhere evident in the first instalment, would eventually be received, the Sibyl gathered her skirts, received her guests, distributed her ardour, spiritual instruction and sympathy in generous armfuls, and braced herself for further huge sales.

Wolfgang Duncker paid £100 for the German translation rights of *Daniel Deronda*, but Tauchnitz pipped him to the post on the Continental reprint, and offered £250, hard cash in hand. Wolfgang remonstrated gently, even called in the old loyalties, but George Lewes proved inexorable. He confirmed the deal with Tauchnitz in a brief letter of polite finality. Wolfgang trotted down the Jägerstraße to moan about the Leweses and their grasping financial tactics. Should he send Max, handsome, charming Max, off to London at once, as a Trojan horse in the subtle war of author's rights? The Sibyl clearly still cherished a tender regard for his younger brother. She always asked after him, in every letter. All the snow had dissolved into muddy slush. Wolfgang shook himself, standing in his brother's hall, removed his outdoor shoes and settled into the new pantoufles, neatly labelled with names for regular visitors, that Sophie had arranged beneath the ancestral bench.

'Max!' he called out, tramping into the salon, without waiting to be announced. Here stood Sophie, radiant with fresh air, still in her riding habit, smelling of horses and lavender.

'He's gone down to the Museum to oversee the loading up of Lucian. Sit down, Wolfgang, and I'll call for coffee.' She described the statue as if it were the philosopher himself. 'After everything we went through to extract him from the Orthodox Christians and then from the Turks, Max doesn't want a disaster to occur right here in Berlin.'

And indeed, the grainy, veined marble body that was Lucian's image, almost certainly taken from life, had traversed many bureaucratic and emotional storms since that day in the dark basilica when Sophie had caressed his foot. The small Orthodox community, ferociously attached to the statue of Saint Lucian, the just Man of God, refused to countenance his removal.

'Lucian was an atheist,' snapped Professor Marek. 'Haven't they read *De natura deorum*?'

'I don't think any of them, except perhaps the priest, can actually read,' said Max, 'and they venerate the statue. They think it's holy. Apparently it's worked many miracles.'

'So much for our sundered brethren in the East,' said the Professor briskly. 'Bribe the Director of Antiquities. And don't let him know what the statue is really worth. Or he'll never let it escape his clutches. Not until he thinks he's got the highest price.'

But the statue's story could not be resolved through bribes with Reichsmarks. One part of the frieze from the *temenos* had already been uncovered by Monsieur Olivier Rayet and sold to the British Museum in London, unbeknown to anyone until it was triumphantly unveiled. Behold, one of the Furies, almost intact, handsome, deadly, swirling, her vital power unleashed. She formed a central part of the north frieze. Professor Marek had unearthed the rest, with a fatal missing figure in the jigsaw. Passionate archaeological recriminations, conducted through letters, journal articles and newspaper columns, were delivered as righteous salvos in the months that followed. The offer of an exchange came from the British Museum by urgent telegraph. Your statue for our glorious morsel of frieze? Who would get the better deal from this arrangement, Berlin or London?

By the 1870s a minor war of national collections, now well under way, as the new museums of Northern Europe expanded and bulged, exploded into patriotic spasms of pique and envy, usually expressed in fulminating editorials. The Old World pillaged fresh victims from the Mediterranean, Egypt, Asia and the Far East. Beautiful objects, restored, repainted, sometimes fraudulent, set out upon their travels, to end their days, carefully labelled in huge halls with high ceilings. The extraction of the statue from the tiny ruined basilica became ever more urgent.

Professor Marek, always dynamic and inventive, now blossomed with ideas. He hired a gifted Italian sculptor and set him to work with an enormous block of marble. Six months later, as the modern Lucian hove into view, flat on his gigantic back, wedged in straw on the ship's deck, no one could immediately tell the difference, but the ancient version, blackened, chipped and missing several fingers, suddenly seemed a poor substitute for the gleaming resurrected saint, whose brave arm and completed hands reached out towards the seven ruined columns on the cliff, as if he longed for home. Professor Marek, his expression a perfect mask of piety, attended the incense-laden consecration of Saint Lucian.

Sophie retold the entire story, while pouring coffee and distributing cake to Wolfgang, who had flung his books and papers down upon her carpet. He had grown up in this house. He felt comfortable, at home, and untidy.

'So! Our philosopher is en route to London? I assume Max will go with him?' Wolfgang wondered how he could use the statue to entrap the Leweses.

'And I will too. We'll come back with the missing Gorgon from the frieze. And of course Max wants to oversee the packing and the transporters. At every stage.'

'Ah, so you are accompanying the statue party?' Wolfgang dipped into the gateau, which had a warm taste of ginger. And how could he exploit the beautiful Countess, who had now become something of a photographic celebrity, to extend his advantage over the rapacious English?

'I've never been to London! Mother and Father used to go frequently when we were small and come back with a selection of tutors and governesses.' Sophie wondered at the English, reputed to be so polite, remote and unknowable, and utterly unlike Miss Arrowpoint as was, who bubbled with warmth and suppressed laughter, when she wasn't being serious and intense about interpretations of Schubert. Her eye fell upon Wolfgang's heap of papers, and there, peeping out beneath the mass, lay the first hundred pages of *Daniel Deronda*.

'Mrs. Lewes! Her new book!' Sophie pounced.

'Just the first instalment. I'm reading Book II at home. It's unlike any of her earlier books. You'll need a dictionary to get through it. But you'll enjoy reading about some of our close acquaintances. Klesmer and Miss Arrowpoint are in there. Named, too. I suppose she has their permission. Klesmer comes out of it as a bit of a hero. He gives the heroine what for when she puffs herself up as a singer. Here you are.' And so Wolfgang handed over the poisoned chalice, amused at Sophie's unfeigned curiosity and delight.

When he had gone Sophie oversaw the kitchens, placed her orders for dinner, retreated to her rooms upstairs, pulled off her boots and dismissed the maid. Then, still wearing her unbuttoned riding jacket and wide skirts, she sat down to read.

> Was she beautiful or not beautiful? And what was the secret of form or expression which gave the dynamic quality to her glance? Was the good or evil genius dominant in those beams?

Sophie read on, appalled, for the opening episode of the young woman gambling rose up before her in insolent accusation; there she was, her irresponsible recklessness, the pawning of the necklace, the young man who stalks her steps, the September day, the long tables, the scene of dull, gas-poisoned absorption, that afternoon, now nearly four years past, reworked, remade, becoming more vivid with every sentence. But the Sibyl's heroine, foolish, reprehensible, lost again and again and again. Sophie sat, scarlet and trembling, awash with shame and rage. As she reached the end of the second chapter, hardly noticing the transformation into fiction, she actually read the message as she had originally received the handwritten note, with her own name inserted over that of the Sibyl's ambiguous heroine.

> A stranger who has found the Countess von Hahn's necklace returns it to her with the hope that she will not again risk the loss of it.

Sophie read not one word more. She hurled the slender volume away into a corner of her warm room and sat staring into the fire, her palms damp and shaking. She felt utterly naked and exposed, her young heart ripped open. Max! What did Max know? For one terrifying moment she believed that Max had sanctioned the book, to teach her a lesson. But she jettisoned this strange idea at once. Max loved her more than his own soul, of that she was quite certain. And so far as he was concerned everything she did was wonderful just because she did it. But why then was this evil witch so jealous of her happiness? She remembered the message Mrs. Lewes had sent upon their wedding day and how it had disturbed her beloved Max. What strange power did the writer have to intimidate and unsettle people she hardly knew? And why did she fling Sophie's youthful folly back in her face, and in so public a fashion, with an image distorted and broken? Why had she redrawn the scene so that the lovely gambler wagered all, and lost?

She wanted me to lose, to lose my money, my necklace and my husband. She cannot bear it that another woman should have beauty, youth, wealth and still be loved. She wants to punish me.

And perhaps, in thinking this, Sophie stumbled upon a truth that remained entombed in the writer's unconscious mind. The Sibyl's heroines are young women with everything to learn and everything to lose. Dorothea, short-sighted, obtuse, deluded and idealistic, learns who her husband really is the hard way, by marrying him. And finds herself chained to an old man, who is very far from being a 'great soul'; he is fraudulent, mean-spirited and vindictive. Gwendolen

Harleth, vain, self-satisfied, egotistical, naïve and confident, is almost destroyed by her husband, the monstrous Henleigh Mallinger Grandcourt, and by the plot of *Daniel Deronda*. Most authors use the plot to punish their characters. Thomas Hardy is famous for doing just that. But who is that woman in the Sibyl's novel, the woman who lurks on the edge of the tale? Who is the discarded mistress, demanding justice for herself and for her bastard children? Remember that the Sibyl never married George Henry Lewes. This woman's fate might have been hers. Some malevolent ill-wishers hoped that it would be. Here stands Lydia Glasher, baying for blood. Would Grandcourt ever have married her? Who knows? Her curse upon the heroine comes good: *You will have your punishment. I desire it with all my soul.*

The older women in the Sibyl's books are startling creations: unfettered, unleashed, seeking their prey and hungry for vengeance. Had Sophie von Hahn possessed all the elements in the story she would have seen this, and proudly taken their part. A fierce passion for justice and a curiously English understanding of fair play reigned in Sophie's heart. There is a great deal of unmapped country within us, which would have to be taken into account, as an explanation of our gusts and storms. Sophie shared many things with the Sibyl; both women blazed with the desire for knowledge, a desire that reduced milder forms of curiosity to mere politeness. Both women grasped their lives, fortified by an unyielding common will, convinced that what they did and said mattered and echoed beyond their small circles and concerns.

Some say the Sibyl was fragile, insecure, lacking in confidence and self-esteem. But do frail and timid women decide to be atheists, challenge their fathers, refuse to go to church, educate themselves to an astonishingly high degree, run off to London, live abroad on their own, fling themselves at married men, beguile women too, and clearly enjoy doing so, edit distinguished literary journals, learn Hebrew, write fiction that will live for ever as long as we remember how to read, become rich and famous, and think for themselves?

Ah, that's the key, the power of independent judgement. Sophie and the Sibyl tested everybody else's judgement against their own. Both women believed in their inalienable right to discriminate and decide, and both were inclined to accept their own opinions. Both women loved getting their own way. Never give up! Neither woman had any intention of ever doing so. A crisp modernity defined their approach: no shame, no guilt, no fear, no hesitation. And no quarter.

Well, what happened next?

❧

Sophie's warm sitting room, filled with mementoes of equestrian achievements, with large double windows overlooking the bare gardens, not yet quite risen from their winter grave, led into the bedroom she shared with Max, who had his own dressing room beyond. She prowled once round the bedroom, searching for a handkerchief and weighing her fears and suspicions. Then she poured clear, cold water into her washing basin and scrubbed her burning face. Outside, dusk settled over the smoke rising from thousands of freshly built fires. Wary as a cat, Sophie approached the first instalment of *Daniel Deronda*, which lay in a fluttered heap behind an armchair, smoothed the pages and slid it carefully into one of her leather travelling cases. She had not decided what to do, but knew the book constituted undeniable, published evidence. As she set off down the staircase she heard Max crashing through the door, bellowing at the servants.

'Has the Countess come home?'

He saw her descending towards him and pounded up to the first landing in a climactic sequence of bangs and creaks.

'Sophie! The statue is all packed and ready for the train. It's locked in the depot with two men on guard. Dearest! Whatever is the matter? You've been crying.'

And this immediate recognition of any glint of pain or trouble in her open face and red-rimmed green eyes reassured her completely. He loves me, he loves me not, he loves me. And he has nothing to do with this vicious treacherous book. Max embraced his wife, suddenly riddled with unease.

'It's all right.' Sophie told the truth, if not the whole truth. 'I've been reading a novel. And I was so affected by the story that it made me cry.'

Husband and wife mounted the stairs, their arms around one another. Sophie stood on safe ground. Max never read novels, or at least she had never seen him do so.

❧

Two days later Max, Sophie, Professor Marek and a little court of acolytes set out for London, their trophy safe in straw, guarded in the goods van. Wolfgang saw them off at the Hauptbahnhof, then went home to write a torrent of calculated adulation to the Sibyl. He composed the letter in his odd stilted English. Max, he had to admit, could write a more fluent, graceful hand, but was not so adept at flattery, and Wolfgang counted on Lewes reading the letter first.

> My dearest Madam Lewes,
>
> Your extraordinary new book has become the event of the month for me. I had not thought that the elegance and sophistication of *Middlemarch* could be surpassed, but I am at present devoured by curiosity to see what will become of the unfortunate little Jewess and our noble hero, Deronda. Pray take pity on your most passionate German admirer here in Berlin and allow me to request the forthcoming proofs from Mr. John Blackwood. Our translator, the one you have approved, is already at work, but of course, not a word will reach the public until he has received the benefit of your astute linguistic advice and you have given your imprimatur. This novel is magnificent, dear madam, the opening scenes masterly, your little minx Gwendolen as captivating as she is dangerous. What will be her fate and how will

the two meeting streams of this great work be bound together? As you see, I think of little else.

Mr. Lewes apprised me of the arrangements you have agreed with Tauchnitz, and while I regret that we shall not have the pleasure of promoting the original in the Continental reprint this time, I trust that you will not forget us when the Cabinet edition of the Collected Works is to be considered. Nothing would give me greater pleasure, or be a higher honour, than to publish you here, in both languages.

(There, thought Wolfgang, that should do it. Be a gentleman. No recriminations. Don't mention figures at this stage. He dipped his pen again into the glass well.)

Max, as you no doubt already know from the *Times* reports, has carried off a little coup with his discovery of the original statue representing Lucian. I shall never forget your comments on the famous *Fragment* when you discussed that unsettling work here with Max, in this very office. He has become a more stable and dedicated person. I firmly believe that this is due to your influence, for after his journey to Stuttgart all those years ago, he returned, chastened, transformed, more serious and responsible. Your wisdom, madam, transfigures lives, and raises our sights to the ideals we might achieve, enables us to become better men.

('Transfigures' sounds convincing. She has a religious turn, and likes to see herself as a saviour.)

Max is at present on his way to London in company with his young wife and the great Professor Marek. They are transporting their rare find to the British Museum, and hope to return with the bas-relief of the *Erinys*, who forms part of the glorious frieze, also discovered at Miletus and at present incomplete. He longs to see you and Mr. Lewes again, and I trust he will bring back word of your good health and steady progress towards the completion of this glorious book.

I remain, madam, your loyal and devoted publisher
Wolfgang Duncker

(There, that should plant the seed for future negotiations. I've set out my stall and I'm open for business.)

Wolfgang patted the letter with his blotter, read it over again, checked for the duplication of flattering adjectives and then prepared the evening post, while his clerk made a fair copy. Wolfgang kept track of every obsequious phrase; he liked to think that his delicate insinuations were well judged.

(I haven't sounded bitter or reproachful; softly, softly, that's the way. Lewes is bound to read this out to her, as it's billowing with compliments. Have I laid it on too thick? No, nothing here I can't honestly repeat. The new book is powerful, no denying it, but why on earth does she have to drag in the Jews?)

❧

Professor Marek's younger sister had married an Englishman, a man not overeducated in classical languages, but good-natured and rich. The couple maintained a large white house in Regent's Park, complete with carriages and stables, not half a mile from the Priory. Marian Evans and George Henry Lewes purchased a forty-five-year lease on this house at No. 21 North Bank, for £2,000 in August 1863, and had lived there ever since. The Priory stood on the edge of the canal, embedded in a garden of roses. Sophie and Max had therefore settled on a London perch uncannily close to the Sibyl's lair.

Sophie, enchanted by the dynamic bustle of the London streets, wrote to her dear Mama and Papa that the multitudes churning up the mud, both in carriages and on foot, made Berlin's wide boulevards seem comfortable and empty of all urgency. She loved the theatres, luminous in gas light, she watched the prostitutes in the Haymarket, gaudy as tropical birds, working the crowds. She galloped round the park on her host's horses, enjoying the early white frosts, which gave way to ravishing floods of narcissi and yellow *jonquilles*. The London spring foamed over garden walls in white brushes of lilac, and thick green buds. But the greatest excitement for the young Countess presented itself in mechanised form: her hostess possessed a small fleet of bicycles.

She had a high-wheeler, later known as the penny-farthing, which she couldn't ride, and a *vélocipède* that her husband had purchased in France. This astonishingly heavy machine sported a cranked axle, like the handle of a grindstone, which could be turned by the feet of the rider. Sophie read the accompanying instruction booklet. 'The rider who wishes to stay upright and in command would be wise to pedal as rapidly as possible or take a spill in consequence.' Once on board and held straight by two grooms Sophie padded out the saddle with a small cushion. After several inconclusive wobbles round the stable yard the intrepid Countess enrolled for an intensive course of lessons with a well-known bicycling expert. They battled with the oily *vélocipède* until she could handle corners unaided. Max watched, appalled, as his wife whirled away at speed.

1. Always look where you're going. (She didn't.)
2. Always sit straight. (Well, she always did that, especially at table.)
3. Pedal evenly and use both legs. (Her boots vanished in a circular blur.)
4. Pedal straight. (Corners, corners, Countess. Lean.)
5. Keep the foot straight. (Both feet.)
6. Hold the handles naturally. (Of course!)
7. Don't wobble the shoulders. (Never!)
8. Hold the body still and sit down. (Sophie was anxious to keep her cushion firmly beneath her.)

9. Don't shake the head. (At this point her hat flew off. Max chased after his wife, who was even now flying over the winter potholes in a torrent of ribbons, cheered on by the footmen and grooms whose democratic spirit had begun to alarm him.)
10. Sophie, Sophie, your hat!

She bicycled away round Regent's Park alongside Professor Marek's enthusiastic little sister, delightfully unchaperoned.

'It's quite a craze among the ladies, Max,' grinned the vivid little Professor. 'But don't worry. As soon as our young Countess is in *anderen Umständen*, or as the English put it, an interesting condition, we'll persuade her to give it all up.'

Max blushed and rubbed his chin.

❧

The statue's size caused a furore in the Museum, not because of the niche for which it was destined, and into which it fitted perfectly, but because the Director of Antiquities had set his heart on a theatrical coup, in which the veiled figure of Lucian would suddenly be unveiled, emerging from a mass of swirling red drapes to ecstatic exclamations. But the marble form settled so snugly into the designated space that removing any form of veil, let alone the heavy red velvet cape, already lying folded and ready, proved practically impossible. A screen? A curtain? Various solutions were proposed, then rejected. No screen tall enough could be procured at short notice, the curtain would have to go round a corner before the philosopher could be entirely revealed, and the necessary rails with runners needed an Isambard Kingdom Brunel to perfect the contraption. Lucian stared blankly at the gaggle of great minds, none as distinguished as the philosopher they honoured, who stood assembled before his mighty toes, disagreeing with one another, like new pupils seeking enlightenment.

And so it fell to Sophie, Countess von Hahn, addressing her Professor with ringing decisiveness, to slash the Gordian knot.

'But didn't Lucian teach in the marketplace at Miletus? So that everyone, even the poorest weavers and farmers, and all the artisans who worked in the port, could hear what he said? Well, why are we trying to hide him now? He taught in the open air. He said that hidden and secret things were dangerous. Aren't we here to celebrate him and his philosophy? Not to devise some vaudeville trick?'

At this point, the Director of Antiquities, who disapproved strongly of uppity young women speaking out of turn, felt himself criticised and tried to intervene. Professor Marek tapped his elbow. Sophie bounded on.

'Why don't I weave a crown of laurels for him? As if he were an athlete or a victor at the games. He was a decathlon champion in his youth, wasn't he? And we can lay flowers at his feet. Then anyone who comes in early can see him in all his splendour.'

Sophie cherished a possessive interest in the statue. In her imagination Lucian still belonged to her. She had first touched the greening feet of the worshipped saint in the dark church and known at once who he was, and while she may have been written out of history in the academic papers she still queened it over all others in the popular magazines and expensive memorial photographs. She gazed up at the curiously naked marble face; the body modestly clad in his toga of office, now immaculately cleaned, the features webbed with emotions and judgements. Professor Marek kissed the Countess's gloved fingers. Her father's money gave her the right to speak up whenever she chose.

'Once more, *chère Madame*,' he said in French, 'you show us the way that leads to glory.' To the assembled scholars and the Director of Antiquities he announced in English:

'I find this idea charming. Flowers, of course, we must have flowers. I propose that the Countess's suggestion be adopted at once.'

Max led his wife aside, capturing her hand, and stared at her, astonished. Her living beauty glowed, fair and luminous, before the cobalt blocks of the Assyrian warriors, pinched from Mesopotamia.

'I had no idea that you had already read the *Letters to Myriam* – Lucian's letter on secrets and the pernicious effect of the anger that is never spoken. I'm reading that section at the ceremony. In English and in Greek.'

'But I haven't.'

'You haven't? That's not possible. You just quoted him verbatim. *That which is hidden and secret is always dangerous, because it serves an undeclared interest.*'

'I didn't say exactly that. It's just a coincidence. And anyway, Max, that's not a sacred piece of wisdom, it's just common sense.'

Sophie kissed his cheek and grinned.

'Come on, let's go to the market and buy armfuls of bay leaves and red tulips.' Red spring flowers, she had already decided, would set off the philosopher's massive marble toes to perfection. And everyone seated before him at the ceremony would be gazing at his feet.

In fact the bay leaves had to be filched from the Royal Botanic Society Gardens and wound into a crown by the cook, who devised a cunning method of holding it all together with a shaved branch of pyracantha.

'If he was still alive this would prick his forehead like the crown of thorns,' said Sophie, holding the thing at arm's length. 'You go on ahead with this and the tulips, Max. I'll get dressed and have a rest. But I'll be down there for the inauguration ceremony by two o'clock. I hope the afternoon won't be too dreary. There's very little natural light in that gallery.'

She packed the laurel crown into a hatbox and waved him off in the front hall. Then she marched into the library, built up the fire with her own hands, despite the housemaid's anxious circling patter, and climbed the movable stairs to the top shelves, looking for Lucian's *Letters to Myriam*. And here they were, the bilingual edition in English and Greek. Sophie sniffed the unread volume, all the pages still uncut.

She rang for a paper knife, pulled her chair close to the fire, kicked off her damp boots and sat down to read. 'Letter VII: On Lies, Secrets and Silence'. Myriam understood Greek and Latin. Some said she was a Jewess, welcomed into Lucian's household, a fugitive from the wars in Palestine. Other sources described her as a Christian, a convert who had known the first disciples. One thing remained certain, she had become the philosopher's adopted daughter, and he had set her free, of his own volition. No child he chose would ever be his slave. The *Letters to Myriam* embodied his teachings on ethics, the metaphysics of daily life and the common good. References to the early practices of Christianity, scattered throughout the texts, ensured that the *Letters* remained topical, scoured by historians and theologians for evidence to prove their numerous theses. Sophie ploughed through a third of the turgid introduction, then gave up and sliced open the very pages Max deduced that she already knew.

All at once the clarity and distinctiveness of a unique, unsilenced voice spoke directly to her, as if she listened like the freed slave, the philosopher's only daughter.

> That great anger within you, that remains unacknowledged and unspoken, will corrode and destroy your soul. Did you not tell me the story of your master, the rabbi who drove the money-lenders out of the temple at Jerusalem, armed only with a scourge of small cords? And did he not also drive out the sheep and the oxen, and poured out the changers' money, and overthrew the tables? So too should you drive out your anger. Confront that passion within you, and transform its force into a river you control, and you will no longer be its slave.

This fragment of wisdom from Lucian, addressed to an unknown woman in the first century, suddenly acquired an echo that seemed sinister and pertinent. London is the city of the Sibyl. Where is the woman who has held me up as vain, foolish and shallow, a just target for the world's derision and contempt? Sophie kicked the fender with her stockinged foot. In the distance she heard a bell ringing and ringing through closed doors. Then the maid appeared, clutching a folded note.

'It's a message for the gentleman, Madam the Countess.' She bobbed in the doorway. 'The boy said it was urgent, but didn't need an answer.'

'Oh.' Sophie looked up, stretching out her hand for the letter. 'What is it?'

'I don't know, ma'am. But it's from Mrs. Lewes at the Priory.'

Sophie snatched the letter from the maid, flung Lucian upon the hearthrug and tore it open, ripping the Sibyl's careful steady writing in the process. Her face changed as she read, as startled and affronted as Our Lady herself, accosted by the angelic messenger. Sophie, far from mastering the lurking anger that bubbled within her, now burned with a pure, white rage.

My dearest Max,

Were I strong enough to attend the ceremony at the Museum this afternoon, nothing would prevent me from congratulating you in person. To think that you have discovered our beloved Lucian who means so much to us both! My delight in seeing you after all these years would make my presence at this particular celebration a temptation indeed, but I am most unwell with an infected tooth. Mr. Lewes will be there to applaud you on behalf of us both. However, I trust that you will call at the Priory before you return to Berlin. My satisfaction in learning that you have at last found your vocation, and have indeed become the famous scholar and adventurer I always longed to honour and admire is indeed a high reward. You have fulfilled all my hopes and expectations.

My dearest Max, if you but knew how deeply I wish to efface any misunderstanding that might still divide us. You have shown nothing but reverence and esteem towards me and I treasure our friendship. My affection for you remains unchanged.

Kindest Regards
Marian Evans Lewes

What was it that unleashed Sophie's colossal rage? The fact that she was ignored? Unmentioned? Her discovery of the statue in the basilica unacknowledged? Her passions and ambitions written out of the official recorded history, yet distorted in the Sibyl's grandiose prose, and held up to be jeered at and belittled by the fashionable world? Should she sit by, powerless, while this antique dame wrote intimate little letters to her husband? Well, whatever it was that exploded in Sophie's heart, a fierce sense that she had been wronged urged her to don her boots, thunder into the hall, bellow in French for her straw hat and long coat, hurtle out of the main doors, clutching the fatal letter with its innocent address printed on the crest, and bound away down the quiet road in the direction of Regent's Park Canal.

'Sophie? Sophie!' called her impotent hostess.

But Countess Sophie von Hahn would not, could not, now be stopped.

❦

The house stood well back from the road: two storeys, high windows and the roses, bristling with fresh shoots, arched before the main doors. The pointed white gables gleamed above her. Sophie paused at the gateway, intent as the Avenging Angel, and looked down at the address in her gloved hand, which she now unfolded like the seventh seal. The Priory – yes, this is the place. She swung on the doorbell and heard it pealing through the house. A tiny maid, with curious, knowing eyes looked up at her, clearly expecting a different face. Sophie instantly stepped inside, and to the maid's obvious alarm, closed the outside door behind her.

'I am very sorry, madam, but Mrs. Lewes is indisposed and can see no one. Mr. Lewes has gone to a ceremony at the British Museum. I'm very sorry, but –'

Sophie cut her short and practically pushed her into a Chinese jar that served as an umbrella stand.

'I'm perfectly aware that Mr. Lewes is out. Tell your mistress that her German publisher, Maximilian Reinhardt August Duncker, needs to speak to her on urgent business.'

A foreign whisper in Sophie's accent startled the maid who lost confidence in her role as Cerberus, the guardian of the gateway. Unscrupulous and forearmed, Sophie handed over Max's visiting card. Shaking her head doubtfully the little maid sped off up the staircase, indicating that Sophie should wait in the morning room. Green wallpaper, comfortable chairs, occasional tables, hand-painted botanical studies, elegantly framed, Sophie waited for thirty seconds, and then set off after the maid, catching up with her on the second landing.

'But, madam –'

'Go on. Announce me. Say that I've brought an important message from Max. She will see me. She's expecting a reply.'

With uncanny prescience Sophie knew that her husband's name would prise the Sibyl out from beneath her afflictions, and raise her cage of prophecy from the Delphic abyss. The maid knocked and entered the great drawing room. Sophie stepped inside the door and paused, assessing the battlefield. Theatrical drapes, pulled back a little, revealed the full extent of the room. A slender, bowed figure in a white lace cap with a poultice tied round her face sat bent double on the sofa, apparently mending a rug. The famous pendulous jaw remained quite concealed, but the nose, spotted red and purple, projected forth. The great head, apparently too weighty to lift, rose tentatively in acknowledgement of the unwelcome intrusion. The maid scuttled up to the Great Lady, pressed the card into her hand, muttered an unintelligible apology and fled, closing the drawing-room doors behind her. Sophie, lurking by the curtains, heard only one word – 'Max!'

And that name had a magical effect upon the shrunken, morbid shape. The Sibyl straightened, turned, and attempted to rise, her shawl slipping back upon the cushions. All the blinds, pulled half-down, created shadows across the carpets. In the murky dark the two women peered at one another, in appalled surprise.

'*You* are Mrs. Lewes?' Sophie strode forward. She intended her opening salvo to be fierce, rational and unanswerable, but her voice boomed like a cannon in the still, fetid air, her tone scornful and incredulous. Was this pale shade really the great sage to whom all Europe bent the knee? And there was no dancing ape-man to shield and protect the famous writer now. She faced one of her most ardent readers, whose rage, unchained, shattered the silence.

'I would not wait downstairs only to be told to go away again. I've waited long enough for an answer to my letter. That letter I wrote to you over four years ago, the letter you never answered. And I am returning this incautious message you sent to my husband expressing your undying affection. So you at least have been fully answered. You did not have the decency to return my letter to me. Nor did you answer it. You gave it to my husband to make trouble between us.'

She flung down the crumpled note at the Sibyl's feet. Two white lines appeared on either side of the writer's purple nose. She was wearing spectacles. Had Sophie, now standing before her, back to the light, taken the trouble to observe her antagonist closely, she would surely have seen a frail old lady, ravaged by toothache. But the young Countess, hat straight as a cardinal's, a shimmering demon incarnate, busy exorcising her anger in a manner never envisaged by the philosopher Lucian, had no intention of pausing, even to draw breath.

'I am Sophie, Countess von Hahn, and you have written me into the opening chapters of your new book – a thing you had no right to do. I accuse you of stealing one moment of my life and of distorting the facts. You are not just. And you are not honest. I once admired your books and now you have disappointed me.'

The Sibyl sank back upon the sofa, as if bludgeoned into the cushions. This accusation proved too preposterous to comprehend. Who on earth had allowed one furious, articulate reader to blaze through her quiet drawing room with her voice raised? And who was this young woman after all? What possible connection did she have to Max? The Sibyl's toothache created a mist in her brain. This room served as her audience chamber, her throne room, the sacred space where her disciples bowed down before her, paid homage to her genius, waited quietly to be granted a moment beside her, a little breath of comfort and guidance from the elderly deity. And where was her mountebank? Her ardent keeper, her defender against unhinged enthusiasms? Her deepest fears rose to the surface, and stuttered out from her swollen jaw.

'You have judged me,' she whispered, 'you scorn me for who I am, for how I have lived. You presume to know how I have suffered.'

The Sibyl answered another tribunal, where she had been judged in absentia, not the one before her. The present confrontation collided at a crossroads. But Sophie stood her ground. She had not stormed the Priory to discuss the Sibyl's situation or the writer's feelings, but to give vent to her own. Her savage cry could be heard all down the stairs, where the servants, gathered at the foot, gazed upwards, transfixed with curiosity and alarm.

'No, you're wrong. I don't judge you for what you've done or who you are. And frankly, I don't care what you've suffered. Why should I care whether you are, or are not, legally married to Mr. Lewes? Plenty of people live like that in Germany. I wouldn't be so small-minded. I wasn't brought up to think about other people in such an ungenerous way. But you, you are not generous. If I had been you and had your choices before me, I would not have written your books in the way that you have done. I would not have told women to be satisfied with self-sacrifice, convention and subservience. I would not have lived one life and believed in another.'

And with that Sophie turned on her heel, flung open the drawing-room doors, and then slammed them behind her. The thud of her boots on the descending stairs vibrated back through the great house. The servants scattered. The Sibyl sat rigid in the half-light, clutching Max's card, her scorned and loving letter fluttered at her feet, her eyes dimmed.

One way and another the Furies had crossed her threshold.

END OF CHAPTER FIFTEEN

CHAPTER SIXTEEN

recounts a Terrible Succession of Melancholy Events.

One thing still puzzles me about this extraordinary encounter. The Sibyl, supposedly a fountain of transparent confidences, confessing all to her devoted little man, never told Lewes anything about this stormy interview. When he returned that evening, jubilant, and full of amusing tales, eager to describe the ceremony and the pompous Director of Antiquities, he found her, collapsed upon the sofa, in a state of great distress. But even as he comforted her and called for warm milk, he never suspected that more lay behind the tearful wails than the prospect of a bad night and aggravated toothache. Poor Polly, that tooth will have to come out. I can't bear to see your pale, drawn face. Why, your cheek feels quite hot. Let me send for some ice, then at least we can cool that reddened swelling. Come, lean on me. There, there, you should be in bed. Oh, but you missed some fine performances. Our boy Max recited Lucian in Greek!

Sophie, however, had been observed leaving the Priory. Ah, yes, the watchful spy lurking near the canal counted the minutes of her visit, and then set off, close behind the brilliant Countess, matching her stride and studying her clothes. Behold Edith Simcox, whose passion for the Sibyl was so overwhelming that she was reduced to skulking in hedgerows, hoping to gather up scraps of information from the servants or a glimpse of her idol in the windows. Edith delivered fresh flowers that very morning, and several loving messages to aid the

Sibyl's progress with her toothache. But she, the faithful lover and disciple, was not admitted to The Presence. So who was this straight, slender girl, unchaperoned, got up in expensive, fashionable dress and a startling straw hat, who strode straight into the sanctuary, without even bothering to scrape her boots?

Edith Simcox polished her spectacles, and quickened her pace. Sophie, still volcanic with rage, would not have noticed cannon to the right of her, or cannon to the left of her, and certainly never noticed the concentrated surveillance of a nondescript thirty-two-year-old woman in a camel jacket and a felt hat haring down the path behind her. But Edith Simcox, now transformed into the passionate huntress, a pack of hounds baying in her heart, convinced herself that she had captured a younger rival in her sights.

Who was Edith Jemima Simcox? She was, quite literally, a shirtmaker, who founded a women's shirtmaking cooperative with her friend Mary Hamilton. She was a businesswoman, a writer, and a social reformer. And from 1876 until 1900 she kept a Journal, a personal, secret Journal, not intended for publication, which she called *Autobiography of a Shirtmaker*. And therein, with unselfconscious, excessive, unhinged emotion, in a style that still seems complex, intricate and embarrassing, she recorded her passion for another woman, a woman twenty-five years older than herself, a woman who was the most famous writer of her day, Marian Evans Lewes.

Simcox first met the Sibyl in 1872, when the idealistic shirtmaker was busy preparing a review of *Middlemarch*, and for the next seven years she haunted the house and traced every move the writer chanced to make. She frequented the drawing room, whenever she could get in, the gardens and the nearby streets whenever she couldn't. She wrote love letters, then tore them up, sent little notes filled with declarations, embroidered treasures, armfuls of forget-me-nots; this unchecked, immoderate obsession transformed her into a suppliant whose behaviour made her utterly ridiculous. The Sibyl received all homage gracefully, but made it clear that the depth and extent of Edith's affection would never be returned or reciprocated. Did the great lady find herself moved by Edith's tendency to fling herself upon the rug and kiss her darling's feet? The beloved moved her slippers out of reach, flattered, but irritated. Edith went on loving; she too could not be stopped.

We barge into other people's lives, desperate to make ourselves heard, to have our feelings noticed, our rage and blame taken into account. Sophie had just done the same thing. She discounted the Sibyl's point of view entirely. And had no idea whatsoever that she had unleashed a hornet's nest of jealousy in the pounding breast of Edith Simcox. Sophie whirled through the front doors of her host's mansion leaving Edith stranded in the street, hoping to snatch a word with the coachman, the housemaid or the delivery boy, anyone she could pump for information. What luck! Here comes a florist with a barrow, bearing red tulips.

The lady of the house? No, she's already gone to the Museum for the ceremony. The lady who just went in? That's the German Countess, married to the famous archaeologist who found the statue. I've brought these flowers for her. Ah! Edith had read all about the discovery in *The Times*. So that woman is the radiant Countess who dominated the photographs. She's far more beautiful than I am. Younger, too, and much more fashionable. Edith charged back towards the Priory, that magnetic lodestone upon which all her thoughts were bent. She patrolled the far side of the street, studying the bedroom blinds, ignoring the oncoming rain.

Edith loved the Sibyl too well to reproach her, even in the privacy of her most secret thoughts, but the galling facts could neither be avoided nor denied. The Countess had walked straight in, when she, Edith, the devoted lover, with years of faithful service behind her, had been unkindly refused entrance. This cross must be borne, but it proved a heavy load to haul up and down the street as the chilly spring evening drew on, with all its lights and shadows.

We think of the Victorians facing death in a rustle of black plumes, many carriages trailing the wet streets in procession, black bows tied to the cab drivers' whips, the blinds and curtains firmly closed. A murmur of gloomy prayers, black crêpe dresses, and weeping mourners dominate the domestic interiors of Victorian novels, pages littered with deathbed scenes and uplifting final moments. They are all there on my bookshelves, desperate to convince me that every single cliché is perfectly true. No one seems to die in a torrent of faeces or yellow vomit. And even if they do there's a cleaned-up lying in state, usually in the dining room or the front parlour, the heavy scent of lilies cloaking the sweeter stench of putrefaction. Only the very rich bothered to have their dead embalmed.

Who faces death in the triumphant certainty that they are bound for better shores than these? No more did then than do now, I rather think. Frederick William Robertson, an Anglican priest, for whom Emma Darwin, beloved wife of Charles, had a good deal of time, preached the following sermon in 1852.

> Talk as we will of immortality, there is an obstinate feeling we cannot master that we end in death; and that may be felt together with the firmest belief of a resurrection. Brethren, our faith tells us one thing, and our sensations tell us another. Everyone who knows what faith is knows too what is the desolation of doubt. We pray till we begin to ask, Is there one who hears, or am I whispering to myself? We hear the consolation administered to the bereaved, and we see the coffin lowered into the grave, and the thought comes, What if all this doctrine of a life to come be but the dream of man's imaginative mind?

If men of faith were men of doubt, how did our agnostic intellectuals of the 1870s face their own deaths, believing, as the Sibyl did, that this was the Final Parting from all that was dearly beloved, from familiar faces and scenes, from the cat and the furniture, shelves of fingered volumes, an unfinished manuscript, a garden where we once gathered in the roses? Were they heroes, facing the void? Did no one blink or flinch as the agony approached? Or were they all stalwart, proud and as courageous with certainty as Marcus Curtius, gazing into the Roman abyss, before he dared the final bound?

Nineteenth-century symptoms of illness are tantalisingly, indeed infuriatingly, vague. G.H. Lewes is often described as 'feeble', 'delicate' and 'ill'. Whereas the Sibyl suffered from dyspepsia, and disabling headaches: bad headache, ordinary headache, bilious headache, theatre headache and constant headache with added nausea. In addition, she came down with bodily malaise, feeling unwell, feebleness of body, constant dull pain, deep depression, feeling weak and generally ailing. In her Journal, on 1st January 1876, she records: 'All blessedness except health.' By 1877 the bulletins concerning health take a darker turn. 16th March: 'Since I last wrote G. has had an illness of rheumatic gout and I have had a visitation of my renal disorder, from which I am not yet free.' By June 1878 she reported that her Little Man was suffering from 'suppressed gout and feeling his inward economy all wrong'. In fact, George Lewes was dying from bowel cancer.

Lewes suffered from piles, cramp and diarrhoea, presumably streaked with blood. His pains, intermittent but severe, didn't stop him singing Rossini, with great spirit, but began to change his appearance. One of their visitors reported that Lewes looked as if he had been 'gnawed by rats'. Cancer, like tuberculosis, haunted the deathbeds of all sorts and conditions of men, one of the many nineteenth-century diseases that dared not speak its name. Sir James Paget examined his wealthy patient and described his terminal ailment as 'thickening of the mucous membrane'. The black cells cast their shadow through his body, and began to creep inside, then occupy all his vital organs. Astonishingly, his energy survived. On 21st November 1878, after an encouraging visit from Sir James, Lewes drove out to post parts of the manuscript of what was to be the Sibyl's last book, to Blackwood in Edinburgh. But on the next day, 22nd November 1878, when Edith Simcox finally gained admittance to The Presence, the joyous pleasure she anticipated lay already dashed to pieces. 'Monday came at last, but hardly the greeting I had dreamt of: the first thing I saw was Lewes stretched upon the sofa, and in concern for him I lost something of the sight of her.' Edith realised at once that he was dying.

She laid siege to the housemaids. 26th November 1878: 'On Monday the doctors were there and he was very ill. It seems that he must die – and then her life is one blank agony and – if that mattered – mine too.' 28th November 1878: 'This morning Sir James Paget thought him a shade better. I did not dare to go and ask and came to the house this morning with a deadly fear – perhaps he will recover? I dare not hope, I only know that if he dies the world will have nothing left for her.' Lewes himself, who had not been told that he was dying, still hoped that his illness, which he described as 'a fluctuating sickness with much malaise and headache', would pass. But by nightfall on 29th November 1878 he had begun to sink away. At half past three in the afternoon of 30th November Edith Simcox roused the white-faced maid, who told her that there was no hope. Edith waited on the road, walking back and forth. The doctors gathered in their carriages and stood talking outside the gates. Edith approached them. 'I asked was there no hope. A tall man – probably Sir James Paget – answered kindly, None: he is dying – dying quickly.'

Her next entry on 1st December reads as follows: 'He died at a quarter to six – an hour and a half after I left the house. She sees no one, is in hysteric agonies. I can only think of her with dread.' George Henry Lewes, the ape-like dancing master, the vibrant buoyant Little Man, cheated of the knowledge of his own death, and yet extravagantly mourned, was swept away to be buried in the Dissenters' section of Highgate Cemetery. Mrs. Lewes did not attend the funeral, but Edith Simcox visited the grave on 5th December 1878, and found 'the desolate new mound. Two white wreaths were on the grave and

I laid mine of heather between them.' Edith Simcox remained faithful, not just to the Sibyl, but to both of them.

❧

Max arrived in London early in January 1879 to participate in the preparations for an International Archaeological Congress. He received stern orders from Wolfgang to pay his sorrowful respects to the grief-stricken author, and thus Max found himself standing at the Priory gates, mid-morning, in bright frost and sunlight, gazing up at the pointed gables and dark thorns of the barren roses. He rang the bell and stood for several minutes, shifting his weight from foot to foot. A tall man with a reddish beard, dressed in deep mourning, came striding towards him. Enter John Walter Cross, financial adviser to the Lewes household, and so intimately cherished that the Sibyl called him 'Dearest Nephew'. Cross clearly counted as family to the older couple. The two men identified themselves, then shook hands. Nobody came to the door.

'She sees no one,' said Cross, looking up at the shuttered windows, 'but I have called almost daily.'

'My brother sent our condolences of course, as soon as we heard.' Max did not want the financial adviser to think that the Sibyl's German publishers had been remiss or in any way disrespectful to the sacred memory of the Beloved Husband. 'But we did not even know that Mr. Lewes had passed away until we read it in the German papers. He is of course very famous in our country as the biographer of Goethe. Many of his works are translated. Mr. and Mrs. Lewes are both greatly honoured and respected in Berlin.'

Johnny Cross's expression of set gravity mellowed a little, gratified. The maid appeared at last in a gust of steam, and reported that her mistress had been out that morning and taken a turn in the garden. She felt the better for it.

'Give her our love,' said Johnny Cross, and Max left his card, unable to think of anything suitable to write upon the back. In fact, he breathed again, mightily relieved that the Sibyl would admit no one. What could he say to her? He had not set eyes upon the lady since that fatal night in the autumn gardens at Stuttgart. Nor had he ever read that loving message of reconciliation and forgiveness which Sophie flung back in her face. He had prepared a formal speech of course, but now, delighted that it would not be delivered, he turned to his companion of the doorstep, with a face glowing in the cold. After a moment's discussion the two men decided to take advantage of the bright day and walk across Regent's Park together.

Something hectic and unsettled emerged from the strange huge man. His powerful physique, like a great cone of polished obsidian, seemed to shudder as he marched ahead, leading the way across the bridge. Two long lines of grief in his vigorous young cheeks gleamed stark and deep as he raised his face to the sun. He adapted his stride so that he and Max walked abreast and made it clear that he wanted to talk. Max knew how to listen, and his hesitant formal English transformed him, on this occasion, into a professional confessor. Thus, the sad torrent of misery that poured forth from the Sibyl's financial adviser, a normally reticent man, fell upon sympathetic ears.

'My dearest mother,' murmured Johnny Cross. His voice broke and his stride faltered, Max supported him gently at the elbow. 'My very dearest mother lay mortally ill just as Mr. Lewes sank close to death, and within a mere nine days she was gone. Forgive me, sir, the burden of my loss weighs hard upon me.'

He produced a handkerchief. Max concluded a rapid diagnosis of the case. Mr. John Walter Cross had lost both a father and a mother in the space of a fortnight, and was now clinging, desperate, to the wreckage of this last attachment. The Sibyl, he went on to explain, meant everything to him, he had counted upon her understanding love, and comfortable words, but the dark veil of mutual grief had descended between them.

'Our lives are utterly changed. We have both lost our counsellors, our daily support. Even ordinary objects become double in our vision, sir. I cannot look upon cushions, teapots, an armchair, without missing the hand, the bent head and white hair beneath the cap, that should be there, and no longer is. Mrs. Lewes cannot bear to leave the rooms they once shared. How well I understand her.'

The pipes at the Priory froze and burst in the blizzards of that freezing winter. Cross narrated this disaster, that would once have shaken the Sibyl to the core, but now household matters shrank to trivialities, for her 'everlasting winter has set in'. Marian Evans Lewes now confronted the starkest, most brutal trial of her entire life. The Final Parting that she had so dreaded, the rupture that wrenched her fragile happiness from her grasp, had come at last, leaving her naked of all philosophy. She reached the bleakest of all shores and gazed upon the endless ocean, until love and fame sank to nothingness.

'She is very wise,' Johnny Cross continued, 'a wise woman indeed. But she is not herself. Our friends are all anxious at this absolute, enforced seclusion. Her nerves are shattered. And I fear that the servants are not discreet. I am told that howls and screams are heard from her apartments. She will not be consoled.'

Johnny Cross would not be consoled either. He paused, tottered, and passed a hand across his forehead.

'Sir, you are not well.' Max transferred his walking stick to the other hand and braced himself, should the giant begin to topple, right there amidst the barren trees and crusted mud upon the pathway. But Johnny Cross recovered himself.

'You are very kind. I'm afraid that I have burdened you most disgracefully with my troubles. The sensation of bereaved disbelief is ever present. I sleep little. And my love for her is boundless. She is an exceptional woman.'

Max no longer knew if Cross was speaking of his dead mother or the living Sibyl.

'Mrs. Lewes is admired by all who know her,' said Max in lowered, cautious tones.

And then again, he saw before him the great forehead, the head inclined, the magnificent clear grey eyes, the godlike sensation of understanding and forgiveness, the certainty of unconditional love. She looks into all hearts, knows all desires before they are spoken. She traces the patterns of our very thoughts, before they take shape within our brains. This stranger to me loves her beyond measure. He is in thrall to the woman who is all pity and compassion, the woman who will have forgiven me for my indiscretion and my too hasty words before I slept that night. He loves her as I loved her. And then at last Max could be honest with himself. He loves her, and I still do.

❧

They were followed, of course, by a not-so-young woman stepping smartly down the winter paths, pattering over the frosty grass and turned earth. Edith Simcox hovered too far back to catch a word of this exchange, but she deduced the intimacy of the conversation from the way the two men leaned together, their hats almost touching.

END OF CHAPTER SIXTEEN

CHAPTER SEVENTEEN

in which Fortune once more turns her Wheel.
A Birth and a Marriage are joyously reported.

Well, our story has reached the freezing days of January 1879. The Sibyl, shrouded in grief, will see no one. Johnny Cross has poured his pain all over Max, the handsome German archaeologist whom he does not expect he will ever see again. Edith, paddling in filthy slush, stands guard outside the Priory, watching her Beloved's windows. And in the warm rooms of the Berlin household at Wilhelmplatz, battened down against blizzards, for there is a snowstorm coming, the drifts are already burying the northern forests, Sophie strolls to and fro, under her mother's watchful eyes. She is nine months gone, her belly is huge; the waters may break at any time and the miracle of birth will begin.

All Sophie's usual activities have been curtailed or completely forbidden. Her only consolation, for riding has been out of the question for many months, is that ice and winter darkness would make anything other than a trot round the sawdust in the covered school quite impossible. She is reading a letter from Max, already on his way home from London, describing the soft white turning to foul mud in the London streets. He records as much as he can remember of the curious encounter with Mr. John Walter Cross, the sad man, hunched and wretched as a sick crow, tottering across Regent's Park. He describes his relief at being spared an interview with the grieving

Sibyl. He has neither set eyes upon her, nor exchanged one word. What could I have said, Sophie?

What indeed? In her expectant happiness even Sophie relents a little in her resentment towards the Sibyl. Years have gone past, and there have been no repercussions whatsoever, concerning the opening scenes of *Daniel Deronda*. Her father has discussed the book with Herr Klesmer, who roars audibly in praise of the author's depiction of the Jews. The child kicks her hand, the very hand in which she holds the letter. Sophie grins, satisfied, and strokes her belly.

'Shall I ring for chocolate and cakes, dear?' Her mother senses a shift in the emotional backwash from Sophie's skirts. 'Your father will soon be here.'

'I am carrying a son, Mama,' declares Sophie, preening her head and neck as she turns, and letting her shawl fall back.

'Is that so? Well, you are certainly big enough for a boy.' Her mother hopes for a grandson, but is too tactful to say so. She pulls the bell rope, and adds thoughtfully, 'But you never can tell. I was quite big with you.'

❧

And at the same moment on 22nd January 1879, Marian Evans Lewes wrote to Mr. John Walter Cross: 'Dearest Nephew, Sometime, if I live, I shall be able to see you – perhaps sooner than anyone else. But not yet. Life seems to get harder instead of easier.' For indeed it did. G.H. Lewes had made his will twenty years earlier, in 1859. He bequeathed his copyrights in all his work to his three sons and all his other property to Mary Ann Evans, Spinster, who was also named as the sole executrix. His own estate was worth less than £2,000, but her securities were worth more that £30,000. Both houses were registered in his name. Thus the Sibyl, wealthy as she was, owned nothing in her own right, beyond her personal effects. A flutter of litigation must ensue, deeds of transfer, and rearrangements had to be negotiated and put into effect. The Sibyl emerged from her grief-stricken seclusion to organise her accounts. And so, at last, by deed poll, she legally adopted the name of Lewes. This little lie, which had served her so well for decades, became at last a partial truth. Now she really was called Mary Ann Evans Lewes. There were only two witnesses to all these transactions: Lewes's son Charles and John Walter Cross.

On 7th February 1879 she wrote tentatively to Cross, summoning him into The Presence.

> In a week or two I think I shall want to see you. Sometimes, even now I have a longing, but it is immediately counteracted by a fear. The perpetual mourner – the grief that can never be healed – is innocently enough felt to be wearisome by the rest of the world. And my sense of desolation increases. Each day seems a new beginning – a new acquaintance with grief.

At this stage she was still signing her letters 'Your affectionate aunt, M.E.L.' He came to see her on Sunday 23rd February. She had withered into a heap of bones.

But now the Priory doors had opened again to friends and supporters of Lewes's many causes. And therefore also opened to scroungers and parasites, presenting themselves as either indigent or simply presumptuous relatives. Quick, let's touch the rich lady for cash, while she's in a vulnerable state. Play on her famous sympathy for the needy and the destitute; get in there before the others do. Lewes's nephew demanded £100 as ballast, 'to save him from reducing his capital'. She wrote a cheque for £50 on the spot, but someone must have told him what sort of leech he was, as he returned the cheque on the following morning, with an apology. Bessie Rayner Parkes, now Mrs. Louis Belloc, an old friend of many years past, had no such scruples, and requested £500. Herbert Lewes's widow Eliza set sail from Natal, with her insidiously named offspring, Marian and George, expecting to move in with the famous wealthy novelist, and be set up comfortably for life. The vultures had gathered in force.

The Sibyl panicked and sent a desperate note to Johnny Cross at his office. 'Dearest N, I am in dreadful need of your counsel. Pray come to me when you can – morning, afternoon, or evening. I shall dismiss anyone else. Your much-worried aunt.'

She needed not only advice, but also a man of the world who could deal with the voracious, encroaching predatory menace. Johnny Cross had known George Lewes; he was already inside the gates, part of her innermost circle, one of her most devoted followers, acquainted with all her business affairs. When he confessed that he was reading Dante's *Inferno*, with the help of Carlyle's translation, she exclaimed, 'Oh, I must read that with you.' And so the intimate little sessions, with the Sibyl as *magister* and the red-bearded young man as the devoted pupil, began.

Nessun maggior dolore
Che ricordarsi del tempo felice
Nella miseria.

(There is no greater sadness than remembering joyous times in times of grief.)

But her time of joy, like the dust from a chariot seen in the distance, came galloping towards her. By the end of May 1879, installed in her summer residence in Witley, she played the piano once more. Here, she received her frequent visitor, free from the surveillance of the ubiquitous Edith Simcox. Johnny Cross fell, irrevocably, under her spell.

And now we, her readers, encased in future times, become the secret voyeurs. Our moral imperatives are not the same as those of her friends, her admirers and her first critics. We look back, digging in the letters and in the massive three volumes of biographical material, carefully edited by Cross, those laconic Journals where one or two words are lifted out of context, polished and surveyed, and made to mean all kinds of unimaginable things. For sometimes that's all she wrote: one or two words. On Monday 2nd June 1879 she still refers to him as 'Johnny', but by Tuesday 30th September he has become 'Mr. Cross'. Something happened in between. But what? Could it be the 'decisive conversation', mentioned on Thursday 21st August? And what is the significance of that wonderful sentence from her entry on Wednesday 8th October 1879: 'Joy came in the evening.'

I ponder the recorded tributes from our predecessors, her first readers. On Tuesday 29th July 1879 she received a 'beautiful anonymous letter from New Zealand'. But on Wednesday 1st October 1879, 'letter from a madman in Kansas'. So it seems to me that we can choose who we become in relation to her. Do I send her a beautiful anonymous bouquet and wish her every happiness with her handsome financial adviser? Or do I join the madman in Kansas and speculate fiercely on her strange behaviour? What can she think she is doing: inveigling into her web a man twenty years younger that herself, whose closest attachment up to this point appears to have been his mother?

One of her most subtle readers, Rosemarie Bodenheimer, in her book, *The Real Life of Mary Ann Evans*, writes: 'In fact, the Cross marriage is still perfectly misunderstandable because it has no history that would allow us to interpret a choice according to its consequences.' Well said. And there is plenty of evidence there in the archival record to fuel our misunderstandings. The blunt facts are these: on Friday 9th April 1880 she writes: 'Sir James Paget came to see me. My marriage decided.' Note that these two events, the doctor's visit and the momentous decision, may not be related, for some have supposed that they are. She doesn't even say to whom she has decided to be married. Well, why should she say? She wasn't writing for us. And it isn't 'our' marriage, but 'mine'. To me, that does seem interesting. 'My marriage'! On 6th May 1880 she writes:

> Married this day at 10.15 to John Walter Cross, at St George's, Hanover Square. Present, Charles [G.H. Lewes's eldest son], who gave me away, Mr. and Mrs. Druce, Mr. Hall, Willie, Mary,

> Eleanor and Florence. We went back to the Priory, where we signed our wills. Then we started for Dover, and arrived there a little after 5 o'clock.

She signed herself, triumphantly, legally, married at last: 'Mary Ann Cross'. Then she fled away on the boat bound for Europe, avoiding all her friends and the inevitable invidious public comment. Wherefore to Dover? Twenty-five years earlier, she had eloped to the Continent with a married man, trailing scandal in her wake. Now she did the same thing again, creating another interesting ripple of censorious gossip by her legal marriage to a man young enough to be her son.

Johnny Cross, years later, had this to say about their wedding journey through France to Italy:

> I had never seen my wife out of England, previous to our marriage, except the first time in Rome when she was suffering. My general impression, therefore, had been that her health was always very low, and that she was almost constantly ailing. I was the more surprised, after our marriage, to find that from the day she set her foot on Continental soil, till the day she returned to Witley, she was never ill – never even unwell. She began at once to look many years younger.

Oh, did she indeed? I see Mrs. John Walter Cross striding through galleries and churches, marching into museums and cathedrals, carrying Murray and Kugler as guides, once more mistress of the plot, educating her ignorant young companion on points of taste and judgement. And I see Johnny Cross, trailing in the wake of mia Donna, the Sibyl herself, once more resplendent, authoritative, powerful – that's My Lady!

But what has happened in Berlin? For we abandoned Sophie pages ago, big as a house, but confident and fearless in the face of her confinement. Ah, when has Sophie von Hahn ever shown anything but undaunted, careless courage in the face of high fences, high stakes at the gaming tables, or famous English writers? Her waters broke in the night, as she thrashed in her bed, unable to make herself comfortable. Her mother, sleeping in the next room with the door open, screeched for the midwife, who was already downstairs, preparing hot water and clean towels. All the lights in the house appeared in the windows. Max, nursing a minor hangover, sent for the doctor, who traipsed through the snow and arrived at six o' clock in the yellow dark. By that time all the screaming and bloodletting were well and truly over. The afterbirth shot out, and Sophie, indignant at how much the entire process had hurt, despite an elevating mixture of rum and chloral, was cradling her son, Leo, with sinister tenacity. The child, a substantial kicking creature, bright red, wrinkled and grunting, opened his tiny, toothless jaws and yawned.

'You can't hold him yet,' Sophie snapped at Max. 'It's not your turn.'

The midwife, educated in modern medical science, made everybody scrub their hands before they touched the baby. But Max's first adoring kiss engulfed the tiny face in a gust of cigar smoke and alcohol. The old Count rushed down to his cellars and opened a bottle of vintage champagne, nursed, cherished and readied in hope that the first child would be a son. His grandson, and named Leopold, after his own father! Max, my boy, congratulations!

'And what about a glass for me too? I did all the work.' Sophie tried to sit up in bed and failed, her genitals still stinging from the pure spirits with which the midwife had tenderly purged every fold.

'No wine,' commanded the midwife, 'just water and a little warm milk.'

Sophie wrinkled her nose.

Her mother crept in later, once the midwife, recuperating in the kitchens, had left the field clear.

'Here you are, darling. Just half a glass, to build you up a bit. And to celebrate Leo's arrival.'

A winter baby, born on the eve of Candlemas, when the sap stirs in the earth, and the first birds, far away in Africa, stretch out their wings, dreaming of return.

END OF CHAPTER SEVENTEEN

CHAPTER EIGHTEEN

takes place in Venice.

Max managed to reduce their baggage train to three servants: a nursemaid for Leo, a lady's maid for Sophie – and Karl. Karl served as Max's valet, and the family's *garde-du-corps*, but he also dealt with the luggage, tipped the boatmen and porters, even if they were unhelpful and rude, sought out their carriage on trains and shovelled them all in, one by one, procured fresh horses as necessary, and purchased cigarettes for Max. Karl fixed broken things, from parasols to carriage wheels. His shifty, flickering eyes passed over everything at speed, judging scale, volume, distance. The luggage – two huge trunks, several leather cases, three voluminous hatboxes, and a carpetbag – always fitted perfectly into increasingly smaller spaces. Thus, when their party disembarked at the last station before the railway bridge across the lagoon, accompanied by a vulgar horde of jolly English tourists, all screaming with pleasure at their first sight of the distant city, floating in mist, Karl had already located the tiny port, secured the first two gondolas and stacked their chests and boxes neatly in each prow, while the gondoliers leaned on their oars, smoking.

The city, transformed during the Austrian occupation, now had a brand-new railway station and a new bridge, levelled like an arrow to its heart. But the old Count, whose memories of Venice were at least thirty years out of date, insisted that they must approach the city across the green waters and see it first as the painters did, Serenissima, caught between water and sky, palaces and towers rising from the mud. Be sure you take the gondolas, there's nothing like it. You'll be floating into Paradise. So here they were, negotiating a musky little channel between flags and bulrushes; the solid waterlogged stakes, which marked out the deeper waterways, sticking up like cloves. The prows' silver teeth wheeled towards the rocking open deep of the lagoon. Sophie ripped off her gloves, leaned out of the closed black cabin, and trailed her fingers in the lapping green.

'Oh Max!' She gazed at him, her eyes blazing. 'It's warm. It's actually warm.'

All the long northern winter dissolved into this extraordinary wash of opaque green. He gazed at her sensual white fingers stroking the water, the other arm firmly coiled around her son, whose desire to plunge into the deepening lagoon now expressed itself in a series of shouts. Leo could almost speak clearly, albeit with a very limited vocabulary, and was beginning, at fourteen months, to totter at alarming speeds. He now banged his heels against the red-carpeted boards of the gondola.

'*Schnuh, Schnuh*!' he clamoured, his version of '*Schnell! Schnell!*' in a demand for more speed. He had inherited Sophie's decisiveness.

The second gondola, at first close behind, now surged past them. The two maids, neither of whom could swim, clutched one another in distress. The gondoliers, whooping across the heads of their passengers, proposed a race to amuse the gentry, and increased the pace and the strange, sweeping scoop of their oars. Karl lashed the trunks with an extra cord and told the shrieking maids to shut up. The two gondolas, now side by side, bucked and dipped, pummelling the swell. The terrified maids wailed in horror, but their cries, engulfed by the warm wind, faded and died. Max lit a cigar, steadied his hat and grinned at Sophie, who pushed open the slats and the little doors so that the warm air of the green lagoon blew through the cabin. Still clutching Leo with one arm, she waved the other high above her head, her lace sleeve falling back to the elbow, her skin white from winter. Then suddenly, with fabulous ferocity, she screamed, '*Vai, Vai, Vai*!' at the gondolier, as if she had wagered all her fortune on the outcome of the race. A little rush of spray caught the wind; the oarsman leaned into the curve as the gondola skimmed and shuddered over the gentle, rocking tide. Max watched her face, white and flickering beneath her veils, her features awash with joy.

❦

The Hotel Danieli turned its blind, shuttered eyes across the lagoon towards the ivory façade of San Giorgio Maggiore. The gondolas slipped into a tiny channel on the right of the hotel before a damp green jetty where a fleet of uniformed staff fought one another to bear the family and all their luggage into an Oriental interior of arcades, decorated pierced screens, and a lopsided flight of stone stairs. Max checked the guest list to see who was already there. To whom should he send his card? Here were one or two acquaintances, better known to the Countess, and an elderly Professor of Natural History, whose lectures he had attended in Leipzig. The usual medley of rich English aristocrats and a welter of bourgeois names, some of whom they had already encountered at the various resorts, from Interlaken onwards, into the Austrian Alps. He decided on French as the more tactful language in which to address the receptionists, despite the evident invasion of Prussian tourists, and enquired after the sea-bathing facilities on the Lido. Sophie had taken up swimming, equipped with a hat that looked like a fruit basket, and could not be dissuaded from experimenting with bathing machines.

And so began their long warm days of idleness and insouciance. Sophie conducted her usual arguments with the hotel kitchens. What should Leo be allowed to eat, and what, under no circumstances, should he be allowed to touch? She had her fish brought to her at the table, in a raw state, then sniffed and prodded the blank-eyed slab, before giving her gladiator's thumb that all was well and that the sturgeon, turbot, tunny, mullet or sole, for which the lagoon was famous, could now be safely cooked. She listened carefully to the chef's suggestions at breakfast every day, then countered him with proposals of her own. The kitchen staff cheekily called her 'la Contessa', with a roll of the eyes, and were all delighted when it turned out that Frau Maximilian Reinhardt August Duncker and Sophie, Gräfin von Hahn, were actually one and the same. Were they really married? Dozens of clients in the hotel were not who they claimed to be. Everyone, from the manager downwards, shrugged and carried on. Is their cash real and is their credit good? What else matters?

But some very surprising guests strolled into the main salon to enjoy the small chamber orchestra, which performed on a little dais, surrounded by palms in gigantic Asiatic jars. Max found himself bowing to Hans Meyrick, now a rich and successful society portrait painter, on holiday in Venice with a lavish, if elderly, English widow.

'Stroke of luck for me, old chap,' grinned Meyrick, unashamed. 'She wanted a portrait of her dog, and I'd almost finished it when the dog died. So now we're in Venice to assuage her grief. I think she's already mightily consoled.'

'Who on earth is that?' Sophie noted the painter's easy familiarity with all the English, and his expensive, glossy clothes. But she no longer recognised her Homburg dancing partner.

'I suppose we can't be too particular about the company we keep when we're on holiday,' said Max ruefully. 'This hotel takes in all sorts.'

'*Glocken! Glocken*!' yelled Leo, who possessed his own set of bells, and adored the bells of Venice, which sounded on the hour, all across the city.

John Murray's *Handbook for Travellers in Northern Italy* (1877, fourteenth edition) noted the Danieli's slippage from the first rank of hotels in Venice and recommended six other establishments, including the Hôtel de l'Europe (good situation, fine view – no pension). Professor Kurt Marek, accompanied by his London entourage, intended timing their arrival to coincide with Max and Sophie's visit to the Paradise of Cities. But they had decided against the Danieli and were booked into the Hôtel de l'Europe. And so Max set out through the labyrinth of streets and bridges to find out when they were expected. He plunged down a tiny slit between two leaning walls of stone. Within minutes he was lost.

And then another kind of Venice, not the one described in Ruskin, or in Murray's *Handbook*, began to observe him carefully, from behind the shutters and from the top of damp steps. Mid-morning, and a bright blue day far above, yet even the thunderous church bells seemed to retreat and withdraw. The filth underfoot matched the strange stench from the canals, now narrow as arrow shafts and bloodily discoloured, not the fabulous shimmering green which stretched away into the haze, visible from their balconies on the Riva degli Schiavoni. Max stopped, looked deliberately about him to make sure that he was not being followed, and lit a cigarette. He sensed at once that he was being watched.

But no one else appeared behind him. He was alone in an obscure narrow *calle* in a city he did not understand. He waited for a moment, trying to identify the smells, and shrinking in disgust from the piles of discarded clothing, paper and faeces heaped in damp corners. A rat, unhurried and unafraid, slunk past his boots and sank into the canal.

'*Scusi, signor.*' The low voice materialised beside him in the doorway. A thin black hand with painted red nails and many bracelets presented an unlit cigarette. Max smiled. So! He had discovered the Venetian pleasure grounds, quite by accident. No immediate danger threatened, and all he stood to lose was a match. The hand brushed his fingers with practised and suggestive gentleness. The voice tried several languages.

'*Merci.* Thank you. *Danke schön.*'

I should walk on now. Nod. Bow very slightly. But something about the prostitute's throat caught his attention; a sequence of smooth dark hollows, visible through the fine white lace across the shoulders. The figure in the doorway, veiled, exotically plumed, overdressed in red satin with white lace trim, that had, in places, seen better days, leaned back, blowing a fine white puff of smoke into his face. The tobacco masked the putrid odour of the canal. He glimpsed two red eyes behind the dim lace, patterned with tiny flowers, summing him up. I am being priced. The rich German visitor is hooked and landed. How much should I ask? Then one hand reached up to lift the veil and he found himself gazing into an extraordinary black face, exquisitely fine, wide, high bones, Oriental rather than European, with a long curved nose, huge eyes, the lids painted red.

'How much?' asked Max, mesmerised.

'The signor will pay.'

Then the black hand shot out like a clamp, catching Max's grey-gloved fingers and forcing them downwards into the satin folds. Max fumbled for the prostitute's genitals, alarmed at his own instant arousal, and without thinking, stepped into the shadowed doorway. A shiver of shock and pure, unambiguous desire flooded through his arse and legs as he clasped two swinging testicles and a hardening penis. The creature before him, both woman and man, looked up into his face, offering a challenging flash of gold, the lower lip pierced. Max's hat slipped back and wedged between his head and the wall as he sucked the dark mouth and smooth cheeks. The prostitute flicked the un-smoked cigarette into the narrow channel of water, unbuttoned the client's trousers with three swift tugs, then rubbed the engorged pink tip of his sex up to a groaning climax, as rapid as it was intense. Max's mind clung to the last sane thought he had. I should walk on now. Nod. Bow very slightly. Leave at once. The sharp smell of the prostitute's body mingled with the rotting stench from the alley's corners.

He parted with many more Reichsmarks than he would have given in Germany and received in return some sweetly whispered directions to the Hôtel de l'Europe, that fronted the Grand Canal, but whose back door opened on to another little *calle*, less than ten minutes' walk away. The Venetian pleasure grounds were all around him, nuzzling the theatres, galleries, churches, restaurants, hotels. One step aside from the thronging sights, the miraculous monuments to Art and God, lay the unlit places, where the gas light never came, where no one swept the stone pavements, where the gleaming belly of the city thrived on piled refuse and passing wealth.

Dazed and horrified at himself, Max strolled into the grand foyer of the Hôtel de l'Europe, aware that he had stepped on to a stage lit for the performance, and that he was only playing a part. Professor Marek and his family, five in all, were expected within days. They had reached Innsbruck on 31st May. Max flicked through the list of visitors, looking for German guests. As his eyes skimmed down the residents he passed over a common enough English name; among the seven families who had checked into the hotel the day before, Wednesday 2nd June 1880, was a couple without children: Mr. and Mrs. J.W. Cross.

❧

Apart from brief canters round the paddock on her aunt's estate and one abortive trip to the opera where her concern for her son forced her to abandon the celebrated soprano in the interval, Sophie never let Leo out of her sight. They employed a nursemaid, who adored him, and accompanied her to church and on walks through the parks and gardens. They both enjoyed pushing the new, London-built perambulator, a Gothic device, with a menacing black hood and giant wheels, suspended like a carriage, to ensure maximum comfort and a rocking sensation for the miraculous infant. The old Countess viewed the contraption with horror and declared that it resembled a sarcophagus on wheels.

'Nonsense, Mama. It's the latest thing.'

Sophie was determined to raise a modern baby. She investigated all the most recent methods and gadgets. Her son shared pride of place with the horses as her greatest love, to be fed, groomed, watered and exercised. He accompanied her everywhere. Where he could not be received, she would not go. Max found himself diminished in consequence; she asked for Leo first.

But now, in Venice, away from home for the first time in years, and confident that the child, who shook off every illness with energetic rapidity, was happy and safe, she dared to leave him for a few hours and arranged to meet Max in the Accademia. Whoever passed through the floating paradise without inspecting the pictures? She stepped briskly into their gondola, arranging her creamy veils and shawls against the sharp wind gusting across the lagoon. Sophie did not care to negotiate the hordes of vendors and beggars who clustered round the doors of the hotels and the Basilica. One importunate woman had dared to stroke Leo's head. Sophie poked her savagely with the point of her parasol, but immediately thereafter, horribly penitent at her own lack of charity, had given the shrivelled creature a coin. The Countess von Hahn developed a metaphysical repulsion for poverty and grovelling abjection; a quality directly related to the fact that she had been born into a wealthy household and lacked for nothing. The beggars disgusted her, especially those who claimed to be abandoned soldiers, and who displayed their sabre scars and pink stumps, all that remained of their amputated limbs. The world settled back into beauty, light and distance from the rocking, dipping roll of the black gondola. The appalling beggars remained on shore and the distant domes, *palazzi* and *campanili*, which, if inspected closely, appeared dilapidated, speckled with fungi and rogue weeds, glowed once more, as alluring as their reputations, exotic, ravishing.

Sophie tramped into the Stygian shades of the Accademia and tried hard, in the half-light and dingy caverns, to make out what she was supposedly admiring on the walls. The rooms were dense with tourists, clutching guidebooks and parasols. Some traipsed faithfully after a licensed *cicerone* who explained the gloomy beauties high above them. Sophie attached herself to one such party for a moment, but rapidly concluded that the guide, assuming the idiocy of everyone clustered before him, simply handed out a basic Bible lesson. He explained who everyone was in the frozen scenes from Scripture, and tried to guess what they might be doing. She loitered near the group to hear his explanation of the vast painting by Paolo Veronese of *The Last Supper.* This gigantic work, apparently filled with heretical elements, got the artist into trouble. When he was ordered to alter the painting at his own expense Veronese simply changed the title. And wrote in Latin at the top of a pillar: '*fecit D. Covi Magnum Levi-Luca Cap. 5*' – Luke's Gospel Chapter 5, Levi held a great banquet for the Lord. And so the painting became known as *Feast in the House of Levi.* Sophie gazed at two young black men on the far left of the painting, their faces oddly modern and familiar. It's more interesting to look at the margins, she thought, and set about peering into the corners of the giant tableaux, ignoring the dim murk far above.

Eventually she found herself seated before a little row of three tender virgins by Giovanni Bellini, which glowed, small, luminous, and pleasantly within reach. Still no sign of Max! One of the Madonnas sported a floating row of six bright red bodiless cherubs, wedged on clouds, with dwarf wings sprouting from their puffy necks. All three women, dressed in red and blue, clutched their tiny doomed sons with long gentle fingers. What would it be like to love your son, as I love Leo, and know that you would see him die?

A shiver ran down the back of her neck. She pulled her ivory skirts close around her knees and bit her lip. Then she heard a woman's low voice, speaking English, almost whispering.

'The motif of the red cherubs comes from the Pesaro *Coronation* of 1474; they symbolise the divine passion, but also earthly love. And if, my dearest, you come a little closer, for the light is really not very good, you will see the Madonna's particular symbols worked into the landscape behind her. There, that little fortified city symbolises her virginity. She is the fortress that is never taken. This is an exquisite piece, as is the *Madonna degli Alberetti, the Madonna of the Small Trees*, sadly in need of cleaning. The painting was destined for private devotion and almost certainly had candles burning before it. Hence the darkened background. The trees, you can just see them, symbolise the Old and New Testament.'

Sophie froze as the couple passed before her, the elderly woman still slender and upright, her magnificent mane of hair thick and glossy, although streaked with grey. She leaned upon the arm of a much younger man, pale, but robust, his face covered with a thick, reddish-brown beard.

Sophie could not believe the apparition that had appeared before her: the Sibyl. But it was indeed the Sibyl, well out of widow's weeds.

The young woman pulled her veil discreetly over her face and bowed her head in careful homage to the *Madonna degli Alberetti*. But if this was the Sibyl, who was the man? She quizzed his profile, certain that she had never seen him before. The couple paused before the fourth small picture, not signed by Bellini, but attributed to him, his atelier and his collaborators. This discreet square portrait represented three figures in an arid landscape. Sophie buried her nose in the guide: Saint Mark, Saint Jerome and unknown devotee, oil on wood panel, acquired by donation, 1838, from Girolamo Contarini. She heard the man's deep tones, despite the fact that the couple had their backs to her. Two other tourists, a mother and daughter, lined up in front of the Madonnas. Sophie ducked behind them, still seated, her guide-book on her lap.

'And this one, my love? This is the very picture you spoke of?'

'It is indeed.'

Sophie leaned forwards, trying to catch every word as the low whisper flowed on.

'The subject is disputed and has caused many debates. It is in fact a representation of Lucian, the atheist poet and philosopher, whose works were rediscovered and attacked by the ecclesiastical authorities during the fifteenth century. The unknown devotee represents the Jewish maiden, Myriam. This is Saint Mark, who appears to be sharing his lion with the figure that is described in the catalogue as Saint Jerome. But you see, there is no cardinal's hat. Instead there are books, tablets and scrolls. It would be very unusual to have a young woman, albeit one that is richly dressed, as the devotee. The story goes that

Myriam escaped from Jerusalem with Saint Mark as her companion after the Crucifixion; they wandered the Mediterranean, preaching the Gospel of Christ. Myriam entered Lucian's household as a slave, and despite being very young, proved remarkable for her knowledge of languages and powers of healing. I often thought of her when I created Dinah in *Adam Bede*. Look at the way the philosopher inclines towards her. She became his adopted daughter. But he never converted to her faith.'

'The picture seems to suggest otherwise,' ventured the young man. Sophie noted how tenderly he clasped the Sibyl's hand, still encased in black lace mittens, despite the heat. 'He is pointing to Saint Mark.'

'And with the other hand he is indicating his own writing. The Jewish maid faced a choice: the passionate disciple or the Stoic philosopher. The painting depicts that moment of choice.'

Now she could see the Sibyl's long jaw, huge nose and terrifying smile. A wave of rage and repulsion, very similar to the rush of disgust she felt upon being accosted by stinking beggars, knocked Sophie into the shadows. Something indefinable and disturbing looked out from the Sibyl's grave eyes, and lurked in the fleeting smile. A fragile veil was lifted away from her forehead, magnifying the long, thin countenance, the massive jaw and the vast, expressive eyes. The lady is old. The lady is ugly. The lady has wonderful eyes.

'Ah, my dear, we know that he never became a Christian. He died a Roman, and a Roman's courageous death.'

The strange couple turned to continue their tour. Sophie, now transfixed with curiosity, slid stealthily after them, missing nothing, neither the loving pressure of the mittened hand, nor the gentle weight pressed upon the young man's arm. The last words she caught before they turned into the sculpture gallery clinched all her suspicions.

'To see these lovely things with you, my dearest, is a happiness beyond imagining. My joy is now complete.' The Sibyl delivered this declaration in seductive, lowered tones.

Sophie flattened herself against a priapic satyr on a plinth. 'My dearest'? 'Joy'? The Sibyl was childless. This man was young enough to be her son, yet there was no mistaking the sensual tenderness of her tones, or the enthralled devotion of her companion. This cannot be. And yet it is so – her husband hardly cold, and she has already taken another lover! She has hypnotised this young man, like a snake swallowing a toad. La belle dame sans merci hath thee in thrall. Sophie scudded through the galleries, racing for the exit. So that's what she was after when she wrote that loving little letter to my husband. She had her eye on Max! She wanted a younger man. The sexual triangle of *Middlemarch* and the entire scenario of Dorothea, Casaubon and Ladislaw shifted and warped in Sophie's racing speculations. The hideous Sibyl metamorphosed into a witch-like ancient scholar, a Morgana of the Black Arts, armed with her enchantments, predatory, concupiscent. The red-beard is her next chosen victim. Does Max know that she is in Venice? And what would he do if he did?

It never occurred to Sophie that the Sibyl could actually have married Mr. John Walter Cross.

❦

Max saw his wife leaving the galleries, veils flying, boots banging on the pavement, as if the Devil himself tickled her heels. He whirled down the steps after her, but lost her on the wharf, where the gondoliers jostled for customers and tourists thronged the entrance. Karl reappeared at his elbow and informed him that the Countess had taken their private gondola, and was, even now, being rowed back to the Danieli at speed. Max panicked. Leo must have suffered an attack or vomited. Somehow Sophie had received the message, abandoned their planned tour of the paintings, and hurtled back to her son's bedside. This was the only explanation!

'The child's ill, Karl! It must be the heat. Have me rowed across the Canal and we'll run to the hotel through the back streets. I'll never get a gondola.'

They tore across the Piazza San Marco, neck and neck, sweating profusely, sending clouds of pigeons into the air, disturbing the orchestra and jostling the tourists. Max stormed the little nursery on his way up to their apartments, and discovered Leo astride his rocking horse, shouting '*Schnuh! Schnuh!*' and charging directly into the first lines of the enemy host. No, he's not sick, exclaimed the nursemaid in alarm, scrutinising Leo at close range, in case she had missed the first symptoms.

Sophie had reached the hotel well before them. Max found her pacing the balcony, high above the bustle of the lagoon and the smoky little steamers that now chugged up and down the Grand Canal. She had discarded her hat and veils; she barely glanced at Max.

'But nothing's wrong with Leo!' cried Max, catching his wife in his arms.

'Of course not.' She shrugged him off. 'Why should there be?'

Then she stopped and turned, leaning on the stone balcony, and fixed Max with a peculiar glare. He felt the prostitute's hands on his body. I washed carefully. She can't know. Was I being watched? Who could have told her? It is impossible that she could know. Max blanched, then flushed red from forehead to moustache, the colour of a red-brick Gothic church.

'What is the matter, my dearest Sophie?'

He awaited judgement.

'Did you know that Mrs. Lewes is here? Here in Venice?'

'Mrs. Lewes?' Max stared at her.

The last conversation concerning the Sibyl that he could recall was with Wolfgang, who was desperately engaged in protracted negotiations to buy both the Continental reprint and the German translation rights to the *Impressions of Theophrastus Such*, as a single package. 'Lewes was a tight-fisted bastard, but at least you knew where you were. Now I've written to Charles Lewes and finally had a muddled reply from her. She'll get on top of things in the end. She always had a good head for figures. But it's all damnably inconvenient.' Wolfgang's voice receded into the distance, like a passing procession.

Sophie's green eyes snapped, accusing. Max told the truth.

'No, I didn't know. Wolfgang told me that she was sequestered in her summer residence at Witley, somewhere south of London.'

'Well, she isn't. She's here. And she's not alone.'

'Is she with Charles? You know, Lewes's eldest son. And his family?'

'She's with a young man. And it's clear, very clear, for I saw them in the gallery, that he's her *cavalier servente*. Isn't that what they call it in Venice? He's at least three decades younger than she is!'

Max froze, dumbfounded.

'Did you speak to her?' He now realised that he had no idea whether Sophie had ever set eyes upon the Sibyl. But perhaps the writer was famous enough to be recognised everywhere.

'Of course not. She didn't see me. And whoever that man was, he cannot have been Charles Lewes. She wouldn't kill off the father and then take up with the son. Even she wouldn't be that outrageous. She called him "dearest" and clutched his hand.'

But to Max, even in his state of sexual shock and relief that Sophie appeared not to know about his encounter with the black prostitute, this didn't seem decisive.

'I never saw her name in the *Gazzetta di Venezia*. I've been looking out for Professor Marek.'

'They'll be staying somewhere quiet, under an assumed name.'

'What did the man look like?'

'Tall. Big. Athletic. Vigorous. Smartly dressed. He had a great reddish-brown beard.'

Max suddenly saw the grief-stricken giant tottering across Regent's Park in mid-winter: Mr. John Walter Cross. And at the same moment he hallucinated the name he had casually passed over on the ledger before him: Mr. and Mrs. J.W. Cross.

'You're right, Sophie,' Max stammered. The taste of the prostitute's mouth rushed back to him, along with a tidal wave of shame. 'They're staying at the Hôtel de l' Europe –'

'So you did know!' She wheeled round and pounced upon him, snatching at his jacket, her blonde curls lashing his face. 'You did! You lied to me. You knew!'

Max, wrong-footed, taken aback, tried to stroke her shoulders. But she jibbed like a fiery pony, and lunged away.

'Don't touch me,' she yelled. The nursemaid appeared momentarily in the doorway, carrying Leo, and determined upon a parental health inspection, just to prove that there was nothing wrong. Upon seeing her employers flying at one another, all claws out, she retreated, head down, to find Karl, hoping to discover the roots of this uproar.

'Listen to me, Sophie. I didn't know. I really didn't. And I wouldn't lie to you.' (Well, not about that.) 'I'll write to Wolfgang at once and see if he knows anything. But I think the man is the one I told you about. Her financial adviser: Mr. John Walter Cross. The sad man who had recently lost his mother.'

'He's found another mother then, hasn't he?' snarled Sophie, scornfully, slamming her fists down upon the balustrade. 'One who calls him "my dearest" and "my joy"!'

She spun round again. 'That's what Mrs. Lewes wanted. A younger man. Now tell me the truth. Did she proposition you?'

Max had no idea what he felt, let alone what to say to his furious young wife. But in a manner of speaking, he did tell the truth.

'No, of course not. She was married to George Lewes.'

'But she wasn't married. That's why Mama never let me visit her.'

This too, was certainly true. But Max now sensed that he was on safe ground: Sophie didn't know anything about the incident with the prostitute.

'Sophie, Mrs. Lewes isn't rapacious in that way. She's just like lots of other famous people. Like Herr Klesmer. Or Professor Marek. She likes to be acknowledged and admired. But she's shy, so she chooses her admirers. You once admired her yourself.'

'The more fool I. Look where it got me. You never read that book, Max. The one with Herr Klesmer in it. The one about the Jews. I know you didn't. Only three people in the world knew the story of the necklace: you, me, and Mrs. Lewes.' Sophie spat out the writer's former name. Now everything came out. 'She retells our story in that book. She described me playing at the gaming tables. She made me look stupid. And that's what I can't bear. Being portrayed as stupid, egotistical, vain and poor.'

Sophie burst into tears of frustration and rage. Max, utterly baffled, took her in his arms. This time, she did not resist him. Surely Wolfgang would have mentioned the fact that there had been a portrait of Sophie in the novel? He had described Klesmer's surreptitious courtship of Miss Arrowpoint, but never mentioned anything else transcribed from life. Max poured out a vial of tenderness and reassurance.

'Beloved girl, no one would ever dream that you were any of those things. And anyway, your father told me that the gambling scene was based on Miss Leigh, Byron's grandniece. She lost £500 when the Count was playing too. He said it was a painful sight. Besides, you don't lose, you always win.'

Max could not bring himself to actually sit down and read *Daniel Deronda,* and now, after all the trouble that the book had caused, he never would.

'She likes young men,' hissed Sophie decisively. 'I know what I saw this morning.'

'Well, I'll write to Wolfgang. The situation may not be quite as you suppose.'

But Max suspected she was right. There had been no ambiguity in the register of the Hôtel de l'Europe: Mr. and Mrs. J. W. Cross. Sophie, on the other hand, supposed unimaginable things.

❧

Venice possessed a violent reputation for passions and assassinations. Nevertheless a week of sightseeing and sea bathing passed happily without any sign of the witch-like Sibyl or her red-bearded *cavalier servente*. And no violent scenes occurred. Professor Marek and his party fell foul of the heat and remained on the Veneto in a Palladian pleasure dome, a palace with fourteen entrances, all caressed by soft winds. Picnics and gallops on fabulous steeds through tall open fields with the misty Alps above her filled Sophie's days. Leo thrived in the hot climate and seemed quite immune to the mosquitoes. He never gave his parents a moment's anxiety. The Sibyl receded into a remote corner of Max's mind. He hoped, fervently, that, whatever her relation with Mr. John Walter Cross, he would not encounter her unsettling presence, or be forced to act. He paddled well away from the Venetian pleasure grounds and clung to the highway of marital virtue. But he did write to Wolfgang in Berlin, explaining the odd situation and asking for information. There was no immediate reply.

On Wednesday 9th June 1880 Max and Sophie set out in two gondolas to visit the Byzantine basilica of Santa Maria Assunta on the island of Torcello. The party also consisted of the indispensable Karl and Leo's nursemaid. Every eventuality had to be taken into account; the luncheon picnic accessories therefore amounted to several baskets. A cool box, with ice wrapped in sacking to contain the wine, fish pâté, various fruits including apricots, washed several times, game pie, cooked yesterday, only one slice missing, which Max could not resist at breakfast, an entire lobster, packed with long hooks and pincers to extract the meat, plates, glasses, napkins, cutlery, a bottle of freshly squeezed juice for Leo, a canvas screen in case the wind got up, rugs in case the ground proved damp, and two gigantic parasols to ward off sunburn. Sophie rubbed lemons on her arms and hands to prevent them from becoming discoloured. She had been known to wear a Venetian carnival mask to protect her nose, when she walked the terrace in the privacy of their balcony apartments, and had terrified the housekeeper bringing up the flowers. Her sea-bathing outfits covered her from throat to toe; but she had learned to swim in the chill lakes of Brandenburg, and often abandoned the security of the bathing machine to kick out powerfully into the warm sea. All Max could see from the shore was a large brimmed straw hat, fastened with a damp red scarf, rising and dipping in the gentle swell.

'I won't swim today,' she informed Max. 'Leo would want to come in too, and without the floats and the bathing machine it's far too risky.'

'Good.' Max discarded a large basket of swimming equipment. 'We might now fit into two boats.'

Even so, as they drifted across the green swell towards the islands both gondolas lurched dangerously low in the water. Sophie's matching jacket and dress in pale gold and green stripes shimmered against the black. Leo fell asleep, snuggled in her lap. Once again she removed her gloves and let her fingers drift in the dreaming lagoon, keeping her hands carefully in shadow. The long voyage to Torcello in the early day as the distant isles hardened in the mist gave Max the miraculous sensation of approaching Elysium. This is eternity, this endless rolling voyage, gliding through calm waters and a ceaseless rocking green. The great square tower of the Torcello Campanile loomed up as the only marker in the dawn mist. As he gazed at the distant basilica the bells rang out across the marshes, channels and lagoons, over the fishing boats, barges and little leisure yachts, fluttering forwards with barely enough wind to fill the jib.

Sophie raised her eyes from the hypnotic, gentle green and Leo awoke in her embrace.

'*Glocken*,' he murmured sleepily. Bells.

As they approached the narrow jetty Sophie dug out her volume of Ruskin and read the descriptions of the mosaics aloud in English.

'Listen, Max, the Madonna in the apse is surrounded by gold. We have to see "the two solemn mosaics of the eastern and western extremities, one representing the Last Judgement" – oh dear, I hope it's not too fearsome, but then Leo always loves the devils – "and at the other the Madonna, her tears falling as her hands are raised to bless", and "the noble range of pillars which enclose the space between". He says that the whole is "expressive at once of the deep sorrow and the sacred courage of men, who had no home left them upon earth, but who looked for one to come".'

Sophie slammed the book shut.

'I hate all that.'

'What?'

'The wretchedness of this life and the bliss stored up for the virtuous in the next. The pastor pours all that down our throats every Sunday. And I think it's poison. I don't believe in another life as beautiful as this one. It's all clearly lies.'

Max smiled. So did their gondolier, who despite the fact that he understood not a word, liked to watch the Countess working herself up into an outburst.

'I want my happiness here, now, with you and Leo. I don't want to wait.'

'The very fact that you can even envisage joy in this world, Sophie, is a measure of your privilege. You already possess wealth, health and general blessedness.' Max's fond gaze undercut this piece of sententious superiority. 'And you are one of my blessings.'

'Then why can't everyone be blessed? Each in their own way? The pastor says that God is just. But God is not just.'

'If it's any help to your rebellious theology, dearest love, the Greeks never solved the problem of God's justice either. Professor Marek says that's why their gods are capricious: to explain the fact that no providential pattern exists in the world. And no justice either.'

'Did Lucian believe that? Is that why he wouldn't listen to Myriam when she spoke about her Christian faith?'

But Max, startled by this sudden eruption of the atheist philosopher into their holiday idyll, remained silent. He simply reached out for the looped ropes bound to the jetty and steadied the swaying gondola. Lucian and all his works could wait for another day.

Max, Sophie and Leo set out at once for the basilica, leaving Karl to choose a shady spot and organise the picnic. However, as soon as their employers had gone Karl and the gondoliers set off into the marsh flags and bulrushes to find a peaceful spot to piss and smoke, leaving Leo's nursemaid staring at the lobster. Max carried Leo on his shoulders as they tramped up the white path. They merely glanced at Santa Fosca and the remains of the baptistery, then pushed past the gathering beggars into the main nave of the church. At first, in the powerful gleam of the southern lights, high up, pouring through the ten round arches of the windows, Sophie saw only the luminous mosaic on the pavement beneath her feet. A rich and striking pattern of geometric perfection, all in black, white and red marble wheels, lozenges and arabesques, swirling beneath her white canvas boots. The warm brick and white light suggested not sorrow, but joy, present and to come. There were very few other tourists, for they had arrived at Torcello early in the day. Leo chuckled and gurgled as Max set him down upon the precious, cool floor, then the boy hoisted himself up and set off at speed, each tottering step a triumph of motion over balance. His sun hat fell off. Down he went, then up again and away, leaving Max to salvage the tiny boater with its sailor's ribbons.

Sophie now looked up, facing the east, her back to the massive and thunderous *Last Judgement*, which dominated the gigantic west wall above the tiny doorway. Leo toddled straight towards the great gouged vault of the apse, with the single colossal figure of the Virgin, flanked by Greek symbols proclaiming her identity: the Mother of God.

Nothing else challenged her extraordinary presence. There she stands, Queen of Heaven, haloed in gold, showered with gold, standing on a shallow golden podium, her long folded robes fringed with gold. Her right hand points to the golden child, cradled in the crook of her left arm, and in her left hand she holds the white shroud of death.

Sophie deciphered the Latin words unfolding at the Virgin's feet. *Epitome of virtue, star of the seas, doorway to heaven, Mary through her son frees those whom Eve and husband reduced to sin.* Sophie gazed at the names, Mary, Eve. They are named. These are not simply decorative women, there to give pleasure. They are the Bible's heroines, the pivots on the gates, whose actions and decisions changed all our lives for ever. The men are simply generic: husband, son. It's the women who count. This struggle between women marks the spiritual history of the whole world. Beneath the Virgin's pointed slippers a bright window lit the golden dome; on either side the twelve apostles, all on a far smaller scale, frisked through fields of poppies, joyfully embracing their symbols of martyrdom. Sophie felt Leo pulling at her skirts, and bent down to touch the tender, upturned face of her only son.

'Papa!' cried Leo. He decided to drag his mother back to his father, but she resisted him gently.

'No, my love, look up. Look up at the beautiful Madonna.'

Leo peered at the gigantic immobile blue figure, then decided that the pitchforked host of scowling devils which claimed his father's attention presented a more interesting spectacle. He scuttled off in search of Max, who was contemplating damnation on the western façade, and now carried both the tiny hat and a lost shoe. As Leo skipped over the inlaid marble floor, he missed one step, and fell straight into the grey satin folds of another tourist. The lady raised him up, her companion whisked her dangerous parasol with its pretty white flowers out of the way as she set the child upright. Leo beamed up at the ancient lady whom he now took to be his grandmother, turned and pointed his chubby finger in the general direction of his luminous mother, who stood before the altar, drenched in white light, directly beneath the gigantic blue virgin, surrounded with gold. Sophie gazed upwards, transfigured in sunshine and glory.

'Madonna!' he yelped, delighted.

His mother turned round, her face outlined in white light, and found herself facing both the unsuspecting Sibyl and Mr. John Walter Cross.

Max recognised the visitors at once, and, tingling with horror, saw what had happened. He sped down the church towards them. But the Sibyl had not recognised Sophie. She was now near-sighted and stood there, vulnerable without her glasses. She addressed the young woman in French. Above her Sophie glittered in a blaze of white light.

'*Voilà, Madame, votre fils*. I think nothing's broken.'

'Mrs. Lewes! How very extraordinary –' Max jumped in, appalled, alarm rather than pleasure evident both on his face and in his voice. Everybody stared at one another.

The Sibyl switched to German. 'Can it really be you, Max?'

She then glanced at the illuminated figure standing at the centre of the apse. Then this young woman must, almost certainly, be that denouncing venomous harpy who forced entry into my household, and prevented me from sleeping for almost a week. She froze, horrified, all the formulas of politeness dying on her lips. But Johnny Cross recognised Max as the sympathetic gentleman of the frozen gardens and began shaking hands vigorously.

'What a pleasure, sir. A great pleasure to see you again. And in much happier circumstances.'

Sophie murmured an excuse, snatched up Leo and evaporated in two rapid stages, down the nave at full tilt, then out of the door into the brilliant white light and away round the side of the *campanile*. She flashed past the beggars, vendors and hucksters, who had no chance to regroup in importunate postures, and came to rest in a deserted corner overlooking the mudflats and the far lagoon. Her breath pumped out in thick gasps. She leaned against the warm brick of the *campanile* and set Leo down beside her on the browning grass. She noticed the missing shoe.

Max, abandoned before the altar, like a jilted bridegroom, was left with the task of being polite and enquiring after everybody's health. He addressed the Sibyl once more as Mrs. Lewes. She smiled fleetingly, now clearly unsettled and deeply embarrassed.

'We seem doomed to misunderstand one another, Max. May I formally introduce you to my husband, Mr. John Cross, who was indeed a dear friend to Mr. Lewes?'

'But we've already met, dearest,' said Johnny Cross, confused and perfectly oblivious of any awkward atmosphere generated by this chance encounter. Max stared at the Sibyl, open-mouthed. Was she telling the truth? She called the last one husband, when he wasn't. The Sibyl ploughed on.

'We are in fact visiting Venice on our wedding journey. We are staying at the Hôtel de l' Europe.'

'Where we should be delighted to receive you and your wife,' declared Johnny Cross, hospitable but ill-advised. He misread the rapid squeeze of the Sibyl's hand upon his wrist, and went on issuing polite invitations. The Sibyl, desperate to escape and terrified that the vanished harpy would reappear and begin screaming further accusations for all the church to hear, now bowed so deeply that her lace mantilla detached itself slightly from her heavy netted hair, and hung askew. Then she fled from the basilica, Johnny Cross trailing in her wake. Max was left standing in front of the Virgin still clutching his son's hat and shoe. Shunted aside by a guide with a fresh party of tourists, he collapsed in a chair above the crypt, and waited for the storm to pass.

From the far side of the canal that led to the village Sophie watched the odd couple making off in the direction of the jetty. There goes Mrs. Lewes and her *cavalier servente*! She found herself, if not exactly victor of the field, at least the last to leave.

❧

A letter from Wolfgang waited in reception.

Berlin, 6th June 1880

My Dear Max,

She is indeed married! And in church! All London is simmering with the scandal. There was an announcement in *The Times*, but I did not see it. I have, however, received a postcard from Herr und Frau Klesmer simply asking, 'Is it true?' News travels fast, but, it seems, not so fast as to reach you both in Venice. You must call upon them at once and present our congratulations and good wishes. It will be an unlooked-for honour that Sophie cannot have expected – to meet her idol at last! If they are on their wedding journey they will not wish to discuss business. But it would be very helpful if you could get to know the husband. I gather he is her financial adviser, so we may be dealing with him, rather than Charles Lewes, for the Cabinet edition. I have it on good authority that *Theophrastus Such* has sold over 6,000 copies. We must secure the contract if we can. It is therefore imperative that you should show Mr. and Mrs. Cross every courtesy. Flowers perhaps, and a formal message first. She seems to generate controversy whatever she does, whether married or unmarried.

Give Sophie and Leo my love. Keep me informed of everything that happens. This could be a wonderful opportunity for us. And don't fail me, *petit frère*.

Liebe Grüße
Dein Wolfgang

Max waited two days, then sent the flowers surreptitiously, so that Sophie's enduring rage against the Sibyl would not be rekindled. That dreadful business with the necklace in Homburg now lay shrouded in the wastes of past time. Why, that was in the days when he found himself seriously compromised, begging Wolfgang for money! Anyway, the congratulations and good wishes came from Duncker und Duncker, as her German publishers, not from Max himself. He decided that he could keep Sophie circumscribed within the domestic sphere without appearing impolite, or suggesting that the Sibyl still could not figure among the acquaintances of virtuous married women. But he certainly ought to follow up the flowers with a brief visit.

Karl went out spying upon Max's instructions and returned with the necessary information. He had quizzed their gondoliers and, after parting with a small bribe, discovered that the interrupted visit to Santa Maria Assunta had been followed by a trip to Murano, Santa Maria Formosa and then back to the Accademia. On Thursday they had been to San Zaccaria and spent hours peering at the paintings in bad light. On Friday they pounded off to San Vitale and took tea with someone called Mr. Bunney, whom they met again on the following morning in the Piazza, then all three set off back to Santa Maria Formosa, and then on to the Salute. They listened to the music on Sunday in the Scuola Grande di San Giovanni Evangelista, then returned to Mr. Bunney. A Mrs. Bunney now entered the picture, a stout lady with a bright green parasol, who escorted them all to the Manfrin Palace and the Palazzo dei Quattro Evangelisti. They took all their meals in their rooms, avoided the dining hall and never loitered in the foyer. Max mopped his damp cheeks and throat in sympathetic horror at this rapid and inexorable process of cultural consumption. He found himself literally sweating with tourism.

On Tuesday 15th June they went back to the Accademia, but Mr. Cross felt unwell in the afternoon and so they did not go out. Next morning, on Wednesday 16th June, Sophie departed for a day at the Lido with another German family they had befriended in the hotel. Max decided to send up his card to the Sibyl with a little message, wishing Mr. Cross a speedy recovery, and then to beat a retreat. He arranged to have himself rowed to the wharf before the Hôtel de l'Europe, but there was Karl, just outside the Danieli's rotating doors, bristling with fresh information.

'Herr Cross is seriously indisposed, sir. The lady has summoned Dr. Richetti for an urgent consultation.'

The clatter of bells and the mass of morning traffic bringing deliveries of fish and fresh vegetables to the market on the wharf blurred Karl's urgent report. Max hauled him into the gondola and yelled at him to say it all again. So, the young man had fallen in the battle to keep pace with the Sibyl.

Even in the midst of his embarrassed dismay at the church of Santa

Maria Assunta, beneath the ironic indifference of the gigantic Madonna, Max registered the fact that Mrs. Lewes, now a decidedly old lady, had blossomed beneath her appalling mantilla, and marched off down the nave with a bounce in her stride. Her young *cavaliere*, red and sweating, tramped beside her. And it was the handsome athletic red-beard who lay toppled upstairs, not the old frail dame.

A breathless rush through a damp German forest surged across Max's memory of the woman, who still, obscurely, haunted his imagination. He heard Lewes's voice urging him to take Polly out for a canter, and remembered his own chagrin upon discovering that the racehorse rarely proceeded at anything less than a gallop.

'Oh well, that's probably for the best. I won't have to persist with visits. We'll deliver our deepest respects and sincere concern for Mr. Cross's health, wish him a rapid recovery and retreat at once to the Lido.'

Max imagined Sophie's glowing face emerging from her bathing machine as he approached, like the wicked stepmother in 'Snow White', carrying a basket of fresh fruit and a melting bowl of ice cream.

They rocked slowly up to the jetty where a drenched red carpet led directly into the Grand Foyer. A gaggle of English visitors wobbled into their gondolas, exclaiming and fanning themselves. The hotel foyer steamed gently with foliage, a tropical palm court, designed to host Sunday-afternoon concerts. Max stepped aside on to the wooden planks, paused to light a cigarette and give himself time to compose a suitable sentence or two that he could slither into the envelope along with his visiting card. But he had no time to compose more than a single phrase. A great shout went up from the gondolas. He sprang back against the cold stone of the hotel wall in time to see a black figure tracing a giant curved arc in the air, the feet whirling like chariot wheels. The man leaped from the balcony above him, cleared all four gondolas and landed with a gigantic splash directly in the middle of the Grand Canal. Karl, stationed in the outermost gondola, immediately hurled himself into the water. So did one of the gondoliers, who later turned out to be one Corradini, the man employed by Mr. and Mrs. Cross to squire them around on their Venetian visits. Corradini had recognised his employer, flying through the air. For the man struggling to sink beneath the green water, resisting all attempts at rescue, was none other than Mr. John Walter Cross.

Max rushed to help the hotel staff, who hoisted the limp and sodden man out of the water. His shirt ripped open, revealing a hairy, virile, barrel chest, beneath the dripping beard. The sad fellow gave up the fight and lay groaning on the jetty, helpless and dishevelled. He wore no shoes. Max clasped his naked ankles and raised them up to stop them dragging on the marble squares as they transported him into the foyer. Five men, all shouting at once in desperate Italian, carried him rapidly up the stairs. The affair shuddered through the public rooms in a slow motion of whispers and stares. Someone's fallen in. He didn't fall. He leaped. Who is it? Who is it? The banker married to the much older lady. I didn't catch the name.

On the wide landing decorated with worm-white copies of classical statues Max confronted a vision of the Sibyl, gaunt and terrified, visibly aged before his very eyes, as if the magic potion of her energy had been drained away. She uttered a low cry and staggered against Dr. Richetti who clutched his watch chain, as if he too needed support. They rushed the dripping body into the marital bedroom and laid him out upon the rumpled sheets and tossed pillows. Max relinquished the collapsed ankles and found the Sibyl attached to his arm like a dying clam.

'Max, help me,' she whispered.

❦

The San Marco police station classified the incident as a 'suicide attempt' and reported the event in the following manner:

> J.W. Cross, an Englishman of forty years, had been lodged for two weeks at the Hôtel de l'Europe with his wife, a woman over sixty. For some days he had been looking sad and melancholy, prompting his wife to call in a doctor. While they were talking, the husband, in the next room, made the aforementioned attempt on his life.

Max spent the rest of the day composing telegrams and organising their rapid expedition to William Cross, the unfortunate banker's brother, begging him to come at once. Cross himself, doused with chloral, passed out. Max insisted on a little brandy for the shaking, distraught Sibyl. Karl was dispatched to the Lido, where he found Sophie, who had been waiting for hours, expecting Max at any moment, livid with fury, ready to eat the tablecloth, and once she had heard the story, prepared to drown the Sibyl herself.

What happened in those days leading up to The Great Leap? Well, the Sibyl's real identity remained concealed. No hint that the elderly lady married to the mad banker was in fact the famous novelist, known under many other names, ever leaked out in Venice. But Rumour, that fleet-footed creature, raced across the mountains. London society rippled with malicious speculation. Even the police reports noticed the age difference between husband and wife. Had the lascivious demands of the elderly widow simply exhausted the young man? Had the very suggestion that he should enjoy the body of a woman old enough to be his mother rushed him to the edge of the balcony? Did he prefer boys? I'm told Venice is the right place for that. Was there madness in the family? The Sibyl said so. That's what she told the doctor; but genetic insanity lets her off the hook, doesn't it? Had Johnny Cross previously suffered from some kind of personality disorder, and the sudden onset of suicidal melancholy? An earlier incident is recorded, but nothing so serious as the Venetian defenestration. Who knows the truth, especially when it is disagreeable and embarrassing for all concerned?

One thing is certain. By the time Sophie returned to their suite at the Danieli on that fatal day, Wednesday 16th June 1880, in the calm gold of evening, she had convinced herself that the Sibyl, not content with the attentions of one young man, whom she had driven insane and then almost bullied into a watery grave, had now sunk her jealous claws into Max, the second young man, and her next victim. Sophie paced the length of her terrace, four floors above the market down on the quays, ignoring the shouts far below her and the bells from San Giorgio Maggiore. Her loosened hair, still damp and salty from the sea, drying fast on the back of her white muslin housecoat, floated free. She strode like a Valkyrie, glamorous, armed. When Max clattered on to the balcony, without his hat, breathless and ready to face the music, she swung round upon him.

'Well? Explain yourself!'

Sophie's opening blast roared past the potted palms in their terracotta jars.

'Sophie, my dearest, I was there by chance when it happened. I had to help her.'

'She drove him to it.'

'Hardly. I can't believe that. He is seriously unwell. No one can be held responsible.'

The justice of this cut through Sophie's rage, which was fuelled by the perception that she had taken second place to the mighty Sibyl, and been abandoned on the Lido.

'You deserted your family to help this woman who has caused nothing but trouble between us.'

This accusation was true, but struck Max as utterly unjust. He bit his lip. Sophie raged on.

'She has a new husband and another family. Let them help her. Why should she need you too?'

'Sophie, stop. In common humanity I could not do otherwise. Her husband apparently tried to make away with himself. I have summoned his brother, who will be here in two days. Until then she is alone, and needs my help. We are her publishers. We owe her a great deal. Surely you must understand that.'

But Sophie refused to understand. Her uncanny intelligence sifted and judged, not just the facts, but also the emotional yearning behind them, and read the cards correctly. Max remained bound to this old woman, and a web of hidden connections, smuggled without acknowledgement into their married lives, sank like the taproot of an unkillable weed, into the past. Homburg. All this dates from Homburg. She could not identify the nature of the web, but knew that it hung between them, all three of them. Palpable, but unrevealed, the shimmering web vanished in the rising wind from the lagoon.

'And I must go back to her this evening, Sophie.' He stood still, waiting for his wife to capitulate.

'Oh no, you won't!' She actually stood on the toes of his boots. 'You shan't go. I say, you shall not.'

Her gently freckled nose was one centimetre away from his own. Max simply gazed at the woman he loved, his decision steady in his eyes. For a moment he thought she intended to strike him. Instead, she screamed her jealous intransigence, not only at Max, but all of Venice.

'You say she needs you. She's already got a husband. Let him get out of bed and look after her. She married the wrong man, didn't she? And so did I.'

END OF CHAPTER EIGHTEEN

END OF PART TWO

FINALE

for who can quit Young Lives after being long in Company with them, and not Desire to Know what befell them in After Years?

And had Sophie married the wrong man? Some marriages rock back and forth, like a creeper stretched between two trees, an unstable link that never breaks. Her marriage to Max, her childhood sweetheart, proved to be one such and rolled on, turbulent, joyous, explosive – and unbroken. Apart from his passion for the Sibyl, which never entirely dissolved, he neither coveted nor desired any other woman. And as he got older he even dropped the prostitutes. I believe him when he claims that he sought out no further Venetian adventures. Other marriages, like the free union between George Henry Lewes and Marian Evans, seem destined, upon strictly utilitarian lines, to secure the greatest happiness for all concerned; and to produce the conditions within which both parties live profitable and industrious lives. Many people found Lewes insufferably irritating. The Sibyl didn't. And between them they gave birth to the writer herself: Marian Evans Lewes, better known as George Eliot. When Sophie accused her of marrying the wrong man she was not of course referring to her union with Lewes, but to that bizarre if legal marriage to Johnny Cross. Is it against nature to marry a man twenty years younger than yourself when he is a vigorous specimen and you have no teeth left? Well, look at it this way, he collapsed with nervous exhaustion, and she was the one still standing after weeks of gruelling tourism in draughty churches and damp trains.

Cross recovered from his peculiar attack of the melancholy horrors and carried on with the honeymoon. His brother, Willie Cross, arrived in Venice like the cavalry, took over from Max, offering his deepest gratitude and counting on 'Your every discretion, sir', so far as the public and indeed the press were concerned. Willie accompanied the newlyweds back to Austria. I note that Johnny Cross never suffered a relapse, never married again, and lived on until 1924. He remained her faithful banker, and, after her death, transformed himself from grieving widower into Keeper of the Sacred Flame. His *Life of George Eliot*, more or less in her own words, carefully edited, amounts to something more solid than a discreet muslin veil draped over an object of sexual scandal. True, he downplays Lewes's role, and he certainly doesn't point out, as more recent biographers have done, that George Eliot flung herself at more or less every man who took the slightest interest in her. She lured in the women too. Both Mrs. Congreve and Edith Simcox regarded themselves as women in love with another woman. They were given plenty of encouragement. George Eliot loved to be loved. We have had to wait a hundred years for all the lesbian attachments to be revealed, and even now I'll be accused of tendentious anachronism for even mentioning that fatal word, and for suggesting that the great writer herself harboured Sapphic sentiments. No, Cross worshipped his dead wife and defended her against all comers. George Eliot married the right man. Twice.

And as for the writer's famous charisma, well, even Sophie von Hahn recognised the drugged enchantment of the older woman's power. She described her as the Queen of Fairies, or la belle dame sans merci, one New Year's Eve, in her father's drawing room. Max alone among the festive company understood that ballad, which is just as well, for Sophie aimed her song at him. He may have fallen under the witch's spell, but Sophie decided, for reasons she has already given, to resist. George Eliot needed to be adored, but, even more deeply, she longed to be worshipped, revered. And until that incident of the letter, a petition addressed to her god, and for her eyes only, Sophie counted herself among the most ardent of acolytes.

Some readers are delighted to find themselves described in other people's novels; readers of a different temperament immediately contact their lawyers. In the eighteenth century, if proceedings ensued, the publishers, or as they were known then, the booksellers, took the hit and saw their business closed down and their stock confiscated. Mrs. Gaskell had to print some embarrassing retractions, after being too free with her sexual accusations in her *Life of Charlotte Brontë*. Nowadays, if a character decides to issue writs, the writer has to face the music on her own. Sophie wasn't the sort of woman who cowered behind writs; she settled her own scores. George Eliot's last heroine, Gwendolen Harleth, with her dangerous egotism and arrogant stupidity, seemed manifestly so different from the bold and elegant Countess von Hahn, a girl born to inherited wealth and privilege, that no one else ever made the connection between the roulette table in Leubronn and the Casino in Homburg. After all, Sophie wasn't the only young woman leaning over the green tables, her gaze fixed on the red and the black. The one thing those two young women shared was a love of horses. But Sophie felt, and justice in this case is clearly on her side, that the novelist had stolen something from her. For George Eliot certainly stole many things from Sophie on that autumn night in Homburg – her courage, her daring, her success. Sophie looked back, later in her life, and hissed in vindictive triumph: *I never lost, I won.*

Writers often begin their works with a question. Sometimes they keep that question to themselves, or in George Eliot's case they put it right there in the first line. Was she beautiful, or not beautiful? Is that the first question a man asks of a woman? George Eliot created, in Gwendolen Harleth, a spirited, exceptional creature, in order to punish her. Discipline and punish. That's what so many nineteenth-century writers did – punish the women. So the questions are never open-ended, such as, what did she think? How did she feel? What did she do? The consequences relating to that first question, was she beautiful or not beautiful, determine all else in the writer's mind. And sometimes in the reader's mind too. Max doesn't escape the clichés of judging women by appearance either, does he? He first saw George Eliot in September 1872, when she was in her fifties. The lady is old, the lady is ugly, the lady has wonderful eyes. George Eliot is still famous for being hideous.

But I must not jeer at the brilliant dead. Their fate will be ours. Beauty and ugliness alike fade, decay and drop to dust. This is a cruel truth perhaps, but then, as George Eliot brutally pointed out to Edith Simcox, 'Why should truth be consoling?' The writer survived her honeymoon, but she did not survive the year. At first the scene remained unclear – between the old woman and her young *cavalier servente* – which one was seriously ill and needing succour, and which one was bearing up well? Mr. and Mrs. Cross were already on their way back to England when Edith Simcox heard the rumours.

> *11th July 1880*
> Yesterday I was startled by the question, 'Is Mr. Cross any better?' and then a rumour that he was ill – or like to die – of typhoid fever at Venice. It seemed too horrible to be true and yet I hardly dared to doubt it. It was bad enough at best to think of her alarm if he was ill at all.

Dear Edith! Her first thought was always for her darling, the woman she never ceased to love. As she wrote the next day, 'I must love you unchangeably, my sweet.'

Over the next few months George Eliot settled into her usual pattern of letters, visits, piano playing and ferociously intellectual reading. Cross clearly recovered all his natural force. By 2nd November 1880 she records that he was cutting down trees in the afternoon. They began the process of moving house to 4 Cheyne Walk in Chelsea. But she began no new work. Her writing life was over. The last words of George Eliot's Journal were written on Saturday 4th December 1880.

> J. to city in morning. Home to lunch. Went to our first Pop. Concert and heard Norman Neruda, Piatti etc. Miss Zimmermann playing the piano. After

And so it ends, the last sentence left unfinished. Edith saw her for the last time just before Christmas. The writer was suffering from a sore throat. Edith records her visit, and the dreadful event which followed, in her own Journal.

> *23rd December 1880*
> She was alone when I arrived. I was too shy to ask for any special greeting – only kissed her again and again as she sat. Mr. Cross came in soon and I noticed his countenance was transfigured, a calm look of pure *beatitude* had succeeded the ordinary good nature. Poor fellow! She was complaining of a slight sore throat, when he came in and touched her hand, said she felt the reverse of better. I only stayed half an hour therefore; she said do not go, but I gave as a reason that she should not tire her throat and then she asked me to come in again and tell them the news. He came down to the door with me and I only asked after his health – she had spoken before of being quite well and I thought it was only a passing cold – she thought it was caught at the Agamemnon. I meant to call again tomorrow and take her some snowdrops. This morning I hear from Johnny – she died at 10 last night!

Her last whispered words to Johnny Cross were these: 'Tell them I have great pain in the left side.'

Edith Simcox, her love unfaltering, followed her beloved to the grave. George Eliot lies buried in unconsecrated ground in Highgate

Cemetery, and her tomb touches that of G.H. Lewes. Edith recorded that terrible day of loss and final separation.

29th December 1880
This day stands alone. I am not afraid of forgetting, but as heretofore I record her teaching while the sound is still fresh in my soul's ears. This morning at 10 when the wreath I had ordered – white flowers bordered with laurel leaves – came, I drove with it to Cheyne Walk, giving it silently to the silent cook. Then, instinct guiding, it seemed to guide one right all day – I went to Highgate – stopping on the way to get some violets – I was not sure for what purpose. In the cemetery I found that the new grave was in the place I had feebly coveted – nearer the path than his and one step further south. Then I laid my violets at the head of Mr. Lewes's solitary grave and left the already gathering crowd to ask which way the entrance would be. Then I drifted towards the chapel – standing first for a while under the colonnade where a child asked me, 'Was it the late George Eliot's wife was going to be buried?' I think I said yes – then I waited on the skirts of the group gathered in the porch between the church and chapel sanctuaries. Then someone claimed a passage through the thickening crowd and I followed in his wake and found myself without effort in a sort of vestibule past the door which kept back the crowd. Mrs. Lankester was next the chapel – I cannot forget that she offered me her place. I took it and presently everyone else was made to stand back, then the solemn procession passed me. The coffin bearers paused in the very doorway, I pressed a kiss upon the pall and trembled violently as I stood motionless else, in the still silence with nothing to mar the realisation of that intense moment's awe. Then – it was hard to tell the invited mourners from the other waiting friends – men many of whose faces I knew – and so I passed among them into the chapel entering a forward pew. White wreaths lay thick upon the velvet pall – it was not painful to think

of her last sleep so guarded. I saw her husband's face, pale and still; he forced himself aloof from the unbearable world in sight. The service was so like our own I did not know it apart till afterwards when I could not trace the outlines that had seemed so almost entirely in harmony with her faith. Dr Sadler quoted – how could he help? – her words of aspiration, but what moved me most was the passage in the church service lesson – it moved me like the voice of God – of Her: 'But some man will say, How are the dead raised up? And with what body do they come? Thou fool, that which thou sowest is not quickened except it die. And that which thou sowest, thou sowest not that body that shall be, but bare grain – but God giveth it a body, as it hath pleased him, and to every seed his own body.' Awe thrilled me. As at the presence of God. In the memory of her life bare grain – oh God, my God. My love, what fruit should such seed bring forth in us – I will force myself to remember your crushing prophecy – that I was to do better work than you had – that cannot be, my Best! and all mine is always yours, but oh! Dearest! Dearest! It shall not be less unworthy of you than it must. As we left the chapel Miss Helps put her arm in mine, but I left her at the door, to make my way alone across the road to the other part where the grave was. I shook hands silently with Mrs. Anderson and waited at the corner where the hearse stopped and the coffin was brought up again. Again I followed near, on the skirts of the procession. A man – Champneys I thought – had a white wreath he wished to lay upon the coffin and as he pressed forward those behind bore me on, till I was standing between his grave and hers and heard the last words said: the grave was deep and narrow – the flowers filled all the level space. I turned away with the first – Charles Lewes pressed my hand as we gave the last look. Then I turned up the hill and walked through the rain by a road unknown before to Hampstead and a station. Then through the twilight I cried and moaned aloud.

Johnny Cross soon became known in the London clubs as 'George Eliot's widow', but nothing ever shook his dedication to her memory. Max and Sophie extended their family with three more children after Leo, who never remembered the Basilica di Santa Maria Assunta, or the towering Madonna, and never visited Torcello again. But he and his brother and sisters, all of whom grew to be robust, intrepid and adventurous, illuminated the old age of their grandparents, the Count and Countess von Hahn. Sophie became famous for her racehorses, which she bred and trained herself. She also became notorious in Berlin, for wearing bloomers and bicycling. Wolfgang Duncker startled his entourage and caused an explosion of gossip by suddenly, in his mid-fifties, marrying a rich widow, Frau Anastasia von Humblot, a large and opulent lady, some years older than he was. She invested in the publishing house, which grew in fame and prosperity. Max bowed out as the sleeping partner and the firm became Duncker und Humblot. They still exist today. I always trot along to visit them on their stand when I am working at the Leipziger Buchmesse.

Leo never lived to be old. He followed the family tradition and pursued a career in the army that led to his death in the trenches of the Great War in 1915. All that could be found of his exploded body was gathered together by his loyal companions and his parents were told of an heroic death in battle, surrounded with sufficient glory to suggest that he died at the head of a cavalry charge. Max, devastated, engaged a spiritualist to contact his dead son. This medium, who came with excellent testimonials assuring all clients of her spiritual power and the authenticity of her American shaman spirit guide, engendered a bitter dispute within the household. 'Leave the dead alone,' snapped Sophie, shivering with rage. How could her husband sink to such melodramatic unreason? Grief must be borne with that terrible patience no one can teach. Max died of a stroke in 1922. His lined face, still handsome, turned purple over a period of twelve hours. He did not regain consciousness. Sophie mourned him deeply, but never attempted to raise his ghost in a shudder of ectoplasm.

The scene begins to darken.

Sophie von Hahn died quietly at Wilhelmplatz in Berlin at the age of eighty, surrounded by her children, grandchildren and great-grandchildren. Her hair, coiled beneath a black net, gleamed still, just as the Sibyl's hair had done in her old age, thick and magnificent, but quite white. She suffered a little from arthritis in the shoulders, but that was all. An undiagnosed heart condition carried her off. The year was 1934. Hitler, busy consolidating his power in the Third Reich, prepared to transform the debates contained in *Daniel Deronda* concerning the Jews of Germany and all Europe into not merely a shrewd reading of the horror to come, but a prophecy. How did she know? She cannot have known.

George Eliot's writing methods appear to be rational, studious, unsparingly calculated and intellectual; you might even argue, academic. She prepared the ground with careful research, read books in many languages, and gave herself up to lengthy meditation. But she told me that in all she considered her best writing, there was a 'not herself' that took possession of her, and that she felt her own personality to be merely the instrument through which this spirit, as it were, was acting. And I believe her. For there is, in great writing, a sinister power, primitive and overwhelming, whose grasp upon the organs within us unsettles and disturbs. And an imagination such as hers, which causes whole worlds to surge into being, is never safe, nor entirely comforting. Beware the writing on the wall, hostile, unintelligible. For every single letter will remain there for ever, waiting to be read. And beware the imagination which seizes the roots of our times, reads the underground seams, clutches at the pulse of our common blood, then stares, unflinching, into the darkness ahead.

THE END

AFTERWORD

Throughout this tale I have mixed fiction with the detail of real lives in outrageous ways. I have used real names, real documents, existing evidence. And that was always part of my plan. Truth and the imagination are not at odds with each other. This story weaves fictitious characters, both George Eliot's and my own, into the recorded histories of the writer and her entourage. I wanted fiction and history, as the historian Richard Holmes once put it, speaking of the biographer and his subject, to shake hands across time. I intended to write a Victorian comedy of manners, which had, as all comedy must do, a darker and more sinister set of shadows at the edge. For what would it be like, as a writer, to be forced by someone else, someone in some future time, to spend years in the company of people you invented purely for your own pleasure, and to be answerable to them?

The ambiguity of my relationship to George Eliot is noted in the epigraphs. I have always adored her work with a passion not unlike the one Edith Simcox harboured for the lady herself. I doubt that I would have much liked Marian Evans Lewes. But I would have fallen in love with George Eliot in the 1870s, just as I did one hundred years later, and revered her power, both as a writer and as an intellectual. I began reading her last great books first: *Middlemarch, Daniel Deronda* and then, in the summer of 1973, *Romola.* I have read all she wrote many times since then, and I have had the honour of teaching her work to generations of students. But the grain of resentment one writer always feels for another whom she hails as 'Master' – and I use that word advisedly – would not dissolve. I have not loved her unchangeably, as Edith did.

My starting point was the coincidence of my name and that of her German publishers. Duncker Verlag of Berlin did and still does exist. I first noticed the connection while I was reading George Eliot's Journals. She recorded the £30 paid to her by 'Duncker of Berlin'. Duncker is not an uncommon name in Holland and Germany. At that moment I was merely amused, but then the seed began to grow. If someone who bore my name had been so closely connected to the writer I loved, why should I not take his place? Eliot was as fascinated by the relationship of mentor and disciple as I am, both as a subject for fiction and as a personal drama in the drawing room. It is a relationship that recurs in her novels and one that she cultivated in her personal life. She set herself up as a Great Teacher. I have always been one of her disciples. But it is in the nature of the disciple to question and challenge the Master, even as you fight alongside her throughout your writing life.

I have deliberately written a Neo-Victorian novel that follows the method of John Fowles's powerfully awful tale, *The French Lieutenant's Woman*. Fowles's Victorian narrative is set in 1867; his narrator is a thinly veiled version of Fowles himself, whose character, a pompous sexual know-all, speaks from the patronising distance of the late 1960s. My story follows the last triumphant years of George Eliot's writing life, from the autumn of 1872 in Homburg through to her death in London in 1880. My narrator, the other voice in this fiction, is a sceptical young woman of Sophie's age, very firmly based in the present day, that is, in the second decade of the twenty-first century. She has never been as infatuated with George Eliot as I am, and I followed her into the past.

Readers who long to know the truth, in so far as it can ever be known, concerning George Eliot's life, and who wish to disentangle her facts from my fictions, and indeed from her own, would be wise to read the novels first and then, perhaps, begin to read their way around the vast list of biographical and critical studies that exist. Here are the books that made all the difference to me. I wish to acknowledge that debt and record my thanks. My first biographical port of call was, of course, Gordon S. Haight, *George Eliot: A Biography* (Oxford: Oxford University Press, 1968), which I first read in 1976. All critics and scholars studying Eliot's work have good cause to be grateful to him, even when they disagree with his approach and conclusions, as I do. Haight is the editor of the 9-volume edition of *The George Eliot Letters* (New Haven, Connecticut: Yale University Press, 1954–55, 1978). Eliot's first biographer was John Walter Cross, *George Eliot's Life as Related in her Letters and Journals*, 3 vols. (Edinburgh and London, 1885). Her Journals are edited by Margaret Harris and Judith Johnstone: *The Journals of George Eliot* (Cambridge: Cambridge University Press, 1998). Eliot's contemporary biographers are numerous, and over the years I read Ruby V. Redinger, *George Eliot: The Emergent Self* (London: The Bodley Head, 1975), Jennifer Uglow, *George Eliot* (London: Virago, 1987), Ina Taylor, *George Eliot: Woman of Contradictions* (London: Weidenfeld and Nicolson, 1989). Rosemary Ashton is the witty and scholarly biographer both of G.H. Lewes and of Eliot herself: *G. H. Lewes: A Life* (Oxford: Oxford University Press, 1991) and *George Eliot: A Life* (London: Hamish Hamilton, 1996). She gives quite wonderful, persuasive readings of Eliot's works and sends us all, as readers, straight back to the novels. Kathryn Hughes's *George Eliot: The Last Victorian* (London: Fourth Estate, 1999) is delightfully irreverent, and I learned a great deal from Rosemarie Bodenheimer, *The Real Life of Mary Ann Evans. George Eliot, Her Letters, and Her Fiction* (Ithaca: Cornell University Press, 1994). Among the many critical studies of George Eliot's work, Gillian Beer's *George Eliot* (Brighton: The Harvester Press, 1986) was the one I read and reread, alongside her classic work on Darwin, *Darwin's Plots: Evolutionary Narrative in Darwin, George Eliot and Nineteenth-Century Fiction*

(London: Routledge & Kegan Paul, 1983). But the documentary source which transformed my understanding of my 'vindictive little game' remains Edith Simcox's Journal, *A Monument to the Memory of George Eliot: Edith J. Simcox's Autobiography of a Shirtmaker,* eds. Constance M. Fulmer and Margaret E. Barfield (London: Taylor and Francis, 1998). Edith fell deeply and irrevocably in love both with Marian Evans Lewes and with the mind of George Eliot; her journals are devastating in the rawness of the feelings she records. She loved and lost 'the master mistress of her passion'. She was not writing for publication, and she was there.

France 2014

ACKNOWLEDGEMENTS

There is a strong community of Victorian and Neo-Victorian writers, scholars and academics, past and present, whose work has informed and inspired my own. I wish to thank in particular Rosario Arias, Stevie Davies, Christian Gutleben, Ann Heilmann, Mel Kohlke, George Letissier, Mark Llewellyn. I owe a great deal to Merle Tönnies and all the 'academic gals – and guys' at the University of Paderborn in Germany.

Thank you to everyone who helped me complete and produce this book: my editor and publisher Alexandra Pringle and her wonderful team, especially Alexa von Hirschberg; my agent Andrew Gordon at David Higham; Mary Tomlinson for close work on my text and her accuracy and expertise; my German translator Barbara Schaden for her help with the foreign languages. And thank you to Kathryn Hughes for sharing her knowledge of George Eliot and the nineteenth century in such generous ways.

The University of Manchester granted me time away from my usual duties to work on this book. Thank you to my colleagues and students in the School of Arts, Languages and Cultures, and in my own department.

Above all I would like to thank my first readers for their enthusiasm, thoughtful criticism and unfailing support – they are, as always, Janet Thomas and Sheila Duncker.

A NOTE ON THE AUTHOR

Patricia Duncker is the author of five previous novels: *Hallucinating Foucault* (winner of the Dillons First Fiction Award and the McKitterick Prize in 1996), *The Deadly Space Between*, *James Miranda Barry*, *Miss Webster and Chérif* (shortlisted for the Commonwealth Writers' Prize in 2007) and *The Strange Case of the Composer and his Judge* (shortlisted for the CWA Gold Dagger award for Best Crime Novel of the Year in 2010). She has written two books of short fiction, *Monsieur Shoushana's Lemon Trees* (shortlisted for the Macmillan Silver Pen Award in 1997) and *Seven Tales of Sex and Death*, and a collection of essays, *Writing on the Wall*. Patricia Duncker is Professor of Contemporary Literature at the University of Manchester.

www.patriciaduncker.com

KT-169-805
Powys
37218 00403408 3

ALED JONES' FAVOURITE CHRISTMAS CAROLS

Also by Aled Jones

Aled Jones' Forty Favourite Hymns

ALED JONES' FAVOURITE CHRISTMAS CAROLS

Aled Jones

preface
publishing

Published by Preface Publishing 2010

10 9 8 7 6 5 4 3 2 1

First published in Great Britain in 2010 by Preface Publishing

20 Vauxhall Bridge Road
London SW1V 2SA

An imprint of The Random House Group Limited

www.rbooks.co.uk

Addresses for companies within The Random House Group Limited can be found at www.randomhouse.co.uk

The Random House Group Limited Reg. No. 954009

A CIP catalogue record for this book is available from the British Library

ISBN 978 1 84809 120 7

The Random House Group Limited supports The Forest Stewardship Council (FSC), the leading international forest certification organisation. All our titles that are printed on Greenpeace approved FSC certified paper carry the FSC logo. Our paper procurement policy can be found at www.rbooks.co.uk/environment

Design by Peter Ward
Typeset by Palimpsest Book Production Limited,
Falkirk, Stirlingshire
Printed and bound in Great Britain by MPG Books Ltd,
Bodmin, Cornwall

To Claire, Emilia and Lucas – my love

CONTENTS

INTRODUCTION

I suppose if you asked people which particular season they'd associate me with it would be Christmas, probably because I recorded 'Walking in the Air'. I don't have a problem with that because Christmas is my favourite season and this is to do with carols. This seasonal music is fantastic. It uplifts the soul, it makes you feel happy whether you're listening to it belted out on a system in some park, or sitting outside a department store in America, or in a supermarket in a British town. Hearing these songs of Christmas that are all about the birth of Jesus makes you feel glad to be alive.

I've sung carols for as long as I can remember and love doing it. There's spellbinding power in this music. I've vivid memories of school assemblies and concerts where they were sung with great gusto and maybe out of tune; even back then performing them made me feel good. As a small boy I had the opportunity of a lifetime when I sang 'O Holy Night' at the exact spot where Jesus was born in Bethlehem. I was also lucky enough to join Bangor Cathedral as a chorister and we felt special conveying the Christmas message to our congregation through song – people felt festive and they were elated by these magical pieces.

One of the things that has surprised me in writing this book is the really rich variety of types of carol that have been collected by the great carol hunters like Percy Dearmer or Ralph Vaughan Williams. I've tried to reflect some of this variety, selecting some folk carols, lullabies and cradle songs, songs of slavery, Latin antiphons, even a counting game. These carols also span the centuries. The earliest was written round about the ninth century, the latest are modern and recent. I also wanted to have both classics that have stood the test of time and been top carols in the *Songs of Praise* polls and a good number of lesser-known gems.

Quite a few of the carols in this book have a childlike quality about them, which in my view makes them particularly special. That some of the melodies are uncomplicated and easily learned is a good thing. How magnificent that a carol like 'Away in a Manger' is simple enough for a child to sing and understand. Equally wonderful is that 'Away in a Manger' is also a terrific carol to perform as an adult. When I was a child I loved this carol's idea of asking Jesus to be forever at my side and I love that idea to this day. As far as I'm concerned, Christmas would not be Christmas without these musical gifts.

Although not all the carols in this book are my favourites, all of them are here because they have special merit of some sort that is worth putting to you, whether it be well-written words, a wonderful melody, or the fact that they've really connected with human beings. I think it will be obvious which are my favourites, and they will probably be among those of a great many people.

What I like and value are simple, heartfelt melodies, which have words that can touch the soul and bring out the best in us. There's something otherworldly about 'Silent Night', 'Jesus Christ the Apple Tree', 'Away in a Manger', 'In the Bleak Midwinter', for example. They almost have healing qualities, they make you feel better when you're singing them. And it doesn't have to be that you're performing them in a church, or a hall, or a cathedral setting, they can even be sung in the shower. There's something very particular about singing Christmas carols.

I've been given the chance to go out to Israel on a number of occasions and to sing Christmas carols in some of the most religious places in the world. This has had a profound effect on me – it's brought carols to life in a larger and deeper way. I also went to Flanders filming for my ITV programme at the spot where British and German troops would have sung 'Silent Night' at dead of night, with hatred and fear and anger in the air. How could I begin to imagine what it was like for those soldiers to hear that lovely melody being sung? It must have produced in them sadness and longing, and brought back memories of loved ones at home. Once I experienced that feeling out there in Flanders, this carol took on a completely different meaning for me. Before then I'd sung it knowing that it had a fine melody and a good story around it; now it has a gritty reality to it. I've had many such experiences, performing these carols in places where they've changed people's worlds and its been an honour to delve deeper into the lives of some of them for you.

Away in a manger

W.J. Kirkpatrick

A - way in a man - ger, no crib for a bed, The

5
lit - tle Lord Je - sus laid down His sweet head. The

9
stars in the bright sky looked down where He lay, The

13
lit - tle Lord Je - sus a - sleep on the hay.

1

AWAY IN A MANGER

WORDS
Unknown, 1885 (verses 1 & 2),
verse 3 attributed to Charles H Gabriel (1856–1932)
or John Thomas McFarland, (1851–1913)

MUSIC
'The Cradle Song' by William J Kirkpatrick (1838–1921),
'St Kilda' by J E Clark (no dates)
'Mueller' by James Ramsey Murray (1841–1905)

Away in a manger, no crib for a bed,
The little Lord Jesus laid down his sweet head.
The stars in the bright sky looked down where he lay,
The little Lord Jesus, asleep in the hay.

The cattle are lowing, the Baby awakes.
But little Lord Jesus, no crying He makes.
I love thee, Lord Jesus, look down from the sky.
And stay by my side until morning is nigh.

Be near me, Lord Jesus, I ask thee to stay
Close by me forever, and love me, I pray!
Bless all the dear children in thy tender care
And fit us for heaven, to live with thee there.

This is an intense carol with a strong message put across in a way everyone can understand, yet its life-story reads like a whodunnit. Who wrote the words? Who wrote the tune? The origins of 'Away in a Manger' are, as with many other carols, shrouded in doubt.

These days it is accepted that the author of the first two quiet stanzas is unknown. Bishop William F Anderson remembered that while he was Secretary of the Board of Education in England between 1904 and 1908, Dr John T McFarland, then Secretary of the Board of Sunday Schools, dashed off a third stanza. However, earlier in 1892 the book *Gabriel's Vineyard Songs* by Charles H Gabriel includes the selfsame third stanza. So Bishop Anderson's story loses credibility: the alibi is blown!

For decades, the credit for both the words and the music went to Martin Luther who was supposed to have written them for his five-year-old son, Hans. Nothing has ever been found among Luther's works to confirm this. But a clue in his favour is that Luther did write and compose some marvellous hymns, for example 'Out of the Depths I Cry to Thee' of 1523 and 'A Safe Stronghold Our God is Still' (1529). Still, it's generally thought these days that this is a wrong deduction and that the lyrics are based on a poem written for the 400th anniversary of Luther's birth in 1883. Another proposition is that the theory that Luther is the 'culprit' may have been dreamed up for an early and, it seems, effective, marketing ploy: Luther as writer lent the song greater authority than would the anonymous credit 'North American origin'. North America was still a young country and rather short on history. Whatever the truth, Martin Luther has become the red herring in this mystery. Now it looks as if he had nothing to do with either the words or the music.

So, if not Luther, who wrote the music? In December 1945, Richard S Hill, a musical historian, holed himself up in a dusty library and, turning detective, isolated as many as forty-one musical settings for the carol. He investigated further and came up with four likely suspects. These men were mentioned in more collections than the others and were backed by the most evidence. They were James R Murray, 1887, John

Bunyan Herbert, 1891, Charles H Gabriel, 1892 and last but certainly not least, William J Kirkpatrick, 1895.

Once a carpenter (fitting for the man who wrote this heart-warming carol involving a carpenter and his wife), William J Kirkpatrick devoted himself entirely to music after his first wife died in 1878. Fifteen years later, according to a snippet in the *New York Times* in 1893, Kirkpatrick married Sara K Bourne at noon on 23 October that year. We know for sure that in 1895 William wrote a simple piece called 'Cradle Song'. In the UK 'Cradle Song' is usually sung to the words of 'Away in a Manger', its unpretentious tune reminding us of music's power to move.

But with other versions there is less certainty about who composed what. In 1895, the *Little children's book: for schools and families. By authority of the general council of the Evangelical Lutheran Church in North America* was published and 'Away in a Manger' is present, listed as a nursery hymn. Here, and in many publications following, the tune is called 'St Kilda' and the author is J E Clark of whom I can find no further trace. Two years later, on 7 May 1887, James R Murray (1841–1905) compiled *Dainty songs for little lads and lasses, for use in the kindergarten, school and home.* Murray made the apparent mistake of saying the tune is 'by Martin Luther for his children' and of putting his initials where the composer is usually credited. This led to the idea that he had arranged a work by Martin Luther who it was supposed wrote the music and the words. Over the next two years Murray tried to correct this. He published a new edition with his own music transposed into G major with the all-important credits: 'music by JRM'. In the next edition he put his initials only and reverted to his original score.

Murray would have been familiar with the thorny jungle of copyright law and have known that an arrangement of an old song is protected. Many compilers of song collections in the nineteenth and early twentieth centuries assumed old compositions to be in the public domain and would include an arrangement rather than ferret out the original, so infringing the arranger's copyright. Murray committed an own goal by attributing his own arrangement to Martin Luther. After this, many carol anthologies included his arrangement, carrying on the myth he had helped to create.

Then in 1921 a collection was published that would trailblaze the idea that a Carl Mueller wrote the music to 'Away in a Manger'. Little is known of Mueller, and Richard C Hill has suggested that an editor, suspecting that the German priest and theologian Martin Luther was not the composer, made up a name as a plausible substitute for the actual creator or arranger of the piece. To add to this confusion of identity, the equally gentle melody 'Mueller' by, in fact, Murray, was sung to the carol which was first known as 'Luther's Cradle Hymn'. It is this version of 'Away in a Manger' that is most often sung in North America.

As we have seen, in the UK, there is no doubt about who composed 'Cradle Song', the tune traditionally sung to the words for 'Away in a Manger'. It is the American composer William J Kirkpatrick. This version of 'Away in a Manger' was voted fifth out of a top ten of carols in a 2008 UK poll carried out to mark the launch of a Barbie DVD! More than seventy-five per cent of respondents said that singing carols made them feel nostalgic; they associated carols with childhood when Christmas is the most exciting time of the year, so it's not surprising that they chose this as one of their top ten.

On the night of 20 September 1921, William Kirkpatrick, aged eighty-three, apparently told his wife Lizzie (by now he had married for the third time) that he had a tune in his head and would not come to bed until he had written it down. When Lizzie Kirkpatrick awoke later, her husband was not there. She found William at his desk. He was dead. Perhaps this was a fitting close to a long and productive career: after his death Kirkpatrick's wife assigned the rights for 1,049 of his hymns to a publishing company, only a portion of his total output. Whatever the tune William Kirkpatrick heard the night he died, the melody he wrote fifty years before is simply sublime. It's a perfect demonstration that simplicity doesn't have to be boring.

I first came in contact with 'Away in a Manger' at Llandegfan primary school. I remember a feeling of great warmth flooding over me instantly. Singing the song felt really good. It has been one of my favourite carols since that special moment in school assembly all those years ago. I sing it often these days – as often as I can, and I've done so all my career, boy and man, in cathedral settings, concert halls and even in far-flung destinations like Israel.

It's interesting to note that many professional choirs shy away from programming this carol as part of their Christmas concerts and services because it's seen as childlike in its construction. I think they're missing a trick on this one. It's that very childlike quality that means it's a song that connects instantly and paints a vivid picture of the Nativity. When singing it you almost feel like you're there, part of the scene. There seems to be a warm glow around the whole telling of the event.

My favourite verse is the third, which is probably the most childlike: it's a simple prayer for God to be present in all of us from childhood innocence throughout our lives, until we all meet again in Heaven:

> Be near me, Lord Jesus, I ask thee to stay
> Close by me forever, and love me, I pray!
> Bless all the dear children in thy tender care
> And fit us for heaven, to live with thee there.

This carol is a gem. It's one that has had a huge impact on my life and I'm sure will continue to do so.

2

CALYPSO CAROL

'See Him Lying on a Bed of Straw'

Words and Music
Michael Perry (1942–96)

Copyright
Mrs B Perry/Jubilate Hymns

See him lying on a bed of straw:
A draughty stable with an open door;
Mary cradling the babe she bore:
The Prince of glory is his name.

Oh now carry me to Bethlehem
To see the Lord of love again;
Just as poor as was the stable then,
The Prince of glory when he came.

Star of silver, sweep across the skies,
Show where Jesus in the manger lies.
Shepherds swiftly from your stupor rise
To see the Saviour of the world.

Refrain

Angels, sing again the song you sang,
Bring God's glory to the heart of man:
Sing that Bethlehem's little baby can
Be salvation to the soul.

Refrain

Mine are riches from your poverty,
From your innocence, eternity;
Mine, forgiveness by your death for me,
Child of sorrow for my joy.

Refrain

The 'Calypso Carol', or 'See Him Lying on a Bed of Straw' is a modern song, although it is now nearly fifty years since it was composed. The calypso rhythm has led some to assume that this carol comes from the West Indies and perhaps this was underlined when in 1983 the Caribbean island of Nevis issued the song's refrain on a set of postage stamps. In fact Michael Perry, the writer of this carol, was born in Beckenham, Kent in 1942 and wrote this piece aged twenty-two while still at college. His inspiration was a Christmas question put to some young people: 'How would you like to be born in a stable?' Well, 'Calypso Carol' responds, on a bed made of straw in a 'draughty stable with an open door'.

Canon Perry went on to become one of the UK's leading contemporary hymn writers, and this one became his best-known composition through a very mid-twentieth-century mishap. When the tape of a carol service for BBC radio was accidentally wiped, Cliff Richard came to the rescue and recorded an alternative. One of his choices for the recording was 'See Him Lying on a Bed of Straw' and a hit was made.

The lyrics speak of the wealth that Christ has brought to the world and remind us of the significance of his birth. Through the innocent baby's poor beginnings in a 'draughty stable' and his later crucifixion, our flaws and transgressions can be recognised and forgiven. It is important, the song tells us, to remember that Jesus paid a price for our wellbeing. The third out of a total of four verses outlines how our riches – our way of life, not material wealth – are only possible because of Christ's sacrifice: 'Mine, forgiveness by your death for me/Child of sorrow for my joy.'

This carol asks us to reflect on God's message. It is perhaps all too easy to forget that peace or happiness are hard won: others have made sacrifices to make it possible. In the third verse 'Calypso Carol', like many traditional carols, evokes the Angels who witness our daily lives. It asks them to remind us and 'Sing that Bethlehem's little baby can/Be salvation to the soul.'

Michael Perry was a major figure in the religious music world. He was a founding member of Jubilate, an organisation set up in the sixties to offer an alternative kind of song to younger worshippers who were influenced by popular music. Perry was part of a movement to create songs that stepped outside the traditional musical and lyrical expectation of hymns. Such songs are called 'contemporary worship music', or 'praise songs' and have become very much a part of services held in many Anglican churches today. 'Calypso Carol' is an early example of this music.

Besides his work in the church and his busy musical career, Canon Michael Perry did much towards clarifying copyright issues for writers and composers of worship music. He countered the objections of critics who considered that songs written in praise of the Lord should not provide economic benefit to their authors. Jubilate, with which Perry was involved for the whole of his career until his death from a brain tumour in 1996, now represents over seventy authors and composers including David Iliff, co-editor of *The Carol Book*. Since 1966 Jubilate has been a major publisher of praise songs and prayers for many of which Michael Perry was the editor. In 1969 Jubilate published *Youth Praise 2*, one of the leading collections of contemporary worship music. It included Perry's 'Calypso Carol'.

There are varying suggestions as to the roots of the musical style of calypso. However, it is likely the style is of African origin: in the eighteen hundreds, slaves working on plantations were not allowed to talk but they were allowed to sing. The calypso was a way of protesting, of telling stories and communicating news around Trinidad and the other Caribbean islands. The subversive nature of the music alarmed the authorities, who in 1884 banned the playing of skin drums. The calypsonians, undeterred, adopted bamboo as their instrument. When this too was outlawed they resorted to found objects like pans and pots, which they fashioned into instruments. The 1930s saw these develop into the steel bands of today. The steel pan is the national instrument of Trinidad and Tobago and the only acoustic (non-electric) instrument invented in the twentieth century.

So, far removed from the traditional hymn, the calypso might be thought a bold genre for Michael Perry to choose for his carol, which has a typical calypso rhythm. However, he was tapping into the craze for calypso around the world and particularly in the US at that time. This had begun when, in 1956, Harry Belafonte released *Calypso*, an album that included the calypso 'Banana Boat Song', 'Day-O'. This was the first gramophone long-player ever to sell a million copies; it topped the charts for thirty-one weeks that year.

'Calypso Carol' was introduced to me through *Songs of Praise*. I'm sure I must have heard it at some point when I was a child, though we didn't really sing it at school. But it's definitely one I remembered pretty instantly when I heard it on *Songs of Praise*; it's a first-rate example of the result of marrying a good melody with good lyrics. With its upbeat rhythm it raises the spirits and encourages an energy that reflects the excitement of those following the star on that particular night. It has found the right blend of the secular and the religious and has touched our hearts. 'Calypso Carol' was voted one of the UK's top ten favourites in the *Songs of Praise* poll of 2005.

It's a great melody to sing, with a very catchy refrain that needs everyone to give extra volume, especially on the line: 'The Prince of glory when he came'. I don't think it will be one that I'll try to record on my own. I think it definitely needs a choir or a big congregation to deliver it at its best. I love singing it as part of a traditional congregation on

Songs of Praise because the members of the congregation never know how to move or dance or tap their toes or tap their sides – its always a rather uncomfortable moment. Although if you've got a fantastic gospel choir singing it as well, it makes the process a lot easier.

3

COVENTRY CAROL

Words and Music
Anon.

Lully, lulla, thow littel tyne child,
By, by, lully, lulla.
Lullay, lulla, thou littel tyne child,
By, by, lully, lulla.

O sisters too, how may we do
For to preserve this day
This pore yongling
For whom we do sing
Bye, bye, lully, lulla?

Herod, the king,
In his raging,
Chargid he hath this day
His men of might
In his owne sight,
All yonge children to slay.

That wo is me,
Pore child, for thee,
And ever morne and say
For thi parting
Neither say nor singe:
'By, by, lully, lulla.

Lully, lullay, thou little tiny child,
Bye, bye, lully, lullay.
Lully, lullay, thou little tiny child,
Bye, bye, lully, lullay.

Oh sisters too, how may we do
For to preserve this day.
This poor youngling
For whom we do sing,
Bye, bye, lully, lullay?

Herod the king,
In his raging,
Charged he hath this day
His men of might
In his own sight,
All children young to slay.

That woe is me,
Poor child, for thee,
And ever mourn and sigh
For thy parting
Neither say nor sing:
'By, by, lully, lullay.'

Haunting and sad, the 'Coventry Carol' has deep roots and an unusual history. It's said that the melody and lyrics originated in the songs that Bethlehem women sang when they held their firstborn sons during King Herod's reign of terror. It's rare in the history of carols that the ordinary people caught up in the Christmas story speak directly to us. Here it is the mothers themselves who sing this dark and frightened lullaby to their babies: 'Lully, lulla, thow little tyne child'.

The carol was first performed formally in the sixteenth century in Coventry as part of a mystery play called *The Pageant of the Shearmen and Taylors*. The play would proceed through the streets of the town, with the players performing on carts and the audience followed on foot – it must have been quite a sight. It brings to vivid life the Christmas story in chapter two of Matthew's Gospel, which has at its centre the Slaughter of the Innocents.

Herod, the king of Judea, is visited by the wise men who prophesy the wonders of Christ's birth. Wily Herod, who wants to find and kill the baby, says to them: 'Go and search diligently for the young child; and when ye have found him, bring me word again, that I may come and worship him also.' But the wise men, having found the child and presented him with their gifts, are warned in a dream not to return to Herod, and go home another way. Matthew continues in these stark words: 'Herod, when he saw that he was mocked of the wise men, was exceeding wroth, and sent forth, and slew all the children that were in Bethlehem, in all the coasts thereof, from two years old and under.'

The 'Coventry Carol' was performed in the play at the point where the women are singing to put their children to sleep lest Herod's soldiers find them by their crying. A splendid stage direction notes, 'Here Erode ragis (Herod rages) in the pagond (pageant) and in the strete also.' Its music is plaintive, full of the fear of impending brutality, but also the loss felt by the mothers. The play goes on to show what happens next, when the soldiers arrive to murder the children – one of the women stands up to them, flourishing 'the womanly geyre' of her 'pott-ladull'. But her resistance is futile. Then, as Matthew puts it, 'was there a voice heard, lamentation, and weeping, and great mourning'. Written for three voices, the carol would actually have been sung by a boy, and two men, representing the women, which audiences would have been used to.

The Coventry cycle was first mentioned in 1392 but the tune of the 'Coventry Carol' was first recorded in print in 1591 and the lyrics in 1534. Many of the traditional carols we sing today have lost their original tune or lyrics, but this one has kept both. Their author or authors however are unknown and a fire destroyed the manuscript at the Birmingham Free Reference Library in 1879. So in one sense the lyrics we sing today are original, but they are based on poor-quality transcripts and may not be completely accurate. The music has been recovered from a manuscript engraving also considered inaccurate – Thomas Sharp's *Dissertations on the Pageants or Dramatic Mysteries, Anciently Performed at Coventry* . . . (1825). It is a well-known example of a 'Picardy third' (a harmonic device used in European classical music) and is traditionally sung a cappella.

There is much discussion about the meaning of the words – for example, 'And ever morne and say/For thi parting/Neither say nor singe' in the last verse isn't clear. Some writers have changed it to 'ever mourn and may' some to 'ever morn and day'. Other writers have given the meaning as plain 'grieve and sigh'. I sing simply, 'And ever mourn and sigh/For thy parting/Neither say nor sing.' Like other medieval carols, the 'Coventry Carol' is lesser known than the big hits like 'We Three Kings of Orient Are' or 'Hark ! The Herald Angels Sing' (both nineteenth-century). Today it is mostly sung not by congregations in church services but by choirs in Christmas performances – a far cry from the colourful outdoor pageants of sixteenth-century Coventry.

I first got to hear 'Lully, Lullay' at Bangor Cathedral when I was a probationer looking up at the main choristers. It was during one of the Christmas services that I heard this carol which sounded so different to all the others that we sang. It's neither bright and energetic nor similar in vein to something like 'O Come, O Come, Emmanuel!' The melody is like that of no other carol, including the fact that the final chord goes into the major when the whole of the music has been very much in the minor. It's odd to think that as children we used to sing this carol whose lyrics are quite heavy going, being all about the danger that these babies could be in. But the story makes it really, really powerful to sing as an adult. Even now when I perform it I approach it in such a different way to all the others, it's almost as if you need to take greater care with 'Lully, Lullay' because it's so haunting and emotional that it requires more concentration and more from the heart. You've got to delve deep into your soul to bring out the best in this carol.

It's almost impossible to imagine what any of these mothers felt like, or fathers for that matter, under the threat that your child would not just be taken away from you, but would be murdered. The melody line up until the final chord is quite ploddy, it doesn't really do anything out of the ordinary. But then you get this huge shock on the final phrase when you expect the melody to go da da da da da with the final da the same note as the preceding, and it goes da da da da da and the final da goes up with a major leap – something that you're really not expecting. Maybe it's there because on the final chord there's some hope that murder won't be the downfall of your newborn baby and that God will come good in the end – who knows? The carol was performed at a highly dramatic moment near the end of *The Pageant of the Shearmen and Taylors*. I can imagine the lights going down in the performance space and basically just the words and the music telling the story. It doesn't need any gimmicks at all.

Due to a lot of repetition in the words, the 'Coventry Carol' harks back to some of our greatest hymns, which use repetition to great effect. This doesn't happen so often in carols, but in this one it does. It's very still, it's thought-provoking in its construction; it makes you listen.

THE ANGEL GABRIEL FROM HEAVEN CAME

(Gabriel's Message)

WORDS
Basque carol collected by
Charles Bordes (1863–1909)

MUSIC
'Gabriel's Message' arranged by
Edgar Pettman (1866–1943)

Translation by Sabine Baring-Gould (1834–1924)

The angel Gabriel from Heaven came,
His wings as drifted snow, his eyes as flame:
'All hail,' said he, 'thou lowly maiden Mary
Most highly favoured lady.' Gloria!

'For know a blessed mother thou shalt be,
All generations laud and honour thee,
Thy Son shall be Emmanuel, by seers foretold.
Most highly favoured lady.' Gloria!

Then gentle Mary meekly bowed her head,
'To me be as it pleaseth God,' she said.
'My soul shall laud and magnify his holy name.'
Most highly favoured lady. Gloria!

Of her, Emmanuel, the Christ, was born
In Bethlehem, all on a Christmas morn,

The angel Gabriel

(Gabriel's Message)

adapted by
S. Baring-Gould

Traditional Basque

The an - gel Ga - bri - el from hea - ven came, His

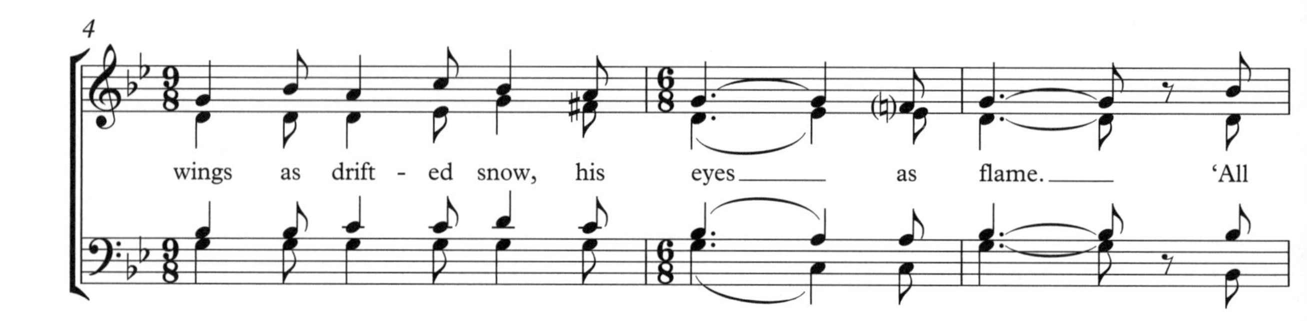
4
wings as drift - ed snow, his eyes as flame. 'All

7
hail' said he, 'thou low - ly maid - en Ma - - ry, Most

11
high - ly fa - voured La - dy, Glo - - - ri - a!'

And Christian folk throughout the world will ever say:
'Most highly favoured lady.' Gloria!

This beautiful, melodic Basque carol brings to life the Annunciation and Mary's lines in St Luke's Gospel: 'Behold the handmaid of the Lord, be it unto me according to Thy word'. The moment when the Angel Gabriel comes to Mary and tells her she will be carrying the son of God must have been like a thunderclap to this 'lowly maiden' Mary. Luke says simply, 'and the angel came unto her'. The carol tells it in splendidly dramatic – and suitably scary – form: 'The Angel Gabriel from Heaven came/His wings as drifted snow, his eyes as flame'. The Angel Gabriel calls Mary 'most highly favoured lady'. The feast of the Annunciation on 25 March was known, and still is in many parts of rural Britain, as Lady Day.

Sabine Baring-Gould wrote standing up. The author of memorable hymns like 'Now the Day is Over' (often heard chiming from belfries) translated 'The Angel Gabriel' from the original Basque carol. Renowned for ten-minute sermons, with which his congregation seemed comfortable, Baring-Gould wrote another of his hits, 'Onward Christian Soldiers', within a similarly short time frame while a teacher at Lancing College near Brighton. He was a multi-talented man. Besides his clerical duties and attending to his brood of fifteen children, he was a novelist and scholar. With so much to do no wonder he had little time to sit down!

Baring-Gould's background was far from calm or uneventful. One of his ancestors, Edward Gould, murdered a man who had beaten him at the gambling table. Edward got off on a technicality familiar to readers of murder mysteries: his counsel proved that a witness could not have identified him by the light of the 'full moon' as the moon had not been full that night. Edward's gambling might have cost him the family seat of Lewtrenchard Manor had he not already mortgaged it to his mother Margaret, known as Old Madame. Margaret Gould disapproved of the religious beliefs of her daughter's husband, Charles Baring (of the banking family) and insisted that he add 'Gould' to his name and that the estate go to her grandson, Sabine's grandfather.

Sabine's father, also Edward, worked for the East India Company. His career was curtailed by a carriage accident and then Edward took the young Sabine abroad. This meant he spent little more than two years in formal schooling. One winter spent in the Basque country may have been the inspiration for his translation into English of this old Christmas carol which he called 'The Angel Gabriel from Heaven Came' or more simply, 'Gabriel's Message'. Unable to transcribe a tune, Baring-Gould sang it to himself until he could remember it and then got a member of his family to note it down.

Baring-Gould's desire to take holy orders was disapproved of by his father, but despite threats of disinheritance in 1864 he became curate at Horbury Bridge in the West Riding and he did take over the estate on Edward's death in 1872. Then in 1881, when his uncle died, he became both parson and squire (squarson) of Lewtrenchard Manor for the last four decades of his life. The manor today is a hotel, complete with the desk at which Sabine wrote 'Onward Christian Soldiers' and with rumours of the ghost of Old Madame; the house is supposedly little changed since Sabine's painstaking renovations.

Sabine's grandson William Baring-Gould was an expert on Sir Arthur Conan-Doyle's Sherlock Holmes. He wrote a biography of this famous, but fictional, detective, *Sherlock Holmes of Baker Street: A life of the world's first consulting detective*, which was published in 1962. Short of material for Holmes' early years, William is supposed to have drawn on the eccentric experiences of his grandfather Sabine for inspiration. An early case of identity theft!

The Basque carol, *'Birjina gaztetto bat zegoen'*, which Baring-Gould translated, was included in the *Archives de la Tradition Basque* collected by the French music teacher and composer Charles Bordes and published in 1895. Co-founder of the Schola Cantorum, Bordes was part of a successful movement to open up the French music scene in the nineteenth century from its focus on opera to music that included plainsong. The Schola Cantorum is now a highly respected institution with alumni such as the cellist Paul Tortelier and composer Cole Porter.

Aside from Bordes' source it's been suggested that the roots of this carol go back to a fourteenth-century Latin chant, 'Angelus Ad Virginem'. There are also several versions of 'The Angel Gabriel', including one by the Victorian poet Gerard Manley Hopkins (1844–1889) called 'Gabriel From Heaven's King' and another by an unknown author, 'The Angel Gabriel from God', which is published in the 1833 edition of *Christmas Carols Ancient and Modern*.

In this and other of his translations, Baring-Gould does not provide a literal English version of the text; instead he captures the essential atmosphere of the original. He reduced the number of stanzas from six in the original to four, and used powerful imagery, writing in fine phrases reminiscent of the Victorian era in which most of his life was lived. Sung with few instruments or with a choir only, not only for the Annunciation, but for Advent and Christmas services of lessons and carols, this is a moving meditation on the magnitude of God's choice of Mary to be the mother of his son and on her humble response to the message that Gabriel brings to her. The words were first published in *The University Carol Book* in 1922 of which the composer Edgar Pettman (1866–1943) was music editor.

Sabine Baring-Gould died a week after Christmas Day, on 2 January 1924. He is buried next to his wife Grace, the mill girl he had fallen in love with when she was 16, in the churchyard across the road from Lewtrenchard Manor. It is to be hoped that after 90 years of a full and productive life, which includes this wonderful carol, this energetic, gifted man rests there in peace.

I think I was first introduced to 'The Angel Gabriel' by the musical supervisor of *Songs of Praise* and I included it on my first Christmas album as an adult, sung to an oboe accompaniment. My favourite verse is the third, which is the only time we hear Mary speak:

Then gentle Mary meekly bowed her head,
'To me be as it pleaseth God,' she said.
'My soul shall laud and magnify His holy name.'

The writing is old-fashioned, but it's still relevant to this day. It's another carol that, without having an obvious melody, is musically both exciting and interesting. My favourite part to sing is definitely the final 'Gloria!' because it's very lilting, very melodic and you can put a lot of different emotions into each of the 'Glorias' at the end of each verse. It's a favourite with choirboys around Christmas because the Lady becomes flavoured as opposed to favoured – and the Lady of course is called Gloria!

Performing this piece of music was definitely one of the highlights of my Christmas tour a few years back during the time I was also doing *Strictly Come Dancing*. This carol just does seem to lilt along and it's a real pleasure singing it. I feel I put my whole soul into it. It's also one of those carols that could never become stale. I performed it forty-seven times over fifty-two nights on that tour and every night found something different within those four verses.

The clever writing of this carol means that musically it grows throughout the verses – the first growing into the second, second into the third and third into the fourth. The words do exactly the same thing, so that every verse has a starting point and then a climax and then you start again and then a climax, start again and to a climax . . . This is carol writing at its best; I like it so much that I gave my son the middle name of Gabriel.

5

DECK THE HALL WITH BOUGHS OF HOLLY

'Nos Galan'

WORDS AND MUSIC
Anon.

Deck the hall with boughs of holly,
'Tis the season to be jolly,
Don we now our gay apparel,
Troll the ancient Yuletide carol.

See the blazing Yule before us,
Strike the harp and join the chorus,
Follow me in merry measure,
While I tell of Yuletide treasure.

Fast away the old year passes,
Hail the new, ye lads and lasses,
Sing we joyous all together,
Heedless of the wind and weather.

Carols are of course associated with Christmas and the birth of Christ. This is not how they started out. At the beginning, carols were pagan and they were sung (and danced) for festivities and rites that had nothing to do with Christmas or Christianity. The medieval church adopted carols to celebrate the major feasts and 'Deck the Hall' is a fine example of carols' long journey of reinvention from pagan festival dance songs through to current Christmas carols.

Until researching this book, I'd not known that the tune for 'Deck the Hall' was Welsh. But it was originally a Welsh dance song dating back to the sixteenth century and sung at Yuletide accompanied by the harp. Yuletide is one of those pagan religious festivals that have been absorbed, like carols, into the Christian church, as in the case of Yule into the celebration of Christmas. Yuletide was originally observed from late December to early January and was placed on 25 December when the Julian, Christian calendar was adopted.

'Deck the Hall' goes right back to the beginning in another way. One of the various interpretations of the origin of the word 'carol' is that it means a dance – a circling dance. 'Deck the Hall' began as just that, a circling dance. On New Year's Eve, revellers would dance in a ring around the harpist, who played answering bars to the verses improvised or remembered by the dancers. It was like a party game – if a dancer could not think of a new verse, he or she would drop out of the dance. It's thought that the 'fa la la la la, la la la la' refrains now sung in the carol replace the harp's responses. And the harp is here in the lyrics, with 'strike the harp and join the chorus'.

'Deck the Hall' celebrates the harp – an instrument understood and appreciated in Wales. The tune was first found in a musical manuscript by Welsh harpist John Parry Ddall (*c.*1710–1782; in Welsh, Ddall means blind, so his name was blind John Parry), but it is without a doubt older than that. It was published in 1784 by harpist Edward Jones, who was an energetic promoter of the traditional music of his native Wales. He gathered more than 200 songs and even supplied prizes for harp-playing at the eisteddfod. For this carol (at the time a dance song), Jones uses the name '*Nos Galan*' (New Year's Eve) and the text of a love song written by the Poet John Ceiriog Hughes (1832–87).

Hughes also celebrated the harp of Wales. He worked for much of his life on the railways, as station master for Caersws railway station. He was celebrated for the simple directness of his poetry; like many Welsh poets, he took a bardic name – 'Ceiriog' – from the River Ceiriog, which flows through the Ceiriog Valley, where he was born. In his home village, the public library contains a memorial inscription to him. He also spent his time pursuing his interest in the folk music and songs of Wales and the harpists who accompanied them, setting these old tunes to his own lyrics. This led to a grand project to publish four volumes of Welsh airs, of which only the first volume actually made it to press in 1863: *Cant O Ganeuon* ('A Hundred Songs').

During the eighteenth century the tune of 'Nos Galan' spread widely, but the Welsh harp was abandoned when Mozart used the tune in a piano and violin duet and, later, Haydn arranged it in the song 'New Year's Night', accompanied by piano, violin and cello.

No one seems to know who wrote the words of 'Deck the Hall'. We do know that the song was carried to North America by Welsh miners who emigrated to the Appalachian mountains of North Carolina, so the words may have American roots. It's clear though that they almost certainly bear no resemblance to the original words sung in the Welsh pagan festival or to the poem by John Ceiriog Hughes. The dance steps of the merrymakers are also lost.

The journey of '*Nos Galan*' continues into Victorian England. The carol was reinvented again when the Victorians started to understand Christmas not as a community event, but as a domestic festival honouring the family, with holly, and gifts, and trees. The Victorians turned 'Deck the Hall' into a traditional English Christmas carol. The first English version appeared in *The Franklin Square Song Collection*, edited by J P McCaskey in 1881.

Due to the pagan roots of carols, for many years the Church was uneasy about singing them. 'Deck the Hall' still wears its pagan clothes well. 'Deck the hall with boughs of holly,' it goes, ''Tis the season to be jolly.' The birth of Christ is not here, but the passing of the old year and the birth of the new are, and both are welcomed joyfully by everyone. Decking the halls with holly is an ancient custom several thousand years old – the Druids, Romans and Greeks all decorated their homes with

this plant. The Druids in particular believed that the holly was a sacred tree – they noticed that it remained green all winter long and thus believed that it was never deserted by the sun. The Romans considered holly to be a symbol of good will and sent wreaths of it to newlyweds as a token of good wishes and congratulations. Holly was also used during the festival of Saturn, which was held each year beginning on 17 December to honour the Roman god of sowing and husbandry.

In the twenty-first century and in the spirit of its pagan origins, 'Deck the Hall' fell into the hands of vandals. *Bart Simpson's Guide to Life* features the following:

Decorate your father's belly
Fa la la la la, la la la la
While he's sleeping by the telly
Fa la la la la, la la la la

Through all its reinventions, 'Deck the Hall' has remained a popular carol – dancing optional. It wasn't one we performed particularly often in primary school and the only time I think I have sung it was as a member of the Bangor Cathedral choir, not in the cathedral setting but in the concert setting at Penrhyn Castle, where we used to give Christmas concerts. It's a little bit too schmaltzy, too jolly for me and I like my carols with a little bit of a story, a little bit of a journey, and let's face it, this one has none of that. But through all its reinventions 'Deck the Hall' has remained a popular carol and the tune has stood the test of time. But, like Bart Simpson, I don't take it one hundred per cent seriously. It's programmed into a concert in order to put a smile on the face and it's one of those moments where you reach across and hold your child's hand and squeeze it gently.

6

DING DONG MERRILY ON HIGH

WORDS	MUSIC
George Ratcliffe Woodward	Jehan Tabourot
(1848–1934)	(1518–93)

Ding dong merrily on high,
In heaven the bells are ringing,
Ding dong, verily the sky
Is riv'n with angel-singing:

Gloria . . . Hosanna in excelsis!

E'en so here below, below
Let steeple bells be swungen
And 'Io, io, io!'
By priest and people sungen.

Gloria . . . Hosanna in excelsis!

Pray you, dutifully prime
Your matin chime, ye ringers!
May you beautifully rhyme
Your evetime song, ye singers.

Gloria . . . Hosanna in excelsis!

'Ding Dong Merrily on High' – or as every chorister calls it, 'Ding Dong' – is one of those Christmas carols that probably everyone has sung during their lifetime and it's a little bit of Christmas cheer in the middle of a doubtless highly focused nine lessons and carols service.

George Woodward, who arranged 'Ding Dong', just missed being a Christmas baby, being born on 27 December 1848 in Birkenhead. He was ordained deacon in the Church of England just before Christmas on 21 December, aged twenty-six. He played the euphonium and his hobbies were bee-keeping and bell-ringing. He must have brought his bell-ringing skills to the writing of 'Ding Dong Merrily on High', keeping the bells swinging with a rhythmic rise and fall. It's a rhythm that is vital for the tune of the carol to succeed and it is the tune here, with its momentum of bells, that creates the dynamism of this carol, sweeping up the singer in a tide of euphoria.

Like many carols, including 'Deck the Hall' and 'The Twelve Days of Christmas', 'Ding Dong Merrily on High', which was first published in *The Cambridge Carol Book* in 1924, has secular beginnings with no seasonal or religious associations. George Woodward dug deep into the history of traditional European folk tunes to source his several carol collections. In this case he found the melody, '*Le branle de l'official*', in a dance manual called *Orchésographie*. Published in 1589, this lively book is presented in the form of a dialogue between a dance tutor and his pupil, a device used today to make dry or difficult information easier to grasp. The editor, Thoinot Arbeau, was a French ecclesiastic, who had a penchant for anagrams, Thoinot Arbeau being an anagram of his real name, Jehan Tabourot.

Arbeau's book covers a range of late Renaissance dances as well as the branle, including the gavotte, the pavane and the volta. Unusually for the time, the musical score is set down one side of the page with the dance steps printed next to the notes. The exhaustive and sometimes exhausting dancing instructions in the *Orchésographie*, alongside woodcut illustrations of dancers in a variety of eye-catching costumes, leave nothing to doubt. The branle appears to be similar to the modern line-dance and each one has a colourful title such as the 'branle of the horse', or 'the torch', or 'the washerwoman'. This 'branle' is danced, writes Thoinot/ Jehan, 'by lackeys and serving wenches', comprising 'little springs' whereby the lackey helps the serving wench to leap into the air. Sometimes the gentility liked to dress down as peasants and shepherds and dance like them too. This was perhaps because with so many intimate moves and steps, it was a good way to meet a future partner!

Despite its sixteenth-century origins, 'Ding Dong Merrily on High' is a carol of an early twentieth-century Christmas. It came upon the scene in the 1924 edition of *The Cambridge Carol Book* where it was arranged by the Irish composer and lecturer Charles Wood (1866–1926) who collaborated with Woodward on many of his books.

During the second half of the nineteenth and the beginning of the twentieth century carols moved indoors: from wassailing in the streets, they were brought into the more formal setting of the church. So 'Ding Dong Merrily on High' is a fine example of the secular dance – an original meaning of the word carol – coming together with the religious to create the inspirational song for Christmas that we think of today as a carol.

Carols have developed over centuries in accordance with cultural or religious shifts, with changes in words and verses. 'Ding Dong Merrily on High' started life in a very different social setting to today's. The carol's flexibility is represented in the variety of artists who have recorded it in differing arrangements. These include John Rutter and the Choir of Clare College, Cambridge, Maddy Prior and Charlotte Church. Alison Moyet's strong and melodious performance in the 1988 French and Saunders Christmas Special is backed by a berobed choir (French and Saunders). Singing with a lusty lack of harmony, they grab their microphone stands and come to centre stage, their soaring voices drowning Moyet's solo.

So, dance and bells and perhaps bees may be influences behind Woodward's compilation of this carol that rings in the powerful mystery of God coming to earth in human form. It brims with the vigorous energy of its secular roots, its tune leading the way.

I first performed 'Ding Dong' not at school, funnily enough – it obviously wasn't very popular in North Wales – but in Bangor Cathedral, and for me, as any chorister would probably tell you, it's always about breath control. I've heard so many choirs singing this piece of music and I was probably guilty of this myself in the early days in Bangor Cathedral, where you'd start the Gloria not having taken enough breath and so when you've got to the end of it you've no breath left to actually finish off the phrase. So the 'Hosannah in Excelsis' would be just a mumble. You feel you've really achieved something quite momentous when you can actually do the Gloria all in one breath without turning green or looking as if you've just run a marathon. It's also all about diction – the words need to be really spat out. And there are plenty of opportunities to roll the rr's: 'rriven wth angel-singing' and 'verrrily the sky' and I remember as a boy soprano not quite understanding what was happening in the second verse when the steeple bells are swung and 'io io io'. I'd sing it with gusto but didn't really get the intricacies of the message of the carol. Even if you don't get it, the chorus particularly tells you what it's all about – glorification and lifting your voice to God in song.

I'm not sure if 'Ding Dong' would be on my top ten list, I think it's probably a little bit too light-hearted and simplistic for my liking. And I don't mean simplistic in the way of 'Away in a Manger'. That simplicity works in its favour whereas this is really just a cheery Christmas interlude. I think lots of choirs record 'Ding Dong Merrily on High' to prove, especially on a Christmas album, just how versatile they can be. There have been some very elaborate arrangements of this carol, where lots of voices sing against one another, and on the whole I think that, though most of the best-known arrangements work, some have been too clever for their own good and by complicating this carol you take away its heart and it's overriding message.

O COME, ALL YE FAITHFUL

(Adeste Fideles)

Words & Music
John Francis Wade (1711–86)

Translated by Frederick Oakley (1802–80),
William Brooke (1848–1917)

O come, all ye faithful,
Joyful and triumphant,
O come ye, O come ye to Bethlehem;
Come and behold him,
Born the King of Angels;

O come, let us adore him!
O come, let us adore him!
O come, let us adore him, Christ the Lord!

God of God,
Light of Light,
Lo! He abhors not the Virgin's womb;
Very God,
Begotten, not created;

Refrain

O come, all ye faithful

ADESTE FIDELES
translated by F. Oakeley,
W.T. Brooke and others

J. F. Wade

O come, all ye faith - ful, Joy - ful and tri - umph - ant, O come ye, O

6
come_ ye to Beth - le - hem; Come and_ be - hold Him,

11
Born the King of an - gels; O come, let us a - dore Him, O come, let us a -

16
- dore Him, O come, let us a - dore Him,_ Christ_ the Lord.

See how the shepherds,
Summoned to his cradle,
Leaving their flocks, draw nigh to gaze!
We, too, will thither
Bend our hearts' oblations;

Refrain

Sing, choir of angels,
Sing in exultation;
Sing, all ye citizens of heaven above;
Glory to God
In the highest;

Refrain

Yea, Lord, we greet thee,
Born this happy morning;
Jesu, to thee be glory given;
Word of the Father,
Now in flesh appearing;

Refrain

It wouldn't be Christmas if we didn't wholeheartedly perform 'O Come, All Ye Faithful'. It's one of those carols that have come to mean Christmas. It issues a personal invitation to witness the momentous event of Christ's birth – 'O come ye, O come ye to Bethlehem/ Come and behold Him/Born the King of angels'. The clear imagery of 'O Come, All Ye Faithful', which tells the story of Christmas from the virgin birth to the arrival of the shepherds and the three Magi, seems to have appeal for everyone, everywhere. It ends with the actual greeting of the newborn Jesus and an offering of praise and adoration to Our Lord now manifest in the world. It is sung with conviction in church services on Christmas Eve or Christmas morning when a celebration is called for and we respond with joyful assent and full hearts.

So it is perhaps strange to discover that this accessible hymn has such obscure origins and that theories abound as to who wrote the lyrics and composed the tune. It has been suggested that the music of 'O Come All Ye Faithful' was adapted by Handel or written by a prominent eighteenth-century Catholic musician Thomas Arne (1720–78). For many years it was an anonymous Latin hymn, '*Adeste Fideles*', possibly written and composed by John Francis Wade, who was the son of a Leeds cloth merchant. If he did write it he may have copied the tune from other sources including, curiously, a 1744 comic opera, *Acajou*, by Charles Favart. John Francis was a Catholic and supporter of the Jacobite cause for the return of the Stuarts to the throne of Britain and, round about 1745–46, during a Jacobite rebellion, he fled to Douai in France. There he perfected his mastery of calligraphy and illumination and scratched a living by making and selling beautiful copies of plainchant and other music, as well as by teaching Latin and church song. He has been credited as the 'father of the English plainchant revival'. It's supposed that he wrote '*Adeste Fideles*' some time around 1740 to 1743. A mystery surrounding 'O Come, All Ye Faithful' is why it became known as the 'Portuguese hymn'. It was regularly sung at the chapel of the Portuguese Embassy in London, and it was suggested that it had Portuguese origins, being composed by King John IV of Portugal (1603–56), 'the Musician King'. Ian Bradley suggests that Marcos Portugal (1762–1830), composer of opera and Chapel Master to the Portuguese kings, wrote the music. Whatever its origins, it grew in popularity from the mid-nineteenth century boosted by its inclusion in the first edition of *Hymns Ancient and Modern* in 1861.

The current text seems to be the work of many hands. The first, second, sixth and seventh verses, the most commonly sung, are based on a translation by Frederick Oakley (1802–80) for his congregation at the Margaret

Chapel in London. Frederick Oakley was keen to restore what he regarded as authentic church worship. He wanted to counter 'frivolous' modern tunes replacing them with tunes from older traditions. Criticism of his ritualistic practices contributed to his decision to embrace Roman Catholicism in 1845. Among those who worshipped at his Chapel, the Margaret Chapel in Marylebone, was William Gladstone, who liked the fact that the worship was both devout and hearty, and approved of the fact that the sermons never lasted for more than twenty minutes.

Verses three, four and five are based on a translation by William Brooke (1848–1917), who became interested in hymnology after entering commercial life. He apparently translated three new Latin verses and inserted them into the Oakley translation, thus forming the basis of the version that was first published in *Murray's Hymnal* in 1852 and which we sing today.

The mystery deepens in the early twenty-first century; Professor Bennett Zon, Head of Music at Durham University, has suggested that this carol contains secret codes from Jacobite times, the work of John Francis Wade. He thinks it masks an ode to Bonnie Prince Charlie, so that the 'all ye faithful' are in reality the Jacobites and 'Bethlehem' is England. Looked at in this way, 'O Come, All Ye Faithful' is about the restoration to the British throne of the exiled King Charles Edward Stuart – the Bonnie Prince – who was born on 20 December 1720. So, Professor Zon argues, the carol's hidden text is 'O come, faithful Catholics, joyful and triumphant, O come ye, O come ye to England; come and behold him born the King of the English – Bonnie Prince Charlie!' The carol would have lost its Jacobite meanings as Catholics gained more religious freedom and the Jacobite cause lost its attraction in the late 1770s. This coincided with Wade's (alleged) first publication of this glorious carol and its steady rise in popularity in churches of many denominations since then.

I sang 'O Come, All Ye Faithful' at school, I sang it in Bangor Cathedral. It's a carol that you really need to be able to perform with other people, best sung as a congregational carol. I've also sung it as a solo and it doesn't really work as well, it's very difficult to get the energy across that's needed, but when you've got like-minded people letting rip with you, then I think the true meaning of this carol comes across. It's performed at its best in St George's Chapel just before Christmas as part of my charity The Story of Christmas when you put the band of the Irish Guards with the descant (descant is musical ornament – it's the melody sung above, and simultaneously with, the main theme) and you've got the Choir of Westminster Cathedral, and a congregation of about 800 people. The way we do it is to break it up so that basically the carol starts with the magnificent fanfare, with all eyes on the horns of the Irish Guards, then as the carol is performed, a procession with the Bishop of London at the back comes to the altar and after

Sing, choir of angels,
Sing in exultation,
Sing, all ye citizens of heaven above;
Glory to God
In the highest;

and the chorus, all of a sudden the light is taken down and the Bishop of London addresses the congregation with the final Lesson. I'll always remember that the first time I did it I was in the company of such fine actors as Judy Dench and Anthony Hopkins and down came the Bishop of London, Richard Chartres, and boomed the final Lesson in his most actorly of voices. You could see every well-known actor turn and face him and all that was going through their minds, which was what was going through mine, the fact that the Bishop of London had a better acting voice than any of those assembled. So what happens is that he reads his Lesson and then the band, voices of the choir, organ, all of us carry on to end the carol with 'Yea Lord, we greet thee/Born this happy morning' and it's a really special moment where you can understand how music is vital to worship. You have the words of the Bishop, which are so important, surrounded by this glorious music composed with God in mind. It's the perfect coming together of words and music in the most perfect of environments.

Many descants have been written for this carol, but I think that the best by far is by David Willcocks. It was published in 1961 in the first book of the *Carols for Choirs* series that we used at Bangor Cathedral. It's majestic, exciting, vocally challenging, and fits beautifully with the original melody. Another testament to this beautiful carol is that it can be performed away from a church or a cathedral setting and still retain its religiousness. I've been very fortunate to sing it in the Royal Albert Hall on many occasions, not just during a *Songs of Praise* Christmas recording but as part of Christmas concerts there and this carol's magnitude makes even the Albert Hall seem like a religious venue.

Another of my memories of this carol is of travelling with my wife, who used to work for the travel industry, flying out to San Francisco before her because the flight she was on was full and actually sitting outside Macy's store in the square in San Francisco with Christmas music coming out of a microphone and the whole of San Francisco it seemed in a good mood and hearing Bing Crosby singing this song '*Adeste Fidelis*', 'O Come, All Ye Faithful'. It was a real moment when you knew that Christmas was coming and there was a reason to be joyful.

Aside from Bing, this carol has been covered by everyone: Andy Williams, John Williams, Sinatra, Dylan, the Three Tenors, the Chieftans, Celine Dion, Enya – the list is endless. But 'O Come All Ye Faithful' is not a carol that I can say I really love to sing. I can't put my finger on why this is, because it has all the ingredients of a fantastic carol: it's majestic, exciting to sing, it has a powerful accompaniment, the words are very positive. But I think that for this carol really to come alive you need more than that somehow; you do need the descant, the brass accompaniment, you do need the blaring organ, and more than anything you really do need a fine congregation.

8

DO YOU HEAR WHAT I HEAR?

Words
Noel Regney (1922–2002)

Music
Gloria Shayne (1923–2008)

Said the night wind to the little lamb,
'Do you see what I see?
Way up in the sky, little lamb,
Do you see what I see?

'A star, a star
Dancing in the night
With a tail as big as a kite,
With a tail as big as a kite.'

Said the little lamb to the shepherd boy,
'Do you hear what I hear?
Ringing thru the sky, shepherd boy
Do you hear what I hear?

'A song, a song
High above the tree
With a voice as big as the sea,
With a voice as big as the sea.'

Said the shepherd boy to the mighty king,
'Do you know what I know?
In your palace warm, mighty king,
Do you know what I know?

'A Child, a Child
Shivers in the cold,
Let us bring Him silver and gold
Let us bring Him silver and gold.'

Said the king to the people ev'rywhere
'Listen to what I say!
Pray for peace, people ev'rywhere
Listen to what I say!

'The Child, the Child
Sleeping in the night
He will bring us goodness and light,
He will bring us goodness and light.'

At Christmas there are many kinds of music, performed in churches, school assembly halls, community centres: all the places where people come together to celebrate the season. We hear Christmas songs on television and in shopping malls and cafes as we go about our lives buying gifts for our family and friends. Traditionally these are the carols that we have known since childhood, but many are not the classic compositions, they are modern Christmas songs. One such is 'Do You Hear What I Hear?'

'Do You Hear What I Hear?' was to be the 'B' side for a single expected to be a hit. The composer Noel Regney wrote the words picturing a new-born lamb. His then wife, the composer and lyricist Gloria Shayne, composed the tune. It's a great story, the fact that it begins with a little lamb, as not many carols do, and the fact that it starts with a night wind telling the lamb, the lamb tells the shepherd boy, the shepherd boy then tells the mighty king and the king proclaims the story of this magical child that has come to save us all. The hook of the whole carol is one single line if you like. It's 'Do you see what I see, Do you hear what I hear, Do you know what I know, listen to what I say' – that's it in its entirety.

It's also a prayer for peace. In October 1962, at the time this song was written, the world was contemplating the very real possibility of nuclear war. Russia had placed nuclear weapons in Cuba, and on discovering this the United States asked for them to be removed. After intense negotiations between President John F Kennedy and the Soviet premier Nikita Khrushchev and their advisers and with the United Nations, the 'Cuban Missile Crisis' was averted. But for several crucial days, people all over the world contemplated the likelihood that they would be killed.

Regney's words were influenced by the sight of the mothers and babies in strollers who patrolled Manhattan's sidewalks. This was not an idealistic notion; the couple wrote the song at the very time that America was poised on the brink of war. Years later Shayne was to remark that when they had written the song neither she nor Regney were able to sing it all the way through. 'Our little song broke us up', she said, 'you must realize there was a threat of nuclear war at the time.'

The crisis was over when 'Do You Hear What I Hear' was released in America shortly after Thanksgiving in November 1962. Its first recording was made by the Harry Simeone Chorale who in 1958 had had a hit with 'The Little Drummer Boy'. Conceived as a 'B' side as it was, 'Do You Hear What I Hear' went on to sell more than a quarter of a million copies over the Christmas season. But it was Bing Crosby's version, recorded on Friday 22 November 1963 – the day that John F Kennedy was assassinated – that made it a worldwide hit.

Many artists since have recorded this song: Bob Dylan, Mahalia Jackson, Whitney Houston, Gladys Knight, Johnny Mathis and Andy Williams are just a few of them. It's a piece of music I didn't know as a child. It was introduced to me by the musical supervisor of *Songs of Praise* as a possible duet, a collaboration I could do with the boys' choir Libera, who were to perform it on *Songs of Praise*. I went into the studio to record it and was bowled over by the melody and the simplicity of the message. I've loved singing it. The most difficult thing in this carol is getting who said what to whom at exactly the right time. Our performance of 'Do

You Hear What I Hear' on *Songs of Praise* went down incredibly well. The whole idea I suppose that here was a man who was probably best known as a boy soprano singing, with young boys, a carol which is very simple and childlike in its creation, really did seem to resonate with the audience. I also love the fact that this carol builds up and up and up as the verses go along until 'Said the king to the people ev'rywhere / listen to what I say! / Pray for peace, people ev'rywhere'. It's glorious, it's the highlight of the carol and then all of a sudden you go back to why we're all there performing it with:

The Child, the Child
Sleeping in the night
He will bring us goodness and light,
He will bring us goodness and light.

It's almost like a Spielberg epic movie in the way it's been constructed. There are some really beautiful moments in it. From using your voice and your performance to portray 'A Star a star/Dancing in the night/ With a tail as big as a kite', but also a child, a child who shivers in the cold. It's built up to be very, very dramatic.

The power of this carol was further brought home to me a couple of years ago when my daughter, who was about seven years old at the time, came home from school having been told that she'd made it into the choir and the piece of music they were performing in the Christmas concert was 'Do You Hear What I Hear?' Just listening to the excitement in her voice, telling me the story of this carol and how she enjoyed singing it was just such a magical moment, which was further enhanced when I was asked by the school then to actually take the solo part myself. I'll never forget until my dying day glancing over and being winked at by my own daughter in the chorus while singing this carol.

9

GOD REST YOU MERRY, GENTLEMEN

WORDS
Anon.

MUSIC
'London', arranged by
John Stainer (1840–1901)

God rest you merry, gentlemen,
Let nothing you dismay,
For Jesus Christ our Saviour
Was born upon this day,
To save us all from Satan's power
When we were gone astray.

O tidings of comfort and joy,
Comfort and joy,
O tidings of comfort and joy.

In Bethlehem in Jewry
This blessed babe was born,
And laid within a manger
Upon this blessed morn;
The which his mother Mary
Nothing did take in scorn.

Refrain

From God our Heavenly Father
A blessed angel came,
And unto certain shepherds
Brought tidings of the same,
How that in Bethlehem was born
The Son of God by name.

Refrain

Fear not, then said the angel
Let nothing you affright,
This day is born a Saviour
Of virtue, power and might,
So frequently to vanquish all
The friends of Satan quite.

Refrain

The shepherds at those tidings
Rejoicéd much in mind,
And left their flocks a-feeding
In tempest, storm and wind,
And went to Bethlehem straightway
This blessed Babe to find.

Refrain

But when to Bethlehem they came,
Whereat this Infant lay,
They found him in a manger
Where oxen feed on hay;
His mother Mary kneeling
Unto the Lord did pray.

Refrain

Now to the Lord sing praises,
All you within this place,
And with true love and brotherhood
Each other now embrace;
This holy tide of Christmas
All others doth efface.

Refrain

The owner of one scant young nose, gnawed and mumbled by the hungry cold as bones are gnawed by dogs, stooped down at Scrooge's keyhole to regale him with a Christmas carol: but at the first sound of '*God bless you, merry gentlemen! May nothing you dismay!*', Scrooge seized the ruler with such energy of action, that the singer fled in terror, leaving the keyhole to the fog and even more congenial frost.

That word 'merry' expresses the uniquely jolly spirit of Christmas. Christmas is on its own as a festival of merrymaking as Dickens knew and conjured up in *A Christmas Carol* (1843) – of togetherness, warm fires, huge turkeys, well-laden tables and religious celebration – of 'comfort and joy' – which is exactly what 'God Rest You Merry' and carols in general were invented to express.

This is also another of those huge Christmas carols, probably one of the top five big ones that you expect to hear every Christmas. Of these Big Sing ones, and here I'm talking about 'O Come, All Ye Faithful', 'Hark! The Herald Angels Sing', 'The First Nowell', 'While Shepherds Watched Their Flocks by Night', I would say that 'God Rest You Merry, Gentlemen' is probably my favourite. It was a first for me in Bangor Cathedral. I remember being transfixed by the melody line. It's a massive

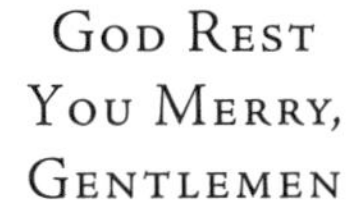

carol from start to finish, and one that tells a story. The angel, the shepherds, they all make an entrance into this carol.

Its history is, as with so many carols, rather convoluted and sometimes controversial. It's generally agreed to be a folk carol, grown out of the rich carol tradition of the West of England, with its origins in the eighteenth or nineteenth century. Drawing on its West Country origins, William Sandys' *Christmas Carols, Ancient and Modern* (1833) is the main source for the version we sing today. Hugh Keyte and Andrew Parrott in their *New Oxford Book of Carols* offer us three tunes, the Sandys version as well as the 'London' tune, also known as 'Chestnut' in John Stainer's arrangement in *Christmas Carols New and Old* of 1871. Of John Stainer, Arthur Sullivan said bluntly, and memorably, 'He is a genius.' Stainer was an organist and composer, best known of course for his work *The Crucifixion*. He set high standards for Anglican church music, which are still influential today. He sang in the choir of St Paul's Cathedral, and I think there's a house in the choir school there that's still named after him. He became organist at Magdalen College, Oxford in 1860 and was made Professor of Music at Oxford in 1889. He was a prolific composer and his arrangements of 'God Rest You Merry, Gentlemen', as well as of 'The First Nowell' and 'I Saw Three Ships Come Sailing In', have become standard versions. Stainer died in Verona at the beginning of the twentieth century. His tune, Keyte and Parrott point out, has spawned many derivatives, including the melodies of 'While Shepherds Watched' and 'Here We Come A-wassailing'. Their third choice is from Ralph Dunstan's *Cornish Song Book* (1929), described by Dunstan rather vaguely as 'formerly popular in Cornwall'.

The question of the whereabouts of the comma in the first line of the carol has caused some confusion. As is so well demonstrated by Lynne Truss in *Eats Shoots and Leaves*, the placing of the comma can change the meaning entirely: in the hymn 'All Things Bright and Beautiful', 'The rich man in his castle, the poor man at his gate/God made them high or lowly' has a whole different meaning from 'The rich man in his castle, the poor man at his gate/God made them, high or lowly';

similarly, there's a different meaning between 'God Rest You, Merry Gentlemen' and the placing used widely today with the comma after 'Merry'. As Ian Bradley, in his excellent *The Daily Telegraph Book of Carols* (2006), observes, these words are probably addressed to the shepherds tending their flocks, telling them to fear not.

Through its life, 'God Rest You Merry' has given parodists pleasure. Its rhyme and rhythm, along with the first two lines, seem to offer these guys the ideal jumping-off point. Ian Bradley notes a parody of 1820, directed at Lord Castlereagh, then leader of the House of Commons, by the journalist William Hone (replacing that first-line comma):

God rest you, merry Gentlemen,
Let nothing you dismay;
Remember we were left alive
Upon last Christmas day,
With both our lips at liberty
To praise Lord C_____h,
With his 'practical' comfort and joy!

Moving swiftly on, to American Jewish ace parodist Allan Sherman ('Hello Muddah, Hello Faddah . . . ') and the song 'Schticks and Stones' in his album *My Son, the Folksinger*, which begins:

'God bless you, Jerry Mandelbaum may nothing you dismay;
Dis May you had a rotten month, so what is there to say?
Let's hope next May is better and good things will come your way
And you won't have a feeling of dismay next May . . . '

Tom Lehrer's song 'A Christmas Carol' includes the line 'God rest ye merry merchants, may ye make the Yuletide pay . . . ' and in 'Merry Christmas, Mr Bean', broadcast on Christmas Day 1992, Bean conducts a brass band, Bean-style, in a rendition of 'God Rest You Merry'.

In 2000, 'God Rest You Merry' didn't make it into the *Church Hymnary*, the hymnbook of the Church of Scotland. Along with 199 other 'traditional hymns and carols', including 'Jerusalem' and 'Stand Up, Stand Up for Jesus', 'God Rest You Merry' was declared by the Kirk to be out of tune with the twenty-first century. Urging modern worshippers to cast aside sentimental attachments, the committee's convener Revd John Bell said: 'There is something unjust if a church includes a hymn which only speaks to the past of those who are singing it and not to the future of those who are being born.' His objections to 'God Rest You Merry' included its exclusivity to the male gender, its archaisms and dubious theology, as well as its claim that 'This holy tide of Christmas/All others doth efface.' Well, in terms of gender, the alternative, 'God Rest You Merry, Gentlefolk', doesn't really work and to exclude according to the Revd Bell's latter point would be to excise quite a few other inspiring carols from the carol pantheon, including 'We Three Kings' and 'In the Deep Midwinter'. Anyway, undeterred, modern worshippers have voted with their voices and 'God Rest You Merry, Gentlemen' has remained a favourite, sixteenth in the 2005 *Songs of Praise* poll and lustily performed by carol singers at Christmastide.

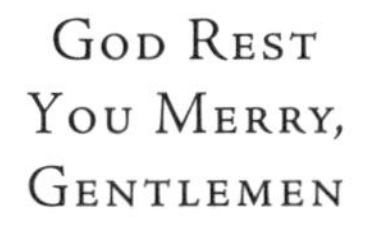

The melody line of 'God Rest You Merry' creates a feeling of mystery. It's not obvious in any way, but it leaves a lasting impression on you when you sing it. It's also an unusual melody. Even though the first four lines are quite repetitive, it then goes somewhere totally different and is only brought back on line by the chorus, to a melodic line which gives the impression that you've heard it somewhere before, but you haven't. The melody line is incredibly strong as well, another Big Sing. You need a lot of energy to get through it. If it's sung in a lacklustre way, the refrain after every verse can be really tiresome. You need to keep that energy up and use body and soul to put across the message of 'Tidings of comfort and joy'.

Here is another carol with a terrific David Willcocks descant, which we used to sing in Bangor Cathedral, and the choir of Westminster Cathedral sing it in 'The Story of Christmas'. It's greatly enhanced by the involvement of the congregation. I am going to try and do this as a solo piece on my next Christmas album but God knows how it will turn out. I usually leave out the second verse in performance. So it's actually a six-verse carol that requires great stamina in the singing of it.

One thing I love about 'God Rest You Merry' is that coming together of the congregation, praising God in unison. At the final verse on the line, 'And with true love and brotherhood/Each other now embrace,' you always get people looking around at one another and there's a wonderful feeling of Christmas within either the church, chapel or concert hall where it's being performed.

O COME, O COME, EMMANUEL!

Words and Music
Eighth-century
Latin Advent Antiphons

Translation
John Mason Neale (1818–66)

O come, O come, Emmanuel!
And ransom captive Israel,
That mourns in lonely exile here
Until the Son of God appear.

Rejoice! Rejoice! Emmanuel
Shall come to thee, O Israel.

O come, Thou Rod of Jesse, free
Thine own from Satan's tyranny;
From depths of Hell Thy people save
And give them victory o'er the grave.

Refrain

O come, Thou day-spring, come and cheer
Our spirits by Thine advent here;
Disperse the gloomy clouds of night
And death's dark shadows put to flight.

Refrain

O come, o come, Emmanuel

VENI EMMANUEL
translated by J.M. Neale

Traditional

O come, o come, Em - man - u - el, And ran - som cap - tive
5
Is - ra - el, That mourns in lone - ly ex - ile here, Un -
10
- til the Son of God ap - pear. Re - joice! Re - joice! Em -
15
- man - u - el shall come to thee, O Is - ra - el.

O come, Thou Key of David, come
And open wide our heavenly home;
Make safe the way that leads on high,
And close the path to misery.

Refrain

O come, O come, Thou Lord of Might,
Who to Thy tribes on Sinai's height
In ancient times did'st give the Law,
In cloud, and majesty, and awe.

Refrain

'O Come, O Come, Emmanuel!' is a very old work, probably our oldest Christmas carol, going right back to the eighth-century monasteries. It's a hymn for Advent, which was translated in the nineteenth century by the great hymnologist John Mason Neale from an old monastic psalter of that early period. The writer is unknown – probably a scholarly monk or priest with a deep knowledge of both Old and New Testaments. He designed its verses to be antiphons sung in Latin during vespers through the last seven days of Advent. One verse would have been chanted each day, and its words have in them that excitement of the anticipatory soul during the days and nights leading up to Christmas Eve.

'O Come, O Come, Emmanuel!' crosses biblical time, with the Old Testament predicting the events of the New. Somehow the carol collapses the ages that have passed between the prophecies and their fulfilment in the Incarnation. It's full of Old Testament images and references. Isaiah's prophecy (11:1) that the Messiah will be born into the line of King David's father Jesse, for example: 'a shoot will come up from the stump of Jesse; from his roots a Branch will bear fruit'. The Key of David comes again from Isaiah (22:22): 'And the key of the house of David will I lay upon his shoulder; so he shall shut, and none shall open'. It has a large and hopeful message, that the coming of Emmanuel (meaning 'God with us') will fulfil God's great promise to deliver us from the world. Musically it's not a typical carol, it's more religious-sounding melody-wise than all the others because of its background. The original chants of those monks can still be heard in the music of this song and its original words would have had great impact on the people of its times, who had little access to the Bible and its teachings. Its strong and spiritual nature has carried it through into modern days, modern audiences, and many languages.

John Mason Neale translated this Advent hymn as 'Draw nigh, draw nigh, Emmanuel' in 1851, then revising his translation to the version commonly sung today in 1853. Neale had taken orders in the Anglican church in 1841. He was high church in his sympathies and his Roman Catholic leanings were received with suspicion and some hostility. This may explain why he was never granted a pastorate in London – instead he was sent to the Madeira Islands and then in 1846 was allocated a lowly position as warden of Sackville College, an almshouse in East Grinstead. He never gave up on God or his calling though and in 1854 on an annual salary of just £27 he co-founded the Society of Saint Margaret, a female order of the Anglican Church, dedicated to nursing the sick. The Society continues today and is based in Boston, USA, where there are currently twenty-seven sisters, two dogs and five cats in the community. From this position he also established an orphanage, a school for girls and a refuge for prostitutes in East Grinstead.

Suffering in his life not only from religious opposition but also from ill health, Neale was nevertheless an energetic researcher who studied every Scripture-based writing he could find. It was while he was doing this research that he found the Latin chant '*Veni, veni, Emmanuel*' in a book called the *Psalterium Cantionum Catholicorum*. Realising its importance, he immediately translated it into English and, put together with a fifteenth-century French Plainsong processional tune originating with a community of French Franciscan nuns living in Lisbon, it was published

initially in England in the 1850s. Later cut to five verses, 'O Come, O Come, Emmanuel!' grew and grew in popularity throughout Europe and America.

'O Come, O Come, Emmanuel!' has been covered by many artists, including Sufjan Stevens, Belle and Sebastian, Joan Baez and Enya. 2006's BBC Young Chorister of the Year William Dutton has also recorded it. In 2009 Bono, lead singer of U2, recorded a version of 'O Come, O Come, Emmanuel!' with new words and called it 'White As Snow'. It is written from the point of view of a soldier dying from a roadside bomb in Afghanistan. It is supposed to last the length of time it takes him to die. It has a quiet power and sadness that is true to the carol.

> Where I came from there were no hills at all
> The land was flat, the highway straight and wide.
> My brother and I would drive for hours
> Like we had years instead of days,
> Our faces as pale as the dirty snow . . .

I first came into contact with 'O Come, O Come, Emmanuel!' as a chorister at Bangor Cathedral, although we didn't sing it very often. My most vivid memory of this carol is that when I was performing *Strictly Come Dancing* a few years ago, I was also on tour, my largest tour ever. It was a Christmas tour around the British Isles, I think forty-seven concerts in fifty-two days, while also learning all my routines on *Strictly*. So during the day I would rehearse with my partner Lilia Kopolova for about seven hours wherever I was in the country and then that evening I would do a concert. Actually what was wonderful was that during the day, because I was so busy with the dancing, I wouldn't concentrate on the concert and then in the evening, when I was busy doing what I do best, which is singing, I wouldn't be thinking about the dancing. So each worked as an antidote to the other if you like.

I would start my Christmas tour with 'O Come, O Come, Emmanuel!' and such is the power of the piece of music that we started with the whole stage in darkness and I would sing the first verse offstage, unaccompanied. So all you would hear was the voice coming from nowhere: 'O Come, O Come, Emmanuel!/And ransom captive Israel'. And then during the second verse I would walk onto the stage and perform the rest of the carol. It worked a treat as a way to start a concert: you're asking God to join with you in what you're doing and the third verse in particular: 'Disperse the gloomy clouds of night/And death's dark shadows put to flight/Rejoice! rejoice! Emmanuel/shall come to thee, O Israel' banishes all negative thoughts, and what lies ahead – hopefully in the case of the concert I did – is a joyous celebration of Christmas music, which is exactly what it was. For me personally it was a great way of starting a concert because even though I had a string quartet and harp and guitar and piano and various other instruments and support artists – the lot – what I liked more than anything was that at the start you wouldn't even see the performer, all you heard was the voice and that was all that was important. And then my connection with the music didn't need any frills, didn't need any gimmicks. I just let the music stand for itself.

The reason why this carol is so popular is, I'd say, because it's a real dream to sing. It's an unusual melody line, not as simple as some of the other very well-known carols, which I've called childlike in this book. This is a lot more cultured as far as the melodic line is concerned and I think that's what adds to its mystery. I suppose that this is why it's not in the top five favourite carols, because it has that element of mystery and it's not obvious in any way.

GOOD KING WENCESLAS

Words
J M Neale (1818–66)

Music
'Tempus Adest Floridum'
('It is time for flowering'): Anon.

Good King Wenceslas looked out
On the feast of Stephen,
When the snow lay round about,
Deep and crisp and even;
Brightly shone the moon that night,
Though the frost was cruel,
When a poor man came in sight,
Gathering winter fuel.

'Hither, page, and stand by me,
If thou know'st it, telling,
Yonder peasant, who is he?
Where and what his dwelling?'
'Sire, he lives a good league hence,
Underneath the mountain,
Right against the forest fence,
By St. Agnes' fountain.'

'Bring me flesh, and bring me wine!
Bring me pine logs hither!
Thou and I will see him dine
When we bear them thither.'

Page and monarch, forth they went,
Forth they went together,
Through the rude wind's wild lament
And the bitter weather.

'Sire, the night is darker now
And the wind grows stronger;
Fails my heart I know not how,
I can go no longer.'
'Mark my footsteps, good my page,
Tread thou in them boldly:
Thou shalt find the winter's rage
Freeze thy blood less coldly.'

In his master's steps he trod
Where the snow lay dinted;
Heat was in the very sod
Which the saint had printed.
Therefore Christian men be sure,
Wealth or rank possessing,
Ye who now will bless the poor,
Shall yourselves find blessing.

'Good King Wenceslas' is as close to musical theatre as Christmas carols can get. I've performed it with the choir of Bangor Cathedral and it gives the boy soprano the opportunity to spit out the words, especially 'Deep and crisp and even', as well as 'Gathering winter fuel'. And then of course the men come in deep with 'Hither, page, and stand by me,/If thou know'st it, telling', hamming it up like mad and I've heard it done by many a cathedral choir who do the same sort of thing. It's almost as if with the serious Christmas carols like 'The Shepherds' Farewell' and others that really do need to be sung well, this is one you can get away with hamming it up a little bit.

As a young child I didn't really know what some of the words meant, but you know I always had a glint in the eye as did all my colleagues in Bangor Cathedral at the age of twelve when we used to sing:

> In his master's steps he trod
> Where the snow lay dinted;
> Heat was in the very sod
> Which the saint had printed.

It was later in life that I came to understand the true meaning of the words. The final verse which I've just referred to ends beautifully:

> Therefore Christian men be sure,
> Wealth or rank possessing,
> Ye who now will bless the poor,
> Shall yourselves find blessing.

There are some great descants by Derek Willcocks, which really set that last verse alight.

The life story of King Wenceslas himself (*c.* 907–935) is the stuff of fairy tales, complete with wicked family members. In fact Wenceslas, or Vaclav, to give him his native name, was not a king. For fourteen years, until he was murdered by his brother, he was Duke of Bohemia, now part of the Czech Republic. The poor chap was dubbed 'the father of all the wretched' by the Bohemian priest Cosmas of Prague. After his death, Otto the Great, Emperor of the Holy Roman Empire (912–973), is supposed to have conferred on him the grander title of king in recognition of his philanthropy, and he was canonised. His remains are still in Prague's St Vitus' Cathedral, where there are murals by a fifteenth-century Bohemian painter, the Master of the Litoměřice Altarpiece, that show Wenceslas distributing alms to the poor and working in the fields.

Wenceslas' father died when he was thirteen. He was brought up by his Christian grandmother Ludmilla – also to be canonised – who, with her husband the first Duke of Bohemia, converted Bohemia to Christianity. Drahomíra, the mother of Wenceslas and daughter of a pagan chief, may have tried to convert her son to paganism. Ludmilla thwarted her and, jealous of the power her mother-in-law had over her son, Drahomíra hired two assassins named Tunna and Gommon to murder Ludmilla. Legend has it that they strangled her with her own veil.

When Wenceslas came to power he sent his mother into exile as punishment, although he later reprieved her. This act of compassion did not lead to a family reunion. Instead in September 935, Wenceslas was killed on the orders of his brother, Boleslav, who had been brought up by Drahomíra. Boleslav repented and he promised he would educate his son, born on the day of his brother's murder, as a clergyman. This remorse may have been influenced by the displeasure of the Emperor Otto.

Our familiarity with the story of Wenceslas and with this festive and popular carol is down to the great hymnologist and writer John Mason Neale. In 1849 he published a fictional tale about the king and four years later followed it with the song.

In 1853 'Good King Wenceslas' was published in *Carols for Christmastide*, co-authored by Neale with the Reverend Thomas Helmore, musician and Vice-Principal of St Mark's College, Cambridge. It is likely that Neale had written the lyrics published there for 'Good King Wenceslas' at the same time as his story. This is one of eleven religious tales for children in a volume entitled *Deeds of Faith*.

The events of 'The Legend of Saint Wenceslaus' (the English spelling of his name) take place on Boxing Day. You really feel the cold in this story of personal sacrifice in the snow and freezing frost and it complements the Christmas story. On this day alms were distributed (probably in boxes) to the poor and gifts were given to tradespeople. The story opens with Wenceslas sitting at a window in his palace as the sun sets, dusk gathers and night falls. We can perhaps understand how the peace of watching the changing of day to night could help the king find connection to the workings of God.

By the light of a crescent moon Wenceslas spots a figure pulling at a bush in the snow and sends out his servant Otto to investigate. Otto reports back that Rudolph the swineherd is scratching for fuel for his cold and hungry family. Wenceslas tells Otto to fetch food and, much to Otto's horror for he thinks it's a job for servants, Wenceslas insists on carrying the wood himself. Otto refuses Wenceslas' offer to go to Rudolph's dwelling alone and heads off with him into the icy cold, copying his master's refusal to dress up warmly. Neale tells us that Wenceslas 'desired to feel with the poor, that he might feel for them'. Soon the servant is numb and can't walk. Wenceslas suggests he literally follow in his footsteps and Otto discovers that the ground where Wenceslas has trodden is warm with the 'fire of love that has kindled in him'. The king and his servant complete the journey and deliver the provisions.

Perhaps Neale felt some empathy with Wenceslas. He too lived by his principles. His devotion to high-church worship led to the restoration of his chapel (at his own expense) to include open benches, a cross, two candles and a rood screen and caused him to be 'inhibited' by his bishop for thirteen years. This meant the poor at the almshouse in Sussex, where he was warden for the last twenty years of his life, could not receive the sacraments. The Bishop of Chichester considered it his duty 'to stop Mr. Neale from continuing to debase the minds of the poor people with his spiritual haberdashery'. Only nine years after John Henry Newman had encouraged Roman Catholic practices in his church and then converted to Catholicism, Neale had aroused suspicions that he was an agent for the Vatican intent on destroying the Anglican Church.

In 1853 Neale and Thomas Helmore had been given a collection of Latin and Swedish songs, the *Piae Contiones* of 1582. It was a songbook that must have appealed to Neale, being a product of medieval Catholic culture. Some of the songs, such as '*Gaudete*', are still popular. An English version of *Piae Contiones* was published in 1919 with a preface and notes by George Ratcliffe Woodward, the author of 'Ding Dong Merrily on High'. Oddly, given the chilly images conjured up by his lyrics, Neale chose the tune '*Tempus Adest Floridum*' ('It is time for flowering'), a thirteenth-century spring carol, to fit to his words.

There have been many recordings of 'Good King Wenceslas'. In 1963 it featured in several renditions on the first *Beatles Christmas Record*, with festive messages from the Fab Four. The disc lasted five minutes and ended with a chorus of 'Rudolph the Red-Nosed Ringo'. Joan Baez has recorded it, as have the Choir of King's College, Cambridge and Joan Sutherland with the New Philharmonia Orchestra. I recorded 'Good King Wenceslas' as a boy with the BBC Welsh Symphony Chorus on an album called *Aled Jones: The Christmas Album* in 1985.

Neale's story of the kindness and humility of a monarch is fiction. Little is known about Duke Vaclav of Bohemia although he is associated with many miracles and is now the patron saint of the Czech Republic. Nevertheless, it's the sentiment that counts and John Mason Neale wrote a tale and later a carol that dramatically illustrate an act of charity by a good king that still has the power to move us.

12

HARK! THE HERALD ANGELS SING

WORDS
Charles Wesley (1707–88) and George Whitefield (1714–70)

MUSIC
Felix Mendelssohn (1809–47)

Arranged by W H Cummings (1831–1915)

Hark! the herald angels sing,
'Glory to the new-born King,
Peace on earth and mercy mild,
God and sinners reconciled.'
Joyful, all ye nations rise,
Join the triumph of the skies;
With th'angelic host proclaim:
'Christ is born in Bethlehem.'
Hark! the herald angels sing
'Glory to the new-born King.'

Christ, by highest Heaven adored,
Christ, the Everlasting Lord,
Late in time behold him come,
Offspring of a virgin's womb.
Veiled in flesh the Godhead see,
Hail the incarnate Deity!
Pleased as Man with man to dwell,

Jesus, our Emmanuel.
Hark! the herald angels sing
'Glory to the new-born King.'

Hail, the heaven-born Prince of Peace!
Hail, the Sun of Righteousness!
Light and life to all he brings,
Risen with healing in his wing.
Mild he lays his glory by,
Born that man no more may die,
Born to raise the sons of earth,
Born to give them second birth.
Hark! the herald angels sing
'Glory to the new-born King.'

What a double act! Words by Charles Wesley, music by Mendelssohn. You expect this carol to be world class and it is. 'Listen to those angels!' cries Wesley's 'Hymn for Christmas Day'. Mendelssohn's melody, soaring aloft, welcomes to earth Jesus our Emmanuel. Charles Wesley has left us a legacy of literally hundreds of fine hymns and at least two of his carols, 'Lo! He comes, with Clouds Descending' and 'Hark! The Herald Angels Sing' have remained great favourites. Wesley was an inspired craftsman, and a passionate poet, whose words to 'Hark! The Herald Angels Sing' display his deep conviction and his ability to wonder at the event of Christ's birth. His first hymn was written on the day of his conversion on 21 May 1738 and it opens 'Where shall my won'dring soul begin?'

Wesley's wonder had many forms; alongside his more serious works like 'Love Divine, All Loves Excelling' or 'Forth in Thy name, O Lord, I go/My daily labour to pursue', many of his poems celebrate mundane and earthly matters, like children teething, Handel's birthday or the courage of his cat:

I sing Grimalkin brave and bold
Who makes intruders fly
His claws and whiskers they behold
And squall and scamper by.

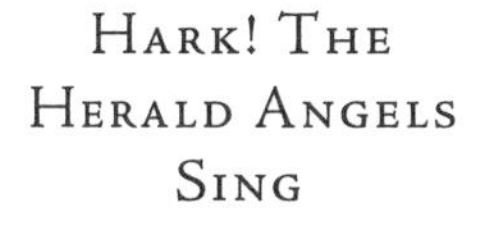

'Hark! The Herald Angels Sing' was first published in 1739 with the opening lines: 'Hark, how all the welkin rings/Glory to the King of Kings'. In 1779 John Wesley included it in his *A Collection of Hymns for the Use of the People Called Methodists*. At this time there was a new demand for hymns and it was the Methodists who brought them back into church services. Much to the annoyance of his elder brother John, then leader of the new Methodist movement started by Charles at Oxford, the poem was altered in 1753 by the Calvinistically inclined Methodist George Whitefield, whose advocacy of slavery the Wesley brothers opposed. He cut out two of the verses and substituted for Wesley's first lines the opening we sing today. Perhaps it was Whitefield that John was referring to when he grumbled that those who 'do my Brother and me (though without naming us) the honour of reprinting many of our hymns ... are perfectly welcome to do so, provided they print them just as they are'. He proposed a solution, that these 'many gentlemen' print in the margin Charles's words, 'that we may no longer be held responsible either for the nonsense or the doggerel of other men'. Charles too was unlikely to have welcomed Whitefield's changes. More adjustments followed through the years. By the early nineteenth century 'Hark! The Herald Angels Sing' was usually sung in four-line stanzas. Then in the 1850s, the three or four verses were grouped together, each forming eight lines with a choral-type melody, to became the version we know today.

John Wesley wouldn't have approved of this modification:

Hark! The herald angels sing,
Beecham's Pills are quite the thing.
Two for a man and one for a child
Peace on earth and mercy mild.

Sir Thomas Beecham was a renowned conductor of the London Philharmonic Orchestra, but at one time the name Beecham was known in households for one reason only. Thomas's grandfather Joseph invented Beecham's powders, which made the family very rich. This wealth freed Thomas to pursue a career in music. Beecham's was one of the first businesses to grasp the value of advertising; nowadays sumo wrestlers convey strength of efficacy, but in the late 1800s, so it was rumoured, hymn books donated by Beecham's to a parish in South Shields carried the above rendition. This Joseph Beecham denied. Nevertheless, according to the National Archives, pedlars were hired to sing this version of 'Hark! The Herald Angels Sing' up and down Britain.

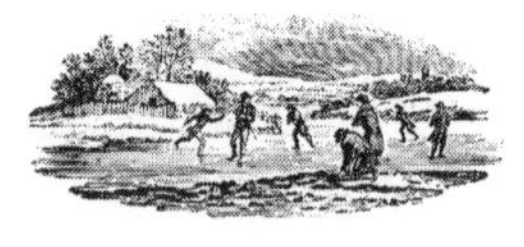

What gives any song the special quality that moves the singer and the listener is the dovetailing of a great tune with inspiring words. In the 1850s Wesley's words would find their perfect musical match. Dr William Hayford Cummings (1831–1915) began his singing career (as I did), when he was still a boy. Aged seven, he was a chorister at St Paul's Cathedral, and in his teens he was an organist at the Waltham Abbey parish church in Essex, where he wrote his arrangement of 'Hark! The Herald Angels Sing'. He had other talents; he wrote the first biography of Purcell, for instance, and he was an expert on Handel, but his obituary in the *Musical Times* remarked that as a 'composer he cannot be said to have made any special mark upon his generation'.

This perhaps unnecessary observation does not tell the whole story. Cummings has made an impression on many generations. One day in the 1850s he was flicking through Felix Mendelssohn's *Festgesang*, a work of four movements for male chorus. Mendelssohn had composed this as an occasional piece for the 1840 Gutenberg Festival in Leipzig celebrating the 400th anniversary of the invention of printing. Cummings was taken with a melody in the second movement, repeated in the fourth. He realised it would go with 'Hark! The Herald Angels Sing'. Mendelssohn had stipulated that his lively composition would be enjoyed by secular singers but was not suited to sacred words. Unaware of this, Cummings put Mendelssohn's music to Wesley's words and in 1856 the 'Hymn for

Christmas Day' we now sing was published. Inclusion in the first edition of *Hymns Ancient and Modern*, published in 1861 by a committee of clergy called the Proprietors, would seal this carol's happy partnership of lyrics and melody.

In 1885, the Revd James King set out to establish the Great Four Anglican Hymns in a survey of favourites conducted for his *Anglican Hymnology*. King attempted to arrive at the best ever hymn by gathering 52 hymn books from around the world and analysing their content using a weighting system of scores. He failed to find a number one: no hymn got a unanimous vote from all the books, but he did find four hymns that tied, with fifty-one 'votes' each. Two of them were by Charles Wesley: 'Lo! He Comes with Clouds Descending' and 'Hark! The Herald Angels Sing'.

Sir David Willcocks, King's College's Director of Music for seventeen years from 1957, made another adjustment to the carol – to its music this time. He introduced a harmonisation for the organ and a soprano descant for the last verse. This version is usually included in the Festival of Nine Lessons and Carols at King's College, Cambridge, where Dr Cummings, like Harold Darke, was once an organist. A recessional hymn, it is sung at the end when broadcasting has finished and the choir and clergy file out. David Willcock's descant is probably the greatest of its kind and probably David Willcock's own greatest descant. It's sublime and really does bring you closer to Heaven.

'Hark! The Herald Angels Sing' has been recorded by stars from outside the choral or classical world, such as Frank Sinatra, Johnny Cash and Mariah Carey. It is sung in the movie often shown during Christmas, Frank Capra's *It's a Wonderful Life* (1946), which, like carols themselves, celebrates the joy of living. And with discordant gusto the kids' choir belt through it in an episode of *South Park*.

Perhaps Charles and John Wesley, keen to see the right of worship and communication with God open to all, would have been gratified to witness the power of this carol to move millions nearly three centuries after its original publication.

I sang this carol first with gusto when I was at primary school, then with a little bit more finesse when I was in Bangor Cathedral Choir. It's the carol equivalent of a hymn like 'Guide Me Oh Thou Great Redeemer', in the way that you need quite a lot of stamina to get through it. It's a big sing, a big ask, a big commitment. It starts on full power and then builds to even greater glory throughout every verse. Used very often as a recessional, during our Nine Lessons and Carols we do exactly that in our charity performance in St George's Hanover Square and I'm always literally cream crackered by the time I get to the back door of the church, having let rip during this one.

I may be castigated for saying this, but I really do think this carol is at its best when it's performed by a full cathedral choir to the glorious organ accompaniment. I've recorded it as a solo artist with choir accompaniment and it does work even then, just probably not as well. I didn't record it as a child – unbelievably. I don't know whether it's because of my chorister background, but whenever I see this hymn on a sheet now at a service or at a charity event, my heart sinks a little bit because it is an incredibly difficult sing. As I've said, you really do need to have lungs of steel and also a major amount of stamina. This isn't something you can come to lightly, you've got to give your all, vocally, body and soul when you perform 'Hark! The Herald Angels Sing'.

13

O HOLY NIGHT

Words	Music
Placide Clappeau (1808–77)	Adolphe Charles Adam (1803–56)

O holy night! The stars are brightly shining,
It is the night of the dear Saviour's birth.
Long lay the world in sin and error pining,
Till He appeared, gift of infinite worth.
A thrill of hope, a weary world rejoices,
For yonder breaks a new and glorious morn,
Fall on your knees! Oh, hear the angel voices!
Oh night divine, O night when Christ was born;
O night, O holy night, O night divine!

Led by the light of faith serenely beaming,
With glowing hearts by His cradle we stand.
O'er the world a star is sweetly gleaming,
Now come the wise men from the Orient land.
The King of kings lay thus in lowly manger;
In all our trials born to be our friend.
He knows our need, our weakness is no stranger,
Behold your King! Before him lowly bend!
Behold your King! Before him lowly bend!

Truly He taught us to love one another,
His law is love and His gospel is peace.
Chains he shall break, for the slave is our brother

O holy night

Placide Capeau
translated by J.S. Dwight

Adolphe Adam

O ho - ly night! The stars are brightly shin - ing, It is the night of the dear Sav - iour's
5
birth. Long lay the world in sin and dark - ness pin - ing, Till He ap - peared, gift of in - fin - ite
9
worth. A thrill of hope the wea - ry soul re - joic - es, For yon - der breaks a
13
new and glor - ious morn; Fall on your knees, O hear the an - gel
17
voic - es! O night di - vine, O night when Christ was
21
born. O night, O ho - ly night, O night di - vine!

And in His name all oppression shall cease.
Sweet hymns of joy in grateful chorus raise we,
With all our hearts we praise His holy name.
Christ is the Lord! Then ever, ever praise we,
His power and glory ever more proclaim!
His power and glory ever more proclaim!

'O Holy Night' is by way of being a paradox. It is the most beautiful of carols, composed by the man who wrote the flowing music for the ballet *Giselle* and written by a French poet. It came in at fourth place in the 2005 BBC *Songs of Praise* poll and its place in the hearts of people who love carols is assured. But, but, 'O Holy Night' is not often sung by congregations in church services and is a rarity in books of hymns and carols. It's a gift to a solo performer and you are more likely to hear it crooned by balladeers Nat 'King' Cole and Perry Como, or recorded in the US by country music singers like Martina McBride or John Berry. It's a favourite with opera stars: Joan Sutherland and Luciano Pavarotti have given the carol memorable renditions and Welsh mezzo-soprano Katherine Jenkins shattered a glass chandelier above her head while singing it recently.

Nevertheless, this carol has frequently been kept outside the church door. This is not unusual in the life stories of carols. Churchmen have often suspected that they are not quite religiously respectable. You can find a few more instances of this in my choice for this book, where carols with pagan origins or those accused of political incorrectness come up, and occasionally with carols that do not mention Christ himself. So why is this most religious of songs, which considers the birth of Jesus and the redemption of human beings, seen by some as an undesirable at Christmas? In this instance, the answer could lie in the tendency of carols to reflect the tenor of their times; a few of our most famous carols do express coded opinions on contemporary events: 'O Come, All Ye Faithful', for example. One answer lies perhaps in the third line of the third stanza: 'Chains he shall break, for the slave is our brother/And in His name all oppression shall cease.'

Placide Clappeau, who wrote the poem '*Minuit, Chrétiens*' on which 'O Holy Night' is based, was a freethinker. He was raised in the small town of Roquemaure, near Avignon in the Rhone Valley, and in a region where wine is a religion, he was destined to follow in his father's footsteps into the wine business. But a painful event changed the direction of his life. When he was eight years old, he was accidentally shot in the hand by a friend. His hand was amputated and, thus disabled, he changed direction to study hard and gain a literature degree in Paris. While earning his living in the wine trade, he was also writing poetry, as well as being the mayor of Roquemaure.

But Placide also had socialist, republican and anti-clerical leanings. Like other nineteenth-century creators of carols, from Charles Wesley to Christina Rossetti, he was opposed to slavery and the slave trade that supported the prosperity of his country. This slipped into a line of his poem.

Another reason why 'O Holy Night' has not found its way into many hymnals could be that both Placide Clappeau and its composer, Adolphe Adam, had their reputations attacked by churchmen in their native France for being unbelievers. It's been claimed that Adam was in fact Jewish and Clappeau was of course damned as a freethinking radical. The story goes that on 3 December 1847 Clappeau was about to embark upon a business trip to Paris when the local parish priest asked him to write a Christmas poem. About halfway to Paris, Clappeau apparently became inspired and wrote the poem, '*Minuit, Chrétiens*' or 'O Holy Night'. When Clappeau arrived in Paris, he asked a friend of a friend, Adolphe Charles Adam, to compose a tune for it. Adam had studied at the Paris Conservatoire and was then at the height of his career as a composer of comic opera. His operas, like *Le Postillon de Lonjumeau* and *Si j'étais roi* are hardly known today, but his ballet *Giselle* is famous. He'd also written songs for the Paris vaudeville and earned his living as organist. He'd even played the triangle in the orchestra of the Conservatoire. He wrote the tune to

Clappeau's poem in a few days and '*Cantique de Noël*' received its first performance at midnight mass in Roquemaure parish church on Christmas Eve 1847. Adam later called their carol '*la Marseillaise religieuse*': the religious national anthem of France. Despite resistance from the French clergy, the carol was a success, first in France and then abroad after it had been published in an English version in 1855. Its beauty had won the day.

'O Holy Night' is treasured in the United States, thanks to John Sullivan Dwight's translation (1812–93), which has become the standard version. Dwight was a Harvard graduate, Unitarian minister for 6 years then a music journalist and critic. He edited *Dwight's Journal of Music* for 30 years and lived most of his life in and around Boston and made a home at the Transcendentalist community of Brook Farm, Massachusetts. Like Clappeau, he held strong anti-slavery views and perhaps that is why he was drawn to this carol and translated it so sensitively.

Two, apocryphal, stories about this carol are worth telling. The first is that it figured prominently on Christmas Eve in 1870 during the Franco-Prussian War. Apparently a French soldier suddenly and unexpectedly jumped out of the trench and sang 'O Holy Night'. Instead of firing at him, his German adversaries sang a German carol (reputedly Martin Luther's '*Vom Himmel hoch, da komm' ich her*', 'From Highest Heaven I Come to Tell') in response. The other, short, story is that 'O Holy Night' was the first ever music performed live on radio. It was broadcast by Reginald Fessenden who played the tune on his violin for ships at sea on 24 December 1906 from his radio station in Massachusetts.

I first got to perform 'O Holy Night' when I went out to Israel as a boy soprano. I was recording three programmes for BBC1, two for Easter, one for Christmas, and I was dressed up in my cassock and ruff from my cathedral, and when it came to recording 'O Holy Night' I was actually going to be miming to the music I had recorded in Cardiff, but in all the relevant holy places in Israel. I remember 'O Holy Night' was being sung/mimed to in the exact spot where Jesus was born in Bethlehem. I think it's called the Church of the Nativity and it's really a cave. What an honour to be performing in this place. But there's a story that goes with it. I was out in Israel with the BBC Welsh Chorus and they'd finished work for the day so they were going back to the kibbutz to swim, but unfortunately I had to go and do the 'O Holy Night' performance. So there was a part of me that wanted to get it done as soon as possible so I could jump in the pool with the whole chorus who were having a whale of a time. But also it was incredibly warm everywhere we were filming in Israel. On TV you see me dressed in cassock and ruff. You'd think that what I was wearing underneath was a shirt and tie and smart pair of trousers but all I was actually wearing was a pair of shorts, not even a top, such was the heat.

It's a carol that's meant the world to me ever since then and it's actually the carol that brought me back to singing as a man. I was asked to perform it on *Songs of Praise* and I went down to the home of Robert Prizeman, who's the programme's music supervisor, and we recorded the adult version of 'O Holy Night' specially for the *Songs of Praise* performance. Well, Robert also had my boy soprano recording there and he played both at exactly the same time. It was uncanny: the voice, the phrasing and the interpretation of the piece were *exactly* the same as a man as they had been when I was a boy. So this gave me hope, if you like, that I could be a professional singer again. The feeling and emotion I had as a boy had come back to me as a man. I'd done musicals and quite a few concerts but the joy I had of singing as a boy, the instinctive joy, had not been there as an adult but came back with this piece, 'O Holy Night'.

Since then I've sung 'O Holy Night' in concert many times and I've even been back to Israel to perform it again. It's able to move an audience greatly. One performance I did on *Songs of Praise* was filmed by a really talented producer called Medwin Hughes who had the idea of starting with me as a boy singing that carol in the cave in Bethlehem, and then zooming out to me in a live concert situation performing it – I think at Birmingham Symphony Hall – as a man. There is a part where the young Aled is singing with the slightly older and fatter Aled. And the feedback that came when that programme went out was so strong: people really, really loved it. So it's a carol I've had associations with since I was a very very small boy.

'O Holy Night' is a joyous carol to perform, the words and music complement each other beautifully. Lines such as 'A thrill of hope, a weary world rejoices/For yonder breaks a new and glorious morn/Fall on your knees! . . .' are very dramatic; looking back, my performance as a boy in the cave in Bethlehem was also rather dramatic and I remember feeling quite embarrassed that I had my hands clasped together giving it my all. It's a carol that requires you to be positive and you need to give everything you've got when you're performing it.

It's funny, sometimes some carols work better than others on stage in a concert scenario, and this is one that really does work. You can end a Christmas concert easily with 'O Holy Night'. It's that powerful and I suppose for me it's a carol that will always take me back to those early days in Israel; how fortunate I was to be singing in the actual place where Jesus was born. This beautiful carol tells that story, so having the opportunity to sing it in the exact spot was a real honour.

IN THE BLEAK MIDWINTER

Words
Christina Rossetti (1830–94)

Music
Gustav Holst (1874–1934),
Harold Darke (1888–1976)

In the bleak midwinter
Frosty wind made moan,
Earth stood hard as iron,
Water like a stone;
Snow had fallen, snow on snow,
Snow on snow,
In the bleak midwinter,
Long ago.

Our God, heaven cannot hold him
Nor earth sustain;
Heaven and earth shall flee away
When he comes to reign:
In the bleak mid-winter
A stable-place sufficed
The Lord God almighty,
Jesus Christ.

Enough for him, whom cherubim
Worship night and day,
A breastful of milk
And a mangerful of hay;

Enough for him, whom angels
Fall down before,
The ox and ass and camel
Which adore.

Angels and archangels
May have gathered there,
Cherubim and seraphim
Thronged the air;
But only his mother
In her maiden bliss
Worshipped the Beloved
With a kiss.

What can I give him,
Poor as I am?
If I were a shepherd
I would bring a lamb;
If I were a wise man
I would do my part
Yet what I can give him,
Give my heart.

'In the Bleak Midwinter' has been in my soul since I was nine years old when I first sang it in Bangor Cathedral as a probationer. This carol is not a cheery offering to accompany mince pies and mulled wine; Christina Rossetti's words provoke a sombre mood. Her poem 'A Christmas Carol' appeared (with odd timing) in the January 1872 edition of the American magazine *Scribner's Monthly*. *Scribner's'* editor advertised the poem, somewhat coyly, as 'a little poem in my breast-pocket – wise in a sort of child-wisdom, sweet and clear and musical as the sunset chimes . . . yes, and cheerier, for it celebrates that first Christmas morning.'

Still, he paid Christina the liberal fee of £10 for her little poem.

There are certain carols that when you hear them really do get you in the mood for Christmas. The minute you hear 'In the Bleak Midwinter' it's as if a warm glow comes over you and you eagerly anticipate the great event. Rossetti's choice of title perhaps evoked the warmth of Charles Dickens' story of Scrooge and the Cratchit family, written for Christmas 1843. Dickens' novella had a purpose – to rejuvenate the old Christmas traditions that people had enjoyed before Cromwell's icy hand cancelled Christmas celebrations. New customs were coming in for Christmas in his and Christina Rossetti's time; sending greetings cards, for instance, or dressing the Christmas tree while outside the window snow lay deep and crisp and even. There is something very Dickensian in this carol. It perfectly sets the scene for Christmas. You feel safe when you're singing it; that all is good in the world for those three very special minutes.

Christina Rossetti was born 20 days before Christmas 1830, described by her father Gabriele as having a round face, 'like a little moon risen at the full'. She grew up in a close and loving Italian family. Her father was a poet and political exile, who had fled from the kingdom of Naples with a price on his head. Her younger brother, the poet and painter Dante Gabriel, was a leading member of the Pre-Raphaelite Brotherhood. Her mother Frances, full of 'commonsense and modesty', was a devout Anglo-Catholic, and Christina was also deeply religious. This shy woman was in her life and her work a brave protagonist. She opposed slavery, rescued prostitutes and was active in the movement for animal rights. She was also a visionary poet. Virginia Woolf wrote of her, 'Modest you were, still you were drastic, sure of your gift, convinced of your vision.' Christina Rossetti died as she was born, close to Christmas, on 29 December 1894, of cancer.

Rossetti takes poetic licence by placing Christ's birth in a wintry landscape, white with deep snow. There's a big pile of hay in the stable, enough for the traditional ox and the ass – and a camel for good measure. She had an unrivalled ear for music, but she did not intend either 'A Christmas Carol' or her 1885 'Christmastide' (which became the carol

'Love came down at Christmas') to be set to music as carols. The free rhythm of her poem wasn't considered easy to set to music, but there are two memorable arrangements for it. Gustav Holst put Rossetti's words to music for *The English Hymnal* of 1906. Holst, whose astrologically inspired orchestral suite *The Planets* gave him the celebrity he loathed, was, like Rossetti, a poorly child and adult. He was a little accident-prone as well – in 1923 he suffered concussion having fallen backwards off his podium. Again like Rossetti though, neither ailment nor accident could sap his creative energy and he continued to teach and compose up to his death in 1934. The piece he wrote for Rossetti's poem is called 'Cranham' after the village outside Cheltenham from which his mother's family came. The little house where he wrote it is now fittingly called 'Midwinter Cottage'. His simple, evocative tune must take its share of credit for the popularity of this carol.

Harold Darke wrote his music to Rossetti's poem three years after Holst when he was just twenty-one and a student at the Royal College of Music. Born in London, he was an organist by profession. He was organist at the Church of St Michael, Cornhill in the City of London for a good fifty years and while at Cornhill he gave over 1,800 organ recitals at Monday lunchtimes for an enthusiastic audience. This, the Cornhill Lunchtime Organ Recitals series that he began in 1916, is the longest running of its kind in the world, and continues to flourish today with Jonathan Rennert the current organist. One of the things I love about the Darke music for 'In the Deep Midwinter' is its beautiful, delicate organ accompaniment. He also seems effortlessly to have met the rhythmical challenges of Rossetti's poem.

Recently, Bob Chilcott, formerly a member of the King's Singers, has written a choral setting for 'In the Bleak Midwinter' called simply 'Midwinter'. His version was, I expect, brought to prominence by the King's College Choir because they sing it in their Nine Lessons and Carols, broadcast to millions around the world each year. Fitting to its origins this, because Harold Darke was himself a conductor of the choir during the Second World War.

'In the Bleak Midwinter' has twice been voted a Christmas number one. In 2005 it knocked 'Silent Night' off the top spot in a *Songs of Praise* poll. In 2008, Darke's arrangement was judged favourite of the UK and US music directors who contributed to the *BBC Music Magazine* poll.

I was at once struck by the sheer perfection of this carol. It's definitely one of my top three favourites of all time and what's testament to this carol is that I like the melody by Holst and the one by Darke equally. Recently the *Songs of Praise* producer managed very cleverly to put on a performance I was involved in at the Royal Albert Hall (it's always in the Royal Albert Hall – always the Big Sing!) where we incorporated both melodies. They have similarities and were of course composed really close together in time. The congregation sang the first couple of verses to the Darke melody and then yours truly was to take the solo in the third verse to the Holst melody. Well, I was the only one who managed to mess it up because in the middle of the Holst, I crept into the Darke melody, which is very easily done. And this carol will be included on my new album at Christmas, probably the Holst melody this time round all the way through.

This is a carol that takes you on a journey where you can really use every aspect of colour in your voice and performance. It's almost like a theatrical carol. You're setting the scene in the first verse, where the earth is hard, water's like a stone, winds are moaning and snow is falling, not just a little, but snow on snow, snow on snow. It's like the first chapter in a Harry Potter book, you just want to read on to find out what happens next!

The most lyrical of the verses is the third. It's the one where the singer in you can really come out. It's full of rhythm changes from 'In the bleak midwinter/Frosty wind made moan' to, in the third verse:

Enough for him, whom cherubim
Worship night and day,
A breastful of milk
And a mangerful of hay;

Enough for him, whom angels
Fall down before,
The ox and ass and camel,
Which adore.

This is just a different rhythm, which falls beautifully within the voice. The fourth verse is usually missed out in my performances anyway, so I go from verses one, two and three into the final 'What can I give him/ Poor as I am?' I know people love singing this carol; I do anyway. Because it's a fantastic sing, it's a beautiful melody, wonderful words, but also the final verse brings it all back to being humble – the fact that if you were a shepherd you'd have given one of your flock, if a wise man you'd have done your part, but all you can give is your heart. This is reinforced right the way through the carol. If you sing it with honesty and an open heart, you can't go wrong.

I've performed 'In the Deep Midwinter' so many times. It's a crowd pleaser but also a performer pleaser. There are so many of these carols that I sing to hopefully make an audience smile but also because I absolutely love singing them.

15

IT CAME UPON THE MIDNIGHT CLEAR

Words

Edmund Hamilton Sears (1810–76)

Music

Richard Storrs Willis (1819–1900),
Arthur Sullivan (1842–1900)

It came upon the midnight clear,
That glorious song of old,
From angels bending near the earth
To touch their harps of gold:
'Peace on the earth, good will to men,
From heaven's all-gracious King!'
The world in solemn stillness lay
To hear the angels sing.

Still through the cloven skies they come,
With peaceful wings unfurled;
And still their heavenly music floats
O'er all the weary world:
Above its sad and lowly plains
They bend on hovering wing;
And ever o'er its Babel-sounds
The blessed angels sing.

Yet with the woes of sin and strife
The world has suffered long;
Beneath the angel-strain have rolled
Two thousand years of wrong;
And man, at war with man, hears not
The long-song which they bring:
O hush the noise, ye men of strife,
And hear the angels sing.

And ye, beneath life's crushing load,
Whose forms are bending low,
Who toil along the climbing way
With painful steps and slow,
Look, now! For glad and golden hours
Come swiftly on the wing;
O rest beside the weary road
And hear the angels sing.

For lo! the days are hastening on,
By prophet-bards foretold,
When, with the ever-circling years,
Comes round the age of gold;
When peace shall over all the earth
Its ancient splendours fling,
And the whole world give back the song
Which now the angels sing.

Edmund Sears wrote this powerful anthem for peace in December 1849 four months before his fortieth birthday. In his *Sermons and Songs of the Christian Life,* Sears places 'It Came Upon the Midnight Clear' right after his sermon based on the biblical text Hebrews 12:1 concerning the doctrine of angels:

> Seeing we also are compassed about with so great a cloud of witnesses, let us lay aside every weight, and the sin which doth so easily beset us, and let us run with patience the race that is set before us . . .

His great cloud of witnesses, the multitude of the Heavenly host, take centre-stage here and carry the Christmas message of peace on earth, good will to men. They are wonderfully bird-like, dynamic angels: 'Still through the cloven skies they come/with peaceful wings unfurled . . . They bend on hovering wing'.

Edmund Hamilton Sears was born in 1810 in Sandisfield, Massachusetts. The town was founded upon a rural economy, and when they tried to introduce other industries, these failed when a planned railway line fell through. Perhaps growing up in a township so recently settled, Sears was aware of the fragility that such a community has. He was brought up on a farm, the youngest of three boys, and chose to become a Unitarian minister.

At the time he wrote this carol Sears was a pastor in Wayland, Massachusetts. 'It Came Upon the Midnight Clear' was published in the *Christian Register* of 29 December 1849. Then in 1850 Sears asked his friend, the American composer Richard Storrs Willis to set his words to music. The resulting composition is called 'Carol' and in 1875 it appeared in Sears' *Sermons and Songs of the Christian Life*, in which he reminds us that our lives are witnessed, we do not act in isolation or unobserved: 'Your home may be humble, apart, alone; but if a good life is lived there, it stands in the centre of an amphitheatre thronged with heavenly multitudes, all bending towards you and breathing their spirit into yours.'

The social message carried in these verses was in line with Sears' faith and with the Unitarian church's anti-war sentiments. Because Unitarianism teaches belief in the sole personality of God, rather than the doctrine of the Trinity, the words in this poem do not describe the birth of Christ or make Christological references. This might have meant it was easier for those Unitarians who did not view Jesus as divine to sing it. However Sears himself believed in the divinity of Jesus and 'Calm on the Listening Ear of Night', the carol for which he is also known, does have the Nativity at its centre. It is still popular in America, though not often sung in the UK.

Like Gloria Shayne and Noel Regney, the writers of 'Do You Hear What I Hear?', Sears wrote 'It Came upon the Midnight Clear' for a world in which prospects for peace seemed threatened to be eclipsed by the savagery of war. It is sometimes suggested that he was influenced by the revolutions in Europe at that time and by a recent war between America and Mexico between 1846 and 1848 over right of possession of Texas. But unlike 'Do You Hear What I Hear?', Sears' poem makes a direct call to humanity to 'hush the noise' and to live in peace with one another.

Sears first preached the sermon that precedes his poem 'Carol' in 1865 at the end of the American Civil War which had raged since 1861. He would have been mindful of 'the thousands of martyrs, the flower of the country' who gave up their lives. It was a time when, after so many casualties, the value of peace would have been held high in the hearts of his congregation.

In the UK 'It Came upon the Midnight Clear' is sung to a different melody. Arthur Sullivan, one half of Gilbert and Sullivan, reworked a traditional carol from Herefordshire that was reportedly sent to him by a friend. It was likely that Sullivan, himself an agnostic, was attracted to Sears' humanist Unitarianism. His tune was titled 'Eardisley', after the Herefordshire town (it is also known as 'Noel'), and the resulting arrangement was published in *Church Hymns* in 1874 with the credit: 'Traditional Air rearranged'.

When this carol was first published in Britain, in Edward Bickersteth's *Hymnal Companion to the Book of Common Prayer* of 1870, it underwent changes that give it a more Christocentric feel. Bickersteth took out the third verse and rewrote the fifth as follows:

For lo the days are hastening on,
By prophets seen of old,
When with the ever-circling years
Shall come the time foretold,
When the new heaven and earth shall own
The Prince of Peace their King,
And the whole world send back the song
Which now the angels sing.

Then in the next century Erik Routley's 1961 *University Carol Book* changes the last five lines of this new version to:

Came round the day foretold,
When men, surprised by joy, adored
The prince of peace, their king;
Come all who hear! Join in the song
Which men and angels sing.

So, as with many carols and hymns, this song with its powerful melody and words that move us has come on a journey to become what we sing today, but over the last hundred and sixty years its core message has remained unchanged. Christ's coming is of course a time to celebrate, but Sears' words ask us to remember that this time it signals a call to service. The angels have witnessed two thousand years of conflict among humanity: 'It Came upon the Midnight Clear' voices their plea for peace on earth and challenges us to listen and to take responsibility to stop our wars.

JESUS CHRIST THE APPLE TREE

WORDS
Anon.

MUSIC
Elizabeth Poston (1905–87)

The tree of life my soul hath seen,
Laden with fruit and always green:
The trees of nature fruitless be
Compared with Christ the apple tree.

His beauty doth all things excel:
By faith I know, but ne'er can tell,
The glory which I now can see
In Jesus Christ the apple tree.

For happiness I long have sought,
And pleasure dearly I have bought:
I missed of all; but now I see
'Tis found in Christ the apple tree.

I'm weary with my former toil,
Here I will sit and rest awhile:
Under the shadow I will be,
Of Jesus Christ the apple tree.

This fruit doth make my soul to thrive,
It keeps my dying faith alive:
Which makes my soul in haste to be
With Jesus Christ the apple tree.

This carol was introduced to me by J Mervyn Williams and Hefen Owen, producers of most of my albums as a boy. Invariably I'd meet up with the organist that was going to accompany me on my albums on the morning of the recording and I remember them saying, 'How do you feel about recording this album?' Well, I'd never heard this one before. But after going through it a couple of times with the organist I knew it was something I could do justice to.

The mysterious lyrics of the piece are by an American author who remains unknown. He or she was probably living in New England in the 1700s as the lyrics first appeared in *Divine Hymns, or Spiritual Songs: for the use of Religious Assemblies and Private Christians* published in 1784 by Joshua Smith, a lay Baptist minister from New Hampshire. Apple trees were grown widely in New England and this might have provided the inspiration for the song, or maybe the lyrics are a meditation on the verses from the Song of Songs (2:3): 'As the apple tree among the trees of the wood, so is my beloved among the sons. I sat down under his shadow with great delight, and his fruit was sweet to my taste.'

The setting of the carol I used to sing is by Elizabeth Poston, who is a twentieth-century English composer born on 24 October 1905 at Pin Green, Stevenage. Her father died in 1914 when Elizabeth was nine. Her mother Clementine then took her and her brother to live at Rooks Nest House, which was also the childhood home of E M Forster, who lived there between 1883 and 1893. It's the house on which Howards End, the setting for Forster's novel of the same name, is based. Elizabeth Poston lived at Rooks Nest House for the rest of her life, and in a neat connection, it was there that she wrote the score for the 1970 television production of Forster's novel.

Both Peter Warlock and Ralph Vaughan Williams mentored Elizabeth Poston during her studies at the Royal Academy of Music in London. She travelled during the 1930s studying architecture and during her travels she, like her mentor Vaughan Williams, collected folk songs. She came back to England at the beginning of the Second World War and began a new career in radio broadcasting for the BBC, becoming Director of Music in the European Service.

During the war Elizabeth Poston went underground, working for the British Government using gramophone records to send coded messages to allies in Europe. She never revealed the exact nature of this work and it remains secret to this day. Poston had a role in the creation of the BBC Third Programme, which became Radio 3 and between 1955 and 1961 she was the president of the Society of Women Musicians.

Her melody is enchanting to sing and is ideally suited to a boy chorister's voice. It's very much in the same vein as 'Once in Royal David's City' in being very exposed but also giving opportunities to really soar with the melodic line. I recorded it on my Christmas album back in 1985 as a boy soprano. It was a favourite of Robert Runcie, the 102nd Archbishop of Canterbury; actually I think it was sung at his funeral. Poston's setting is in the key of C major and there aren't any accidentals in the score so it gives it a really folk-song-like sound, very pure and also means you can put your own stamp on it: there's no strict metre, you can play around with the time, which gives you carte blanche on performance. And that's what I used to love about it, the blank sheet. When I sat there with the organist that morning we were able very, very quickly to create something I was proud of. I'll record it as an adult as well and hopefully I will be as lucky this time round. Such is the melody of 'Jesus Christ the Apple Tree' that I used to sing the first couple of verses unaccompanied, I've even sung it all unaccompanied. It doesn't need an organ accompaniment, or strings, or anything gimmicky. All one needs is the purity of the voice and the passion of the performance.

O little town of Bethlehem

P. Brooks

O LITTLE TOWN OF BETHLEHEM

Words Phillips Brooks (1835–93)

Music 'Forest Green' by Ralph Vaughan Williams (1872–1958),
'Wengen' by Henry Walford Davies (1869–1941)

O little town of Bethlehem,
How still we see thee lie!
Above thy deep and dreamless sleep
The silent stars go by.
Yet in thy dark streets shineth
The everlasting light,
The hopes and fears of all the years
Are met in thee tonight.

O morning stars, together
Proclaim the holy birth,
And praises sing to God the King,
And peace to men on earth;
For Christ is born of Mary,
And, gathered all above,
While mortals sleep, the angels keep
Their watch of wondering love.

How silently, how silently,
The wondrous gift is given!
So God imparts to human hearts

The blessings of his heaven.
O holy child of Bethlehem,
No ear may hear his coming;
But in this world of sin,
Where meek souls will receive him, still
The dear Christ enters in.

Where children pure and happy
Pray to the blessed child,
Where misery cries out to thee,
Son of the mother mild;
Where charity stands watching
And faith holds wide the door,
The dark night wakes, the glory breaks,
And Christmas comes once more.

O holy child of Bethlehem
Descend to us we pray;
Cast out our sin and enter in,
Be born in us today.
We hear the Christmas angels
The great glad tidings tell:
O come to us, abide with us,
Our Lord Emmanuel.

On Christmas Eve 1865, Phillips Brooks, an American Episcopalian priest, stood in the field outside Bethlehem where the angel of the Lord is said to have appeared to the shepherds. He had taken a year's leave of absence from his Holy Trinity Church in Philadelphia to do a world tour and, stopping off in Jerusalem, he picked up a horse and rode it from there to Bethlehem. He was deeply moved by his moments in this field and by the five-hour service in Bethlehem at the Church of the Nativity on the supposed site of Jesus' birth. He said,

> I remember standing in the old church in Bethlehem close to the spot where Jesus was born, when the whole church was ringing hour after hour with splendid hymns of praise to God, how again and again it seemed as if I could hear voices I knew well, telling each other of the *Wonderful Night* of the Savior's birth.

Later, in 1868, after returning home to Philadelphia and drawing on this experience, he wrote 'O Little Town of Bethlehem' for the children of his Sunday School to sing at Christmas.

Phillips conveys beautifully the quiet streets of a small town in the middle of the night. Unusually in the writing of carols, which tend to trumpet their celebrations, this one is gentle and dwells on the contrast between the hushed setting and the wondrous thing that is happening there. He gave his verses to his organist, Lewis Redner, asking him to compose a tune for it. Lewis couldn't, try as he might, find the melody, but the night before Christmas he woke with the music 'ringing in my ears, full formed and harmonized'. He jotted the notes down and went back to sleep. The tune is called 'St Louis' after him and it is still the standard one in the US.

Phillips Brooks was born in Boston. He was over six foot six, a man of great physical presence and spiritual strength. When giving sermons, his delivery came in lightning bursts – it's said that he spoke at a rate of over 200 words a minute; one wonders how his congregation kept up! He was also a committed humanitarian and reformer and an admirer of Abraham Lincoln. At the age of fifty-six he was made Bishop of Massachusetts, but died eighteen months after his consecration in 1893.

'O Little Town of Bethlehem' was brought to Britain by W Garrett Horder, in his *Treasury of Hymns*, 1896. It has been set to two melodies, both of which I enjoy. It became a favourite of carol singers when set to Vaughan Williams' arrangement of a tune of an English folk song, 'The

Ploughboy's Dream'. As an enthusiastic collector of folk melodies, Vaughan Williams travelled the countryside, meeting the people who were still singing them. He recovered a treasure trove of songs. This one was sung to him in 1903 by Mr Garman, a farm labourer of Forest Green near Ockley in Surrey and Vaughan Williams renamed the melody the more mundane 'Forest Green' after the village. Carol singers love to sing this carol in the open air; its picture of Bethlehem under the stars could easily be transferred to imagining an English village.

Another version is by Henry Walford Davies. This marvellous tune is called 'Wengen' and is the one usually performed in the Nine Lessons and Carols at King's College Cambridge. Sir Walford Davies was an interesting character with a long and varied musical life. He was born on the English/Welsh border in Oswestry, the seventh of nine hildren of John and Sarah Whitridge Davies, and the youngest of their four surviving sons. His father was big in the local music scene and he encouraged his family to make music, so Henry and his siblings grew up playing any and every instrument they could get hold of. Henry's talents as a singer were recognised and, with some discomfort to his Nonconformist family, he became a chorister at St George's, Windsor. So at the age of twelve he was singing a gruelling fourteen services a week – as well as going to school of course. Walford Davies (his middle name Walford was his grandmother's maiden name) was also a talented organist and held the position of organist of the Temple Church in London for twenty years. He succeeded Sir Edward Elgar as Master of the King's Music, remaining in the job until 1941. His choral arrangement of another carol, 'The Holly and the Ivy', became famous through its broadcast performances in the King's College carol services.

Walford Davies was a great proponent of making classical music accessible to the masses and he found his ideal platform during the 1920s and 30s with his popular BBC series called 'Music and the Ordinary Listener'. He died in 1941 in Bristol, and is buried in the cathedral grounds there.

I've been associated with this carol since I was at Bangor Cathedral.

It explores deep meaning yet it also shows its origins as a work written for children – as many carols were. There's an internal rhyme in each verse that recreates a lovely chiming almost nursery-rhyme quality, as in the first: 'Above thy *deep* and dreamless *sleep*' and then 'The hopes and *fears* of all the *years*.' It's full of contrast as far as dynamic is concerned. The first verse is silent, otherworldly. The reality comes to you in the third verse, again, when I'm involved in it, performed very quietly, in a still fashion. The last verse can be organs blazing with a descant. It's all about casting sin out and living as pure a life as you possibly can. But even in a world of sin, as long as you've an open heart, Christ will enter.

You also have to have quite good breath to sing this carol. There are lots of lines that go over into other lines. For instance in the first verse:

> Above thy deep and dreamless sleep
> The silent stars go by.
> Yet in thy dark streets shineth
> The everlasting light,
> The hopes and fears of all the years
> Are met in thee tonight.

Every two lines are basically one line, and it's the same all the way through.

My favourite lines towards the end of verse three are 'Where meek souls will receive him, *still*/the dear Christ enters in'; the meaning slipping from one line to another with a simple stress that speaks volumes.

I've had the pleasure of performing 'O Little Town of Bethlehem' on two occasions in Israel, once as a boy, and then I got to perform it in Bethlehem for the television programmes I was producing for the BBC and recently for my programme for ITV discovering the stories behind the carols.

The Bethlehem I experienced as a man was very, very different to the Bethlehem I was introduced to as a boy. The place has changed beyond all recognition. There was more of an innocence in the Bethlehem of old, whereas today it's a bustling, busy place, which made the carol

even more poignant. I was filmed in the centre of the town, with cars going past, horns hooting, people shouting. And there am I in the middle miming 'Oh little town of Bethlehem/How still we see thee lie.' Ironic, really.

But there's something magical about singing 'O Little Town of Bethlehem' in Bethlehem itself. As a child in the school congregation or if you're lucky enough to sing in a choir, you have no idea really what Bethlehem would be like. As a child I had my own preconceived idea and I remember saying to my mum and dad that I could not quite believe the fact that I actually was in Bethlehem, singing a carol about Jesus' Nativity in the place where he was born. It was a surreal – and life-changing – experience.

JOY TO THE WORLD

Words
Isaac Watts (1674–1748)

Music
'Antioch' Lowell Mason (1792–1872)

Joy to the world! the Lord is come:
Let earth receive her King!
Let ev'ry heart prepare him room,
And heav'n and nature sing!

Joy to the earth! the Saviour reigns:
Let men their songs employ,
While fields and floods, rocks, hills, and plains,
Repeat the sounding joy.

No more let sins and sorrows grow,
Nor thorns infest the ground;
He comes to make his blessings flow
Far as the curse is found.

He rules the world with truth and grace,
And makes the nations prove
The glories of his righteousness,
And wonders of his love.

In Isaac Watts' book with the breathtaking title: *Logic, or The Right Use of Reason in the Enquiry After Truth With a Variety of Rules to Guard Against Error in the Affairs of Religion and Human Life, as well as in the Sciences* – phew! – he defines judgement as '. . . when mere ideas are joined in the mind without words . . .' while a proposition is when those ideas are ' . . . clothed with words . . .'

So one of Watts' best-known works 'Joy to the World' is by nature more of a proposition than a judgement. Nevertheless, before some gentle judgement is made of a carol that celebrates Christ's Second Coming, it must first be said that it provokes strong emotion, is a joy to sing, and whenever I've sung it as a member of the congregation of *Songs of Praise*, it really does what it says on the tin and makes the whole place come alive.

Isaac Watts is dubbed the 'father of English hymnody' and the 'poet of the sanctuary'. He was not an imposing figure, described two hundred years after his birth as 'Scarcely more than five feet in stature, his bodily presence was weak, his forehead was low, his cheek-bones rather prominent, his eyes small and gray, and his face in repose, of a heavy aspect.' But his precise and clear voice commanded attention and his words and singing voice captured the soul. He was named after his father Isaac, and like his father, who was imprisoned a couple of times for his dissenting convictions, Watts was a Nonconformist. Practically, this meant that he was educated at a free grammar school in Stoke Newington and was not permitted to go to either Oxford or Cambridge.

Watts was let down by his poor health for much of his life. His pastorate in London involved preaching and training future preachers, but when illness led him to cut down on his pastoral duties, Sir Thomas Abney MP, a former Lord Mayor of the City of London, invited Watts to live on his estate in Hertfordshire and in his property in Stoke Newington. There he stayed for most of the time until his death in Stoke Newington in 1748. On the anniversary of his arrival, Watts dropped a note to Abney's widow Mary saying that, having intended to stay one night '. . . I have extended my visit to the length of exactly thirty years . . .'

Free of a level of responsibility and public work, Watts' health improved. In 1719 he produced another publication with a long title, *The Psalms of David: Imitated in the Language of the New Testament, and Applied to the Christian State and Worship*. Here he paraphrases the psalms to suit a Christian audience. The source of Watts' lyrics for 'Joy to the World' is Psalm 98, which tells us to glorify Christ's triumphant Second Coming:

> Let the sea roar, and the fullness thereof; the world and they
> that dwell therein.
> Let the floods clap their hands: let the hills be joyful together
> Before the Lord, for he cometh to judge the earth:
> With righteousness shall he judge the world, and the people
> with equity.

Many of the carols I've chosen for this book tell the story of Christ as a child born to Mary in a humble stable. This one is different. The original doesn't refer specifically to Christmas and it can be sung at many times of the year, but its heading reads 'The Messiah's Coming and Kingdom' and it has become a firm favourite for Christmas.

Watts wrote over 750 hymns, many of them still familiar, including 'When I Survey the Wondrous Cross' or 'Come Let Us Join Our Cheerful Songs'. His poetry is not so well known today; one of his poems for the edification of children,'Against Idleness and Mischief', was shamelessly used by Lewis Carroll in *Alice's Adventures in Wonderland*, becoming 'How Doth the Little Crocodile'. Maybe in revenge for Watts' 'Against Idleness . . . ', a playground parody of 'Joy to the World', popular with American kids, goes with homicidal intent:

> Joy to the world our teacher's dead,
> We barbecued the head . . .

Altogether, Watts' compositions have a straightforward and simple power. He had a natural gift for language and could break down the distance between the singer and the words to create an authentic connection to God and invest the song with personal meaning. He introduced the idea of using poetry that did not come directly from the Bible, but from the worshippers' own experience, which is perhaps a key to the popularity of his verses.

In 1839, Lowell Mason, who wrote over 1,600 hymn tunes and, as choir director and organist, initiated in his church the first Sunday School for Black children in America, wrote the music of 'Antioch' to go with Watts' lyrics. After some difficulties, in 1822 Mason at last found a publisher for the collection of his tunes that, following the British model, took their influence from classical European composers such as Mozart and Haydn. This was published anonymously because Mason was concerned that giving his name would jeopardise his career as a banker!

Mason was much criticised in his native North America for his leanings towards European musical tradition, and his pieces did tend to overwhelm home-grown compositions that were part of a more participatory American tradition. 'Joy to the World' was caught up in this debate; some have found the tune indistinguishable from a melody by George Frideric Handel (1685–1759), raising doubts that it is actually composed by Mason. It has been noted that the tune for the refrain 'And heaven and nature sing' features in the opening statement and accompaniment to 'Comfort Ye' in Handel's *Messiah*, and the first four words echo 'Lift up your heads' from the same oratorio.

Watts' version is not the only one of 'Joy to the World' sung today. William Wines Phelps (1792–1872) an early leader of the Latter Day Saints Movement, better known as the Mormon Church, adapted Watts' 'Joy to the World' with subtle changes around the concept of anticipating the arrival of Christ as opposed to celebrating his actual second coming.

But Watts' rendering continues to be the most popular. There are also other arrangements to add to Mason's, but one very popular one is John Rutter's; he recorded a version in the style of Handel with the Cambridge Singers for their Christmas albums in 1983 (*Christmas Star*) and 1989 (*Christmas with the Cambridge Singers*).

Over the years, this exultant piece has been recorded by many choirs. It has also been on albums by popular artists such as Andy Williams and Boney M. Mariah Carey's rendition included the opening refrain of the version written by folk singer Hoyt Axton which was a number one hit for Three Dog Night in 1971: 'Jeremiah was a bullfrog/Was a good friend of mine.' This has little resemblance to Watts' lyrics or Mason's music beyond the title but like the original it does call upon the audience to take part in its rousing rendition. And I have to include my favourite: punk rock band The Vandals named their 1996 collection of Christmas-themed songs *Oi to the World*.

It is easy to apply the judgement – or is it the proposition, as defined by Watts? – that his carol is truly inspirational.

19

LITTLE DONKEY

Words and Music
Eric Boswell (1921–2009)

Little donkey, little donkey
On a dusty road
Got to keep on plodding onwards
With your precious load.

Been a long time little donkey
Through the winter's night.
Don't give up now little donkey,
Bethlehem's in sight.

Ring out those bells tonight
Bethlehem, Bethlehem.
Follow the star tonight
Bethlehem, Bethlehem.

Little donkey, little donkey
Had a heavy day,
Little donkey carry Mary
Safely on her way.

Little donkey, little donkey
Journey's end is near
There are wise men waiting
For a sign to bring them here.

Do not falter, little donkey
There's a star ahead
It will guide you, little donkey
To a cattle shed.

Ring out those bells tonight
Bethlehem, Bethlehem.
Follow the star tonight
Bethlehem, Bethlehem.

Little donkey, little donkey
Had a heavy day
Little donkey carry Mary
Safely on her way,
Little donkey carry Mary
Safely on her way.

This is a carol I first got to hear in Llandegfan Primary School, although I never played Joseph, Mary or the donkey for that matter. But picture the scene: I was one of the wise men with a tea towel over the head and a belt holding the thing in place.

'Little Donkey' is the sort of carol you only have to hear a few times and it soaks up into your soul; it's very easy to remember, so much so that it's probably one of the favourite carols of my daughter and now my son who's five because it's so accessible to them. And the whole idea of this tired donkey needing our support to get to its destination is a lovely one really. It's also a carol that sets the scene absolutely beautifully for a child. It's saying to this weary little donkey moving slowly through the winter's night not to give up, not to give up, Bethlehem's in sight. 'If you don't believe me there are wise men waiting to help you, there's also a star to guide you, those bells in Bethlehem are ringing out and Mary your precious cargo couldn't get there without you.' The image of Joseph with Mary on a donkey is eloquent, reinterpreted countless times on our Christmas cards and sung in school carol concerts.

The Christmas story has been enriched through its history by many such details and this one is rooted in the Gospel of Luke. Luke tells us that the Roman Emperor Augustus (27BC – AD14) on a tax-collecting spree, ordered a census to be taken of the Roman world. Joseph's ancestral home was Bethlehem, and to be counted, he and Mary had to leave Nazareth and travel more than seventy miles to Bethlehem to register there. It's not actually recorded how they travelled to Bethlehem, but riding a donkey was the most common kind of transport for poor people. It would have been a long, arduous and perhaps frightening journey, especially for Mary who was heavily pregnant, but we can only imagine her feelings about it all as they're not described in the Gospel or in this carol.

'Little Donkey' is a twentieth-century Christmas song. Eric Boswell, who wrote the words and the music in the 1950s, was a Geordie, born in the Millfield district of Sunderland on 18 July 1921, the son of a tailor and a housewife. He started to learn music when he was seven and later studied under Clifford Hartley, a local organist and choirmaster. He trained as a physicist and was employed by Marconi Electronics during the Second World War. He began writing songs during this time and was inspired to write 'Little Donkey' because he wanted to provide a simple song for children to sing: 'I racked my brains to think of aspects of the Christmas story that hadn't been sung about and came up with the idea of the donkey riding into Bethlehem.' The story goes that when he took it to his music publishers he bumped into Gracie Fields, who not only liked it, but said there and then that she wanted to record it. Our Gracie, who was then sixty-one, found Boswell's complex original tune difficult to sing, so he simplified the song for her, which was the right thing to do because it became a top twenty Christmas hit for her in 1959 and the year following reached number three in a version by Nina and Frederik. Among many other cover versions, the Beverley Sisters, Vera Lynn and the George Mitchell Minstrels have recorded 'Little

Donkey'. It's also on Dame Vera Lynn's current Christmas album and was even performed at the *Songs of Praise* Big Sing in 2008. It took its place alongside two standards, 'Ding Dong Merrily on High' and 'Hark ! The Herald Angels Sing'.

Eric Boswell apparently had mixed feelings about 'Little Donkey'. Although delighted that he had composed such a popular carol he felt that it perhaps overshadowed his other achievements. He was a songwriter, who had written 'I'll Know Her' for Matt Munro, and was well known in the north-east of England for his funny songs in the Geordie dialect such as 'I've Got a Little Whippet' and 'The Social Security Waltz'. But 'Little Donkey' was such a commercial success (it's even available as a ringtone) that Boswell never had to worry about money. It's tempting to imagine that his story was behind the plot of the film of Nick Hornby's *About a Boy* (2002), where Will Freeman played by Hugh Grant is able to have a leisurely, work-free lifestyle because his father had earned a fortune in royalties by writing a Christmas song that was played annually in supermarkets across the land.

Eric Boswell died just before Christmas in 2009, aged eighty-eight.

I can't think of this carol without seeing the school assemblies with hundreds of children sitting cross-legged giving a plodding performance of this quite plodding carol. I absolutely love it: love the melody, love the words and that it takes the child to remind the little donkey: 'you're nearly there'. It's very positive. I also have great affection for the chorus:

> Ring out those bells tonight
> Bethlehem, Bethlehem.
> Follow the star tonight
> Bethlehem, Bethlehem.

Carols like 'Away in a Manger' are also childlike in their construction and regarded by some musicologists as childish, but 'Away in a Manger' can still be performed in a performance setting whereas it's a little more difficult with 'Little Donkey' because it's now so associated with children singing it. I have recorded it myself as an adult and you do feel a little bit guilty taking away from the children a carol that so obviously belongs to them. I think in this instance the childishness is in the words, but I've been to Israel quite a few times and seen many a sad, tired-looking donkey so it may be that Eric Boswell was onto a good thing.

And such is the testimony to this carol that it can work even when it's being sung in a primary school assembly with not necessarily a music teacher, but someone with maybe only grade two or three on the piano jogging along as accompaniment. It still has a real magic and a special quality of Christmas – that is Christmas at its best as seen through a child's eyes. Perhaps the attraction to schools of 'Little Donkey' is also that it's only one octave in range for the singer and very, very easy to play. Its beauty is its simplicity. Also, what credit to this carol that people think it's a traditional folk song that has been around since the dawn of time, when actually it's a modern carol that's only been popular for the last fifty years or so.

20

THE LITTLE DRUMMER BOY

WORDS AND MUSIC
Katherine K Davis (1892–1980), Harry Simeone (1911–2005)
and Henry Onorati (?)

'Peace on Earth' words by Alan Kohan (1933–),
music by Larry Grossman (1938–) and Ian Fraser (1933–)

Come they told me pa-rum-pum-pum-pum
A new-born king to see pa-rum-pum-pum-pum
Our finest gifts we bring pa-rum-pum-pum-pum
Rum-pum-pum-pum, rum-pum-pum-pum.

Come they told me pa-rum-pum-pum-pum
A new-born king to see pa-rum-pum-pum-pum
Our finest gifts we bring pa-rum-pum-pum-pum
To lay before the king pa-rum-pum-pum-pum
Rum-pum-pum-pum, rum-pum-pum-pum
So to honour him pa-rum-pum-pum-pum
When we come.

Little baby pa-rum-pum-pum-pum
I stood beside him there pa-rum-pum-pum-pum
I played my drum for him pa-rum-pum-pum-pum
I played my best for him pa-rum-pum-pum-pum
Rum-pum-pum-pum, rum-pum-pum-pum
And he smiled at me pa-rum-pum-pum-pum
Me and my drum.

Peace on earth, can it be
Years from now, perhaps we'll see,
See the day of glory,
See the day, when men of good will
Live in peace, live in peace again.

Peace on earth, can it be
Every child must be made aware,
Every child must be made to care,
Care enough for his fellow man
To give all the love that he can.

I pray my wish will come true
For my child and your child too.
He'll see the day of glory,
See the day when men of good will
Live in peace, live in peace again.

Peace on Earth, can it be
Can it be.

The words for this song, originally 'The Carol and the Drum', came to its author in 1941 while she was trying to take a nap. Katherine K Davis (1892–1980), American composer and pianist, had the feeling that the words wrote themselves. It was not long before most music publishers started to put two other names, Henry Onorati and Harry Simeone, beside Davis in the writing credits (perhaps overstating their contributions). They each provided an arrangement of Davis' song. Onorati wrote his in 1957 for a recording which missed Christmas so was not released. The following year Simeone was asked by 20th Century Fox Records to produce a Christmas album. He formed the Harry Simeone Chorale and recorded his own arrangement under a new title, 'The Little Drummer Boy' – it was a hit. Simeone and his Chorale went on to have another with his arrangement of 'Do You Hear What I Hear' in 1962.

'The Little Drummer Boy' tells of a poor boy who can only offer the sound of his drum to the baby Jesus. Although it might be thought unwise to bang a drum up close to a newborn baby, Jesus rewards him with a smile of gratitude; the drummer boy has given Jesus his true self. To offer our skills and our abilities is worth more than to lavish expensive gifts that cost us nothing but money. The snowbound 'In the Bleak Midwinter' also celebrates humble and honest generosity as an expression of devotion in a complementary way to this modern carol.

In essence the story of the drummer boy echoes an oft-related twelfth-century tale. A juggler is reprimanded for singing vulgar songs outside a monastery. He is taken inside where he repents and joins the Order. One day he watches other monks laying rich gifts before the newly sculpted statue of the Virgin Mary. The boy is poor and has no presents to offer her. Late at night he creeps into the chapel and performs a juggling act at the foot of the pedestal. The statue comes to life and the Virgin blesses him, in some versions with a smile, in others with a rose. As Mary ascends to Heaven she beckons to the juggler to follow her. He drops dead and does as she commands. Witnessing this miracle, the monks declare him a saint.

In 1892 Anatole France published this story as '*Le Jongleur de Notre Dame*' and in 1902 Jules Massenet turned it into an opera of the same name.

Bing Crosby made his first recording of 'The Little Drummer Boy' song in 1962. Any seasonal song was safe in Crosby's hands, who had had his big Christmas hit with Irving Berlin's 'White Christmas', performed by Bing in the 1954 movie *White Christmas*. This was no exception. The recording is still available today, as it was then, on Crosby's *I Wish You A Merry Christmas* 1962 album.

Then in 1977 there was what many consider to be one of the oddest pairings in duet history. The then glam-rocker David Bowie joined up

with Bing to perform 'The Little Drummer Boy' for a recording of Crosby's Christmas Special in a hot September. The makers of the Special took advantage of Crosby's tour of Britain to film the show in the UK. On his arrival at Elstree Studios, to the set of a fake medieval castle supposed to be Crosby's home during his stay in Britain, David Bowie threw the producers into confusion when he announced that he disliked the song. He did not want to sing it. Writers Ian Fraser, Larry Grossman and Alan Kohan found a piano in the studio's basement and got to work.

They wrote 'Peace on Earth' in an hour and a half.

The melody and lyrics are a counterpoint to the original song and follow after Davis' last verse. Bowie agreed to sing the new version. The two men's voices create a smooth and soulful harmony and theirs turned out to be a match made in Heaven. For some years this new song was available only as a bootleg copy. In 1982 it was released as a single and it went to number three in the UK on Christmas Day.

Six weeks after recording the song, on 14 October, Bing Crosby had a fatal heart attack on a golf course in Spain.

Other artists who have sung 'The Little Drummer Boy' include the Von Trapp family, Marlene Dietrich, Nana Mouskouri, Boney M and Whitney Houston, who sang it with her daughter Bobbi Kristina Brown.

What a year 2008 was. I'd been asked by TOGGS, Terry's Old Gals and Geezers, to do a charity single of the Bowie/Crosby arrangement with Terry Wogan taking Bing's part. I'd never recorded 'The Little Drummer Boy' as a child and, to be brutally honest, it wasn't my favourite carol. I love the message in the carol that we are at all times to be the best that we can be, and at all times to be ourselves. I think that's a fantastic message, which I've tried to be true to throughout my life. And it's not every day that you get to go into the studio with Sir Terry Wogan. That's exactly what we did. He'd finished his morning programme at 9.30. By ten o'clock we were facing one another in fits of laughter, recording this song. Miraculously and without really thinking about it, because, let's face it, Terry's far too busy to be thinking about Christmas carols, he was completely himself on this. He knows he hasn't got the greatest voice in the world, maybe not the greatest voice in Britain, maybe not even the greatest voice in London, or in the studio that day. He delivered it as Terry Wogan would so that the innate message of the carol came through. It also shows off Terry's rich voice beautifully, the fact that he's been on the radio for so many years, the fact that his voice resonates with so many people – that vibrant, ringing tone was there in the recording of the carol. His weighty voice paired with my more lyrical, higher voice suits the song well. There's a part where we sing together and the blend is fantastic.

I've always joked, as has Terry on the radio, that he's my illegitimate radio father, therefore I am his illegitimate radio son and when we were in the studio together, it really was a feeling of father and son. He's somebody I look up to massively on the radio and it was quite nice seeing him out of his environment and actually in mine – roles were reversed somewhat; usually he's in the studio and I'm there with my tongue lolling out worshipping the ground he walks on because I think he's one of the greatest broadcasters in the world, so to see the roles reversed was quite interesting.

The highlight of the carol for me again, even going back to the recording with Sir Terry, is the counter melody I get to sing against his pa-rum-pum-pum-pums, especially because the words are really poignant for this day and age: 'Peace on earth, can it be/Years from now, perhaps we'll see/See the day of glory/See the day, when men of good will/Live in peace, live in peace again.' Then the final verse, as if both reiterating and bringing in a more religious aspect of it: 'I pray my wish will come true/For my child and your child too . . .'

So – a perfect carol for these times and little did we know that by going into the studio we'd create a single that actually got a higher ranking in the charts than a Christmas song I'm most well known for, which is 'Walking in the Air'. 'Walking in the Air' got to number five in the charts, while this got to number three, and if it weren't for being up against *The X Factor* winner Alexandra Burke, then I think we would have got to number one. (In fact, on physical sales alone we would have been number one by miles – she was ahead by 200,000 on download.) But we got to record the video in Cliveden House hotel and to my dying day I'll remember walking out of Cliveden to find that the production team had sprayed this fake snow everywhere. I looked into the Cliveden restaurant from outside and could see that there were three tables occupied by people having lunch, two American tables and I think a business couple from Britain, and their jaws were on the floor because they couldn't believe that they were actually seeing fake snow in Cliveden on a beautifully sunny day and Sir Terry Wogan and myself dressed in woollen coats, and scarves, and hats. It was a surreal scene. Needless to say we signed lots of autographs that day.

It was a wonderful experience being involved in this carol and I never realised it would be so popular until Chris Evans, who has more energy than anyone I've ever met, took it upon himself to make it Christmas number one. He would be ringing me constantly saying 'What happened today? Who've you got involved now?' So I managed to get a record company to record it and release it and then a promotions company to look after it. Every night Chris Evans would have a 'Little Drummer Boy' update and I think his audience by the end were fed up hearing it, but it was an incredible Christmas and a very, very exciting time. Wouldn't it be good if the message of this simple carol one day did come true?

ONCE IN ROYAL DAVID'S CITY

Words
Cecil Frances Alexander (1818–95)

Music
Henry John Gauntlett (1805–76)

Once in Royal David's city
Stood a lowly cattle shed,
Where a mother laid her baby
In a manger for his bed.
Mary was that mother mild,
Jesus Christ her little child.

He came down to earth from heaven
Who is God and Lord of all
And his shelter was a stable
And his cradle was a stall;
With the poor and mean and lowly
Lived on earth our Saviour holy.

And through all his wondrous childhood
He would honour and obey,
Love and watch the lowly maiden
In whose gentle arms he lay.
Christian children all must be
Mild, obedient, good as he.

For he is our childhood's pattern:
Day by day like us he grew;

Once in royal David's city

C.F. Alexander

H.J. Gauntlett

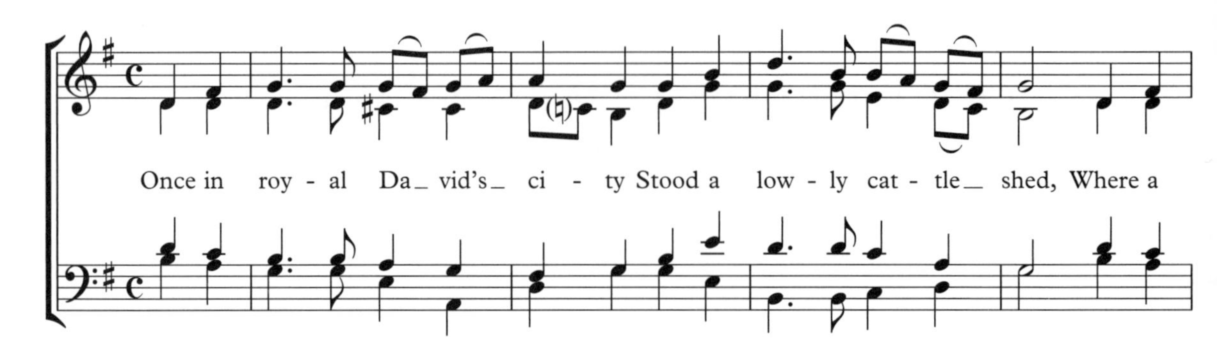
Once in roy - al Da _ vid's _ ci - ty Stood a low - ly cat - tle _ shed, Where a

5
moth - er laid _ her _ ba - by In a man - ger for _ His _ bed. Ma - ry

9
was that moth - er mild, Je - sus Christ her lit - tle ___ child.

He was little, weak and helpless,
Tears and smiles like us he knew;
And he feeleth for our sadness,
And he shareth in our gladness.

And our eyes at last shall see him
Through his own redeeming love,
For that Child so dear and gentle
Is our Lord in heaven above;
And he leads his children on
To the place where he is gone.

Not in that poor lowly stable,
With the oxen standing by
We shall see him, but in heaven,
Set at God's right hand on high,
When, like stars, his children crowned
All in white shall wait around.

Probably the most famous carol in the whole book, 'Once in Royal David's City' is famous for so many reasons. Of course this is an amazing carol, a beautiful blend of music and words. But also in the way it's used these days, in Nine Lessons and Carols from King's College, Cambridge for instance, by all accounts it's become so famous that the choristers are always so nervous before performing it and of course the first verse is always sung by a boy soloist. Because of the nerve situation, he is chosen at the very last minute, usually about twenty or thirty seconds before the broadcast, so the nerves don't get the better of the poor chap. The second verse is sung by the choir, and the congregation joins in the third.

Not many people have heard of the carol's author Cecil Frances Alexander, but millions of us naturally have heard her work sung every

Christmas. Perhaps we've grown up singing her best-known poems at school assemblies and in church. Her hymns 'There is a Green Hill Far Away' and 'All Things Bright and Beautiful' have been enjoyed by generations and have caused controversy too (for the story of the debate surrounding 'All Things Bright and Beautiful' see my *Forty Favourite Hymns*).

Since Hildegarde of Bingen put pen to paper in the twelfth century, hymn writing has been considered a suitable occupation for a woman and flourished through the nineteenth century. Like her contemporaries Charlotte Elliott (1789–1871) and Christina Rossetti (1830–94), Cecil Frances Alexander wrote many hymns and poems – about 400 in her case – during the second half of Queen Victoria's reign. She was born in Dublin in 1818 and brought up in Dublin's Anglo-Irish community. Her father managed the estates of the Earl of Wicklow. Cecil Frances had quite a few suitors; her choice was the Reverend William Alexander, whom she married in 1850. William became Archbishop of Armagh and the Primate of All Ireland.

Cecil Frances Alexander was by inclination a teacher. She wrote her *Hymns for Little Children* in 1848. The book included 'Once in Royal David's City'. It became a nineteenth-century bestseller in the UK, where it went to 100 editions, and through the rest of the world. *Hymns for Little Children* was laid out in the form of the Church Catechism. Through its fourteen hymns, Cecil Frances set out to explain the sections of the Apostles' Creed. 'Once in Royal David's City' was the eleventh hymn in the Creed, coming immediately before 'There is a Green Hill Far Away', which explores what the lines 'he was crucified, dead and buried' mean. Cecil Frances made no money from this collection, as she donated her royalties towards the building and maintenance of a school for the deaf in Strabane, which she had founded.

Henry John Gauntlett, composer of the tune called 'Irby' that fits so well with Cecil Frances' verses, was a lawyer until he was forty, when he gave up the law to devote the rest of his life to music. Thenceforth, he made up for the lost time given to legal matters by writing a mind-boggling 10,000-plus hymn tunes. When the muse was absent, he put into action his perception that the organ was an instrument with potential to be a more flexible musical device, patenting a new electrical-action apparatus for it. Gauntlett's invention combined the lightness of touch of the tubular-pneumatic action it was replacing – the means of transferring the action of the keys and the stops to the pipes – with a faster response.

Gauntlett's simple melody was first arranged not for organ but as a piano accompaniment and in 1849 it was published in a pamphlet called *Christmas Carols, Four Numbers*. It did not get the name 'Irby' until it was included in the 1861 first edition of *Hymns Ancient and Modern*. It is not clear why the tune was called this. Gauntlett doesn't appear to have had a connection with any of the places in the UK called Irby, nor with the Irby in Southern Ireland that these days is a few hours' drive from Londonderry where Cecil Frances once lived. The house today boasts a blue plaque commemorating her time there.

Cecil Frances' *Hymns for Little Children* is dedicated to her 'little Godsons'. She is supposed to have written the book in response to their complaint that learning the catechism for their confirmation was boring and difficult. She expresses the hope that the 'language of verse which children love may help to impress on their minds what they are, what I have promised them, and what they must seek to be.' This message demonstrates a Victorian idolisation of childhood, which Cecil Frances subscribed to, and of which 'Once in Royal David's City' is a good example. The human baby Jesus, who cries and smiles as they do, demonstrates to children what they can indeed 'seek to be'.

This inspirational carol still communicates a powerful message, not only to children but to all of us. 'Once in Royal David's City' celebrates the wondrous event that occurred so many centuries ago in Bethlehem; for many this carol signals the start of Christmas.

In my days as a chorister I sang 'Once in Royal David's City' as part of the choir of Bangor Cathedral and I was always bowled over by its majesty, the fact that it can start so quietly and really does build up.

These days my association with this carol is through the charity event that I take part in in Handel's church, St George's Hanover Square, where Westminster Cathedral choristers sing 'Once in Royal David's City' as we process into the church ready for our very own Nine Lessons and Carols. It's an event for which Judi Dench is the President and I'm the Vice President and lessons are read by such actors as Anthony Hopkins, Charles Dance and the like.

As a boy soprano I was very fortunate to perform 'Once in Royal David's City' in Israel in one of two programmes made there by the BBC. I was the guest soloist, so I'd recorded all the music back in Britain, and then I went over to Israel to mime these holy pieces in their environment. It was the morning that I was supposed to be driving to the Wailing Wall to perform the carol, which was being filmed by an Israeli film crew as a joint production between Israeli Television and British TV and this was going to be a special programme for Christmas Eve. We were in the back of the van and two minutes before we arrived at our destination, a huge bomb had gone off so we were sent on a detour. I remember as a boy being in the back of this van with my parents and the British producer, feeling slightly scared to say the least, knowing that I was about to perform what I regarded as an amazing Godlike carol in an area where I thought bombs and hatred didn't really exist. It shows that as a child I wasn't really aware of the dangerous and frightening situation I was in. But once I got to the Wailing Wall there was no sign of bombs or anything like that, just a friendly Israeli film crew with lots of cameras, a crowd of tourists looking on, and a little Aled Jones in grey trousers, blue shirt and a terrible blue bow tie performing 'Once in Royal David's City'. I think it was about seven o'clock in the morning as well. That's an experience that will remain with me forever.

Of the many descants that have been written for this carol, my favourite is again by a person I've been very fortunate to get to know through my life and that's Sir David Willcocks. His descant, especially on the sixth verse: 'Not in that poor lowly stable/With the oxen standing by' is so uplifting, and when you get to the two last lines: 'When, like

stars, his children crowned/All in white shall wait around' with the descant – and I'm very lucky that at Christmas we have the Band of the Irish Guards playing along – you can imagine the scene: a packed church, six hundred people, the Band of the Irish Guards, Westminster Cathedral Choir and congregation all belting out this glorious carol. Then it really does make the hairs at the back of your neck stand up.

22

MARY HAD A BABY

Collected by N G J Ballanta-Taylor (1893–1962)

Mary had a baby, my Lord,
Mary had a baby, oh my Lord,
Mary had a baby, my Lord,
People keep a-comin' an' the train done gone.
What did she name him? my Lord,
What did she name him? oh my Lord,
What did she name him? my Lord,
People keep a-comin' an' the train done gone.
She named him Jesus, my Lord,
She named him Jesus, oh my Lord,
She named him Jesus, my Lord,
People keep a-comin' an' the train done gone.
Named him King Jesus, my Lord,
Named him King Jesus, oh my Lord,
Named him King Jesus, my Lord,
People keep a-comin' an' the train done gone.
Now where was he born? my Lord,
Where was he born? oh my Lord,
Where was he born? my Lord,
People keep a-comin' an' the train done gone.
Born in a stable, my Lord,
Born in a stable, oh my Lord,
Born in a stable, my Lord,
People keep a-comin' an' the train done gone.

And where did she lay him? My Lord,
Where did she lay him? oh my Lord,
Where did she lay him? my Lord,
People keep a-comin' an' the train done gone.
She laid him in a manger, my Lord,
Laid him in a manger, oh my Lord,
Laid him in a manger, my Lord,
People keep a-comin' an' the train done gone.
Who heard the singing? my Lord,
Who heard the singing? oh my Lord,
Who heard the singing? my Lord,
People keep a-comin' an' the train done gone.
Shepherds heard the singing, my Lord,
Shepherds heard the singing, oh my Lord,
Shepherds heard the singing, my Lord,
People keep a-comin' an' the train done gone.
Who came to see him? my Lord,
Who came to see him? oh my Lord,
Who came to see him? my Lord,
People keep a-comin' an' the train done gone.
Shepherds came to see him, my Lord,
Shepherds came to see him, oh my Lord,
Shepherds came to see him, my Lord,
People keep a-comin' an' the train done gone.
Star keeps shining, my Lord,
Star keeps shining, oh my Lord,
Star keeps shining, my Lord,
People keep a-comin' an' the train done gone.
The wise men kneeled before him, my Lord,
The wise men kneeled before him, oh my Lord,
The wise men kneeled before him, my Lord,
People keep a-comin' an' the train done gone.
King Herod tried to find him, my Lord,

King Herod tried to find him, oh my Lord,
King Herod tried to find him, my Lord,
People keep a-comin' an' the train done gone.
Moving in the elements, my Lord,
Moving in the elements, oh my Lord,
Moving in the elements, my Lord,
People keep a-comin' an' the train done gone.
They went away to Egypt, my Lord,
They went away to Egypt, oh my Lord,
They went away to Egypt, my Lord,
People keep a-comin' an' the train done gone.
Traveled on a donkey, my Lord,
Traveled on a donkey, oh my Lord,
Traveled on a donkey, my Lord,
People keep a-comin' an' the train done gone.
Angels watching over him, my Lord,
Angels watching over him, oh, my Lord,
Angels watching over him, my Lord,
People keep a-comin' an' the train done gone.

The origins of 'Mary Had a Baby' have been traced to St Helena Island off the coast of South Carolina. It is a traditional Christmas song and is maybe more a spiritual than a carol.

Spirituals set out to communicate Christian ideals, but they also spoke of the hardship of being an African-American slave and their lyrics were often directly linked to the composer's experience. The spiritual offered slaves an expressive way of sharing their religious, emotional, and physical experiences. The passion of the music could remind its singers that Jesus was always by their side looking after them. Today, in entirely different circumstances, this sense of being connected is still evoked by spirituals.

We owe a debt to the forensic skills of the musicologist N G J Ballanta-Taylor for diligently collecting the words and music of many spirituals, among them 'Mary Had a Baby'. Ballanta-Taylor was building on the work of the abolitionists William Francis Allen (1830–89), Lucy McKim Garrison (1842–77) and Charles Pickard Ware (1849–1921). During the American Civil War of 1861 to 1865, their work with freed slaves on plantations moved the authors to transcribe the tunes and lyrics of slave songs. Published in 1867, *Slave Songs of the United States* was the first and most influential collection of African American music.

Nicholas George Julius Ballanta-Taylor, born near Freetown in Sierra Leone in 1893, was the son of Gustavus Taylor, a ship's engineer who played the violin and organ. Tragically Gustavus died in a shipping accident when his son was ten and although Nicholas was able to achieve a grammar school education in Freetown and pass the entrance exam for a music degree in England at Durham University, he could not afford to actually travel to university in the UK. However his undoubted muscial talent got him a break: he was working as musical director for the Choral Society in Freetown when he met Adelaide Casely-Hayford (1868–1960). Casely-Hayford was also born in Sierra Leone. She was an ardent feminist and advocate for preserving the national identity and cultural heritage of Sierra Leoneans. She was educated in England, to where her father had retired, and then Germany, returning to Freetown after an absence of twenty-five years. Determined to help Ballanta-Taylor's musical career, she took his choral work with her on a trip to New York and later paid for him to join her there. He was given a scholarship to the Institute of Musical Art (now the Juilliard School of Music) and met the philanthropist George Peabody who went on to fund his research into spirituals. Ballanta-Taylor's scientifically rigorous approach to this work has left a significant legacy for musicians and academics alike.

One of those musicians was William Levi Dawson.

Born in Anniston, Alabama in 1899, William Dawson ran away from home at the age of thirteen and joined the Tuskegee Institute in Alabama. This was the only school in the area that accepted African-American students. William paid for his education by working on the school's farm. He played in both the band and orchestra of Tuskegee.

Dawson received international acclaim for his most important orchestral work, *Negro Folk Symphony*. It was the first work of its nature by an African-American composer incorporating authentic African-American folk melodies in a symphonic form. The symphony was premiered by the Philadelphia Orchestra under the direction of conductor Leopold Stokowski in 1934. Life came around full circle for William when he returned to the Tuskegee Institute and was professor there. He developed the 100-member Tuskegee choir, formed by the school's founder, Booker T Washington. While he was their conductor – from 1931 to 1956 – William took the choir out on tour and they gained a worldwide reputation, singing at Carnegie Hall in New York and at the White House.

Although he is best known for his contributions to both orchestral and choral literature, perhaps Dawson's most celebrated works are his arrangements and variations of spiritual songs such as those collected by his near contemporary, Nicholas Ballanta-Taylor. Dawson's many recordings and sheet music have assured that 'Mary Had a Baby' is a well-loved favourite at the festive season. It is part of a rich tradition of Christmas spirituals that include the popular 'Go Tell It on the Mountain', sung by African-American slaves labouring in the fields of the American South. William Levi Dawson died in Montgomery, Alabama in 1990 aged ninety-one.

'Mary Had a Baby' has an upbeat rhythmic tune, which is repeated throughout the song, with a key change midway. For the first few verses it is a classic call and response song: questions are answered with a key phrase, 'People keep a-comin' an' the train done gone', chanted over and over. It's a dynamic image of the crowds flocking – but too late to see the Baby Jesus. There is hidden meaning too. Spiritual songs often contained codes that referred to the situation of the singers. 'Home' was heaven but it was also an imagined haven for slaves, a place free of literal shackles. While in this instance 'train' was the transport used by fugitives escaping to a free country – giving a poignancy to the line that's repeated throughout the many verses of this song. Such 'secret messages' were a powerful path of communication between the singers and their God.

It's a carol I've never recorded before; I don't think it's a song that can only be sung by African-Americans, I think it's a song that's open to anyone. I used to sing it as a boy in school. We never sang all the twenty verses, otherwise our school assemblies would have gone on forever! It's a song that truthfully conveys the gospel arising from the good news that in Bethlehem on that special day Mary. Had. A. Baby – and that baby changed the course of the world forever.

23

MARY'S BOY CHILD

WORDS AND MUSIC
Jester Joseph Hairston (1901–2000)

Long time ago in Bethlehem,
So the Holy Bible say
Mary's boy child, Jesus Christ
Was born on Christmas day.

Hark, now hear the angels sing,
A new King born today
And man will live for evermore
Because of Christmas day.

While shepherds watched their flock by night
Them see a bright new shining star,
Them hear a choir of angels sing,
The music seems to come from afar.

Chorus

Now, Joseph and his wife Mary
Come to Bethlehem that night,
Them find no place for to born the child,
Not a single room was in sight.

Chorus

By and by they find a little nook
In a stable all forlorn,
And in a manger cold and dark
Mary's little boy was born.

Chorus

The three wise men tell old King Herod
We hear a new King born today,
We bring he frankincense and myrrh,
We come from far, far away.

Chorus

When old King Herod he learned this news,
Him mad as him can be,
He tell de wise men find this child,
So that I may worship he!

Chorus

I remember hearing 'Mary's Boy Child' for the first time on my parents' old record player. They'd gone out and bought an album by Boney M and I remembering them playing 'Mary's Boy Child' in our little house in Llandegfan – it was just before Christmas – and it having a tremendous effect on me: the harmonies, the melody line. It was unlike anything I'd heard before and this was from a boy who went to Sunday School and sang his carols and his hymns with gusto every week. But this was something different with a totally different heart and beat to it. And I loved the idea of the chorus that man will live for ever more because of Christmas because as far as I was concerned Chrismas Day was the best day of the year anyway and not just because of the birth of

Jesus but (I'm being honest now) I'd get a new bike, say, and Father Christmas would come, but also that because of Christmas Day we'd live forever, what a great thought. I must have been only about seven or eight when I first heard 'Mary's Boy Child' on that Boney M recording. The story is a lot more real and the verses tell the story in a more modern way than some of the ones I used to hear and sing in Sunday School.

Jester Joseph Hairston was not a household name when he died aged ninety-nine, just eighteen days into the twenty-first century, but he had written a song nearly fifty years earlier that still trips off our tongues. 'Mary's Boy Child' is now played in many public places at Christmas, from community halls to supermarkets. Hairston wrote the piece in 1956. It was recorded that same year by Mahalia Jackson (1911–72), the first gospel singer to perform at Carnegie Hall in New York, whose version was slightly differently titled: 'Mary's Little Boy Child'. Singer and actor Harry Connick Jr (1967–) has also recorded the song under this title.

The following year, in 1957, Harry Belafonte (1927–) included the track on his album *An Evening with Harry Belafonte*, in which he interprets folk music from around the world with songs including 'Danny Boy' and 'When the Saints Go Marching In'. Harry Belafonte became the first black singer to reach number one with 'Mary's Boy Child'. This version was also the first British number one to last longer than four minutes (by 12 seconds) and the first UK single to sell more than a million copies. Purely seasonal however, it stayed at number one for seven weeks then plummeted straight out of the top ten, becoming the first single to leave as swiftly as it had arrived.

Jester Joseph Hairston was the grandson of slaves. He was born in Belews Creek, North Carolina, grew up in Pennsylvania – where generations of his family had worked in the steel mills – and went on to study music at Tufts University and the Juilliard School in New York. In 1937 he became a founding member of the Screen Actors' Guild. He was one of the great choral directors, who found his way onto Broadway and into Hollywood as the conductor of choirs, organising the first integrated choir there, and he had a long movie and TV acting career. One can imagine what his first bit parts in the early *Tarzan* movies were like, but talking later in his life about those roles he said, 'We had a hard time then fighting for dignity. We had no power, we had to take it, and because we took it the young people today have opportunities.' His later movie career was celebrated, from *To Kill a Mockingbird* in 1962, through to *Being John Malkovich* in 1999, just a few months before his death; he certainly earned his star on the Hollywood Walk of Fame.

As composer and arranger, Hairston dedicated himself to preserving the old Negro spirituals and 'Mary's Boy Child' is written in spiritual style. Mary, the mother of Jesus, is remarkably absent from the Christmas carols of our European traditions, coming after the shepherds and angels, and just above the wise men. She is a quiet absent presence nevertheless. Her thoughtful silence surrounded by massed angels and worshipping kings and shepherds is noted briefly and movingly by St Luke: 'But Mary kept all these things, and pondered them in her heart.' But the carol as a musical genre is rich and diverse enough to include everyone involved in the story of the Nativity and Mary takes centre stage as the subject of Christmas spirituals, including, in this book, 'Mary Had a Baby' from St Helena, or 'Mary, Don't You Weep', or 'Mary, Mary, Where is Your Baby?', which Jester Hairston also arranged.

The London Adventist Chorale under its Principal Conductor Ken Burton has performed 'Mary's Boy Child' on *Songs of Praise* with full orchestra. It was also a great pleasure for me to invite them to record this carol on my Christmas carols programme for ITV, produced at St Bartholomew's Church. I asked Ken Burton for his and the Chorale's experience of performing the carol and what it means to him:

'"Mary's Boy Child"', Ken Burton says,

> is a fantastic musical celebration of the Christmas story and very satisfying to sing, thanks to its well-crafted melody. I particularly enjoy the syncopated rhythms and the angular contour of the verse's tune, which contrasts with the hymn-like majestic chorus, a truly powerful moment in the song. Any singer will relate to that wonderful feeling of release when singing a phrase such as that which

opens the refrain of this carol, when the abdominal muscles combine with the most open of vowel sounds to give that brilliant burst of musical energy on the word 'Hark'. What also makes this a significant moment in the song is its connection with the words; the lighter rhythms of the verse characterise the simple telling of the Nativity story using a simple narrative language, whilst the chorus conveys the majesty of Christ. And being of the Adventist faith, the last line 'man shall live for evermore' resonates strongly with my personal belief in the hope of eternal life.

I have known this song practically all my life, and have memories of listening to many recordings of it and getting a warm feeling. It was not always appreciated by many whom I knew felt it was denigrating to refer to the Son of God as 'boy child', which is a colloquial term in many Caribbean islands. Others were uncomfortable about the phrase 'born on Christmas Day'; so whilst I listened to and enjoyed recordings of it, 'Mary's Boy Child' was not typically on the repertoire list, although I personally appreciated the poetry.

The choir (and conductor) recalls the wonderful setting and the amazing buzz in filming for the Aled Jones Christmas carols programme a song that combines the signature warm 'chestnuts roasting on an open fire' type rich-harmony choral singing, with gentle calypso rhythms, classical-style writing, and cascading lines representing myriads of angels joining in the song of praise. The atmosphere allowed the singers to appreciate the song musically and spiritually.

From early childhood memories to when I am old and grey, the song will continue to inspire me.

I agree. I think 'Mary's Boy Child' has stood the test of time: it's a heartfelt and moving song with a catchy tune that lends itself to different rhythms. Its rousing qualities can arouse strong emotions in singers and audience, its roots are deep inside popular music, and it had a real impact on a small boy in Llandegfan.

24

SEE AMID THE WINTER'S SNOW

WORDS
Edward Caswall (1814–78)

MUSIC
Sir John Goss (1800–80)

See amid the winter's snow,
Born for us on earth below,
See the tender Lamb appears,
Promised from eternal years.

Hail! Thou ever blessed morn!
Hail, redemption's happy dawn!
Sing through all Jerusalem,
Christ is born in Bethlehem.

Lo, within a manger lies
He who built the starry skies;
He who, throned in height sublime,
Sits amid the cherubim.

Chorus

Say, ye holy shepherds, say
What your joyful news today;
Wherefore have ye left your sheep
On the lonely mountain steep?

Chorus

'As we watched at dead of night,
Lo, we saw a wondrous light;
Angels singing "Peace on earth"
Told us of the Saviour's birth.'

Chorus

Sacred infant, all divine,
What a tender love was thine;
Thus to come from highest bliss
Down to such a world as this.

Chorus

Teach, O teach us, Holy Child,
By Thy face so meek and mild,
Teach us to resemble Thee,
In Thy sweet humility!

Chorus

Unlike the short simplicity of 'Away in a Manger' or the 'Coventry' and 'Rocking' carols, this carol is a generous six verses, divided by a rousing chorus. It brings to us the astonishing paradox that the baby sleeping in straw in a stable is the God 'who built the starry skies' themselves. It also stirs the imagination with its images. Like 'In the Bleak Midwinter' or 'Still, Still, Still' it pictures a cold, white Nativity. The snowy place conjured into our imaginations here seems a little strange for Bethlehem town, but the whiteness of snow is a simple way of giving the message of purity covering the sins of the world and, in the northern hemisphere at least, reflects the time we celebrate Christmas.

The shepherds are here again; this time they are asked a quite challenging question: someone, perhaps, as Luke's Gospel says, encountering the shepherds returning from the Nativity, 'glorifying and praising God', asks them why they have left their sheep alone 'On the lonely mountain steep?' They reply 'As we watched at dead of night/Lo, we saw a wondrous light.'

Edward Caswall wrote the words for 'See Amid the Winter's Snow'. He was a well-respected translator of hymns, including the hymn for Advent, 'Hark! A Herald Voice is Calling'. He was born in Yateley in Hampshire. His father the Reverend R C Caswall was vicar there and Edward too was ordained as an Anglican clergyman. But he left his living in 1846 to follow John Henry Newman (1801–90), the major figure of the Oxford Movement, into Roman Catholicism. Caswall did not become a priest but joined the Oratory of Saint Philip Neri, a community committed to being independent and self-governing without taking formal vows.

In 1871, Sir John Goss, perhaps better known for his tune 'Lauda Anima' for the hymn 'Praise my Soul, the King of Heaven', put Caswall's words to music. He was born two days after Christmas Day in 1800 as the first year of the new century drew to a close. He was in his seventies when he composed the nicely named tune 'Humility' for the carol. In the same year, 'See Amid the Winter's Snow' was guaranteed a national audience. Henry Ramsden Bramley and John Stainer selected it as a new carol for the second of their series of enormously influential collections, *Christmas Carols New and Old*. They had, as they assured readers, 'made every effort to preserve those compositions which proved their hold upon the popular mind, by their continued use up to the present time'. Goss's advice in the score is that 'See Amid the Winter's Snow' be sung as a solo by 'Treble or Tenor, or alternately'. In the collection, the carol's words are set below an engraving by Edward Dalziel (1817–1905) of snow-free rolling downland, dotted with grazing animals. This is one of many such featured in the collection by the Dalziel Brothers, a renowned family of engravers whose company provided illustrations to the work of the likes of Charles Dickens, Lewis Carroll and Edward Lear during the late nineteenth century.

Henry Ramsden Bramley and John Stainer assert that their selection for inclusion in *Christmas Carols New and Old* is designed to cater for two kinds of worshipper:

> Such carols may afford pleasure to some who are unable to make use of the more difficult productions of modern composers, while those who prefer the latter may perhaps find in the whole collection an adequate supply of words and music adapted to a more fastidious taste.

It's not clear into which of these categories they place 'See Amid the Winter's Snow'. What we do know is that it still captures minds and hearts: it came in at number twelve in the 2005 *Songs of Praise* poll.

In 1920, Caswall's hymn was published in *The St. Gregory Hymnal and Catholic Choir Book* with Goss's name replaced by the credit 'Traditional Melody'. Its editor, the conductor, composer and arranger Nicola A Montani (1880–1948) was a Knight Commander of the Order of St Sylvester, one of the five Catholic orders awarded directly by the Pope. He was also founder of the St Gregory Guild, an organisation devoted to the music of the Roman Catholic church. Montani's arrangement of the carol leaves out Caswall's two shepherds' verses.

Instead he focuses on the devotional aspect of the carol and ends with a verse of his own:

> Virgin Mother, Mary blest,
> By the joys that fill thy breast,
> Pray for us, that we may prove
> Worthy of the Saviour's love.

Thankfully, the shepherds are back in the joyous carol we sing today, putting us singers in touch with our faith.

It's a carol in the same bracket as the Big Five, the ones that you sing out with relish. 'O Come All Ye Faithful', 'Hark! The Herald Angels Sing',

'The First Nowell' . . . It's very simple in its construction, which means everyone can have a go at it, the verses are uncomplicated in their melodic structure and then it comes to the chorus, which is repetitive, monotonous, but again in a good way – it reinforces everything that's fine about this carol, in almost the same vein as our most popular hymns; the chorus is good too in that monotony adds to the message getting drummed home. I must have sung it in Bangor Cathedral. It's not one I've recorded before but I would like to have a go at it as a solo soon. I've definitely sung this carol as part of a *Songs of Praise* congregation and when you are part of the congregation it really does take a lot out of you, it requires 100 per cent commitment.

It's quite modern in its construction, especially the final verse:

> Sacred infant, all divine,
> What a tender love was thine:
> Thus to come from highest bliss
> Down to such a world as this.

It's saying that something as wonderful as Jesus could actually come down to the world he created, so it's a mixture of ancient and modern in a way.

Rocking

translated by
P. Dearmer

Traditional Czech

Lit - tle Je - sus, sweet - ly sleep, do not stir;

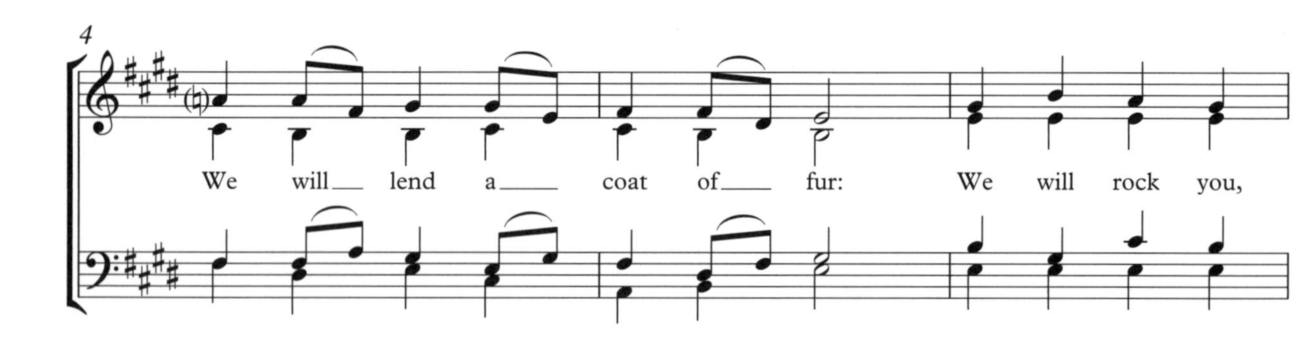
4
We will lend a coat of fur: We will rock you,

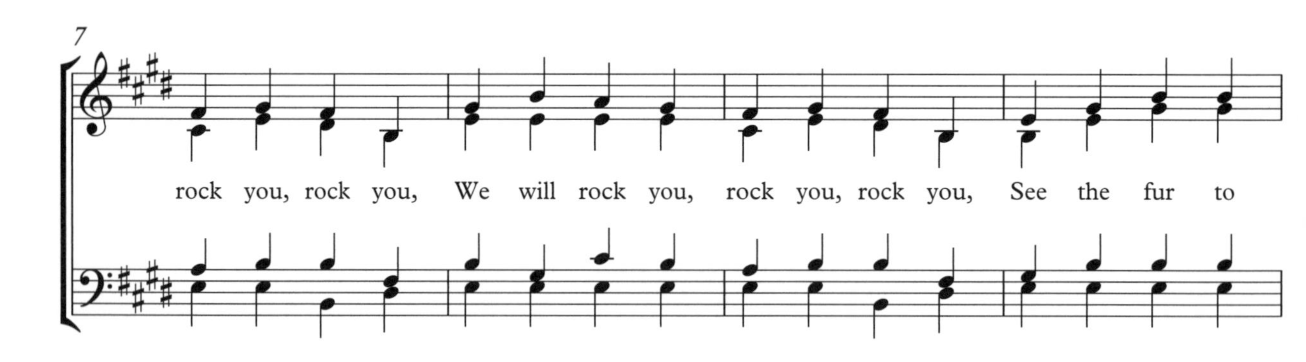
7
rock you, rock you, We will rock you, rock you, rock you, See the fur to

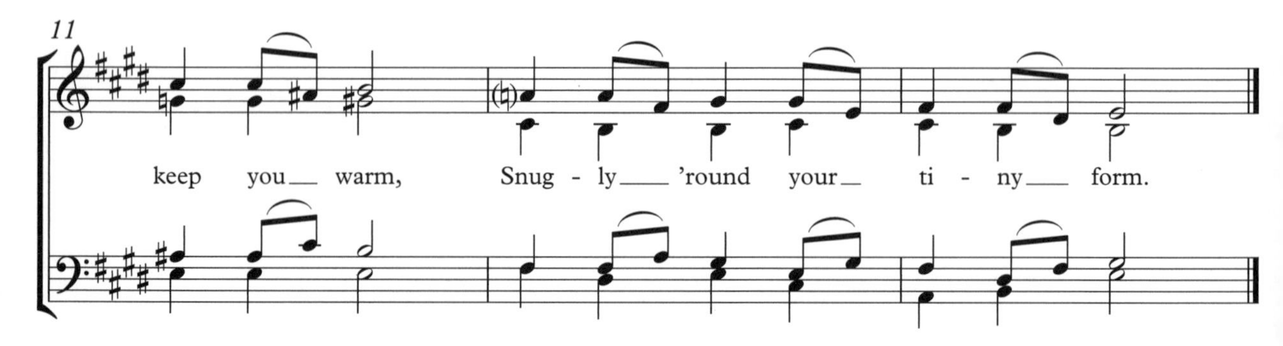
11
keep you warm, Snug - ly 'round your ti - ny form.

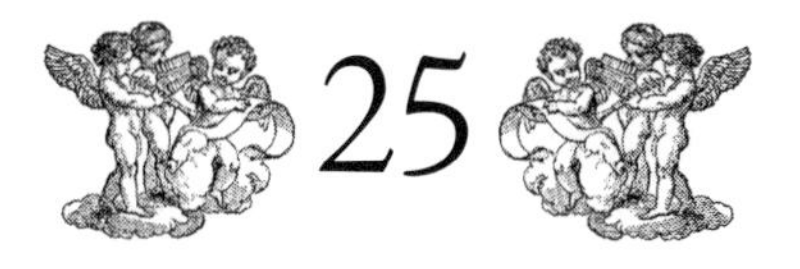

25

ROCKING CAROL

Traditional Czech lullaby

TRANSLATION
Percy Dearmer (1867–1936)

ARRANGEMENT
John Rutter (1945–)

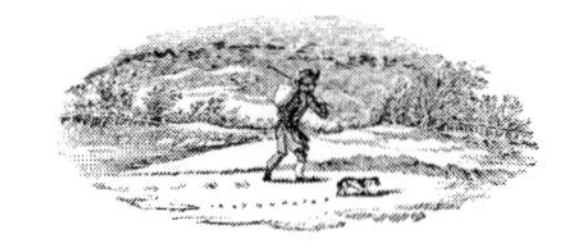

Little Jesus, sweetly sleep, do not stir;
We will lend a coat of fur:
We will rock you, rock you, rock you,
We will rock you, rock you, rock you,
See the fur to keep you warm,
Snugly round your tiny form.

Mary's little baby, sleep, sweetly sleep,
Sleep in comfort, slumber deep;
We will rock you, rock you, rock you,
We will rock you, rock you, rock you:
We will serve you all we can,
Darling, darling little man.

I always associate 'Rocking Carol' a little bit with 'The Coventry Carol'. It's another that really does stay in your mind and your heart. Its stillness is its great quality. This is a carol that could make you go to sleep in the middle of a performance, not in a negative way but because of its beauty. And like other good lullabies, 'Rocking' is really quite sustained – the motion of 'Rock you, rock you, rock you' gives the carol its magical, rhythmic quality.

Christmas carols in the manner of lullabies are found in many cultures, from Austria with 'Still, Still, Still' and 'Silent Night' to the Cossack lullaby '*Spi mladenets, moy prekrasnuy*' ('Sleep baby, my dear one'), and back via England's 'Twinkle Twinkle Little Star' to this lovely Christmas lullaby from Czechoslovakia. It's very old, coming from the late Middle Ages, but it works for any age, its melody and words mimicking the soothing movement of the cradle. It's likely that 'Rocking' originally accompanied the custom of cradle rocking in German churches that spread from there across the Low Countries during the Middle Ages. The cradle stood before the altar, with a brightly coloured Christ Child visible within, and the priest would rock it enthusiastically to the rhythm of the triple-time music of a cradle song.

This lullaby carol was collected in the early 1920s by a Miss Jacubickova as '*Hajej, nynjej*' and translated freely by the master champion of carols Percy Dearmer, for his *Oxford Book of Carols* of 1928. Dearmer and this book saved many neglected English carols for Christmas and other festivals, and brought them together with more recent items. 'Carols,' Dearmer writes in his preface to the book, 'are songs with a religious impulse that are simple, hilarious, popular and modern'. They were always modern:

> The charm of an old carol lies precisely in its having been true to the period in which it was written, and those which are alive to-day retain their vitality because of this sincerity . . . A genuine carol may have faults of grammar, logic, and prosody; but one fault it never has – that of sham antiquity.

He is true to his principles in his version of this lullaby, though his final line, 'Darling, darling little man' has not caught on with everyone, and some have changed it, to for instance 'Son of God and Son of Man'. But I take great pleasure in what Percy Dearmer has done with the words because of their steady rhythm and because of the space he allows: he's using very simple words.

'Rocking' has been arranged by John Rutter, who, like Percy Dearmer, is a lover of Christmas carols – so much so that he's become known as the musical equivalent of Dickens, synonymous with the season. He doesn't mind. 'I've a special place in my heart for its music. It's the first music I remember actually enjoying when I was a kid, and as a member of my school chapel choir the carol service was the high point of the singing year.' Choral conductor, arranger, composer, he wrote his first carol 'The Shepherd's Pipe' when he was eighteen, followed by others including 'The Star', 'Nativity' and 'Donkey' carols. Percy Dearmer would have agreed with Rutter's view that 'they have the most variegated history, from those that go back centuries to those like "Silent Night", which only really became popular when Bing Crosby sang it in *Going My Way* in 1944'. With its ancient origins, 'Rocking' has similarly had the good fortune to be taken up by Julie Andrews in the 1960s. Rutter believes carols are a form of miniature, and 'Rocking Carol' has that quality as well as demonstrating – as both Percy Dearmer and John Rutter believe – that good carols have a way of spanning the years, enjoyed by ancient and modern worshippers.

You can really put your own stamp on a carol like this. I recorded it as an adult, much to the amusement of my producers and also quite a few colleagues who work in the music industry, who were saying it's too simplistic, too boring. I think far from it; it's totally the opposite. You can put your whole heart and soul into every single word in this carol. In the second verse, 'Mary's little baby, sleep, sweetly sleep/Sleep in comfort, slumber deep', you've got three sleeps in the space of two lines and your artistry is to make all those sleeps different and to envelop the listener in your voice, make it sound so safe, so snug. The words are saying, 'See the fur to keep you warm', so it's vocal fur if you like, it's the talent to be able to make the listener or the person watching you perform a carol feel totally at ease, wrapped up in this great feeling of Christmas.

I recorded the 'Rocking Carol' as a boy on my 1985 Christmas album and want to record it again. It's definitely a carol that makes you forget all the woes and the troubles that you have in the world in those three very special minutes. It's comforting to sing and also comforting to listen to.

26

STILL, STILL, STILL

Words
Aled Jones

Music
Anon.

Still, still, still,
Let all the earth be still,
For Mary in her arms enfolding
Hope of all the world is holding.

Sing, sing, sing,
Sweet angel voices sing,
While Jesus lies in manger dreaming,
Seraph choirs from Heaven are streaming.

Light, light, light,
The sky is filled with light,
The holy star its news a-blazing,
Sign of hope for nations raising.

This haunting lullaby from Salzburg in Austria does what it says on the tin; it's very tranquil, poised – everything about this carol just oozes class. And it makes people listen, listen to the message within the words but also the melody is beautiful. Its music was written in 1819, three years after 'Silent Night', another traditional carol from the city where Mozart was born. Beyond these facts, nothing is known of the composer of this carol, which describes that sense of anticipation on the eve of Christ's birth.

The snow-bound setting of 'Still, Still, Still' is a familiar one to carol singers; this one cleverly uses the falling snow to express total silence heralding the birth of the Christ Child – and for the child who is being rocked to sleep to this carol. Snow is silent, yet so hushed and peaceful is the 'eve of our Saviour's birth' that the gently falling snowflakes can be heard.

There are different versions of 'Still, Still, Still'. Some have two verses, others four. Here is the first verse in German:

Still, still, still,
Weil's Kindlein schlafen will!
Maria tut es niedersingen
Ihre keusche Brust darbringen,
Still, still, still,
Weil Kindlein schlafen will.

In 1918, ninety-nine years after this carol was composed, the Wartburg Publishing House in Chicago published the *Wartburg Hymnal for Church, School and Home* edited by the splendidly named Oswald Guido Hardwig. We can find in its Christmas section at number 116 a carol with the first line: 'Hush, Hush, Hush'. In the metrical index this carol is referred to as 'Still, Still, Still' and has been translated by Frederik William Herzberger (1859 –1930). The lyrics are very different to those of 'Still, Still, Still', although it too is about the great event that is to come and is sung to the same melody; this is how it begins:

Hush, hush, hush!
Behold the wondrous light!
Who will appear? The Christ-child dear,
For this, you know, is Holy night.
For this, you know, is Holy night.

The publishing company that produced this hymnal was presumably named after Wartburg Castle in Germany. In this castle from May 1521 to March 1522, the German priest and philosopher Martin Luther (wrongly credited with writing 'Away in a Manger') took refuge at the request of Frederick the Wise after being excommunicated by Pope Leo X for his refusal to recant at the Diet of Worms. (This was the name of the general assembly taking place at Worms, a town on the Rhine River.) It was during this period that Martin Luther, using the name of Junker Jörg (the Knight George), was translating the New Testament into German: the first translation into a modern language for over a millennium.

'Still, Still, Still' has been recorded by a number of artists including Mannheim Steamroller, the American group that fuses classical and popular techniques and has made worldwide sales with its Christmas albums. 'Still, Still, Still' was featured on their 1988 album: *A Fresh Aire Christmas*. Other artists who have recorded this include Charlotte Church, who sings it to an original arrangement by the composer Michelle Hynson. The folk and country artist Mary Chapin Carpenter recorded it on her 2008 *Come Darkness, Come Light* album.

I only came into contact with this great Austrian carol as an adult. I recorded it for my first Christmas album as an adult with Universal Records and the melody is exquisite to sing. Its words may be monotonous, the first line of every verse being the same, so it's either 'Still, still, still' or, in the original, 'Sleep, sleep, sleep/Dream, dream, dream'. We changed the words for my album to the version above. I don't understand why this carol is not more popular, it should be taught in every school.

'Still, Still, Still' is also very easy to sing, no difficult parts at all. The third line of every verse is the most drawn out and gives the opportunity to really open out with the voice. My favourite line is the fourth, it's the highlight of the piece if you like, starting by being very, very quiet, very still and building up to all the light of heaven shining and the holy star telling this incredible news.

I performed this carol on *Songs of Praise* and the producer had the

idea of my being in a primary school in the dead of night. So all you see is me walking from classroom to classroom. It was filmed over a very long period of time, with the camera on a track so that it could pull back through the school. The children were preparing for Christmas but they weren't there: in the depths of the night it was very still and there was just one lone figure walking in this place.

It was wonderful seeing how much expectancy of Jesus coming into the world there was in that one primary school. They had brightly coloured paintings around the walls, Christmas trees in the corners, streamers everywhere. During the day it would have been full of merriment, laughter and energy; in deepest night it was eerily quiet, which was perfect for this carol.

In my particular recording of 'Still, Still, Still' I play around with the musical arrangement of the third and fourth lines of the third verse, and the melody I created really does seem to work with this carol. This is the carol's highlight, leading from the simplicity of 'Light, light, light/ The sky is filled with light', into hope with 'The holy star its news a-blazing'. I can't praise this carol enough. It would probably be in my top three.

I've heard many choirs do this, as well as solo performances, and one of the most momentous for me was listening to Bryn Terfel singing it in the Royal Albert Hall. Here was a giant of a man with a huge, huge voice effortlessly singing this motionless carol. He didn't move, his arms were by his sides all the way through, and out of his mouth just came this glorious voice singing this mesmeric carol.

27

THE SUSSEX CAROL

'On Christmas Night All Christians Sing'

Words and Music
Anon.

On Christmas night all Christians sing
To hear the news the angels bring:
News of great joy, news of great mirth,
News of our merciful King's birth.

Then why should men on earth be so sad,
Since our Redeemer made us glad
When from our sin he set us free,
All for to gain our liberty?

When sin departs before his grace,
Then life and health come in its place.
Angels and men with joy may sing,
All for to see the new-born King.

All out of darkness we have light,
Which made the angels sing this night:
'Glory to God and peace to men,
Now and for evermore, Amen'.

Also known as 'On Christmas Night All Christians Sing' or 'On Christmas Night True Christians Sing', this carol tells how all Christians rejoice at the coming of their Redeemer and their salvation – and the minute you start singing it, it puts a smile on your face.

'The Sussex Carol' first appeared in print as 'Another short carol for Christmas Day' by Luke Wadding, a seventeenth-century Irish bishop, in his *Smale Garland of Pious and Godly Songs,* which he published in 1684 shortly after his consecration to the diocese of Ferns, County Wexford. Otherwise, there is little known about Luke Wadding's life and we don't even know whether he wrote the carol himself; it's more likely that he recorded an earlier composition from medieval sources. Versions of the carol differing considerably from Wadding's original text appeared in print in both 1790 and 1847.

William Studwell, writing about 'The Sussex Carol', is puzzled by the English 'curious custom of naming some of their folk carols after the places of their supposed origin'. There are no such things as 'Provençal Carol', 'Catalan Carol', or 'Kentucky Carol', he points out. Well, yes, we do this, often recognising the place where a carol has its roots, or where it was first performed. In this book, for instance, there's the 'Coventry Carol', so-named because it was part of the Coventry Mystery Cycle. To be found as well, leafing through the literature, there's the bucolically titled 'Exeter Boar's Head Carol', various wassails, including 'The Somerset Wassail', 'The Gloucestershire Wassail' and more. Writers and composers of hymns and carols too, often name their compositions after a place in Britain that has special meaning for the words or tune. This was also the habit of Ralph Vaughan Williams' *An Oxford Elegy, On Wenlock Edge*. 'The Sussex Carol' was discovered in Sussex and written down by Vaughan Williams and Cecil Sharp, who heard it being sung by Mrs Harriet Verrall of Monks Gate. Vaughan Williams really loved Christmas and had a lifelong passion for carols, for their freshness, beauty and nobility, an enthusiasm that came from the pleasure he took in folk songs. He understood that these were being undermined by increasing

literacy and printed music in rural areas, so in an attempt to halt the decline of the folk song, he and Sharp, the founding father of the folklore tradition in England, travelled the length and breadth of the countryside collecting hymns and carols from the noted singers of the time like Harriet Verrall, transcribed them and in so doing preserved them.

It is not known where the version sung by Harriet Verrall to Cecil Sharp and Ralph Vaughan Williams came from and the words she sang differ widely from the original recorded by Wadding. However, it is this version that was printed in the *Journal of the Folk-Song Society* in 1905 and has since been taken up by many carol books including *The Oxford Book of Carols* of 1924. In this respect 'The Sussex Carol' is similar to other carols in the history of its origins – there is no true agreed original, rather, the provenance of the words and music is a process of various adaptations from different sources, chance encounters and timely publication. This is especially true of carols with folk origins, such as 'The Sussex Carol' and 'Deck the Hall'.

The history of the tune we now sing to the 'Sussex Carol' is also unknown. Although the text has been found with many tunes, the one that has become standard is 'Christmas Night', which Harriet Verrall used. Vaughan Williams took it down and arranged it for unaccompanied singing in 1920 with seven other traditional carols. He must have been impressed by Harriet Verrall – he also heard her sing 'Who Would True Valour See' to the stirring tune of 'Monks Gate' – a melody named after a place – which he also arranged for congregational singing. 'The Sussex Carol' does not have a standard refrain – instead, each verse comprises two couplets. The first is repeated, usually performed in unison voices. The second couplet is sung once in harmony, usually with three or four voices.

Harriet Verrall lived with her husband Peter in Monks Gate, later moving to Horsham. She seems to have possessed the largest store of songs around that area. Her husband was also a singer and they often sang to each other for their own pleasure by the fire in the evenings. Harriet Verrall died in 1918 aged sixty-three and Peter Verrall a few years

later. In the *The West Sussex Village Book*, Tony Wales mentions that the Verralls were buried together in an unmarked grave in Hills Cemetery, Horsham.

I often wondered, both as a chorister and then as an adult, whether, if Ralph Vaughan Williams hadn't heard Harriet Verrall singing this beautiful melody, 'The Sussex Carol' would have been lost to us forever. But this has to be one of my favourite carol melodies because it's so immediately appealing. It's got a great lilting rhythm and it's also pretty simple in its structure. There are great arrangements from David Willcocks and also Philip Ledger, both of King's College, Cambridge and I don't think there are any other great arrangements, not compared to those anyway.

I think it's a carol that you don't have to be a massively strong believer to get the most out of. It's to the point and cleverly written. Each verse tells a mini story in its own right and you don't need more than four verses to tell the whole story through to the final verse:

> All out of darkness we have light,
> Which made the angels sing this night:
> 'Glory to God and peace to men,
> Now and for evermore, Amen.'

I don't think it can get any better really, we have light and because of that the angels are singing and just to cap it off we get the final two lines, and 'Amen'!

It's difficult sometimes to get the most out of fast-paced carols vocally and in terms of performance, but this one is totally different. You have the instant gently swinging melody in the first two lines and then in the second two lines of each verse you really open out and express more through the voice and also the phrasing really comes into its own in those third and fourth lines. It's not one I've recorded thus far but all that's about to change with the release of my Christmas album, 2010, and this one is definitely among the first on the list. It's a carol that also works tremendously well with brass accompaniment, which we've had on *Songs of Praise* quite a few times. I don't know why, but there's something quite magical about the congregation singing a Christmas carol like this one with the brass alongside. It's almost as if the music brings you closer to Heaven.

28

THE FIRST NOWELL

Words and Music Traditional Cornish carol

Adapted and arranged by Davies Gilbert (1767–1839)

The first Nowell the angel did say
Was to certain poor shepherds in fields as they lay;
In fields where they lay keeping their sheep
On a cold winter's night that was so deep.

Nowell, nowell, nowell. nowell!
Born is the King of Israel.

They looked up and saw a star,
Shining in the east, beyond them far;
And to the earth it gave great light,
And so it continued both day and night.

Refrain

And by the light of that same star,
Three wise men came from country far;
To seek for a King was their intent
And to follow the star wherever it went.

Refrain

This star drew nigh to the north-west
O'er Bethlehem it took its rest,
And there it did both stop and stay
Right over the place where Jesus lay.

Refrain

Then entered in those wise men three,
Full reverently, upon their knee,
And offered there in his presence
Their gold and myrrh and frankincense.

Refrain

Then let us all with one accord
Sing praises to our Heavenly Lord,
That hath made heaven and earth of naught,
And with his blood mankind hath bought.

Refrain.

Nowell is from the French 'Noël', meaning Christmas of course, and this is one of those carols which, if you didn't hear it at Christmas, you would feel you'd missed out. It's among a handful that the choir does breathing, or sleeping, or eating: it's Christmas and you hear 'O Come, All Ye Faithful', 'Hark! The Herald Angels Sing', 'Silent Night' – and 'The First Nowell'.

Together the shepherds of St Luke's Gospel and the wise men of Matthew's book follow the light of the travelling star. It is likely that this carol first appeared in 1823 in Davies Gilbert's *Some Ancient Christmas Carols*. It next appeared ten years later in William Sandys' (1792–1874) volume of *Christmas Carols Ancient and Modern*, published in 1833. Both marked the beginning of many such collections by editors who were contributing to the new kind of Victorian fireside Christmas that came about over the following decades of the nineteenth century.

But 'The First Nowell' has medieval beginnings, possibly as far back as the thirteenth century, and the version we are familiar with is thought to be of Cornish origin. Some regions of England – Cornwall in particular – have developed their own carol tradition. In his introduction to *Lyver Canow Kernewek* (*The Cornish Song Book*, published in 1929), Ralph Dunstan describes various groups of Cornish carols, notably folk carols, the Redruth-Camborne Carols sung in mining communities across the county, and that good old catch-all, 'miscellaneous'. 'The First Nowell' may well belong to a variant going back to medieval tunes in Cornwall. Dunstan comments that the words for 'The First Nowell' in his collection come from an old Cornish broadside that, printed in Helston, was hawked around the county by pedlars for a halfpenny. He remembers actually seeing one of these stuck on cottage walls near his home.

Davies Gilbert, who collected the version known today, was born Davies Giddy. He later changed his surname to that of his wife Mary-Anne in order to inherit her uncle's estate in Sussex (the contents included shells, fossils, a telescope, conversation stools and a ewe in a glass case).

Gilbert's love of the history and culture of Cornwall fuelled his knowledge of ancient songs from that county and has meant that carols such as 'The First Nowell' have been preserved for so many generations. In his preface to the collection, Gilbert pointed out that carols had been sung in private homes on Christmas Eve and on Christmas Day in the churches throughout the West of England up to the end of the eighteenth century – when carol singing in England was otherwise out of fashion and favour. He wanted to preserve them complete with any false grammar, 'as specimens of times now passed away, and of religious feelings superseded by others of a different cast'. This is not an unusual motivation for carol collectors, including the great Percy Dearmer, but on a more personal note, Gilbert also wrote that he was preserving them as well because they had given him such childhood delight: 'On Christmas

Eve at seven or eight o'clock in the evening cakes were drawn hot from the oven; cyder or beer exhilarated the spirits in every house; and the singing of Carols was continued late into the night.' As Davies Gilbert intended, 'The First Nowell' can take us back to the 'delights' of a magical childhood Christmas; it's a song about the wonder of the Nativity that many of us have sung.

Davies Gilbert died on Christmas Eve 1879 aged seventy-two years. He had lived a life full of energy and activity. He was by no means a typical hymn collector, being an engineer and a scientist, and sometime President of the Royal Society of Science. He also found the time to be Member of Parliament for Helston (where he grew up) and then Bodmin over twenty-eight years. He was a writer too; maybe it's a sign of the breadth of his knowledge, and typical of the polymath age in which he lived, that he published (a strong candidate for the most unusual, certainly the longest book title of the year) *On the vibrations of heavy bodies in cycloidal and in circular arches, as compared with their descents through free space; including an estimate of the variable circular excess in vibrations continually decreasing*!

'The First Nowell' is not short of critics. Comprising what is, without much variation, basically one tune in the verse that's repeated in the refrain, there's reason to wonder whether the melody is one section of another tune. Possibly it was the treble part that, lost in transcription, was mistaken for the main melody. One idea was that the words for 'The First Nowell' were once sung to the tune for 'On Christmas Night All Christians Sing' and they do fit the music for this carol.

The question of how many shepherds there were has created confusion. The Gospel does not specifically state that there were three, while some legends speak of four. In the medieval mystery play *Play of the Shepherds* there are four, called – rather like Hobbits or Shakespeare's rude mechanicals – Harvey, Tudd, Trowle and Hancken.

Putting aside these doubts and debates, it's an inspiring carol often chosen for services at Christmas. It was in the line-up for the first Nine Lessons and Carols at King's College, Cambridge in 1918 when it was sung after the Ninth Lesson and on another occasion placed after the

Seventh. It was a carol I first performed in Bangor Cathedral during my time as a chorister there.

'The First Nowell' was one of several that British composer Christian Victor Hely-Hutchinson, born on Boxing Day in 1901 (died 1947), used for his 'Carol Symphony', noted for its opening variation on the theme of 'The First Nowell'. Fans of John Masefield will know it as the music for the BBC's 1984 television adaptation of his *Box of Delights* and for radio's *Children's Hour* dramatisation, broadcast both during and just after the Second World War. It's been recorded by many artists, from Bing Crosby on his *White Christmas* album through to Bob Dylan on his 2009 seasonal *Christmas in the Heart*. I've also heard it performed by the Australian children's group the Wiggles.

This is what you call a 'crowd-pleasing carol'. Due to the repetitive way in which it's constructed I suppose the melody does stick instantly in the mind. Again as with many carols, it's a Big Sing. There are lots and lots of verses – no one's suggesting that you do all of them otherwise you'd be in performance all night. I think it's also one of those carols where, though it's slightly overlong, the refrain absolutely does save it. It gives the congregation an opportunity to really, really sing out 'Nowell, Nowell, Nowell, Nowell/Born is the King of Israel'. It doesn't get simpler, but that simplicity gives you the opportunity through voice to praise God and the chorus is quite majestic and to the point.

I'm about to record 'The First Nowell' on my new Christmas album and I have to say it's with some trepidation, because I'm not sure how I can maintain interest throughout and I'm still not sure whether it will work as a solo piece because it needs that whole congregational input. When you hear the organ accompaniment start and everyone stands up, you're sure you're on safe ground. It's one of those carols that has seeped into your bloodstream, it's in your heart, it's in your soul, you don't really have to think when you are performing it. I suppose there's a lot to be said for that.

29

SILENT NIGHT!

(*Stille Nacht!*)

Words
Joseph Mohr (1792–1848)

Music
Franz Xaver Gruber (1787–1863)

Silent night! Holy night!
All is calm, all is bright.
Round yon virgin mother and child,
Holy infant so tender and mild,
Sleep in heavenly peace,
Sleep in heavenly peace.

Silent night! Holy night!
Shepherds quake at the sight.
Glories stream from heaven afar,
Heavenly hosts sing Alleluia
Christ the Saviour is born!
Christ the Saviour is born!

Silent night! Holy night!
Son of God, love's pure light.
Radiant beams from thy holy face
With the dawn of redeeming grace,
Jesus, Lord, at thy birth.
Jesus, Lord, at thy birth.

Silent night

J. Mohr

F. Gruber

Si - lent night, ho - ly night, All is calm,

7
all is bright. 'Round you vir - gin, moth - er and child,

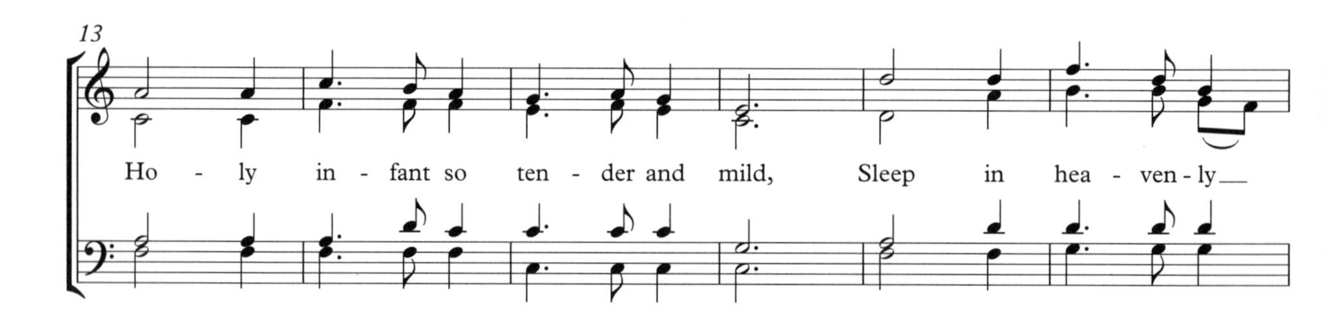
13
Ho - ly in - fant so ten - der and mild, Sleep in hea - ven - ly

19
peace, sleep in hea - ven - ly peace.

From the little town of Oberndorf where it was composed to Tahiti and Greenland, Latvia and Taiwan, '*Stille Nacht!*', 'Silent Night!' is the world's most popular carol. It has been translated into at least 250 languages, arranged for many instruments and is an essential part of Christmas.

'Silent Night!' so often wins surveys of Britain's favourite carols that its place at the top is pretty stable; it was also the favourite of twenty-one per cent of entries to a December 1996 Gallup poll, way ahead of the runners-up 'Away in a Manger' and 'O Come, All Ye Faithful'. A hard one to beat.

How '*Stille Nacht!*' came to be written is a fine, if fictional, tale. On Christmas Eve 1818 the organ in the parish church of the little Lower Austrian (now Bavarian) church of Oberndorf had given up the ghost. Presented with a list of carols for his congregation and no organ accompaniment, the enterprising curate Joseph Mohr (who played the guitar) and assistant organist Franz Xaver Gruber between them quickly wrote a carol to be sung at midnight mass on Christmas Eve with guitar accompaniment. Various interpretations of the reason for the organ's temporary disablement include rust and the nibbles of a mouse at the organ's cables. The mouse's point of view on the creation of '*Stille Nacht!*' has been dramatized on TV, narrated by actress Lynn Redgrave.

Sadly, this story doesn't add up. There's a manuscript in Joseph Mohr's handwriting that shows he actually wrote the words to the simple poem '*Stille Nacht!*' in 1816, while he was a curate in the Austrian alps, inspired by the little villages peppering the surrounding mountains, peaceful and lit by the stars.

'*Stille Nacht!*' is an Austrian/Bavarian folk song for the midnight service. Like 'Rocking Carol', it would have been sung by the crib placed in the church for the Christmas period. It certainly has the calm, spiritual quality of a lullaby. There are many such songs, but what Mohr and Gruber did was produce a carol that has captivated countless people's hearts from then to now.

The story continues with Gruber, a kind and trusting man, liberally distributing copies of his carol, often without bothering to add his name to it. One of these came into the hands of a glove-maker and folk-music enthusiast Josef Strasser. He was part of the family Strasser singing group, who performed the carol as a 'Tyrolean folk carol', newly unearthed. Sounds familiar . . . Tyrol . . . family singing group . . . In fact the Von Trapp family singers of Robert Wise's *The Sound of Music* (1965) won the music festival presented in the film in Salzburg, a few miles from Oberndorf.

The Strassers sang the carol at a concert in Leipzig in December 1832 and it was published by an A R Friese, as the last of his 'Four Authentic Tyrolean Songs' for soprano soloist or four voices with optional piano accompaniment. Mohr and Gruber had to turn to the law and the courts to reclaim the authorship of '*Stille Nacht!*'.

Joseph Mohr was born in Salzburg on 11 December 1792. His mother was poor, a young woman making a meagre living as an embroiderer when she met his father Franz Mohr, a soldier, who abandoned her, one imagines, when he learned she was pregnant. It wasn't easy for an illegitimate boy to make his way in the world, but Joseph's musical talents were recognised; he chose the religious life, and was ordained in 1815. As curate for the pilgrimage church at Mariapfarr in the Austrian Alps, he wrote the six-stanza poem that became '*Stille Nacht!*' and while priest at St Nicholas, he befriended Franz Gruber, a local teacher who was also assistant organist in the church, and together priest and organist composed '*Stille Nacht!*' Gruber, the son of linen weavers, born in Hochburg in Upper Austria, who dedicated most of his life to church music as choir director, singer and organist, described '*Stille Nacht!*' as 'a simple composition'.

First translated into English around 1858 by Emily Elliott for St Mark's Church in Brighton as 'Stilly night, holy night', the carol has since had many translations. Minister and hymn-writer John Freeman Young (1820–85) of Pittston, Maine, is credited with translating the three-verse carol that is most widely sung today.

Popular in America, 'Silent Night!' was for a time considered vulgar in England and omitted from most books of hymns and carols. Bing Crosby came to the rescue and brought it to millions when he sang 'Silent Night!' in the 1945 film *The Bells of St Mary's*.

'Silent Night!' has been performed by a multitude of other artists in just about every musical genre. Enya sang it in Irish, Andrea Bocelli in Italian, Mahalia Jackson gave it the gospel treatment, Fleetwood Mac's Stevie Nicks sang it solo. Mannheim Steamroller, the group founded by Chip Davis and known for their modern renditions of Christmas carols, recorded an instrumental version, and on their *Parsley, Sage, Rosemary and Thyme* album, Simon and Garfunkel recorded their own offering, '7 o'clock News/Silent Night'. Here they sing the carol to the accompaniment of items reporting murders, and a newscast about the Vietnam War. The beauty of the singing and the song, backed by broadcast news of death and destruction, is particularly disturbing.

Going back to the beginning of this lovely carol, St Nicholas's Church in Oberndorf was demolished in the early twentieth century. A little 'Silent Night Memorial Chapel' now stands on the site. On that spot and throughout the world in hundreds of languages, 'Heavenly hosts sing Alleluia' for 'Christ the Saviour is born'.

'Silent Night!' is another one I've performed since I was at school and definitely in Bangor Cathedral. I think it comes into its own when sung as a solo piece. You really do feel that you have more of a connection with the Nativity itself and with God when sung solo. I've done it as a duet with Hayley Westenra in concert and with choirs; I've performed it with orchestra and, as an adult, on my third album. I really do think that when you strip away this carol, it truly comes into its own and these days all you really need is a guitar accompaniment, which is exactly how it was composed. So I'm very thankful to the mouse for eating away at the organ pipes.

Recently on the ITV celebration of Christmas I went out to Israel and explored some of the stories behind the carols. I was very fortunate to mime 'Silent Night!', not out in Israel, which was where most of the programme was done, but in Flanders, where so many British soldiers had lost their lives in World War I. By all accounts this carol was sung in the trenches, in no man's land. There was a truce for a matter of moments, where the German and the British soldiers stopped fighting and eerily all you heard coming across no man's land in the bitter cold, in a time of desperation, were the German troops singing '*Stille Nacht!*' and coming back at them was 'Good King Wenceslas' from the British soldiers. Two fighting armies had been hard at it trying to kill one another and then, because it was Christmas, they decided to stop and they played a game of football and sang carols. Such is the power of a carol like this that when I was there in Flanders I could actually begin to imagine what it was like for those soldiers. In the middle of so much hatred and brutality something as beautiful as '*Stille Nacht!*' was sung.

My first live performance of '*Stille Nacht!*' was on German television when I was a young child in the prime of my boy chorister career. I went over there with my accompanist from Wales, Annette Bryn Parry, probably one of the finest accompanists ever to have come out of Wales. We really were on holiday in our hotel, playing table tennis together, going swimming, and we were to perform on the number one TV show in Germany, which had interviews, a game show element, a panel of people talking – and lots of different music. On that particular programme the London Community Gospel Choir were also performing. I was there to sing '*Stille Nacht!*' in German, with Annette accompanying on a very, very dodgy keyboard, which they provided for us.

Well, being used to television in Britain and being looked after by a German representative, there was no rush getting to the rehearsal. She remarked that, 'Oh, just like British television, we'll be running late.' We arrived ten minutes late for the rehearsal and the producer came running up to me (I was only thirteen at the time) and berated me for my lateness. He said, 'We're not going to let you rehearse any more because you don't take it seriously.' I was bright red, mortified, because even at that age I really did pride myself on being a professional; after all, I'd been told there was no rush to get to the rehearsal. So I apologised, grovelled – a lot – and gave the performance of my life on the live broadcast of the show.

The following week, I was sitting next to Boy George – as you do – at a rock and pop awards event in London at the Grosvenor Hotel and I regaled him with this tale. And he said, 'Oh, I was on that programme the week before – they did the same thing to me. I turned round to them and said, "If you don't let me rehearse, I'm going" and took the next plane home.' This I think is the difference between me and Boy George: I grovelled in the classical style, saying 'I'm terribly sorry, I'll do a good performance for you, promise!' Whereas Boy George, in rock 'n' roll style, turned round and said, 'Sod you all, I'm off.'

My favourite verse, without doubt, has to be the third. It gives you the opportunity to open up with the voice on the first two lines:

> Silent night! Holy night!
> Son of God, love's pure light.

Then I always in performance take the third line back in dynamic completely with

> Radiant beams from thy holy face
> With the dawn of redeeming grace,
> Jesus, Lord, at thy birth,
> Jesus, Lord, at thy birth.

That's a kind of moment between me and God when I'm performing the carol. It's a one-on-one if you like. I feel that I'm connecting with that one person. It's the beauty of this carol that it can be enjoyed by the masses, but actually when I'm performing it, selfishly I feel that it's a piece of music where I have this connection with God.

WHILE SHEPHERDS WATCHED THEIR FLOCKS BY NIGHT

Words
Nahum Tate (1652–1715)

Music
Arrangement by
William Henry Monk (1823–89)

While shepherds watched their flocks by night,
All seated on the ground,
The angel of the Lord came down,
And glory shone around.

'Fear not,' said he (for mighty dread
Had seized their troubled minds),
'Glad tidings of great joy I bring
To you and all mankind.

'To you in David's town this day
Is born of David's line
A Saviour, who is Christ the Lord;
And this shall be the sign:

'The heavenly babe you there shall find
To human view displayed,
All meanly wrapped in swathing bands,
And in a manger laid.'

Thus spake the seraph; and forthwith
Appeared a shining throng

Of angels praising God, and thus
Addressed their joyful song:

'All glory be to God on high,
And to the earth be peace;
Good will henceforth from heaven to men,
Begin and never cease.'

Together, the carols in this book tell the Christmas story more or less from beginning to end. The central themes and happenings are here – and some subplots as well. Isaiah's prophecy of the coming of Emmanuel features, so do Herod's nefarious schemes and the coming of the three kings. The journey to Bethlehem on a little donkey and the birth in the stable are of course included: Mary, Joseph and baby, surrounded by Magi, shepherds and sheep, an ox, an ass, even in Christina Rossetti's carol – a camel! And the story continues through the massacre of the innocents and the Holy Family's flight into Egypt.

The shepherds in particular crop up frequently. In 'See Amid the Winter's Snow', for instance, they talk about following the star to find Jesus; in 'The First Nowell', the selfsame star guides them and the three kings to the stable in Bethlehem, and in 'The Shepherds' Farewell' they see off the Holy Family on their journey back home with words of encouragement and comfort. The shepherds of Christmas refer maybe to Christ the Good Shepherd; they perhaps also represent us, ordinary human beings, members of congregations and choirs, a flock, and never more so than in this carol. These shepherds are simple folk, who are scared stiff when the angel of the Lord swoops down in a blaze of light giving them headline news. 'Fear not,' he admonishes, then brings along a terrifying throng of singing angels. Quite an event for an ordinary shepherd to deal with.

First published in 1700, 'While Shepherds Watched their Flocks by Night' comes from Luke's Gospel (2:8–14) when that angel appears to the shepherds resting in the field and gives them 'glad tidings of great joy' of the coming of Christ. Popular – and parodied – it tells a story and the angel speaks directly to the shepherds and to us, a rare thing in a carol. This directness maybe contributes to its appeal as one of our most popular carols, and it's clear and simple for children to sing with joy.

'While Shepherds Watched their Flocks by Night' is also one of England's earliest carols. From the beginning of the sixteenth until the eighteenth century, the singing of hymns and carols was practically non-existent in most of England. Instead, church congregations sang versified forms of the Psalms, which came to be considered rather crude and un-poetic in nature. In 1696, two Irishmen, Nahum Tate and Nicholas Brady, collaborated to undertake a new metrical version of the Psalms with higher literary standards than hitherto. It was Nahum Tate, one half of this partnership, who wrote 'While Shepherds Watched Their Flocks by Night', paraphrasing Luke's verses. The Anglican Church accepted his work and for eighty-two years it was the only carol that had the church's stamp of approval, until 'Hark! The Herald Angels Sing' was added to the approved list in 1782.

Nahum Tate was the son of an Irish clergyman who went by the name of Faithful Teate. Unsurprisingly Nahum changed his surname to Tate when he moved to England. He was considered to be a distinguished if eccentric poet and writer for the stage and John Dryden was his friend. His achievements for the stage included adapting a libretto for Henry Purcell's opera *Dido and Aeneas*. He also had the curious habit of rewriting Shakespeare's plays. His version of the tragedy of *King Lear* had a happy ending, with Cordelia alive and well and married to Edgar; he also changed *Richard II* so that every scene, he said, was 'full of respect to Majesty and the dignity of courts'. This didn't seem to worry his contemporaries and he was made Poet Laureate in 1692. But he fell victim to excessive drinking and died in 1715 in Southwark, where he had taken refuge from his creditors.

Many small changes have successively been made to the original text of 'While Shepherds Watched their Flocks by Night'. The 'swathing bands' of verse four, for example, have been substituted by the more modern 'swaddling clothes' or 'swaddling bands'. In Scotland there is a completely different first verse:

> While humble shepherds watched their flocks
> In Bethlehem's plains by night
> An angel sent from heaven appeared
> And filled the plains with light.

Another variation sometimes performed is 'As shepherds watched their fleecy care'. Like children before and since, I was guilty as a child in school of parodying this carol many times:

> While shepherds washed their socks at night
> All seated round the tub,
> A bar of Sunlight soap came down
> And they began to scrub.

Or alternatively:

> While shepherds washed their socks by night
> And hung them on the line,
> The angel of the Lord came down
> And said, 'Those socks are mine!'

I remember being told off quite severely at Bangor Cathedral as a relatively new chorister when I nudged my compatriots and dared them to sing the sock-washing variant. I feel sorry now for the choirmaster of the time because he'd been there for many, many years and every Christmas must have lived in dread of some smart chorister coming out with the wisecrack of singing the alternative words – very boring.

The number of competing tunes for this carol must be a record. An estimated 100-plus have appeared in print. One of the most popular is

'Winchester Old', a psalm tune first published in 1592 and arranged by William Henry Monk some time before 1874, popular perhaps because its strong beats convey the rhythm of Tate's words and it has a fine descant. Monk was an important person in the history of hymnody, being the first ever musical editor of the highly influential first collection of *Hymns Ancient and Modern* of 1861 – a bestseller that has sold millions through its successive editions. He made his living as organist for churches across the map of London, including St Peter's Church in Eaton Square, and St Paul's Church, Portman Square, and was organist and choirmaster at St Matthias' Church in Stoke Newington. But he was also composer of memorable hymns and carols. He wrote the tune to Cecil Frances Alexander's 'All Things Bright and Beautiful' and the lovely 'Eventide' for 'Abide with Me', as well as a selection of other melodies including the oddly-titled 'Martyrdom' by Hugh Wilson in 1800 and 'Shackelford' by Frederick Henry Cheeswright in 1889. A parish organist in Lancashire, Robert Jackson, wrote 'Jackson's Tune' for the carol and that remains popular there. In Cornwall the carol is popularly sung to 'Lyngham', a tune usually associated with 'O For A Thousand Tongues to Sing!' and many other tunes are still sung to Tate's words by village carollers in Yorkshire, most notably 'Foster' or rather, 'Old Foster', more like a couple of ales, which maybe explains why 'While Shepherds Watched their Flocks by Night' is carolled particularly in local pubs!

Even though the melody is really nice to sing and the words are wonderful, 'While Shepherds Watched their Flocks by Night' is not among my favourites; it's neither one thing nor the other. It doesn't quite hit the majesty and grandeur of 'O Come All Ye Faithful' or 'Hark! The Herald Angels Sing', nor is it a mood-enhancing carol. It is what it is. Some of the verses can be quite clumsy; the only one I really enjoyed singing as a boy was the third:

'To you in David's town this day
Is born of David's line
A Saviour, who is Christ the Lord;
And this shall be the sign:

This is, though, what you'd call a perfect congregation carol, a carol to get everyone singing. It's instantly recognisable, it's one that anyone in Britain has sung at some point during a school assembly and it is testament to the words and the melody that you probably have to hear it only a couple of times and you feel that you know it. Lots of the carols in this anthology itself would love this to be the truth about them.

'While Shepherds Watched' really did come to life for me recently when I had the opportunity of performing it out in Israel. I was sitting in the shepherds' fields and we'd been filming for quite a while and the sun was just setting and there was one particular recording we did as dusk fell when I really did feel what a privilege it was to be in the fields in Israel where the shepherds would have been when they experienced what they did. It was quite a surreal experience. I almost re-lived the second verse and imagined how I would feel if an angel came down while I was sitting there minding my own business, so it always puts a smile on my face now when I hear

> 'Fear not,' said he (for mighty dread
> Had seized their troubled minds),

It's as if they see the angel, they panic like mad and the angel says, 'Hey, don't worry, I'm only here because I've got some good news for you.' They go, 'Oh that's fine then, fire away.' I'm not sure that my head would be so easily turned, I think that that angel would have had to explain a lot more.

I think all of these carols that are simple in their telling of a story should be commended for the fact that their creators can actually tell the story of the Nativity, probably the greatest story in the world, in four or five short stanzas – this is a real testament to their writing skills.

31

THE SHEPHERDS' FAREWELL TO THE HOLY FAMILY

WORDS
Anon.

TRANSLATION
Paul England (dates not known)

MUSIC
Hector Berlioz (1803–69)

Thou must leave thy lowly dwelling,
The humble crib, the stable bare.
Babe, all mortal babes excelling,
Content our earthly lot to share.

Loving father, loving mother,
Shelter thee with tender care.
Loving father, loving mother,
Shelter thee with tender care,
Shelter thee with tender care.

Blessed Jesus, we implore thee
With humble love and holy fear,
In the land that lies before thee,
Forget not us who linger here.

May the shepherd's lowly calling
Ever to thy heart be dear.
May the shepherd's lowly calling

Ever to thy heart be dear,
Ever to thy heart be dear.

Blest are ye beyond all measure,
Thou happy father, mother mild;
Guard ye well your heav'nly treasure,
The Prince of peace, the holy child.

God go with you, God protect you,
Guide you safely through the wild.
God go with you, God protect you,
Guide you safely through the wild,
Guide you safely through the wild.

This is an intimate song of the shepherds voicing their love and concern for the Holy Family who are leaving Bethlehem to escape Herod's wrath. It's achingly beautiful, but in a great way so that you can really put your heart and soul into singing it.

It is a short work for orchestra and chorus that's part of a larger choral oratorio by Hector Berlioz, called *L'Enfance du Christ*. Berlioz was a key figure of his time, friend of Victor Hugo and Alexandre Dumas, and a champion of Beethoven, then unheard of in France. His father wanted him to become a doctor and he spent two unsuccessful years fulfilling his father's wishes and training in medicine before performing his own flight into music.

Oddly for such a meditative composition, 'The Shepherds' Farewell' began life as a stand-alone piece and a party joke and was the seed from which grew one of Hector Berlioz's finest works. By the age of forty-seven he had become frustrated with the reluctance of audiences and critics to appreciate the modernist nature of his music. To his chagrin they considered it to be discordant and bizarre. This lack of recognition was more than irritating; it meant he had no regular income and was extremely hard up. In October 1850, Berlioz had written a short organ piece for the autograph album of his friend the architect Joseph-Louis Duc, under the fictitious name of Pierre Ducré. He reworked this piece to his own text as '*L'adieu des bergers a la Sainte Famille*' or 'The Shepherds' Farewell to the Holy Family'. He then decided to trick the critics and the audience by passing off 'The Shepherds' Farewell' as a tune 'in the antique style' by this fictitious seventeenth-century composer Pierre Ducré and supposedly written in the year 1679. His plan worked. He conducted the work on 12 November, at a concert of the Grande Société Philharmonique de Paris and it was enthusiastically received by all. His British biographer David Cairns observes that Berlioz was told by Joseph-Louis Duc that 'a society lady of his acquaintance, a connoisseur of ancient music, had declared that "Berlioz would never be able to write a tune as simple and charming as this little piece by old Ducré."'

Nonetheless the cool response to Berlioz's work continued. Many put the success of 'The Shepherds' Farewell' down to a change of style adopted by Berlioz to win approval. He was at pains to point out that any change was due to the touching subject matter and nothing else. In a postscript to his memoirs he explains:

> In that work many people imagined they could detect a radical change in my style and manner. This opinion is entirely without foundation. The subject naturally lent itself to a gentle and simple style of music, and for that reason alone was more in accordance with their taste and intelligence. Time would probably have developed these qualities, but I should have written *L'Enfance du Christ* in the same manner twenty years ago. (*J'eusse écrit* L'Enfance du Christ *de la même façon il y a vingt ans.*)

Berlioz described *L'Enfance du Christ*, the oratorio of which 'The Shepherds' Farewell' was the seed, as a *trilogie sacrée* (sacred trilogy). It tells the story of Herod's genocide and Mary and Joseph's painful and arduous flight to Egypt to take refuge in the city of Sais. Berlioz took his narrative from the second chapter of the book of Matthew, and composed what many consider to be one of his gentlest and most endearing scores. Untypically he specified a smaller orchestral force than usual. 'The Shepherds' Farewell' comes in the second section, 'The Flight into Egypt', which is itself divided into three parts. Berlioz added a tenor part '*Le repos de la Sainte Famille*' ('The repose of the Holy Family') and then set an overture before both this and the original 'Shepherds' Farewell' to form what we know now as '*La fuite en Egypte*'.

The writing of the three-part oratorio did not start at the very beginning. 'The Flight into Egypt' was published in 1852 and performed in December the following year at Leipzig. This was so well received that, on the advice of his friends, Berlioz added more to his composition, topping and tailing it with the last section '*L'arrivée a Sais*' and finally the opening section, '*Le songe d'Hérode*' ('Herod's Dream'). The entire sacred trilogy took four years to complete.

Berlioz was married twice, the first time to the Irish actress Harriet Smithson (1800–54) who inspired his *Symphonie Fantastique* written in 1830. They had a son, Louis, born in 1834. Louis' death in 1867 was a terrible blow to his father who by then had already lost many of his friends and family. It prompted him to burn many of his papers, and he died only two years later.

Perhaps because Hector Berlioz turned to the music of other countries such as Britain and Germany for inspiration he is still to this day treated with some indifference in his native land. In 2003, two hundred years after his birth, it was proposed that his remains, buried between his two wives in the Cimetière de Montmartre, be moved to the Panthéon. This idea was blocked by Jacques Chirac, then President of France, because he considered it too soon after the body of Alexandre Dumas had been moved there. Opponents of the idea have come from different sides: some felt Berlioz was not a Republican, others that his wish to be beside his wives should be respected. The decision on this matter is still pending.

In the UK, affection for Berlioz is maybe due to the conductor Colin

Davies, who has recorded all of his work, including two renditions of *L'Enfance du Christ*, one on vinyl in 1977 with Janet Baker and a CD nearly thirty years later: a live recording with the London Symphony Orchestra and the chamber choir Tenebrae in December 2006.

This wonderful piece lasts little over five minutes. It depicts a deeply moving episode in the story of the Nativity, giving a vivid account of the shepherds gathering by the crib and bidding Jesus goodbye. They urge him not to forget their lowly selves and utter a prayer for Christ's safe future. It's all the more poignant because we know how unsafe that future will be. It's often sung as part of a carol service as well as within the oratorio to which it eventually came to belong.

I first sang this piece at Bangor Cathedral and it is a beautiful marriage of words and music, one that I'll be recording on my 2010 album for Christmas, I expect, as a duet between me and a choir.

I think it has probably one of the nicest carol melodies that we've got and it's not an obvious melody. I love the introduction: like the carol itself it's not conspicuous, it's very simple and is almost as if it is coming from a shepherd's pipe – the sound of the pipes and horns in the accompaniment too give it a sense of the pastoral. It's very, very simple and you don't really expect this searingly beautiful melody to come through, but then it does and it's just the most joyous piece to sing: open long phrases and sublime melody, especially during the end of each verse, where you repeat the last two lines. There the words are also at their strongest, so repeating them three times reinforces their message:

Loving father, loving mother,
Shelter thee with tender care,
Loving father, loving mother,
Shelter thee with tender care,
Shelter thee with tender care.

I also love the final verse: 'God go with you, God protect you/ Guide you safely through the wild.'

I hear this carol every year as it's part of our charity event in St George's Hanover Square. I think this is one of the pieces of music that the Westminster Cathedral Choir do so well. Their exposed boys' voices at first, then joined by the male voices. They also sing it in French, and even if you're not fluent in French the meaning of the words comes across because it's so well written. Hearing a choir of top boys' voices singing it is a real treat for me at Christmas and I think it is one of the carols that really does set up the true meaning of the festival for me.

32

THE TWELVE DAYS OF CHRISTMAS

Words and Music
Anon.

Musical arrangement by Frederic Austin (1872–1952)

On the first day of Christmas
My true love sent to me
A partridge in a pear tree.

On the second day of Christmas
My true love sent to me
Two turtle doves,
And a partridge in a pear tree.

On the third day of Christmas
My true love sent to me
Three French hens, Two turtle doves,
And a partridge in a pear tree.

On the fourth day of Christmas
My true love sent to me
Four calling birds, Three French hens,
Two turtle doves,
And a partridge in a pear tree.

On the fifth day of Christmas
My true love sent to me
Five gold rings, Four calling birds,
Three French hens, Two turtle doves,
And a partridge in a pear tree.

On the sixth day of Christmas
My true love sent to me
Six geese a-laying, Five gold rings,
Four calling birds, Three French hens, Two turtle doves,
And a partridge in a pear tree.

On the seventh day of Christmas
My true love sent to me
Seven swans a-swimming, Six geese a-laying,
Five gold rings, Four calling birds,
Three French hens, Two turtle doves,
And a partridge in a pear tree.

On the eighth day of Christmas
My true love sent to me
Eight maids a-milking, Seven swans a-swimming,
Six geese a-laying, Five gold rings,
Four calling birds, Three French hens, Two turtle doves,
And a partridge in a pear tree.

On the ninth day of Christmas
My true love sent to me
Nine ladies dancing, Eight maids a-milking,
Seven swans a-swimming, Six geese a-laying,
Five gold rings, Four calling birds, Three French hens, Two turtle doves,
And a partridge in a pear tree.

On the tenth day of Christmas
My true love sent to me
Ten lords a-leaping, Nine ladies dancing,
Eight maids a-milking, Seven swans a-swimming,
Six geese a-laying, Five gold rings, Four calling birds,
Three French hens, Two turtle doves,
And a partridge in a pear tree.

On the eleventh day of Christmas
My true love sent to me
Eleven pipers piping, Ten lords a-leaping,
Nine ladies dancing, Eight maids a-milking,
Seven swans a-swimming, Six geese a-laying,
Five gold rings, Four calling birds,
Three French hens, Two turtle doves,
And a partridge in a pear tree.

On the twelfth day of Christmas
My true love sent to me
Twelve drummers drumming, Eleven pipers piping,
Ten lords a-leaping, Nine ladies dancing,
Eight maids a-milking, Seven swans a-swimming,
Six geese a-laying, Five gold rings,
Four calling birds, Three French hens, Two turtle doves,
And a partridge in a pear tree.

'The Twelve Days of Christmas' belongs to those magical Christmases of childhood. It was a real treat for us at Bangor Cathedral if during the Christmas period we were allowed to sing this. One point we'd usually get to was a real joy because if you were an established chorister, you'd always look across at the probationers who were starting their life in the Cathedral choir and didn't have a clue what the words were or how to keep them in time – because it's quite a tricky song from that point of view – a choristers' joke. But it was also a stressful sing for all of us. For the Nine Lessons and Carols service we had three carol books to use and were constantly flicking from one book to another, to another and another all through the Nine Lessons and Carols. And invariably a chorister, usually me, would drop a book or a page or a bookmark, much to the anger of the choirmaster.

I've always loved this carol though because it portrays vivid pictures in your mind. It's not every day you get to sing about turtle doves, or maids a-milking, or lords a-leaping, or ladies dancing!

It's likely that the origin of 'The Twelve Days of Christmas', which dates back at least to its first publication in England in 1780, was a festive feat of memory and of maths to be sung by everyone together on Twelfth Night (hence the twelve days), the feast of the Epiphany. A cumulative song, it is often listed as a nursery rhyme and is a fine game, building as it does from one item up to the twelve along with all the previous items attached.

The words that we sing today were printed in 1864, but the earliest known performance of the song was in 1842 by James Halliwell-Phillipps, an English scholar. In the early twentieth century the composer Frederic Austin, best known for his restoration and production of John Gay's *The Beggar's Opera*, wrote an arrangement that included his own melody from the verse 'Five gold rings' onwards. Austin's version has now become standard.

A lot of people have speculated about the genesis of 'The Twelve Days of Christmas', which is not an obviously religious carol. The real meaning could be hidden within the verses like a code according to one interpretation, each of the gifts holding religious significance. The 'true love' of the carol is not a generous, if rather impractical, admirer, but is God who gives wonderful gifts to 'me', meaning all of us. But why go to the trouble of concealing these things deep in a Christmas song for children? The hypothesis is that 'The Twelve Days of Christmas' was

created by Catholics during a time (1558–1829) when they were not allowed to practise their faith openly and when the only legal church was the state, Anglican, church. This song would not raise the suspicions of non-Catholics and the articles communicated in this way would help Catholic children growing up to remember central elements of their faith. The references suggested are:

- The partridge is a reminder of Christ. A mother partridge will pretend injury to decoy predators from her helpless nestlings and literally give her life for her children. The pear tree symbolizes the cross.
- Two turtle doves are the Old and New Testaments of the Bible.
- Three French hens: in the sixteenth century these birds were affordable only by the rich; they are signs for the three great gifts of faith, hope and love (1 Corinthians 13:13).
- Four calling birds are the four Gospels, Matthew, Mark, Luke and John.
- Five gold rings are the first five books of the Old Testament or the Torah. These books were treated by the Jews with reverence and were considered more valuable than gold (Psalm 19:10).
- Six geese a-laying. Eggs are a symbol of new life and the geese mark the six days of creation. God spoke the word and brought forth life.
- Seven swans a-swimming are the seven gifts of the Holy Spirit (Romans 12:6–8): prophecy, service, teaching, encouraging, giving, leadership and mercy.
- Eight maids-a-milking equal the eight Beatitudes of Jesus (Matthew 5:3–10), which nourish us as milk does.
- Nine ladies dancing represent the nine fruits of the Holy Spirit (Galatians 5:22–23): love, joy, peace, patience, kindness, goodness, faithfulness, gentleness and self-control.
- Ten lords a-leaping are the Ten Commandments (Exodus 20:3–17). Lords were men who carried social authority.
- Eleven pipers piping match the eleven apostles who stayed loyal to Jesus and the pipes express the people joyfully following their message.

- Twelve drummers drumming beat out the twelve vital beliefs that set us apart as Christians that are in the Creed of the Apostles.

It is tempting to go with this neat explanation. The numbers seem, as it were, to add up. However there are arguments against this idea, among them that this interpretation was a way for Christians to claim as one of their own what is actually a secular song. For example, all the items could just be birds: the calling birds might be a phonetic misunderstanding of 'colly' birds, a term used for blackbirds; gold rings are maybe 'goldspinks', the Scottish name for goldfinches, the mysterious pear tree could come from the French word for partridge, *perdrix*.

Who knows? Also, there are lots of variants of the gifts themselves in areas of Britain and beyond. In France for example, this carol is all about food, featuring wood pigeons, rabbits, ducks, hares, turkeys, hams, legs of mutton, partridges with cabbage, salads, and to complete the feast, twelve full casks of wine!

It is also possible that 'The Twelve Days of Christmas' was religious and inspired by number carols like 'The Seven Joys of Mary' or 'The New Dial', which takes the hours of the clock to relate Christian concepts. The folk song, 'Green Grow the Rushes-O', closely related to 'The New Dial', also has many concealed religious references. Whatever the truth of the matter, it's packed with glittering images.

I've performed this carol in *Songs of Praise* at the Royal Albert Hall as part of the Big Sing. It was a trio: Connie Fisher, who won BBC TV's *How Do You Solve a Problem Like Maria?* programme, and Ray Quinn of course, who was also on *The X Factor* (and came second to Leona Lewis). So to have these two reality TV performers and myself singing in the Albert Hall to a thousand people this particular piece was very strange. I remember Connie and Ray being very, very confident and saying that they knew the words and which part each was singing. And me of course in the middle. Going back to my chorister days I knew that first they hadn't sung it before publicly and then that they were the probationers.

Of course, what happened? Ray got his words wrong and Connie forgot that she was singing about four calling birds and instead sang about two turtle doves, so we could have got into a right mess. But the audience who were in the Hall that day for that recording loved the fact that we got it wrong. I think it added to the whole feeling of merriment that was already in the building. You can't but smile when you're performing carols.

The great thing about 'The Twelve Days of Christmas' is that even if you do mess it up you always know that you're going to get one line right and that's 'Five gold rings'. After that it's up to you, but that's the middle of the carol if you like, where all forces should come together in time. I have to be honest and say that I don't really take this carol that seriously. It's probably not one of my favourites, it's a bit of fun. It's very repetitive, and doesn't take you on a journey in any sense of the word. It hasn't got the majesty and triumphant aspect of some of the others, like 'Hark! The Herald Angels Sing' or 'O Come, All Ye Faithful'. It also lacks the mystery or the heart of something like 'O Come, O Come, Emmanuel' or 'Silent Night'. But it's a good little bit of Christmas froth.

FURTHER READING

Allen, William Francis; Ware, Charles Pickard; Garrison, Lucy McKim, *Slave Songs of the United States* (Oak Publications, New York, 1965)

Bradley, Ian C, *The Daily Telegraph Book of Carols* (Continuum, 2006)

Cairns, David, *Berlioz: Volume Two: Servitude and Greatness, 1832–1869* (University of California Press, 2000)

Dearmer, Percy; Vaughan Williams, R; Shaw, Martin, *The Oxford Book of Carols* (Oxford University Press, 1928, paperback 1964)

Jacques, Reginald and Willcocks, David, (eds), *Carols for Choirs 1* (Oxford University Press, 1961)

Keyte, Hugh and Parrott, Andrew (eds), *The New Oxford Book of Carols* (Oxford University Press, 1992)

Marsh, Jan, *Christina Rossetti: A Literary Biography* (Jonathan Cape, 1994)

Perry, Michael (ed.), *Carols for Today* (Hodder and Stoughton, 1986)

Reeves, Marjorie and Worsley, Jenyth, *Favourite Hymns: 2000 Years of Magnificat* (Continuum, 2001)

Roseberry, Eric (ed.), *The Faber Book of Carols and Christmas Songs* (Faber, 1983)

Routley, Erik, *The English Carol* (Oxford University Press, 1959)

Sandys, William, *Christmas Carols Ancient and Modern* (Richard Beckley, 1833)

Studwell, William, *The Christmas Carol Reader* (Harrington Park Press, 1995)

Vaughan Williams, Ursula, *R.V.W: A Biography of Ralph Vaughan Williams* (Oxford Lives, Oxford University Press, 1993)

Watson, J R, (ed.), *An Annotated Anthology of Hymns* (Oxford University Press, 2003)

ACKNOWLEDGEMENTS

Firstly, to my family, Claire, Emilia and Lucas for their love and support. I would be nothing without you. Love and thanks to Philippa Brewster for her never-ending positive nature and helping hand. To Georgina Capel and Anita Land for being them (scary at the best of times)! To Wendi Batt for being my right hand lady – cheers. To Trevor Dolby, Nicola Taplin and all at Preface and Random House – sorry for always being late and thanks for everything. To Peter Ward for the text design and Charlotte Abrams-Simpson for the jacket. To all at *Songs of Praise*, thanks for the great times. Thanks also to my publishers the Music Sales Group. To Adrian Sear and all at Demon Music Group who will be releasing a Carol CD to accompany this book. And a huge thanks to all the talented musicians and lyricists who came up with these festive treasures. Happy Christmas!